Elements of Magic
House of Xannon 5

Copyright © 2017 Melinda VanLone.

All rights reserved.

Published by: WrittenHouse Publishing, Gaithersburg, MD

This is a work of fiction. Names, characters, businesses, places, events and incidents are either the products of the author's imagination or used in a fictitious manner. Any resemblance to actual persons, living or dead, or actual events is purely coincidental.

ISBN-10:
ISBN-13:

Cover Illustration: Carrie Osborne

Cover design and book layout: Book Cover Corner, www.bookcovercorner.com

VanLone, Melinda.

Elements of Magic / Melinda VanLone

Visit the author website: www.melindavan.com

ELEMENTS OF MAGIC
HOUSE OF XANNON BOOK 5

Melinda VanLone

WrittenHouse Publishing

Tallahassee, Florida

Also by Melinda VanLone

House of Xannon

Stronger Than Magic

Finding Flame

Promise of Magic

Taking Earth

Elements of Magic

Raegan Reid Case Files

Raegan Reid: Rifter

Rifter For Hire (coming soon)

—1—

Tarian Xannon swam like a prizefighter, punching the water with every stroke and punishing the waves with every kick—but the ocean fought back. The waves felt empty and endless and relentless. Every splash and every crash against her body and against the shore reminded her that something…someone…was missing.

She depended on the ocean to soothe away bad moods, but today it did just the opposite. Instead of joy and a sense of all-is-right-with-the-world, she battled worry, frustration, and irritation.

She wanted her daughter back. Now.

Daric Voltain, her lover, best friend, and a father to her child, floated nearby, arms splayed out like an awkward puppy trying to keep his balance on ice. Tarian tried to stop the grin from spreading across her face. The man she loved, the man she relied on to be calm, strong, and steady, looked vulnerable, alarmed, and more than a little desperate.

Tarian flicked water at him and didn't bother trying to keep the giggle out of her voice. "You don't have to stay out here. I'll relax more if I don't have to worry about you drowning."

"As if you ever relax. Especially not today. Not without some sort of serious distraction." His voice was laced with sexual innuendo. He paddled over to her, fighting off the next wave with surprising ease for someone so obviously out of his element. A hint of cinnamon filled the breeze, a sign that he'd used his Air abilities to steady himself. "And us Air users aren't helpless in water. We just don't like being surrounded by waves of it."

"I don't need a distraction. I'm nothing but distracted today."

"You definitely need a distraction." The light in his eyes reminded her of a kid anticipating a present. "Question is, what would distract the Keeper of Water in her own element?"

Something flashed through his eyes just before his hands tightened on her shoulders and he pushed her down, hard. She gasped as ocean rushed to cover them both.

Daric shoved again, forcing them well below the next wave. His hands on her shoulders sent tingles into interesting places.

She grabbed his neck and pulled him in for a long, slow, extremely wet kiss. Her talent with Water and Air formed a bubble around their heads that provided a barrier of oxygen against the ocean, giving them time to savor the contact. She wrapped legs and arms around him and squeezed tight. His nether regions responded with an instant salute. She pressed herself against it, liking the hard feel of him poking into her most sensitive body parts.

Daric's hands drifted from her shoulders around to her back and down. Tarian kneaded the muscles along his arms while she savored the feel of his hands on her body, the warm caress of water, the heat of his erection against her girly bits. She thrust her tongue deeper into his mouth, enjoying the taste of salt and mint she found there.

His hands dove into the top of her bikini bottoms, squeezing, teasing, promising. She wanted to take him up on that promise. She pictured them entwined, using the momentum of the ocean to fuel their passion and their joining.

But then other images infiltrated her thoughts and filled her mind with how her daughter, Ember, looked yesterday. One day away from her first birthday, Ember already had a head full of hair and curious sapphire eyes that didn't miss much. She was dressed in a soft blue jumper with a white undershirt that showed off the deep brown innocence of her skin. She'd been pure, precious, and absolutely adorable. The kind of adorable that could melt the polar ice caps.

Ember had nestled into the arms of a slick, dark-haired daemon with a slimy smile. He looked arrogant, proud, and self-satisfied as he took Tarian's daughter through a travel portal to his home for visitation. Just thinking of that look on his face made something beyond frustration and anger surge through her body straight to her brain where it stole all reason and thought and replaced it with a burning desire to set something on fire.

She couldn't stand the deal they'd made. She couldn't stand how he had the right to take her daughter, even for twenty-four hours. Mostly she couldn't stand that the daemon in question, Ruarc, was one of Ember's fathers. It wasn't like she could ever undo that one simple truth. Her daughter was the result of a ritualistic joining between Tarian and three men. Or, actually, two men and one daemon. It was the Xannon way. Multiple fathers for the Scion meant no man would ever be able to claim the Dolphin Throne. And she certainly hadn't minded the time spent with Daric and Alex, Ember's third dad. She'd liked…no, loved…

both of them. But Ruarc…love was not the word she'd use to describe her feelings about him. Not even close.

Daric's hands on her face brought Tarian out of her thoughts and back to the present. She looked into Daric's eyes, so full of compassion and support and love, and resented Ruarc for interrupting their moment. It wasn't fair to blame him, but it was that or blame herself.

Tarian pulled away from Daric, the mood shattered. She saw the passion, regret, and understanding at war on his face. She touched her lips briefly to his, hoping it felt like the apology it was meant to be, then pulled him upward until their heads broke the surface. She let the protective bubble of air release, and the salty, fishy, briny air rush in.

Daric wrinkled his nose against it and wiped water off his face. "You're worrying over nothing, you know."

"It's not nothing."

"Ember is fine." Daric kept his arms moving to stabilize himself against the tide.

"I put my baby into the arms of a daemon. He could be telling her anything. Teaching her anything. He could be, hell, turning her…I don't know. Daemon. Something."

Daric circled his arms around her. "Ruarc loves her. You know he does. He wouldn't hurt her any more than I would."

Tarian used a push of Water energy to stabilize both of them, a reflexive muscle memory thing she'd done since she was Ember's age. "You're a good man. He's not. He's a liar and a cheat. There has to be a way out of that stupid agreement."

"He doesn't lie. Cheat, maybe." Daric paused, as if considering his words. "It's binding, Tari."

"There could be a way."

"There isn't." Daric said the words with flat conviction. "He swore to protect her with his life. Even if he doesn't value her, he values his own life. He wouldn't risk it. That Agreement was a damn good one, considering."

"I don't trust him."

"That's obvious." Daric glanced longingly at the shore. "We should go get ready."

"Not yet." She pressed her lips to his, both to silence his argument and to prolong the inevitable. It would be nice to spend just one day in Daric's arms without worrying about her daughter, the state of magic, the world, or her mind. Just one day. Was it too much for the Keeper of the House to ask?

She broke the kiss and rested her head on his shoulders and her arms around his neck. From this vantage point, she saw the entrance of her home and the Sentinels standing guard. The electric tingle of the invisible barriers, meant to keep out intruders, raced along her nerves, and in the distance Oahu teemed with humans newly doused with magical energy.

She knew the chaos they dealt with. She'd visited many times since the night magic fell. She'd seen the panic firsthand. The incredible storm dumped power all over the world, but not evenly like a blanket of snow. More like a tornado that destroyed the house to the left and to the right but somehow left one in the middle unscathed.

So many struggled with new abilities. So many others struggled against them. Some resented the fact that magic passed them by so much they fought any who displayed anything even remotely connected to energy manipulation. She'd brought magic to the world, but in one fatal moment she'd destroyed balance. One step forward, a giant leap back.

Tarian pushed Daric toward black sand safety. "You're right. I need to work off this tension. I'm going for a swim."

Daric hesitated. "There's only a few hours left."

"I won't be long."

"Riiight." He drew the word out, his way of telling her he didn't believe a word she said. But he turned and swam toward shore using powerful strokes aided by a push of Air.

She waited until he stood on the beach, his feet far enough away from the edge that she knew he wouldn't, couldn't, attempt to follow her, then dove back under the surface.

She boosted her speed with a mix of Air and Water energy, heading away from him, her home, and the reminders of her daughter.

Ember. Her baby. The child she hadn't wanted but now couldn't imagine life without. Ember in Ruarc's arms. In his home. Ember with the Mayfanata, daemon known for selfish disregard for anything that didn't benefit themselves. Devious, cunning, tricky bastards.

Tarian shook her head, making the water swish in her ear canals. Her damn thoughts refused to stay behind on the shore.

Tarian swam further forward and down. Her heart rate rose to match the tension in her mind. She swam harder.

She'd gone maybe half a mile when something bumped her elbow and her mind filled with an ancient voice.

Race.

She turned to the dolphin bobbing his head up and down in the water next to her. He chattered, eyes glinting in the blue-green water before diving down in clear invitation.

I don't have time, Roger. The protest didn't have any real desire behind it. She'd come to the ocean to relax, recharge, and forget what made her so anxious that she hadn't eaten or slept for almost twenty-four hours.

On second thought...

She dove, flipping her body into position with a push of magical energy from Water, her strongest element.

Roger circled and bumped her foot, then shot past, his body a dark gray streak that instantly merged with the shadows.

Cheater. She pulsed Water, then Air, and used them to form a catapult that launched her deeper into the ocean after the dolphin. If they raced far enough and fast enough and long enough, maybe she could out-swim her thoughts.

—2—

An hour later, Tarian stepped from the ocean onto the black sand and gathered a small pulse of Air, her secondary talent, to dry off. Behind her, Roger leapt his goodbyes before vanishing under the waves. The Ancient took a small piece of the calm she'd managed to gain during her swim in the ocean with him, leaving a hole instantly filled by unease.

Daric tossed a towel to her. "Not bad. I thought you'd be gone longer."

Tarian wrapped it around her body and stepped up the path to the house. "There's a little girl about to come home who needs a birthday party."

"Ruarc's not due back with Ember for another two...no, two and a half hours."

"It's her first birthday. I want it to be special."

"You know she won't remember it, right? She'd be happy with a shiny bow and an empty box."

Tarian didn't answer. Now that she'd left the soothing calm of the ocean, she couldn't shake a growing sense of dread. Something was wrong. Very wrong. Monumentally wrong. She was sure of it.

She just had no idea what.

She led the way into the house and down the hall toward her private rooms in silence, lost in her thoughts again.

Two and a half hours.

That meant Ember had been gone now for twenty-one and a half hours. It felt like twenty-one and a half years. A century in the arms of the daemon who'd tricked her, manipulated her, and wormed his way into her life and her womb. He'd had an agenda. She'd known it when they made the Agreement, and her feelings hadn't changed in the last year. He might be one of Ember's fathers. He might be under Agreement to ensure Ember's safety. It didn't make Tarian feel any better.

When they reached her bedroom, Daric grabbed her arm to stop her. "You can't break an Agreement, Tari."

"I didn't say I would."

"I know what you're thinking. I can tell by the look on your face."

She pushed the door open and moved inside the bedroom, heading for the shower. "I never said I wanted to break it. I said I wanted out of it."

"Same thing."

She tugged the towel off and let it drop to the floor. "No, it's not." She turned her back on him and went into the bathroom, hoping he'd just drop the subject. She'd never break an Agreement. Not just because the penalty in this case was death, but because she'd made a promise. She didn't break promises.

Still.

"There has to be a way to get Ruarc to let it go."

Daric leaned on the bathroom counter and watched her with interest as she stripped off her bathing suit. "Not in a thousand years. I know I wouldn't, if I were him."

"You're not." She stepped into the shower. "It's possible.

Right? If we both agree?"

Daric paused so long she thought he might have left the bathroom. She peeked around the wall to find him contemplating the floor with a worried wrinkle across his forehead. When he looked up, his eyes held so much compassion and understanding she ducked behind the wall again.

"Right?"

"It's possible. But I've never seen anyone actually do it. And Ruarc isn't the type to just let something like that go."

"I just have to convince him."

"Sure. Convince the man he doesn't want to see his own daughter."

"She's not his."

"She is. He contributed. It counts."

She glared at the faucet. It had the nerve to just sit there being useful. "He doesn't deserve her." She shoved her face into the water to drown out the words.

"Give him a chance. He might surprise you."

"Sure. And fish can walk on the beach."

"Some can, you know."

"You know what I mean." She twisted the faucet until the temperature was near scalding. Steam filled the space instantly. She stewed as water pounded the salt off her skin.

The heady scent of cinnamon reached her a second before Daric's arms pulled her close. Her back melded with his front, and the length of him molded to her. He kissed her right ear, his breath warming her insides in a way the ocean simply couldn't match.

"He's kept her safe. I'm sure of it. And that's the most important thing. Right?" He turned her to face him, tilted his head in the way he had that usually helped lighten her mood.

"Right?"

"I guess." Her instincts continued to pound, pound, pound. Whatever the angle or agenda, she was positive Ruarc hadn't kept it secret as a happy surprise. It was a time bomb set to explode in her heart, and there was no way to disarm or escape and no way to run or to duck or to hide.

"What exactly do you think he's up to?"

"I don't know. I just don't know. But something. I can feel it. Here." She shoved a fist into his stomach for emphasis. "I feel it like I can feel my own pulse."

Daric pulled her close. "Let's get ready for her. You'll see. He'll bring her back exactly when he should, and it'll all be fine."

"I hope so."

Daric was wrong. She knew it. But she didn't have to argue with him. They'd both see soon enough.

When they emerged from the shower, Tarian grabbed the first clean pair of jeans she found, added a new black shirt with the phrase "Kick Ass" in white across the chest, and pulled on combat boots. Daric raised an eyebrow at the look but said nothing as she worked the tangles out of her hair with a vengeance they didn't deserve.

They were dressed and halfway down the hallway to the kitchen in under fifteen minutes. She wanted to check on the party setup. There'd be cake and ice cream, and Calli had sewn a cute new outfit for the birthday girl. They'd have lunch, then open the mountain of presents that had accumulated in a corner during the last week. Then maybe cake and some playtime on the beach.

Clomp thud clomp thud. Pause.

Then a faster beat. *Clomp clomp clomp clomp.*

Tarian put a hand on Daric's arm to stop him. "Something

must be up."

"Or maybe someone really needs to use the bathroom." Daric poked her arm.

She laughed. "I seriously doubt that." He was trying hard to lighten her mood. She loved him for making the effort, even in the face of obvious grumpiness.

It didn't take long for the stomping feet to appear. Alex, her lifelong friend and now official Advisor to the Keeper, rounded a corner at full speed, nearly hitting the wall as he navigated the turn. When he spotted them, he slid to a stop, his boots squeaking on the smooth stone floor.

«*Chica*, you gotta see this." The urgent bite to his tone sent a thrill up her spine.

"What's wrong?" She and Daric followed Alex back down the hallway and through the side door to the receiving hall, the center of power for the entire house and the home of the Dolphin Throne itself.

Although the throne was now little more than a chair, since the medallion for which it was named was now firmly lodged in Tarian's chest, it was still a damn impressive one. It embodied authority and leadership and tradition in a way she couldn't manage on her own. She wasn't shy about using that to her advantage when needed.

"It's Texas. There's buildings missing. Just wait. You need to see it. It's freaking unbelievable. I ain't ever seen…just wait." Alex speed-walked across the room, clomping over the symbol of a tree, her own personal mark embedded in the middle of the space, skidding to a halt in front of the monitors mounted on the far wall. They formed a five-by-four grid, each showing a different view of either the house, the grounds, or various news programs. Magic married technology and gave birth to a next-level surveillance system.

She missed the tapestries that used to hang there.

"Check it, number seven. And eleven." Alex pointed.

Daric grunted. "Four and five now too."

"What the hell?" Tarian gestured. "Turn up the sound."

Alex turned up the volume. The very pale, obviously concerned, news anchor on monitor seven continued mid-sentence.

"...just moments ago. As you can see, the effect is catastrophic. Three city blocks of downtown Fort Worth have been leveled. Fires rage out of control. Officials are urging everyone to shelter in place until it can be determined what or who caused the explosion."

The camera panned away from the reporter to show the scene. What used to be buildings were now raging bonfires. Flames obscured everything, but it was obvious something large had exploded. Tarian had seen pictures of nuclear bombs leaving less devastation.

Something behind the reporter caught Tarian's eye. Black marks etched the ground. Flames danced, but it was the way they danced. As if they beckoned the viewer to come closer. "What the..."

"You seen it too?" Alex tapped the closest monitor directly on one of the dancing flames. "That ain't normal."

"Where's the rubble?" Daric asked, then gestured to another monitor. It showed a different angle from the rest. The camera had been positioned closer and more directly behind the largest fire. "There should be mountains of it."

Tarian focused on the area to the right of the largest bonfire. "Is that...it looks like..." She squinted. Blinked. Shook her head in denial. It couldn't be.

A reporter appeared in the scene, his face stricken with fear and maybe just a little excitement. "It's a man. There's a man standing in the middle of the freakin' flames." He gestured frantically for the camera to pan the area, and after a jostling that might have been the holder stumbling on something, it obliged.

"No ordinary man could do that." Daric said. "Some magic newbie combust?"

"It's not a newbie." Tarian pointed at one of the monitors. "That's Lasair."

"The Fire Ancient?" Alex leaned toward the monitor and squinted. "You sure?"

"Positive." Tarian watched Lasair as he strolled from flame to flame. They lapped at his body like puppies, eager to please.

The camera panned left to keep Lasair in view. Lasair paused and stared directly into it. He tilted his chin down significantly, then his mouth moved. She could swear he said, "Keeper." He raised an eyebrow and glanced at the flames. Then mouthed another word, "Danger."

Tarian blinked.

"What the hell is he doing?" Alex moved to another monitor, as if it might offer an explanation the others couldn't give. "What game's he playing?"

Tarian turned up the volume on the one showing Lasair. "As you can see, the man appears to be unaffected by the flames. Emergency crews say the fire is burning too hot to approach and they must wait for it to burn itself out. In the meantime they've established a safe perimeter, and a SWAT team is attempting to communicate with the man. It's possible this is a terrorist who plans more havoc. Or, authorities say, this could be just another in a string of strange incidents caused by the unusual storms last year and resulting in energy waves we've seen causing chaos across the country. At the moment, we do not know if the man intends more harm..."

Alex turned off the sound. All of the monitors now showed various views of the scene, but Tarian was sure their words were much the same. A year since she'd unleashed magic on the world, and nobody knew what to do with newfound abilities. Nothing had stabilized, and lately it seemed the chaos had grown. As if some invisible hand stirred the pot, encouraging things to slosh out the sides and splash into the flames.

"Think he did this?" Alex turned to face her. "Fire is chaos. Maybe he was bored?"

Tarian watched Lasair slowly walk away from the area, his body blending with the surroundings until he disappeared. She shook her head. "Not his style."

"We can't rule it out," Daric said. "We should at least ask him."

"Yeah, right." Alex snorted. "How we gonna interrogate a Fire Ancient? He don't gotta play nice, Daric. He don't gotta play at all."

Tarian turned her back on the monitors. "He looked concerned."

"How could you tell?" Alex raised an eyebrow.

"He was investigating. Not instigating. There's something causing this that's very dangerous, and he wants me to check it out. If something magical caused those fires, and he didn't do it, he'd want to know what did." Tarian thought back to her brief interactions with the Ancient. "He helped me when I thought Ember was dead. He could have ignored the whole thing, but he didn't. Trust me. He wouldn't do this on purpose. And he wouldn't show himself unless..."

"He wanted to be seen." Daric nodded. "But why?"

"To get my attention. He knows we watch." Tarian crossed to the steps of the platform and sat on the top step to think. "He said Keeper. And danger."

"Where'd the buildings go?" Alex walked slowly along the wall of monitors, studying first one, then another. "Daric's right. No rubble. So where'd they go?"

"We need to find out. We can at least stop the fires...they need to be fought with magic, not fire trucks. They aren't ready for this. And Lasair can't do it. He can't stop a fire once it starts." Tarian glanced at the clock. A little under two hours before Ruarc would return with Ember. She looked at the monitors. Running headlines screamed "Terror in Texas" and "Fires Burn the Heart of Texas." She knew the words used would only get more dramatic the longer the flames lived. The area was large, but the fires looked manageable for someone possessing strong talent with Water or Air. Even a strong Earth talent could snuff them out.

She rubbed the Water Artifact beneath her shirt. It warmed, and a trickle of Water energy flowed out. It circled around her, tickling her senses with an aroma of sea spray before fading. She had more than enough power to stop these fires, if they didn't spread any further and she acted fast enough. It wouldn't take long. It better not take long. She glanced back at the clock and sighed. Ember would be safe even if they weren't here to greet her on arrival. Texas? Not so much.

"Alex, get Calli for me? I might need her to boost me in case that fire gets bored and moves. And ask Kia to wait here for Ember? Just in case. We have less than two hours, and I don't want her coming back to an empty room."

She could do this. She could check out the scene, see what caused the explosion, put out fires, and be home in time for her daughter's arrival. She could. She had it all under control.

She did her best to ignore the growing feeling that somewhere a tightly wound ball of string was unraveling.

Tarian, Alex, Daric, and Calliope emerged from travel a block away from the crowd gathered to watch the fire burn. A gaggle of reporters broadcasted from the left, separated by a small space and crime scene tape from the fires.

The area buzzed with activity. Firefighters, police, ambulances, and sirens swarmed the streets like bees hunting sweet nectar. A team of firefighters pushed forward, their faces grim, hose aimed at the closest, smallest blaze. Water rushed forward, landed with a hiss on the flames, and evaporated. The fire flared higher, forcing the firefighters to duck and back away. From the expressions on their faces, it looked like a dance they'd tried before. Tarian shook her head. They'd never put it out that way.

Behind them stood a curious, frightened, fascinated crowd of onlookers ranging in age from toddler to teetering.

Teams of police tried to push the gawkers back, but as soon as one section shifted backward, another surged forward to take its place.

"If this crowd panics, the fires will be the least of the worries," Daric muttered.

"Let's make sure they don't." Tarian turned to her sister. "Can you do something about this Calli?"

Calliope's signature fresh, clean scent spilled out as she used her empathic abilities to survey the mood nearby. "Maybe? There's a lot of them. It would be easier with Macari, but I might be able to do enough. If you don't take too long. But I couldn't boost you at the same time."

A stern-looking cop, clearly just out of training by the lack of wrinkles on his face, waved a hand at Tarian. "You all need to move back. You don't belong up here. It's dangerous. Move on now. Back behind the line. Or better yet, go home. We got this."

"Really? Don't look it to me, man." Alex shook his head. "Looks to me like you need help."

"That's not for you to worry about. Now please. Step. Back." The cop waved with one hand while the other moved to rest on the weapon at his side, fingers twitching.

"You itching to shoot me or something?" Tarian smiled her I-mean-you-no-harm-we-come-in-peace smile. "Why don't you go get your supervisor. Tell him the Keeper is here."

The man remained clearly unaffected by her charm, and his hand tightened around the butt of the gun. "Keeper of what? You stupid or somethin'? Why don't you do what you're told, sweetheart. Back behind the line."

Alex stepped forward to put himself slightly in front of Tarian. "Hope that gun has magic bullets, 'cause you're gonna need 'em." His arms flexed.

The officer's face clouded. He looked at Tarian, and recognition traveled across his face like a rusty freight train gaining speed. "You're some of *them*." He put so much derision in the word that it sounded like the worst possible thing in the world to be. "You got no business being here. You people with so-called magic. One of you prob'ly caused this. I ain't gonna ask you again. Get on back." He half-pulled the weapon.

Alex grabbed the officer's hand and squeezed until the officer let go of his weapon. He twisted the man's arm behind his back, holding him in a tight grip. "Relax, dude. I don't wanna have to break your arm. We ain't got time to heal you. We got fires to put out."

Tarian sighed and turned to Calliope. "Start with him maybe?" She studied the crowd, from the official to not-so-official. How many thought like this guy? She didn't have time to worry about it, not with these fires still threatening all of downtown Fort Worth. She pictured herself wrapping the fool up in a net of Air and hanging him above the fires like a pig on a spit. She wouldn't. But she wanted to.

The most frustrating thing about the fall of magic had been the reaction by those who remained untouched. Some of those who'd been drenched by magic fumbled their way along, doing more harm than good as they learned to cope. Others flat-out denied it had happened, with dire consequences. Most of those who'd been skipped reacted like this cop. Jealous. Fearful. Hateful. A reaction of the have-nots to the haves.

Their terror of the unknown and inexperience did more than cloud their judgment—it destroyed their ability to think and reason. They often lashed out at anyone with even a hint of magical ability, no matter who, no matter the consequences.

The attitude had made it incredibly difficult to educate those suddenly gifted. Progress the last year had been slow, painful, and annoying.

Tarian rubbed the medallion, stoking a surge of energy. "Go to it, Calli. Do your best."

Daric pointed at the nearest bonfire. "They aren't growing at all, so they aren't fed by anything. They're tied off like a web.

We just need to smother them. Earth and Water both work for that. And Air, if we use it strategically. What if we split up? Tari, you go left, using Water and Air. Alex can go right. I can go back and forth between you, lend a hand wherever. And Calli can keep the crowd and officials calm while we work. It's only three blocks. Without opposing force, this should go pretty fast."

Calliope touched the officer's arm and smiled, depositing love like a cedar tree sheds pollen. He stopped struggling immediately. "You can go now, Alex. This nice man is going to show me how they're set up. Right?"

The officer nodded slowly, then escorted Calliope away, looking bemused.

Alex whistled. "Think she gave him a double whammy."

Tarian chuckled. "He needed it. Uptight ass. Okay, let's do this. We have a birthday party to get to."

The three of them nodded at each other and fanned out. Daric and Alex both pulled energy as they circled the flames to the right, leaving a trail of cinnamon and wet grass wafting behind them.

Tarian waited until the group of police and fire officials all clustered around her sister, obviously enthralled by her talents. Her sister made an excellent snake charmer. The entire crowd looked stoned.

When she was sure they no longer watched, Tarian quickly circled around to the left of the largest fire.

She stepped closer to it, and the fire snapped at her, sending a wave of oxygen-sucking heat that made her choke. She backed away, crafting a shield of Air to block the worst of the heat as she went. It wasn't enough. Her lungs burned with every breath she struggled to take. The fire consumed all available oxygen, burning hotter and higher than any normal fire could have managed.

Anyone trying to get close enough to fight the blaze would have died long before they had a chance to succeed.

Tarian reached for more power and formed a helmet of Air around her head like she would in the ocean. She had to take several long breaths before her heart and lungs stopped screaming.

She continued around the fire, keeping a safer distance. When she reached the back of it, she discovered why this particular blaze was the largest. It danced in the middle of what used to be a square, but now looked more like an urban desert, with pavement and asphalt instead of sand. One of the smaller nearby fires flickered and pranced toward this central point like a toddler learning to walk.

The flat emptiness continued for several blocks behind the fire. In the distance, train tracks and what looked like a large bar or nightclub remained untouched. A crowd had gathered, some people standing on top of cars to get a better view.

The gap between herself and the onlookers felt enormous. They might as well be an ocean away, an impossible distance to cross. She knew it was just the cop's attitude that made her feel that way. She was isolated and alone and more apart from the human world than ever. Magic fell, and instead of making things better for those who'd been living in secret, it had made things much, much worse. Or at least, that's how it seemed from what she saw on the news.

She wondered if those watching had been touched by magic. If they liked the gift or rejected it as a curse. If they embraced magic or feared it. If they feared her.

She wondered what to do about it if they did. Then she realized the only thing she could do was show them that magic itself was not good or bad. It was as natural as the sun. In the end, it was the one channeling the power who determined good or evil.

Tarian turned back to the inferno. The fire she targeted completely blocked her view of the crowd, Daric, and Alex. She needed to smother it, with the least amount of splash possible. She could throw an ocean of water at it, but once released it would rush through the fire and onto the waiting people. Not good.

She circled to the left, looking for something to use to block a water surge. No trace of building material remained. No scrap of metal. No heap of brick. Nothing.

She tried to imagine the force it had taken to dissolve so much, so quickly, but couldn't. Even the destruction of the Stulos, the strongest magical constructs she'd ever seen, had left traces of the surroundings behind. Her mind raced ahead to what this might mean. Someone or something this powerful...

She shoved the thoughts ruthlessly to the background. No time. Fix this. Get home. Think later.

Right.

She'd have to suppress the fire and then try to place a shield on the other side to stop the water before it hit anyone. If she forced it to the sides, it should run down the streets and into the storm drains rather than surge like a tidal wave. She hoped.

Tarian squared her shoulders and readied herself to pull power through the medallion.

Before she could focus her thoughts, something flickered in the middle of the square, left of the bonfire. Tarian squinted, looking for whatever had caught her attention. She thought it might be more fire. Perhaps whoever started it waited to strike again.

Heat turned the entire scene into a wiggly surreal painting. The haze made it difficult to make out details, but the square looked empty aside from the fire. She watched for a full thirty seconds. Nothing.

"Lasair? You there?" Tarian continued to stare at the space. The Ancient didn't answer. She hadn't expected him to. She was sure he had gone. He wouldn't want the chaos that naturally surrounded him to make things worse.

She waited another few seconds, then turned her attention back to the fire. This one wasn't overly large and seemed self-contained. It would take a surge of Water but nothing too big. She hoped.

One thing seemed sure—there was no way a fire this stable flattened three city blocks. Whatever left the fires behind had to be the culprit. The fires were the side effects, not the cause.

Flicker.

A pulse of energy moved past her, like a gust of wind. It made her arms tingle.

She spun, trying to catch whatever it was.

A spot in the distance looked hazy and wiggly, like heat sometimes looks above the asphalt on a really hot summer day. But the spot was nowhere near the bonfire she'd hoped to put out. It wasn't Lasair. At least, she didn't think it was.

She walked toward spot. It had been *something*, dammit. She wasn't imagining random flickers or that gust of energy. And air didn't just sparkle like that. Not without help.

Hints of burnt ozone and charcoal filled the air, exactly as she would have expected from any fire. But nothing else. Whatever caused the flicker, and the fires, didn't leave any kind of signature trace behind like a human usually did. Either it was someone very good at hiding their tracks, or it wasn't caused by a human at all. Either way, the last thing they needed was more fires.

She took another step toward the hazy spot and paused again. Something tempted her nostrils. She couldn't place the scent. It was too faint and overwhelmed by the heavy odor of burnt asphalt.

She took another step, then another. Paused. Something tickled her nose again. She didn't dare move closer to the phantom flicker until she knew what she faced. She couldn't detect any active magic use and yet something danced just out of sight.

"What the hell." Tarian sniffed again. Something new wafted on the breeze. Something raw. Wild. Concentrated. Something that tickled with familiarity, like déjà vu or a distant memory.

She inched forward. The scent strengthened. Power played with the hair on her arms. The air rippled. She stared at the spot, expecting a travel portal to form or Lasair to appear.

Nothing.

She glanced around. Fire to the right, empty street to the left. She took one more step, and energy surged. She dodged to the side as a flash of lightning hit the asphalt where she'd been standing. She rolled and scrambled to her feet. Her palms stung, and she smelled burnt hair.

"Great." She rubbed her hands on her jeans to remove the worst of the small pebbles. When she returned her attention to the area in front of her, it looked like someone had blown the world's largest soap bubble. It floated about three feet off the ground and measured about four feet in diameter. It looked slick, oily, and translucent. Inside, blue and red streaks snaked around each other in a sinuously seductive salsa.

"What the...."

Lightning flashed inside the bubble. Sparks from the fire flew toward it as if called. The Water Artifact in Tarian's chest heated and lashed out with a single strand of power. Dolphin cries filled the air as the bolt of energy hit the bubble. The bubble took it in, bulged, and doubled in size. Her heart pounded, adrenaline pushing it past overdrive in under a second. She scrambled to pull back on the energy spewing from the medallion, but the artifact appeared to have other ideas. It continued to feed the bubble.

"Tari, look out!" Daric's voice sounded distant and frantic.

Tarian threw her arms up to shield her head and ducked just as the bubble exploded. Cascades of water burst out in a raging tidal wave that swept toward her like a tsunami.

Daric wrapped his arms around her and a shield around them both. Rushing water struck it and fountained into the air like a geyser.

"Move!" Tarian pulled on Daric's arm, tugging him backward and away from the area just as the water crashed back to earth. It splashed down and gushed outward to envelop the largest bonfire, then rushed on to eat several smaller ones. Steam hissed and filled the air with wet, hot mist. The water extinguished fires and rushed onward as if extremely late for a very important meeting.

Tarian gaped, unable to reconcile the flat streets of a Texas city with the raging waterway they'd suddenly become. Her heart pounded hard enough to march in a parade. The medallion, however, quieted as if nothing had happened. A warm tingle remained to remind her, but that was all. Her own energy reserves hadn't been tapped at all.

"What the hell was that thing? Never seen you make something like that before." Daric panted in between the words, breathless.

"I didn't. It just...showed up." She looked from the now empty air to the gushing water. "I don't get it. What made it pop? Did you do that?"

Daric hunched, hands on knees, trying to get his breath back. "Not my element. I thought you did."

She took a deep breath, trying to calm the race her heart seemed to be running inside her veins. "Hell no. I thought about using Water like that, but I didn't want it running off down the street. Last thing we need. A bunch of onlookers drowned by magic."

They stood ankle deep in water. Tarian watched as more bonfires winked out, each swallowed by the torrent. In the distance, she saw the fires sink into the ground and vanish. "Looks like Alex got the rest."

Daric turned, slowly surveying the area. "Whatever made it pop, it worked. Nice. Messy, but nice."

Tarian followed his gaze and saw what he meant. No trace of fire remained. No buildings. Just wet street, wet sidewalk, and black smudges where buildings once stood. Three blocks of downtown Fort Worth now lay clean and bare, pristine and untouched.

"Creepy. It's like nothing ever lived here," Daric said.

She couldn't help but stare. It wasn't even a ghost town of abandoned buildings or a dystopian area filled with bomb remnants. She looked behind them at the crowd gathered several blocks away. They looked agitated, pointing and talking in groups. She couldn't tell if they were excited that the fire was out or freaked out about the water and obvious use of power, or both.

Daric walked toward the center of the square, to stand where the bubble had hovered. "I can feel some residual energy, but it's already dissipating. Doesn't feel human at all."

"It's not." Tarian sniffed. No hint of power remained either. "Unbelievable. So much power I can still taste it. But no evidence that it was even here."

"What's it taste like?" Daric sounded amused.

"Like the air tastes when someone burns fish and then leaves it to rot in the coals." She rubbed her arms. The remaining power in the air tickled the hair, but otherwise passed harmlessly over her. "Did you see the bubble?"

"Not at first. It looked like you were staring at nothing. But when I got closer, I could see a ripple and saw the lightning. Felt the surge. What the hell was that?"

«No idea." She gulped down oxygen, wishing it would clear the taste of salty soot out of her lungs. "It smelled almost natural. Undirected. Not like when a human channels an element through themselves. More raw." She sniffed the air, trying to remember. It seemed familiar, somehow. But she couldn't place why. "I could swear I've smelled it before."

Daric sloshed back through the water toward her. "Did you see anything else? Anyone?"

She thought about it. "I saw a flicker. When I went to investigate, it, the artifact..." She paused, remembering. "I'm not sure, but I think it defended me."

They heard a shout and turned to see Alex hurrying toward them.

"We better get. The crowd's freaking out."

Calliope splashed toward them, her face full of alarm. Firefighters and police followed just behind her, weapons drawn, grim faces ready for a fight that didn't exist anymore. "Tari, I can't hold them. There's too many. They saw the water and panicked."

Tarian quickly opened a travel portal to Xannon and gestured at it. "We're done here."

—4—

When they arrived back in the entry alcove for the house, they found Letta Roberts, holder of the Earth Artifact, Philadelphia detective, and newly minted lead for the Magical Law Enforcement Office, waiting. She'd been there awhile, if the way she tapped her foot and the impatience written across her face were any indication.

Tarian closed the travel portal in the face of the officer they'd met when they first arrived in Fort Worth. The angry look of shock that flashed through his eyes just before it snapped shut was extremely gratifying. "You'd think they'd be grateful. Most of them had some level of magic. Only that first guy didn't get a drop. You'd think they'd all welcome the extra weapon to fight crime." She looked at Letta, dressed in the torn jeans and leather jacket she wore when she worked in the tougher sections of Philadelphia. She looked ready for a fight. Or a rave. "Somehow I don't think you're here just for the birthday party."

"That's one reason." Letta took in their bedraggled appearance at a glance. Her lip twitched. "Who won?"

"The fire." Tarian raised an eyebrow at her. "What's up?"

Letta fell into step as Tarian led the way to the receiving hall.

"Got something strange in the new park in the Mansion District. Thought maybe you should take a look. Can't make out what it is, but it don't feel right."

Tarian paused. "Define strange."

Letta took out her phone, tapped it a few times, and held it up. "There's two of 'em. They don't show up much in the picture, but they feel funny. I get too close, I feel like they pull on me. Like they trying to suck my soul or something."

Tarian studied the video. It showed the new fountain in the center of Mansion Park. Several blocks of the district had been destroyed when magic fell. Tarian had charged Letta with putting it right, and the woman had managed to create something beautiful to fill the void, with Alex's help and a lot of money from anonymous donors.

A translucent bubble filled with strands of white and blue bobbed slowly up and down next to the fountain. With the water splashing behind it, the effect was quite picturesque. If Tarian hadn't just come from a fire that she was sure had been caused by one of those things exploding, she might have said it was beautiful. As it was, it represented a bright bobbing bit of worry.

"Shit." Tarian jerked her head toward the receiving hall, then continued with faster footsteps.

"You know what it is?" Letta asked, keeping pace. Daric, Alex, and Calliope followed close behind, passing the phone from one to the other.

"Bubbles of evil," Alex said, handing the phone to Daric.

"They aren't evil," Calliope said. "They're just...pockets of energy. Though I'll admit I didn't get a close enough look to know if it was sentient."

"That thing exploded for no reason," Alex said.

Daric glanced at Tarian. "Oh, I'm sure there was a reason. We just need to figure out what."

"Hey, it wasn't my fault." She held up her hands in protest. "The medallion reacted to whatever that bubble was. I didn't tell it to." She walked toward the doorway to the receiving hall, but Calliope stopped her before she could enter.

"It reacted? Did you see how the bubble got there?" Calliope asked.

"Not really. I saw flickers."

"How many?" Letta asked.

"Just the one. I think." Tarian glanced back at Daric for confirmation. He and Alex both nodded. "It was more than enough."

When they entered the receiving hall, Tarian spotted a teenage girl waiting in the center of the room and waved at her. "Hey, Kia. Thanks for waiting."

"Ain't no bother, Ms. Tari." Kia took in their appearance with interest. "I seen the news. Y'all okay? You look a bit done over."

"No more'n usual." Alex stopped at the first set of monitors, his arms crossed over his chest as he studied them. "One bubble did all them fires? Ate all them buildings?"

Calliope sat on the top step of the platform in front of the Dolphin Throne and leaned forward to support her head in her hands. Her eyes drooped, as if she hadn't slept in weeks. "I doubt it. There had to be another, right? I mean, that one unleashed a lot of Water, didn't it? Not Fire?"

Tarian sniffed, remembering. "The air smelled like Fire when we got there. Maybe it did both?"

«Fire *and* Water? In some sort of, what, shield type thing? Fire's never used to make a shield." Calliope looked doubtful.

Tarian shrugged. It sounded ridiculous. They weren't the two elements most likely to hang out together in nature by any stretch. But she didn't have any other explanation.

"Any idea where it came from?" Letta asked.

«No," Tarian said.

"Maybe it just sprang up," Alex said.

"Power don't spring. That ain't how it works." Kia touched one of the monitors, her delicate fingers tracing the scene where fires once ravaged.

Tarian moved closer. "What do you mean?"

Kia looked at Tarian. Her eyes always held more wisdom than someone that young should possess, but now they looked deeper than the darkest part of the ocean. "Power ain't created or destroyed. It be shifted around and channeled, but not made new. Not from scratch. All the elements started balanced. That's how they meant to be. And they all still be here. The same ones as the beginning. Just not spread even. Not since the rain."

"I did screw things up that day, didn't I?" Tarian returned her attention to the monitors. "All that energy plopped down like that was bound to cause trouble. Not sure destroying the Stulos was the smart thing to do, looking back."

"They weren't balanced neither, Ms. Tari. They was an illusion of it. Them Stulos had to come down sooner or later." Kia smiled, and it lit a spark in the depths of her eyes that Tarian thought could hypnotize someone if they stared long enough. "Least this way, you can help with the after."

Calliope joined them to stare at the screens depicting downtown Fort Worth. "How many more bubbles are there? You say there's some in the park in Philadelphia? They aren't showing that on the news yet. Think those will explode too?"

"I hope not." Tarian glanced at the clock. Excitement rushed through her body. "Five minutes. Shit, we cut that close."

Tarian moved to the center of the room and stopped just

short of the symbol embedded in the stone floor. Ruarc had been given special access to that location, so that Ember's return would be as safe as possible.

Letta joined Tarian and held out her hand. "It might be nothing, but when I got close to one of the bubbles, I felt a tug. Like it wanted to pull me in, or maybe pull energy from me. It kinda freaked me out, so I backed up. But I noticed the prism I made for Ember started to glow, and it feels different now. Like it's charged or something. What do you think?"

Tarian glanced down at what Letta held out, then looked again. And again. A diamond nestled in the palm of her hand. A golf-ball sized diamond. "Is that...?" The thing sparkled and glistened and preened against Letta's dark skin, looking exactly like a diamond would look. A really big, incredibly unbelievable, crystal clear, flawless rock. The kind only Bill Gates could afford to buy. Or maybe Warren Buffet. Or J. K. Rowling.

"Holy shit." Tarian took it and held it up to the sunlight. It was honed into an oval shape that grabbed the light, danced with it, and spit it back out in a rainbow of colors that swirled around her hand.

Calliope gasped.

Alex whistled.

Daric reached out to touch it, with reverence.

Kia clapped. "Oh, Ms. Letta, you outdid yo-self. It's perfect."

Finally, Tarian realized she should say something. But all she could manage was "Holy...wow."

Letta cleared her throat. She seemed uncomfortable with the attention but pressed on with her point anyway. "It seemed to me the bubble was a bit smaller the next time I looked at it. Just a bit. Not that big one I showed you, the other one. It's off by that cluster of new trees."

Tarian turned the diamond over in her hand, seeking any sort of magical signature. It was so dense, it had next to no Air energy at all. Stone usually contained a significant portion of Air. The more porous the stone, the more Air it used.

There was a hint of something more, but she couldn't quite grasp what. "The bubble was smaller, because of this? Why?"

Letta shrugged. "Dunno. Just seemed like before I got there, this was just a rock. And after, it glowed. Like it absorbed something from that bubble."

Tarian looked from the diamond to Letta. "It absorbed energy?"

"Just a rock?" Alex sounded amused. "Damn, girl. That ain't just a rock. That'd be like calling the Grand Canyon just a crack."

Daric leaned in for a better look at the prism. "How'd you make this?"

Letta glanced at Kia, then away again, her cheeks flushing. "I just ask. Something I learned that night it rained. Kia told me to ask the stone what it wanted to be and...I don't know. I just...did it."

They all turned to look at Kia, who beamed at Letta like a proud schoolteacher at a prize student.

"Kia? How'd you know?" Tarian asked. Kia's history remained a mystery. They knew her mother, a current resident of the prison below the room they stood in, to be a selfish, overly religious woman who swore she'd conceived Kia in the backseat of a model of car with the same name.

Despite that, Kia had matured into a fourteen-year-old wise woman with an unusual talent for insulating magical energies. She'd spent the last year studying magic and playing babysitter to Ember. Until Ember learned to harness her own talents, Kia served as an excellent safety gate.

"It ain't no mystery, Ms. Tari. Don't you do the same with your talents? I know mine, alls I gotta do is touch skin to skin. Makes a connection. And I just pray for it to fortify, like it says in the Bible. Mama always calmed if I asked for it nicely."

"I've never thought about it. But I'm pretty sure prayer has nothing to do with my...talents." Tarian caressed the diamond. Her fingers glided across the cool surface. Curious, she formed a small droplet of water from the surrounding atmosphere and let it fall on the stone. The diamond soaked the water drop into itself, absorbing the moisture and the energy that created it, leaving nothing behind. A pinpoint of light deep inside grew brighter for a second. Her fingers tingled, and she felt the faintest hint of a pull on her own energy. She cut off her flow, and the glow subsided. She turned the rock in her hand. It caught the light and sparkled, an innocent diamond once more.

"What the hell?" She frowned at it, then at Alex and Letta. "It's a sponge?"

Alex shrugged. "Earth absorbs."

Tarian handed the diamond back to Letta. "Even without that, people will pay a fortune for something that gorgeous."

Letta grinned. "It ain't for sale. It's for Ember. For her birthday. I figured it being a prism and all, she might like it since it sparkles so much."

Tarian stared at her. "You can't be serious. You'd give that to an infant barely a year old?"

"Well, it ain't like she'd swallow it. And I figured, the way her talent works, this won't cause any harm since it don't send out no energy for her to absorb." Letta cast her eyes down to the stone in her hand. "I have bigger ones," she muttered.

"Really? How big?"

Letta cupped her hands as if holding a baseball.

Daric laughed. "Nice."

"Damn, girl." Alex sounded admiring. "I ain't ever done something that cool. You gotta show me how to do that."

Tarian glanced at the clock. One minute. All thoughts of prisms, diamonds, bubbles, and fire flew out of her mind. "It's time!"

They all clustered in anticipation near the center of the room, next to the symbol.

Alex poked Tarian in the shoulder. "Try to be nice, yeah?"

"I'm always nice."

Alex snorted.

"Usually."

«Right.»

Tarian glared at her best friend. "Bite me."

Alex looked away, not even trying to hide the smile on his face. Tarian poked him in the ribs.

The room fell silent as the clock ticked the last few seconds away.

Five.

Four.

Three.

Air churned in the center of the room. A funnel formed, thick and heavy. Soon it obscured the symbol on the floor, the anxious faces, and the monitors on the wall. It swirled, bent, then coalesced into something more solid. Something tall and angular. The something turned into Ruarc, who emerged with his arms full of a squiggly toddler.

Toddler.

The word chased itself in her mind, feeling foreign and out of place.

Toddler. Not Ember.

Tarian stared. Definitely Ruarc. Same slick black hair. Same deep blue eyes. But there was something in his expression. She didn't know what that look meant, but she knew it wasn't good.

She stared at the little girl burying her face against Ruarc's neck.

Girl.

The word girl chased the word toddler in her mind, but neither held any meaning.

"Keeper. As agreed, I've returned our daughter exactly on time."

"That's not my daughter." The words rushed out of her as if they were bullets from a gun. The kind of bullets that could rip through Kevlar and flesh and bone and explode to make mincemeat of internal organs. A flash of heat raced through her stomach and up to her face and colored the room a hazy, angry red.

Daric stepped forward. "What the hell are you trying to pull?"

Tarian blocked Daric. "Stop." She focused on Ruarc. "Bring my daughter here. Now."

"This *is* Ember." Ruarc turned the girl toward Tarian, confusion on his face. "Look at her."

The girl leaned back into Ruarc's arms, eyes wide, thumb in her mouth. She looked startled. Wary. As if she faced a wild animal and wasn't quite sure if it would be friendly.

"What the fuck..." Letta said.

Tarian waved a hand to silence her.

Ruarc watched her, as wary as the girl. He looked around at those waiting as if they would somehow join him against a mad woman. "It's Ember. Why would I bring any other? It would break the Agreement. And as you see, I have not done so. I remain alive."

When no one responded, Ruarc tried again, sounding more than a little frustrated. "What is wrong? Has something happened here? Is it safe?" He pulled the girl closer as if to shield her with his body from an attack.

"Tari..." Calliope put a soft hand on Tarian's arm. "He's telling the truth. It's her."

"No." Tarian shook her head, stunned and unable to comprehend. The room turned upside-down and spun lazily, like a top near the end as it wobbled, about to fall over. "No. No. No."

"Yes, Ms. Tari. She's right. That be your daughter, sure as I'm standing here. She got your eyes." Kia smiled at the little girl. "I'd know them big beautiful eyes anywhere."

Tarian stared at the round sapphire eyes.

My mother's eyes. Calliope's eyes.

"No...no," Tarian whispered. She put her hand over her mouth to stop herself from screaming.

Daric took Tarian's other hand and squeezed, hard. "Breathe, Tari."

Ruarc put his lips near Ember's ear and whispered.

Ember frowned. "Mama?"

Time stretched and yawned and reached into the corners of Tarian's mind, teasing her with a truth that ripped through her brain and then clawed a path to her stomach. She wanted to throw up. She wanted to scream. She wanted to deny everything. This could not be happening. It would not happen. It must not.

She stared at the girl and tried to force her brain to make sense of what she saw.

Failed.

This child was a year older than Ember. At least. Thoughts flitted around in her skull, making no sense at all. Slimy things wormed their way through the hole in her stomach and churned. Her mouth felt full of dry kelp.

Ruarc glanced around the room. When he spoke, it was in a quiet controlled tone, as if afraid of spooking a horse. "I can see you are...surprised...by the phase difference."

"Surprised?" Tarian put a hand over her mouth to stop anything else from coming out. It didn't make sense. Nothing made sense. How could this possibly make sense? There was no way this toddler could be her daughter. No way in hell.

Beside her, Alex made a noise that might have been a word, or it might have been a warning. The kind of sound a dog makes just before it bites.

"What the hell did you do, daemon?" Letta looked to Tarian and Daric. "Did y'all know this would happen?"

Daric, Alex, and Calliope all spoke at once. Their voices rose like a rock concert, growing continually louder, filling the room with noise.

The noise frightened the girl. She cowered backward, seeking refuge in Ruarc's chest. He soothed her, murmuring quietly and patting her back as any father would do. The bond between them was undeniable.

Tarian closed her eyes and blocked out the noise. She focused on the scents and signatures in the room. Daric's cinnamon wrapped around her, comforting and warm as always. Calliope's forest breeze. Letta's rich earth. Alex's deeper moist grass and rock. Ruarc's cooler fresh breezy scent.

Underneath it all lay a soft blend of cinnamon, sea spray, sunshine, and mountain breeze that flitted through the air and explored like a butterfly. It touched here and there, brightening the room with its presence.

Tarian reached for her tracking sense, afraid of what it would tell her. Not wanting to feel it, but desperate to know. The second she focused on her daughter, the bond between them snapped to attention, a link so bright it ached, because they stood so close. Her ability to track someone never failed.

"Ember," Tarian whispered.

The room fell silent. When Tarian opened her eyes, she found everyone watching her, including Ember. The part of her heart that beat only for her daughter cracked just a little, the pain of it swelling up to her eyes. "Ember." She said it louder. It was a statement, not a question.

The look of relief that crossed over Ruarc's face and body would have been comical any other time. He remained wary, but he nodded. "Yes. I've returned with your daughter as agreed."

Tarian looked from Ruarc to Ember. When she'd last seen her daughter, just twenty-four hours ago, Tarian had waved goodbye to a one-year-old with short hair wearing a blue jumper.

Today, a toddler watched her with the same deep sapphire eyes. A toddler in a dark blue dress with red laces along the front. A toddler with a ponytail that brushed her shoulders. Calliope squeezed Tarian's arm. A rush of something cold flooded her body, followed by heat and a shot of adrenaline that sent her heart racing. Words circled her brain and finally joined together to create a sentence that pushed past her lips in a low, hoarse whisper. "What have you done?"

—5—

Tarian's question seemed to confuse Ruarc. His brows furrowed, and for the first time since she'd met him he look worried. Genuinely worried. As if he had no idea what she was talking about.

She rejected the thought and the body language immediately. He knew damn good and well what he'd done. He'd known the second he made the Agreement with her a year ago. Her stomach dropped to her toes as the realization hit home. This was it. This was the loophole she hadn't known existed. This was what had been bothering her ever since they made that Agreement. The thing that had eaten holes in her nerves the past twenty-four hours. The thing that threatened to rip her world to shreds.

Tarian struggled against a landslide of emotions. "How... what...she..." Tarian coughed, the dryness in her mouth and throat at complete odds with the wetness in her eyes. She couldn't make her lips form the right sounds. The right words. Thoughts swirled, but none of them formed complete sentences that she could speak. They were bits and pieces, reflections of anger, betrayal, confusion, and pain pain pain. The kind of pain that gripped the heart and squeezed squeezed squeezed. Her hands moved, as if emphasizing all the words she couldn't say.

Calliope gripped her arm and poured soothing comfort amplified by her special talent. "Tari. Tari, please. Stay with us. Stay with me. Tari?" Tarian knew her sister was using empathy because she felt a tiny stream of warmth trying to infiltrate her body. But the warmth glanced off the avalanche of feelings and thoughts like a pebble skipping along the surface of a pond. It barely made a ripple.

Tarian swallowed, hard. Coughed. Swallowed again. She blinked, and the wetness on her lashes dripped down onto her cheek. She brushed it away, angry with it for being there. For showing weakness here, in her own home, in front of Ruarc, of all people. She took a deep breath and managed to ask again, this time louder and more like herself, "What the hell have you done?"

Ruarc took a step backward, toward the monitors that still broadcast news alerts from the recent fires. He glanced at them, then returned his attention to her, clearly dismissing them as unimportant. "I've returned our daughter to her home, as agreed. I promised her there'd be a celebration when we arrived."

He looked from Tarian to Alex to Daric and back again. "Was I...mistaken?"

"Mistake." Tarian repeated the word, feeling stupid and slow. The word itself sounded foreign. "Mistake?"

Ruarc stilled, taking in her appearance. He studied the others, then glanced back at the monitors. Recognition or understanding flashed across his face. "Keeper, has something happened? You look as though there's been an altercation. Is the safety of the House threatened?"

"Something happened. Yes. Something." Tarian's thoughts began to focus. Sluggish and stupid, but they came. Something most definitely happened. She wanted to reach for her daughter. She wanted to hold her in her arms and never let go. She wanted…but she couldn't move. Couldn't think.

"Explain why Ember is not the same as when she left yesterday." Daric's voice was steel and barbed wire. He reached for Ember. She eyed his hands, but instead of moving toward him, she leaned back into Ruarc.

Ruarc glanced at him, taking note of the hostility with a passive raise of his eyebrow. He continued to soothe Ember, who buried her face in his neck. "I presumed you knew about the natural phase difference between the daemon and human realms. I see I was mistaken. A small matter."

The Water Artifact, Tarian's birthright and symbol for her position as Keeper, warmed with her rising need to pounce. It pushed, eager to run loose, as if some force not her own beckoned. For the first time in years, her magic tilted past the point of control. She fought desperately to rein in her temper and her power. Tried to take a deep breath. Choked. Calliope gripped Tarian's shoulders as if to hold her back. She exuded happiness and peace, but it found no place to land.

Daric squeezed her hand so tight she thought it would break. She ripped it away, shaking.

Kia reached for Tarian's hand, her touch so gentle Tarian barely registered the contact. What she did register was a weight pressing in all over body like someone had enclosed her in some sort of bondage and then tightened the laces. The pressure from the Water Artifact stopped. The swirl of uncontrolled power stopped. Her anger continued unabated.

"What the hell, man!" Alex's outrage barely registered.

Ruarc took another step backward, his arms tight and protective around Ember. "Keeper. Perhaps we…"

"Mr. Ruarc, may I see Ember?" Kia released Tarian's hand and stepped calmly between Tarian and Ruarc, her arms outstretched.

Tarian's power and the artifact swung back into motion as if there hadn't been any kind of break at all. They picked up intensity and energy and prowled through her body ready for some sort of call to action.

Ember's face brightened. "Kia!" She lunged for Kia, oblivious of the danger of falling.

Ruarc had no choice but to transfer the child. Kia smiled broadly at Ember and tickled her tummy. Ember giggled with delight.

It was as if the person on the other end of a tug-of-war suddenly dropped the rope. The pull on her power vanished, and suddenly Tarian was in control of the artifact. She rubbed it, surprised. Nothing had ever called power through the medallion before. She hadn't thought it was possible.

Tarian shook her head, desperately trying to clear the fog and her mood. "How?"

Ruarc stared at Kia and Ember, his expression thoughtful and calculating. When he spoke, he kept his voice low, soft, and calm. "We should discuss this away from the child, Keeper." She wasn't sure if he meant to soothe Ember, or herself. It did the exact opposite. Anger flared higher than before.

"My child. *My* child, doesn't *know* me.»

Ruarc frowned. "Of course she knows you. You're her mother. Why wouldn't she? You're frightening her, Keeper. She is extremely sensitive to the moods of those around her. *Especially* her mother's."

Daric put an arm around Tarian's shoulders and squeezed. She felt the warmth and calm his touch always invoked, but it was a feather brushing against a boulder of anguish and anger. He leaned in to whisper. "Your daughter needs you. She doesn't know anything is wrong unless you tell her. Be strong for her. We can sort him out later."

Tarian nodded and took a deep breath. Then another. It didn't help. She'd given the angry beast inside her too much freedom. It would not be stilled. She tried again. Tried to see past the hazy mist of rage to focus on Ember. "Hey, little spark." Her voice came out a high-pitched squeak. She cleared her throat and tried again. "You've grown so much. Let me look at you." She held out her hands to Kia and nodded.

Ember glanced doubtfully back at Ruarc, her lips in a pout.

Ruarc nodded encouragement. "Go on, Ember. Go to your mother."

"Come see me?" Tarian's voice rose even higher. Fear ran cold water through her veins. What if Ember wouldn't come to her? What if Ember... Tarian took another breath to steady her nerves. She was dizzy, and her focus blurred with unshed tears. "Please?"

Kia gave Ember a kiss on the cheek. "Say hi to your mama, sweet girl. She been missing you something fierce." She transferred Ember into Tarian's arms. Ember looked doubtful but went without protest. Kia remained close enough to keep a soothing hand on Ember's arm.

Tarian gathered her close, breathing in the sweet smell of her. It felt so good. So right. Some of the fear in her heart melted with the touch of Ember's soft skin and solid presence. Tarian held Ember slightly away from her for a minute, examining the child's face. "I've missed you, spark." Tears spilled onto her cheeks, but she ignored them. She smiled and kissed Ember's forehead.

Ember reached out a chubby finger and touched one, tracing it down Tarian's cheek. "Sad," Ember announced.

Tarian's throat caught.

Ember leaned close and pressed her lips against Tarian's cheek in a wet kiss.

Tarian closed her eyes and squeezed Ember, hugging her in a tight embrace that made the girl wiggle. "I missed you, baby girl. So much."

"Better?" Ember placed both hands on Tarian's cheeks and tilted her head, looking like an inquisitive puppy.

Tarian laughed despite the emotions still at war in her body. "Much."

Ruarc cleared his throat. "Perhaps..."

Tarian kept her eyes on Ember. "Perhaps what, Ruarc? Don't even think about leaving. We need to talk."

She'd kept her voice soft, but Ember noticed the change in tone and once again looked troubled.

Tarian gave her a hug. "Hey, I have an idea. Why don't you and Daddy Alex and Kia go out to the beach? You can build a castle. I bet Daddy Alex would love to do that. Wouldn't you, Alex?"

Alex started, then understanding flashed through his eyes. "Castles are my thing, sparky. I'll show ya how to build a really big one."

Tarian turned to hand Ember over to Kia. Kia smiled. "Rest easy, Ms. Tari. This'll pass. My mama always said so."

Tarian flashed Kia a smile of gratitude. "We won't be long."

Ember looked from Tarian to Daric to Alex. Her face looked far more serious than a toddler had any right to be. "Sad?"

Alex chuckled softly and kept his voice light. "No, *chiquita*, not sad. Very happy to see you! Let's go see the sand, yeah?" He tickled her tummy, and Ember squiggled in Kia's arms. Kia laughed with her and walked toward the side exit. Alex followed, pausing as he reached Tarian to mutter, "You sure?"

Tarian took Daric's hand in hers and nodded at Alex, unable to trust her voice or her words. Barely contained anger boiled in her throat, making her ears feel hot.

Calliope cleared her throat. "I think I'll...maybe I should stay here."

"She's quite sensitive, Keeper. She will sense your mood no matter where she is on this island." Ruarc raised an eyebrow. "Possibly further. She appears to have inherited an extremely strong talent for empathy."

Tarian looked at her sister. "Maybe you should go with them? Keep her in a good mood? With you there and Kia, maybe she won't notice us."

Calliope looked doubtfully at Tarian, but nodded.

Tarian tapped her foot, waiting for them to exit the room. If she stopped, she wasn't sure what might happen. She focused on the movement, making each one harder than the last, pounding her frustration into the stone beneath her foot.

Alex paused at the door, and with one last nod from her disappeared through it. She waited another minute, to be sure he'd reached the entry hall, before rounding on Ruarc.

"How?" The demand carried with it a threat she didn't have to voice. Her chest heated as the medallion readied itself to meet her needs. Her own power rose to feed her barely controlled temper.

"Tari." Daric gave her hand a warning squeeze.

"Keeper." Ruarc took a step back. "Our Agreement..."

"Won't stop me from killing you," Tarian snarled.

"It should. I think you'd find it a murky area, given that the girl is bound to be affected by the loss of her mother. Or father." His cold eyes looked like steel with a storm rolling through it. "Not to mention other considerations."

Tarian stomped her foot. A shock wave rippled out from her body. "How?"

Ruarc raised an eyebrow as the power brushed him, then shrugged. "When in a domain governed by Air, time currents run differently. One twenty-four-hour period Earth time is approximately one year in daemon terms. A daemon would seem, to a human, to age at an accelerated rate until the age of maturity, at which point the aging would seem to slow to a near stop. This is why daemon appear to live so much longer than humans. Time for us operates on a curve, bent by the force of the element, which creates our domain. I believe some humans have tapped into it, from time to time. A so-called fountain of youth."

Tarian processed the information, growing angrier as he spoke. Thinking back to the deal they'd made, and the look on his face then, she realized the truth. "You knew. You knew this would happen, and you knew I didn't know."

Ruarc's lip twitched.

«Bastard.»

Ruarc half-inclined his head.

"How *dare* you... Never mind. I already know the answer. You fucking coward. You knew if you told me, I'd never agree. You lied to me."

"Perhaps I omitted information."

"It's the same thing, asshole. The intent was the same. To get me to agree to something with less than all the facts."

"In Agreements, each party is responsible. If you did not have the facts, you should have satisfied that need before agreeing." Ruarc pointed at her. "I gave you what you asked for. What you demanded. It was a fair exchange." Ruarc dropped his hand and stood straighter, eyes flashing. "You wanted the Book of Daemon, you received it. You wanted an heir to the Dolphin Throne, I provided. You wanted the Air Artifact, I handed you the key. I did believe you knew this particular anomaly. Surely you or your sister researched my domain before sending Ember with me."

They had, and Calliope hadn't mentioned anything about this little trick of time. They didn't have the Book of Daemon anymore. The human records obviously lacked crucial information. "There's a hidden plot beneath every action you take. It was never about me. Ever. I knew you would have some loophole, some..." She took a deep breath. The full impact of her mistake slammed into her in waves, relentless, insistent, each accusation building and building, threatening to bury her in an ocean of regret.

Twenty-four hours is one year.

He gets her every year.

Every year she'll age two.

Every year she'll spend a year without me.

Every year.

She'll be sixteen in eight years.

Tarian's knees buckled.

It was a mistake of epic proportions. Not knowing this one fact....

She'd screwed herself.

And Ember.

Wave after wave.

Regret.

Anger.

Despair.

Ruarc spoke, but his words were lost in the ocean of pain that swept through her mind and tied her heart into knots. She crossed her arms tight against her chest and the medallion.

"Believe as you will, Keeper. My actions speak for themselves."

Tarian blinked as the words came in loud and clear. She

shook her head to clear the fog. "What?"

Ruarc took a step forward. His eyes bored into hers, burning in their intensity and, she thought, a desire for understanding. "Your daughter has returned alive and well and more advanced than any mere human child would be at this age. What's more..."

Tarian cut him off. "Screw you, Ruarc." All the things he should have said. Should have done. All the things *she* should have said and done. It all slapped her in the face, leaving welts that burned across her cheeks. "You should have told me." She had to force each word out past the lump in her throat. "My daughter...*my* daughter...doesn't know me."

"She knows you as surely as you know her, Keeper. She merely reacted to the shift in your mood. A mood she's surely sensing right now."

Tarian pushed at her power, sending a ripple of pure energy into the atmosphere. Drops of water formed mid-air and splashed to the ground. They hissed as they struck, fizzling out in the suddenly hot room. Fire always surfaced with the worst of her temper.

"Holy shit." Letta stared at Tarian as if she'd grown a second head.

"Tarian!" Daric's startled tone distracted her for a second. But only a second. She licked her lips, struggling to control both emotions and magic. Her thoughts refused to cooperate. Her mouth refused to let it go.

"You stole her childhood, Ruarc. You stole it from *me*. That is *not* part of any Agreement between us. That *does* affect her welfare."

"I stole nothing. I am not a thief." Ruarc took another step back. He managed to make it look casual, rather than the escape it was surely meant to be. Tarian slammed a shield down over the room, a mix of Water, Air *and* Fire that would keep almost anything or anyone in place.

Ruarc opened his mouth, then let whatever he'd been about to say die on his lips. "Keeper..."

"Don't Keeper me, you asshole. I did *not* agree for my daughter to be raised by you. I did *not* agree to lose her entire childhood. If this happens every time you take her." Tarian paused. Images of Ember growing two years for every one swirled through her mind. Ember coming back a teenager with attitude, no longer listening to her mother because Ruarc had been filling her head for a year with innuendo or lies or whatever his agenda had truly been. And that, she realized, was the key. "You wanted to groom her for something. What? What are you planning on using her for? To take over here? Do you plan on ruling over humans?"

Ruarc glared.

"Well, answer! For once, answer a damn question. Tell the truth. Why did you do this? What are you using my daughter for?" Sweat trickled down the side of her face from the rising heat in the room. She ignored it. She ignored the way her shirt clung to her back and the swamp in her armpits. She kept her focus entirely on the bastard's face, trying to catch every nuance. Every change in body posture. Every muscle twitch.

"If you don't calm, she will react. Her power is far greater than we anticipated. She needs daemon training. She's young and cannot control her energy. For now, it responds to her emotional state. I think you'll find an upset mother is something that upsets the child a great deal."

Thunder crashed outside, startling Tarian briefly but not enough to lose her hold on the room or Ruarc. "Fuck you."

"Keeper." For once, Ruarc looked startled. "Please. Calm

yourself. I will explain."

"An Agreement then? A truthful explanation of your plans for my daughter? Your real plans?"

Ruarc glanced toward the door before nodding. "In exchange for your return to calm. Release your power, Keeper. Please. I will stay until you're satisfied with my explanation."

"Agreed." She tried to fill that one word with all the frustration and betrayal and anger that rolled around inside her.

"Agreed." Ruarc looked at the door again as though expecting a monster to storm through it.

The small Agreement took hold as the magic of it mixed with her own and settled like a soft blanket on her shoulders. She shuddered, suddenly cold to the very core. She was so close to the edge. "I...I can't. Release."

Tarian struggled to pull air into her lungs. Her lungs refused to expand. The lights in the room dimmed, and it began to rain inside the room.

"Tari, you have to release," Daric said, his tone alarmed.

Her thoughts churned like a whirlpool in deep ocean, pulling her deep into an abyss she couldn't escape. She pictured Ember, her sweet baby, and tried to imagine her in the room, in her arms. The thought made tears push at her eyelashes. All that she'd lost and would lose slammed into her. Tendrils of power from the medallion forged out into the room, gathering strength.

Terror flooded through her. "I...it's...I can't..."

Letta grabbed her arm and tugged, forcing Tarian down to her knees. "Get a grip! Use the stone."

"Good. Idea," Tarian panted. Letta guided her hands to the symbol on the floor and held them there. The tree with branches that represented her and Calliope, held by Marielle, glowed with their touch. The sight of it sent a sharp aching stab through her heart. She missed her mother so much it hurt. The kind of hurt that couldn't be soothed. What she wouldn't give to be able to ask her mother's advice right now.

Tears pushed past her lashes and down her cheeks. She didn't stop them. "I've lost her. I've lost her."

Daric knelt beside her, his arm going around her shoulders. "She's your daughter. She always will be. You have a connection that nothing can sever. Nothing."

It was exactly what her mother would have said. It was exactly the sort of thing she'd have ignored, back then. But the idea of it, and the memory of her mother, brought a sense of calm that she'd been lacking the last twenty-four hours.

Letta nudged with her shoulder. "Come on, girl. Let it go."

With a sigh, Tarian relaxed, and the power flowed through her hands into the stone floor. The symbol glowed brighter, accepting the overload and dispersing it along lines of energy that spread out into the room. She closed her eyes and let it all go to Earth, the one element she could not control and the second best for grounding, since it would absorb anything given to it without rebounding back out into the atmosphere. When it was done, she sat back, empty of the power overload but filled with regret and sadness.

Her body shook.

Daric pulled her back into his arms. "What a dysfunctional family we are. A daemon, an Irishman, and a Mexican fathered a child...sounds like the beginning of a really bad joke." Daric squeezed her tight enough to chase the last of her inner demons away.

Letta laughed. "Shit, this ain't dysfunctional, man. I seen a hell of a lot worse'n this."

Tarian choked out a laugh that sounded more like a sob, but

it helped release the last of her temper. The shield she'd placed on the room dissolved, letting fresh oxygen rush into the space. She gasped, taking it in a desperate gulp. She hadn't realized how thin the air had become. Her shield had blocked everything, even the flow of oxygen. She took several deep breaths, forcing herself to do it slowly. Methodically. Counting the time in measured beats. One. Two. Three. Breathe. Three. Two. One. Breath.

Stupid. Losing control like that, in front of Ruarc of all people. Stupid, stupid, stupid.

Tarian looked up at the daemon. He watched her with eyes full of concern and something more she couldn't put a name to. If she didn't know any better, she'd have labeled it compassion. But surely not. Not from a Mayfanata. Not from this particular daemon. He never let emotion show. Ever. It spooked her to see it.

"You must love this. Me, on the floor. Weak."

Ruarc's gaze hardened. "No." He turned and stalked toward the door. He covered half the distance, then stopped abruptly. "Do you feel that?"

"Oh...that ain't good." Letta abruptly dropped to her knees and slapped her palms onto the floor. "Oh crap."

"What?" Tarian pushed herself up to standing. All the emotions and power left her off-balance. It seemed like the room shook, but it had to be just her body reacting to the adrenaline. Daric kept a hand on her arm to steady her.

"Earthquake?" Daric looked alarmed.

Tarian frowned down at the floor. "It's just the leftover power."

Letta stood and ran for the door. "It ain't you."

Ruarc reached the exit first. He shouted over his shoulder as he left the room. "Ember!"

Terror ran through her body. "What's happening?"

"She's having a fit," Letta shouted.

"Ember's doing this?" Tarian and Daric raced through the doorway and into the entry alcove. The shaking became more pronounced, causing small pebbles to fall from the ceiling like dusty rain. "She's just a baby!"

Ruarc reached the front door and pounded through it, calling back as he went. "She is limited only by the power around her."

Realization slammed into Tarian, bringing with it stark terror. She'd sent Ember outside with Calliope, and Alex, and Kia. Three extremely strong with their respective elements. Ember's ability made her a power sponge. She could absorb magical energy of any sort. From anywhere. As a baby, she hadn't been able to do much. Her talent had been passive, a latent ability that she didn't consciously direct. It was easy to shield. Or had been, yesterday.

A year ago.

Panic shot through Tarian, giving her heart a shot of adrenaline. She sprinted ahead of Ruarc, out and down the stone steps to the beach. She'd just thrown a ridiculous amount of her own power into the atmosphere and into the ground.

The knot in her stomach grew into a boulder of ice with spikes that tore holes through her heart. The medallion warmed with the rising need inside her to strike out. She fought to control it, but she might as well try to dam whitewater rapids. Something ahead of her pulled and tugged and nudged the medallion to give up its power. Energy trickled out, despite her best efforts to make it stop. She crossed her arms tight across her chest, fists clenched, as if she could use her own body to stop the theft, and ran.

6

Tarian staggered onto the beach, buffeted by a sandstorm with bite. The sting of chunky grains of rock hitting her face made her eyes tear.

"Ember!" she shouted, her voice swept away into the storm, drowned by the avalanche of sand.

Ruarc grabbed her hand and tugged, and at first she pulled back, not trusting his intentions, before she realized he was trying to help steady both of them. He shouted, but the wind stole his words.

Tarian kept her lips shut, lowered her head, and pushed forward, dragging Ruarc and Daric with her. She felt the stirrings of power from Daric and shoved him with her shoulder. When he looked at her, she shook her head no. They couldn't risk putting even more energy into the atmosphere. Ember was only a baby...a toddler. She couldn't handle this much. No child could.

Tarian called out to Ember in her mind. Ember had daemon essence, so she might have inherited their telepathic abilities. *Ember! Little spark, it's all right. I'm here. Everything is okay. Please, Ember. Let it go. Relax, baby. You can do it.*

The storm raged on. Rocks crumbled around them as they

pressed onward. Ember hadn't heard, didn't care for the message, or didn't even understand how she did what she did.

An outside force tugged at her. It fed on the power in her body and in the medallion. Ember's signature circled through and around Tarian, mingled with the sand and sea. The force was stronger than anything Tarian could have imagined from a grown adult, let alone a toddler.

Primal roars of pain penetrated the storm from somewhere just to her right.

"Kia!" Tarian's shout was lost in the storm. "Calli! Alex!" She didn't hear anyone respond.

Tarian dropped Ruarc's and Daric's hands and turned, seeking her daughter's signature. With the sand and the raging sea, it was hard to pin down. She pictured Ember in her mind, the way she'd looked in Ruarc's arms. The smell of her. She tried again, and the connection solidified. Ahead and to the left. Tarian ran in that direction, leaving Ruarc and Daric to follow.

Halfway down the beach, Tarian stumbled and nearly fell on top of Kia. The teen crouched low, her arms over her head, face tucked to her chest. Tarian bent low, putting her lips to Kia's ear. "Are you okay?"

Kia nodded and lifted her head to shout back. "I'm sorry, Ms. Tari. She pushed me away. She didn't mean to. But I lost hold of her. Now I can't break through. She done put a barrier. I can't do nothing with it. I gotta have skin to skin."

Tarian patted Kia's back to let her know it wasn't her fault, then ducked her head and surged forward toward the spot her tracking sense indicated.

She risked a shout, calling Ember's name in the hope her daughter would hear and calm down, and instantly regretted it when her mouth filled with sand. She spit and pushed forward.

It was like surging up a hill made of molasses while wearing roller skates.

She couldn't see anything but whirling sand. Couldn't hear anything but the howling wind and crash of sea. The enormity of the storm...the power of it...Tarian gulped down the rush of fear at the thought of what it could do. What her daughter could do.

The bond she used to track Ember grew stronger with each step until finally she saw a shadow just ahead. A few more feet, and the shadow solidified into a scared, sobbing sand sorceress.

Ember hovered several feet above the ground, the eye of the storm, while the world fell apart around her. Her body shook with sobs. Her eyes filled with tears and determination. Her little fists punched as though she tried to fight the sand.

Tarian rushed forward and slammed into an invisible wall. She staggered back a few steps, stunned. She tried again, this time slower, with hands outstretched. When she reached the barrier, she realized what had happened. Ember had learned how to shield, and she'd learned it well. This one appeared made of Water, Air, and Fire. Fire...something nobody ever used in a shield. It was too chaotic, too unpredictable. But the way Fire supported this shield made it strong. Super strong. Strong enough to survive a nuclear blast. Ten nuclear blasts.

The shield would certainly withstand any attempt to remove it, even if it wasn't tied off. The constant stream of energy flowing from Ember fed the shield. Which meant Ember could release it if she wanted. Or if she were distracted.

Tarian couldn't help the surge of pride. Her daughter was already so strong. So resourceful.

So dangerous.

She wondered if her own mother had felt like this. Tarian stood there, wondering how to get through to her daughter without using any more elemental energy. She needed something passive. Something that would connect with the girl but not feed into her frenzy. Something like her tracking sense.

A shiny light bulb went off in her skull. Her tracking sense! She concentrated on the bond that connected her forever to her daughter. The signature, the sweet smell of Ember's blend of all four elements. Standing this close to her daughter, it overwhelmed her nose and pushed out everything else. She let her thoughts trace the bond through the shield.

Ember. Little spark. Let me help. Let me through.

Ember wrinkled her nose and turned her head. The wind faltered slightly. It was enough to encourage Tarian to keep going. She repeated the phrases over and over like a mantra.

Come on, baby, it's okay. Stop crying. Let it go. Let it all go.

Ember rubbed her eyes with her fists. Her lip quivered. And there, in the back of Tarian's mind, a childish whisper hovered, tentative and trembling. *Mama?*

Relief rushed through Tarian's thoughts and out through the bond. *Yes, baby. That's it! What a smart girl you are. I'm here. I want to come see you. Let the wind go, sweetie.*

Mama. Sowwy.

Tarian held out her hands. Ember reached out, but they remained several feet apart, with the invisible wall between them. *Come on, baby. Drop the shield. You can do it. Just let it go. Open your hands and let it drop. Like this.*

Tarian demonstrated with her hands. Ember mimicked the movement. It might be her imagination or wishful thinking, but it seemed like the storm lessened. She took a cautious step forward, met resistance, but managed to push through the wall at last.

Inside the barrier, the air was stale and still. Ember's face had turned an odd shade of bluish purple. Tarian took a sand-free breath but felt something press against her lungs. Inside the shield, Ember had blocked oxygen as well as sand. The girl would suffocate if the shield didn't drop soon.

Ember had mimicked the exact shield Tarian had formed not minutes before against Ruarc, with the twist of Fire for added strength. Tarian fought the surge of guilt and concentrated on the happiness she felt at finding her clever little girl. She held out her hands. "Come with me, little spark."

"Mama?" Ember wrinkled her nose, her eyes still wet with tears. "Bad? Mama sad?"

Tarian closed her eyes for a second. She'd done this. Her own outburst not minutes before had taught Ember how to have her own tantrum. Shame made Tarian's cheeks hot and tears push against her eyelashes. With an effort, she forced her mood toward light and happy. It was like wrenching a sandwich from a starving child. "No, little spark, you're not bad. You're a sweet baby. And you make Mama happy." Tarian smiled into her daughter's solemn gaze. "See? Feel how happy I am that you're home? I missed you, that's all. But it's all better now. Because you're here."

Ember offered a watery smile and reached out. Tarian touched Ember's hand, then stumbled as the ground grumbled and shifted. Sand slapped them as the calm eye of the storm collapsed. Ember dropped as the force supporting her vanished. Tarian lunged forward to catch her, carrying Ember down to the ground and pulling her in tight with relief. "I gotcha. I gotcha."

Ember hiccuped, her body collapsing against Tarian's in complete surrender. Tarian rocked gently, murmuring soothing sounds as she looked for the others. Daric reached them first, dropping to his knees in front of them.

"Is she okay? Are you okay?" His hands brushed sand mixed

with tears off Ember's cheek.

"We're fine." Tarian struggled for a deep breath. "Alex? Calli?"

Daric stood and squinted against the sun and settling sand. With no power pushing it, the wind was dying down, but it still wasn't possible to see very far. Tarian continued to rock Ember, while she tracked her sister. "She's not far. That way." She pointed.

Daric looked where she indicated. "I see her." He bolted forward, his face red and his clothes torn, but determined.

Sand crunched behind Tarian, and she turned her head to see Ruarc approaching. He kept his movements slow and deliberate. His eyes blazed with what looked like an accusation.

Tarian glared back at him and mouthed, "You should have told me."

Ruarc worked his jaw but didn't answer. Instead, he continued his slow pace toward the two of them. Tarian watched him, unsure exactly what his intentions were. He wouldn't hurt Ember. In her mind, she knew. But her heart didn't believe it. He looked more angry than she'd ever seen him. He looked ready to strike.

Something caught Tarian's eye, and she held up a hand to stop Ruarc. She squinted at the area, but nothing was there. It might have been a trick of the light. Reflections of sun on sand.

"Keeper. I am shielding you both. Now." Ruarc held up a hand, palm toward them.

The shield wrapped around both of them before she could protest. It slid neatly into place, blocking them from the dying storm and any other use of power.

With the shield in place, she could see more clearly. Calliope sat a little way up the beach toward the rock wall. Daric knelt beside her.

Alex and Letta both clung to a large boulder further up the

beach. She saw a Caraigg hunched next to Letta, with one hand on her leg. Alex's face had turned a deep red underneath his normal latte-toned skin. The ground shook, and she realized why they looked so focused.

"Is she doing that?" Tarian looked at Ruarc.

He shook his head. "The shield stopped any active use of power."

"Alex!" Tarian shouted. "You got this? Need help?"

"Workin' on it."

Tarian returned her attention to Ruarc. He waited, stoic, his expression smoothed as polished stone. She wanted to scream at him. She pictured herself placing a well-aimed kick in his groin, then launching into an all-out full body assault. When she was done, he'd lay in a bloody, huddled mass that the ocean quickly carried out to sea. The image satisfied a primal urge. She wondered if he could see it. Her lips twitched at the thought.

Something just over his shoulder caught her eye again. A bright flash of something that winked in and out. Tarian locked her gaze on the area. Dread grew with every second she waited. She knew what it was. She'd seen that flash before, just hours earlier. In Texas.

She didn't want to believe it. Surely not.

Something flashed again. She zeroed in on it. The atmosphere bent for a second, then disappeared. Tarian struggled to her feet, holding Ember so tight she protested. "See that?"

"Keeper. Stay within the shield. It's not safe as yet." Ruarc held up a hand to stop her.

"Look behind you." Tarian pointed. "Look!"

Ruarc turned. Behind him, a circle of energy flashed and bent, buckled and boiled. The small circle grew to basketball size and continued to expand. Tarian hugged Ember tightly to her chest, dread rising as the bubble got bigger and bigger and bigger until it formed a larger than life, menacing sphere of power.

7

Tarian backed away as the bubble continued to rise up and expand. The thing quickly blocked the path back into the house, leaving Tarian and Ember caught on the beach with only one way out—the sea.

"Run!" Alex shouted.

Tarian turned, the movement more awkward than it should be with Ember in her arms.

"Keeper, stay within the shield." Ruarc grabbed her arm to stop her. "It blocks the elements and Ember's talent."

Letta, Daric, Alex, and Calliope ran toward them, but stopped just outside the barrier Ruarc had erected. Kia followed behind and stopped several feet away from it, her gaze fixated on the bubble.

Letta grabbed her stomach, her eyes wide. "It's pulling. The artifact…it's tugging on it. Feel that?"

"No." Tarian shifted Ember so she could feel the medallion in her chest. It remained cool. For now. "I think the shield is blocking it."

"Can we put the shield around the bubble?" Calliope asked. Her face wore a mantle of exhaustion that gave her wrinkles, where she normally didn't have any, and dark circles under her eyes.

Tarian turned to Ruarc. "Can we?"

He studied the bubble. "Perhaps. Abereil are often unstable and are highly affected by the environment. I am not certain if using enough power to craft a shield so near to it would destabilize this particular one or not. They do not actively channel elemental energy on their own, but it is still wise to handle them from a distance. I have not seen an abereil in person since I was young, but I remember the devastation that one caused."

"I'm tellin' ya, that thing is actively trying to rip power from my ass." Letta took a few steps backward. "And it's a hell of a lot stronger than the ones in the park."

Kia moved to Letta and quietly took her hand. Letta immediately relaxed. "Thanks, Kia. That helps."

Kia nodded, but remained focused on the bubble, her expression thoughtful.

"Abereil?" Tarian looked to her sister, the bookworm. "You ever heard of abereil?"

Calliope shook her head. "It feels like raw power."

„An abereil is precisely **that,**" **Ruarc said.** "**It is a concentration** of elemental energy. They sometimes form in locations heavy with natural deposits, though not usually without some sort of provocation."

Alex pointed. "There's two. One by the pathway, another by that big boulder to the left."

Tarian's heart thumped hard in her chest. Ember stiffened, reacting to the rising tension. Tarian swallowed hard and rubbed her daughter's back, hoping to soothe her. They didn't need another outburst. Not right now.

Calliope rubbed her arms as if she were cold. "It feels kind of like the Stulos felt, that time in the cave. Right, Tari?"

Tarian thought back to that moment. Dismantling the Stulos had kicked her into labor, so the memory was fuzzy and a little incoherent. She remembered a lot of pain. But the other Stulos, before that, had been raw and awe-inspiring. "Kind of. It's hard to say, this far away."

"Well, you ain't getting any closer," Alex said, his tone grim. "Ain't none of us getting any closer. I gotta get to Frankie. Maybe he has something we can use to get rid of these damn things."

"I can ask the archivists to research it," Calliope offered. "If we can get back into the house."

"No time, Calli," Tarian said. "I have a feeling if I come out from behind this shield, the bubble will explode. That's what it did before."

"Ah, so you *have* encountered an abereil before," Ruarc said. He looked at Tarian with interest.

"Just before you got here. In Fort Worth." She contemplated the abereil. "The artifact reacted to it. I think."

"It looks almost stable," Calliope said, with a tone of surprise. "Look at the way the green and gray snake around each other. Like a living marble or something."

"It's a hella lot bigger than the ones in the park," Letta said. "Don't care if it's stable, it's effing huge."

"And it's full of power." Daric walked toward it, but Kia reached out a hand to stop him.

"Best leave it alone, Mr. D. Best we figure a way to get Ember away from them." Kia flashed a worried look toward Tarian and Ember. "Best we do that fast."

Tarian tensed, her arms tightening around Ember. "Why?"

Kia looked at Tarian, Ruarc, and Ember, her face thoughtful. "Ember's a strong little thing, and she touches all the elements.

The bubble don't. She get close to it, not sure what'll happen. Guessing it won't be good. Might be like what happened to you."

Her words made the muscles in Tarian's legs twitch, eager to run. When she'd taken a step too close to that bubble in Fort Worth, the thing had exploded. And it was half the size of this one. "She's right. We can't stay here."

Tarian imagined the bubble scooping her little girl up and carrying her away, locked forever inside a bubble of energy that continuously fed off her odd talent, and in return multiplied a million times. She pictured the thing destroying entire cities, then shook her head to clear the image. She turned her back on the thing and faced the group. "We have to go. Now."

"Keeper, stay within the shield." Ruarc flexed his hands.

"Take Ember to the safe room," Alex urged.

Tarian struggled to keep a tight grip on Ember, who wiggled and pointed at the ground. "Can't. That bubble's in the way. And I can't make a portal. If I pull enough power to travel, the thing might…Using power might be what caused the fires."

Ember pointed at the bubble. "Pretty!"

The word sent a shiver up Tarian's spine. She looked from her daughter's fascinated face to the abereil. The thing obscured the entire pathway and part of the entrance to the house. The one she'd faced in Fort Worth was half its size and filled three blocks with water when it exploded. The realization of what would happen if this one exploded flooded her with a renewed sense of panic. Images of flames, of tidal waves, of earthquakes filled her mind.

Ember's lip quivered as she sensed Tarian's emotions.

The shield weakened.

"The child…she's taking…the shield." Ruarc's voice sounded as if he were running a marathon. His face reddened and his eyes widened with the effort of maintaining the construct. From the look on his face, it was a battle he was about to lose.

Tendrils of Air and Earth snaked their way through the shield, leaving holes in their wake. Tarian couldn't stop the something-is-really-wrong feeling that welled up in her stomach. She knew it was a mistake the second the feeling took hold because Ember reacted with a loud sob that shook her whole body.

The shield broke.

The bubble bulged outward, the pleasant blues and grays turning dark and dangerous.

"Run!" Kia shouted.

"I'll launch another shield," Ruarc shouted. He stepped in between Tarian and the bubble, his hands outstretched.

She could have told him it wouldn't do any good. She could have mentioned that she'd already tried. That she'd felt Ember's talent take control of the Water Artifact the second the first sob of despair erupted from her daughter's lips. She could have told him a lot of things, if she'd been able to do anything but clutch at her daughter. Ember's pull was too intense, too powerful, and too out of control. It rampaged like a St. Bernard through a dish factory.

Tarian took a step backward, then another. She forced her feet to move, even if it felt like they pushed through a pit of tentacles. Her skin burned with the amount of power flowing over and around the two of them. Ember's body heated as though bathed in flames. It hurt to hold her, but Tarian squeezed her even tighter.

«Ember. Stop. Stop!»

The bubble reached for Ember and Tarian as if it wanted a hug. Tarian saw a spark arc between Letta and the thing. They had seconds, maybe. The bubble would pop. Ember's talent would force it to explode.

Tarian turned toward the ocean. Every instinct in her body told her to run run run. She caught sight of Letta bent double, clutching her stomach. Shadows circled the woman as the Earth Artifact launched into full defense mode.

"Run!" Kia shouted at Tarian, then threw herself on top of Letta.

A Caraigg exploded up from the sand at her feet and grasped her leg. *Run.* A wall of rock erupted between Tarian and the Caraigg. They'd provided a physical barrier, since the magical one had failed. It might buy her a few seconds. Time enough to get to the ocean.

Tarian squeezed Ember tight as she could and ran.

8

Tarian brushed past Ruarc. Power hit the wall of rock formed by the Caraigg and shattered it. Shards flew in all directions. One hit her head like a smack from her tutor. She ignored it, just like she had as a teenager, and kept running.

Power raced them to the water's edge. Tarian felt it along the back of her neck where the hair stood at attention. She smelled the elements that churned around them. Water dominated, but a solid base of Earth and Fire left a salty soil scent as well.

She heard shouts of "Get back" and "Look out!" but ignored her impulse to help. Nothing mattered but Ember. She had to get her little girl as far away from these things as she could.

The Water Artifact pulsed. The abereil responded to each beat with an answering wave of energy.

Pulse. Earth slapped and bumped and pushed.

Pulse. Air swirled and grabbed and tripped.

Pulse. Fire licked and stirred and stoked.

Dolphins just offshore leapt and called. Tarian clung to the sound. If she could just get into the ocean, they'd be safe. The Water Ancients would buffer. They'd know what to do. They'd protect Ember.

If she could just get there.

Behind them, elements merged. She smelled the result—an odd blend of charcoal and fish—a second before a force shoved her forward. Tarian stumbled, nearly dropping Ember. She had to stop and tighten her grip on the slippery ball of squiggle in her arms before she could plunge into the breakwater.

Tarian managed to get knee deep, nearly enough to dive under, when Ember thrust her hands out around Tarian's neck. «No!»

Power pulsed through Tarian's chest and out at Ember's command.

Tarian's Water, Air, and Fire flowed freely into her daughter, mixed with Ember's four elements, and grew and grew and grew until the atmosphere lumbered pregnant around them.

"No, Ember! No!" Petrified, Tarian struggled to move into the ocean. But the force surrounding them kept her feet pinned to the spot, as if glued there. Her arms ached from holding the wiggling toddler who clearly wanted to get down. Ember threw herself forward, trying to break Tarian's hold. Her energy tugged at Tarian's core, dragging Water and Air through the artifact.

"No!" Ember shouted again, her face determined, her nose scrunched in concentration. Tarian's arms tingled just before a blast of all four elements rushed from Ember's hands and rocketed toward the bubble on the beach. Tarian looked back over her shoulder, afraid of what she'd see but unable to look away. A solid mass of Air surrounded a blue Water core, wrapped with Fire and Earth that gave it a surface like a bullet. It flew past Daric and Ruarc and Alex, knocking them aside.

It struck the first and largest bubble. The bubble bulged, boiled, and burst. It sounded like a thousand windows shattered. Sparks shot into the afternoon sky, brilliant and blinding against the sun. The sand beneath it grumbled and shook. The tremor spread, knocking Sentinels off the ridge. A hole appeared, spreading faster than a virus. It filled with something red and steaming, and seconds later, a fountain of lava shot skyward.

Tarian gaped. Lava. Lava over her home. Lava that would destroy everything and everyone. She wanted to stop it. She wanted to rush forward and shield her family. Her home.

She could do nothing.

She'd never felt so helpless. Ember quivered in her arms, her body full of the elemental power she'd stolen from everyone on the beach. The scene in front of her stretched out long and slow, like a movie in slow motion, running at half speed.

Calliope and Kia ran for the water. Letta crouched on the sand as if communing with the ground. Several Caraigg appeared around the sinkhole, their faces turned skyward.

The lava crested, then dropped as if siphoned back to the ground. Sand submerged it, smothering the threat. Caraigg turned toward the second bubble.

The energy everyone channeled crackled. The second bubble doubled in size, the core of it dark and angry.

"Tari, go!" Calliope shouted.

Ember looked toward Calliope, and in the split second that her attention wavered, Tarian managed to move several more steps into the ocean. The water reached halfway up her calf. She was nearly there.

Ember's weight made Tarian awkward and slow. She heard a clap of thunder, then a wave of Air struck like a laser against her back. She fell forward into the rising tide.

Ember cried out and kicked hard toddler feet and punched with hard toddler hands. She turned into an incredibly strong starfish as she struggled against Tarian and the water and the power that beat into her little body.

Tarian fought to provide protection and oxygen as water engulfed them, but her efforts were siphoned away. Ember bucked against Tarian in fear or anger, she wasn't sure which. Tarian felt her daughter gathering energy. It was an odd sensation, a push and pull as Ember's talent took Tarian's power, then amplified it into waves of Air that raged around them and thrust them up and out of the ocean.

Ember's weave of elements shot them skyward. Ember's body became hotter the higher they climbed. Scorching hot. Fires of hell hot.

"Ember, stop. Stop!" Tarian patted Ember's back to distract her. They continued to move up and up and up, until the beach was a mere speck below. The atmosphere was cold and thin and hostile.

Tarian's breath froze in her chest. Too high. Way too high. She shook her daughter, desperate to break her concentration. Ember seemed lost in some other world, deep inside herself. Trapped by talent that knew no boundaries.

The air thinned. Ember's teeth chattered. Tarian tried to put up a block around the Water Artifact, but couldn't. The moment energy left her body, it fed Ember, who magnified it three and four times and returned it with a vengeance. What started as a block became a punch.

Ember's face crinkled with effort. She looked like a marathon runner after two races. Her chubby hands pulsed red, as the power anomaly siphoned down into her. Her daughter's ability to absorb worked overtime, pulling it in with no way to stop. Tarian knew the look, knew the feeling. She could sense what was happening in the way Ember's body had grown rigid and the way her eyes looked distant and unfocused. Ember would burn out.

Or die. They both would. Soon.

Desperate, Tarian slammed a shield woven with Fire around the artifact. The shield flickered, then disintegrated. She tried again. It fizzled.

She needed something different. Something passive. Something more personal. Tarian reached for her tracking ability, the one thing she could do without extra energy. The bond surged to awareness, blinding with the nearness of her subject.

Ember's own ability took hold of the connection and widened it, wrapped it in Air and Fire, strengthened it and expanded it and used it to dive through the artifact, through Tarian's chest and into her brain. Icy tendrils snaked and slithered, poked and pounded. They touched memories she'd forgotten and brought forth thoughts she didn't know she had.

The connection reached further, grasping at moments long hidden from her childhood, then further, to memories that couldn't possibly be her own. People she didn't know. Places she'd never seen.

Ember!

«Mama. Look!"

Ember pushed her nose against Tarian's. Her grin was infectious despite the circumstances. Tarian fought the intrusion at first. But somewhere in the middle of the invasion of her mind, a connection formed, stronger than anything she'd ever tracked. A bond more complete than anything she'd ever experienced. She saw through Ember's eyes. Really saw. Ember looked at her mother and saw an angel. A protector. A sister. A friend. She saw something deeper than Tarian had ever known existed. She saw someone strong. Confident. She saw a woman who could do anything. Who would protect her from every danger. Who would right every wrong. Fix any problem.

She saw a hero.

Tarian's throat constricted, and her eyes filled with tears. She pushed her forehead against Ember's and whispered, "I love you too."

"Hey! What are you two doing way up here?" The high voice pushed into Tarian's mind, and the connection that she and Ember shared shook. "What the stars is going on? Need a hand?"

The intrusion into Tarian's mind faltered, as if confused.

Tarian dragged oxygen into her lungs. It burned. Her eyes swam. "Macari! She's taking too much from me. I can't stop her."

"Oh." Macari put her arms around them, her signature scent of fresh ozone and sunny mountain breeze flooding the atmosphere. "Be ready. I'll block her access to elements. Won't last long."

Macari danced around them, performing a ballet that sent her skirt into a flurry. Her arms were elegant as she spun and wove pure Air into something much more solid than anything Tarian could ever have managed. Air was her secondary talent and definitely not strong enough for this kind of shield. "Now!" Macari sealed the shield around Ember.

The tug on Tarian's artifact stopped. Their bond severed. Tarian gasped against the loss of it. To have such a strong presence suddenly evacuate her mind felt like something very precious had died.

A sonic boom sent shock rippling through Tarian and Ember. It shook them so hard, her grip slipped. The energy that Ember had used to lift and hold them so high dissipated and vanished.

Ember and Tarian plummeted toward the water. Tarian managed to get a buffer in place just before they hit, so when they hit it acted more like a bean bag chair than concrete. Bumpy, but not brutal. They broke through the buffer and into the ocean with a loud splash. She caught a brief glimpse of the shoreline, now more than a mile away, before they submerged and sank, pushed by the weight of elemental power and the pull of the ocean tide.

The shield Macari placed around Ember remained intact. With nothing to siphon off power, Tarian managed to form another shield so they could breathe. She added pressure so they'd continue to sink. Water buffeted and protected and welcomed. Relief washed through her. Safe. They'd be safe here.

Tarian looked at Ember. Her daughter's face contorted with pain or anger or both. She'd turned purple, as if she still fought a battle within herself.

Desperate, Tarian shook the girl, rushing water back and forth over her face. *Ember. Stop!*

Ember blinked. She'd heard the thought. The enhanced connection forged through too much power remained intact. Weakened, but solid. But Ember's eyes remained unfocused. She still wasn't breathing.

Ember! Breathe, baby. Let it go. You're scaring me. Please, baby. Please stop. Let the power go. You can do it.

Ember's face crumpled. Her hands fell, and her mouth finally opened in a gasp and silent wail. If they'd been above water, Tarian knew Ember's face would be covered in tears. Her tiny body shook with sobs.

Her face remained a dangerous shade of purple. Her body was still rigid. Even buffeted by the ocean, Tarian could sense the enormous amount of energy within her daughter. She'd pulled too much. The bubbles, the artifacts, she'd taken more than anyone could hold, much less a toddler. She didn't know how to block or how to command her own abilities or how to release them.

Oh stars in heaven, she's just a baby. She can't do this. Tarian needed help. She didn't know what to do, and there was nobody to ask. How could she show Ember what to do? Her daughter's talent was unique and passive. How could Ember release the overload when she couldn't even speak full sentences?

Despair welled up. Tarian pushed back at it. There had to be a way. She was in her element. Water. It dispersed. She used it all the time for excess energy.

She just needed to show Ember.

The water around them churned as dolphins rushed to them from all sides. One by one, they brushed against Ember. She wasn't sure what they were doing. She reached out to touch one as it passed and caught an image of streams of light extending outward from Ember, through the dolphins and into the ocean.

Roger bumped against Tarian's elbow.

"Help."

He sent another image. Ember, floating in a circle of dolphins. Tarian nodded and forced her hands to unclench. It wasn't easy. She'd been clutching Ember so tight, her fingers didn't want to let go.

She released Ember and watched as her daughter floated freely away from Tarian and into the waiting circle of Ancients. She trusted the ancient creatures. If anyone could help now, it would be them.

Tarian held her breath, fighting panic and exhaustion.

Dolphins circled around Ember, forming a tight ring that undulated and revolved. Water rippled out with their movements, carrying pulses of power with it.

One by one, they pressed in on her to bump Ember with their nose and then rejoin the circle. Each bump caused Ember to convulse.

Thoughts taunted Tarian like terrorists. *She could burn out, right here. Overloaded with power. There'd be no coming back from it. Ever.*

Tarian focused on the bond she held with her daughter. It was a living thing, undulating beneath the waves. It was a solid bond that could withstand any assault, any distance, any length of time. Ember had created something special. Tarian leaned against it, her eyes closed, and sent thoughts through it to her daughter.

"Please, Ember. Push it away. Like the peas." Tarian imagined a plate of peas, Ember's least favorite meal. She pictured them racing away and dissolving into the ocean.

Dolphin after dolphin bumped the little girl. Each one took some power as it passed and released it into the waves.

Tarian groaned with impatience. The movement made a little bubble that drifted past her nose and popped. It gave her an idea.

"Ember, look what I can do!" Tarian made her tone excited and mysterious.

Ember turned, her eyes finally focusing on Tarian. She continued to sob but popped a thumb into her mouth.

Tarian formed "O" with her mouth and blew a bubble. It rose and popped in her face.

Ember flashed a smile. She hiccuped. Sobbed. Hiccuped again. Her face still shone purple, even in the dim light of the ocean. The power pulsated from Ember through the dolphins and then out, making everything around her daughter glow.

"You try it, little spark. Make a bubble. Make it with energy. Like Mama." Tarian formed another bubble with a small bit of Air and let it float up, pop. She made another. And another. This one popped right in her eye.

Ember giggled. She opened her mouth and tried to make a bubble, but nothing happened.

Tarian did another and another, with Ember trying to mimic, until finally Ember got one to pop. She smiled and clapped her hands, delighted. Energy rebounded as it joined the motion of the waves and dissipated.

Roger bumped against Tarian, sending an image of Ember shrinking and a thought. *More.*

Elated, Tarian smiled encouragingly at her daughter. She pushed through the circle of dolphins until she reached Ember, and the two of them made bubble after bubble, while dolphin after dolphin continued to bump into the girl, absorbing more power, and helping her disperse what they didn't take.

When Ember stopped glowing, Tarian pulled her in for a tight hug, relief making her giddy. *"Good job, Ember. Good girl."* She glanced up, wondering what was happening on shore. There'd been two of those things up there. Had Ember taken them both?

She'd never felt so much raw power, anywhere. *No, that's not true.* She corrected herself. *I felt it near the Stulos. Or inside them.* She frowned at the thought. *The Stulos are gone. Destroyed.* That was what had caused the magic storm that soaked everyone with power. That was why humans, most of them, had magic now. *But...something caused those bubbles. Two here. One, or more, in Texas. Some in Philly. How many more? What's causing them?*

One thing was clear. Ember couldn't be anywhere near one.

She put her forehead against Ember's and sighed. Ember's eyes drooped. She burrowed into Tarian's arms and fell into deep sleep, her face and limbs going slack. Tarian looked at the rosy cheeks and swollen eyes and swallowed. Even if her daughter was a year older than she should be, she was too young to deal with an overload like that. Her body would be worn out. She simply wasn't old enough to channel that much power.

Roger brushed Tarian's arm with a fin and sent an image of a giggling, happy Ember. It was a clear enough message. Ember's power had fully dissipated, and she was safe once more.

Her daughter lay heavy against her chest, arms buoyed by the ocean, hair streaming out in all directions like a tiny mermaid. Tarian gave her a little squeeze. *I love you.*

Tarian looked up toward the ocean surface as if there'd be an answer floating there. She'd no way of knowing if it was safe to go back. No telling what had happened to everyone else. Something flickered in the sunlight, glistening like a mirror. Tarian squinted, her arms tightening on Ember.

Another flicker.

Water *bent*, bulging outward, distorting the fish that swam through or behind it.

Tarian's breath caught. It might be nothing. A trick of the light. Overactive imagination. Stress. Excess power still floating around.

Or it might be another bubble forming in the one place she thought safe.

Tarian didn't wait to find out. She pictured the secret hideaway apartment she shared with Daric in Philly, tightened her grip on the sleeping child, and traveled.

9

Tarian stumbled forward a few steps when they arrived, hit a coffee table with her shin, spun, and stumbled a few more steps as she struggled to regain her balance while holding onto Ember. The extra weight in front made her awkward and clumsy.

"Ow! Shit!" She hobbled over to Daric's sofa and collapsed onto it. It hugged her like an old friend, inviting her to lean back and stay a while. Water rolled off them both, creating a salty puddle on the floor and couch. She put her head back, closed her eyes, and took a deep breath. It smelled of cinnamon and man. She breathed it in, trying to relax. Ember lay heavy in her arms, oblivious. Tarian gave in to fatigue.

Warm lips on hers woke Tarian from a deep, dreamless state. She started, her eyes flying open as her grip tightened on Ember. She relaxed when she saw the twinkle in the deep brown eyes looking back at her.

"Glad you're predictable." Daric grinned. "You know none of us can actually search the ocean, right? Not where you hang out. When you didn't come back, your sister had to wade in and wait for a dolphin to come tell her you'd gone. But I had a feeling you'd come here."

Daric gave her another kiss before sitting next to her. "Alex sent Sentinels out looking for you. We really should tell him about our secret place."

"Telling a secret means it's not a secret." She shifted Ember off one arm and shook it to relieve the tingles. "I had to run. Another bubble popped up near us in the ocean. I couldn't just stay there, not with Ember so drained already. And I didn't know if there were more on shore. Were there?"

Daric took her hand in his and caressed it soothingly. It sent tingles to her nether regions. "No. They're gone." Daric touched Ember's cheek. "She okay?"

Tarian looked down at the passed-out body in her arms. "I think so. Roger said she was. She's just tired." She looked at Daric. "She took in so much. Too much. I thought..." She stopped the thought, unwilling to voice it out loud. "Where the hell are those things coming from?"

"Calli is hunting for information in the archives. By the time we got back inside, the news showed more popping up. All in random places, nothing significant and nothing in common."

"Something, or someone, has to be directing them. Right? And what made them explode? I didn't do anything this time. We were shielded, and the artifact..." She trailed off, looking at Ember again.

"I have a theory. Don't know how accurate it is."

"Well. Spill." She looked at him with curiosity.

"Well, the one in Fort Worth was red and gray. There were fires...I'm assuming because one had already exploded. Then you showed up, and suddenly there's water everywhere. A little coincidental, don't you think? I mean, you are carrying the Water Artifact."

She thought about it. "Maybe. You think the colors are significant?"

Daric nodded. "Think about the ones on the beach. Green and gray. And when they popped, lava shot up out of the ground."

"Earth." She hadn't really smelled it, but surely the lava wasn't random. Which meant the water wasn't either. And Ember hadn't been in Fort Worth. "So they're all different."

"Seems like it to me."

"That doesn't explain where they're coming from."

"No. But it explains why they'd explode."

She gave him a nod to encourage him continue.

"They were stable, then Ember's talent kicked in and suddenly they weren't."

"She absorbed energy from them, but not in equal amounts." Tarian looked down at her daughter, lost in thought. She'd done the same thing in Fort Worth, but in reverse. The artifact shot energy into the bubble, but the effect was the same. It overloaded. "It was off-balance. Too much of one thing made it unstable."

No wonder the one in Fort Worth had exploded. So many people new to elemental energy, one of them might easily have unbalanced a bubble without even knowing they were doing it. Like Ember.

"Crap."

"Yeah."

Anxiety rumbled around inside her chest.

Ember stirred against her chest.

"Careful there, Mama, you'll wake the baby." Daric soothed Ember by patting her back. "Here, give her to me and get a shower."

"She needs one too." Tarian hesitated. Her grip tightened ever so slightly on Ember's body.

"She needs to sleep, Tari." Daric leaned back, eyebrows raised. "Where's the trust?"

"It's not that." She closed her eyes. She couldn't even explain this sudden need to hold on to her daughter. She couldn't keep this up. She couldn't carry Ember everywhere, and she couldn't be there every second. Her deal with Ruarc made sure of that. *Bastard.*

The look of understanding that flashed through Daric's eyes made her cheeks heat up.

"Ruarc's never going to let go of that Agreement, Tari. And it's the least of our worries right now. It's a whole year before he gets visitation again." Daric stood, leaned over her, and kissed her lightly on the forehead before he scooped Ember out of her arms. Ember opened her eyes for a half second before closing them again, snuggling against Daric's chest.

Tarian stretched. Sore body parts protested the movement, other parts popped their complaints. "I should tell everybody we're okay."

Daric swayed from side to side, keeping Ember in a happy sleep. "They already know. I told them before waking you. Now go get cleaned up—you smell like dolphin." He winked.

Tarian stuck her tongue out at him, then headed for the bathroom.

She showered, staying a little longer than usual to get the sand and sea off her body. As she was selecting a fresh pair of jeans and T-shirt, she thought about her first visit to Daric's safe house and smiled to herself. Happy moments, filled with lust and getting-to-know-you and an intense feeling of safety. She was glad Daric had the foresight to stash clothes here, just in case they needed a time-out from Duty and Responsibility. They'd had a lot of time-outs over the last year, and she treasured all of them. She'd never tell anyone about this place. It was theirs, hers and Daric's. Nobody else's.

Well, maybe one other person. She'd tell Ember, when the girl was old enough. She pictured a teenage Ember using this place to get a bit of peace and quiet. The two of them popping over for a coffee at PJs. A smile flickered across her lips, then faded. The happy thoughts replaced by worry.

She turned to find Daric leaning against the doorway with a mug in his hand, watching her. She reached for it and sniffed. Coffee. Not PJs, but any would do at the moment.

She took a sip, enjoying the heat and the sting of caffeine before a thought struck and sent a wave of panic through her stomach. "Where's Ember? You left her alone." She pushed past him, nearly dropping the coffee.

"Relax. She's fine." Daric followed. "See?"

Ember lay sleeping peacefully, her face turned toward the back of the sofa. Tarian watched the gentle rise and fall of her daughter's chest, lost in thought. The bond Ember had forged remained strong, a tangible connection that almost burned with the proximity.

Daric pulled her close and brushed the hair out of her eyes. "What's up? You're a million miles away."

"Nothing."

He gave her a look that was full of doubt.

She gave in. "It's just...something happened before, when all the power was bouncing around. She was taking so much in and sending more out. I tried to reach her like a daemon would. You know, in my mind. And somehow...somehow she took my tracking and turned it into a real bond. I can feel it, here." Tarian tapped the side of her head. "It's so strong, it hurts this close to her. I could hear her thoughts, and she could hear mine.

She could see memories. Really *see* them. It was intimate and intimidating and..." Tarian gazed at her sleeping daughter. "I've never felt anything like it."

They stood there in silence, watching Ember sleep. When Daric spoke, his voice was barely a whisper. "Can you hear her thoughts now?"

Tarian shook her head. "I can feel the bond, but no. She's not in my mind right now. I have no idea how she did it. Not sure it's a good thing, but at the same time it was..."

"Amazing," Daric finished for her.

"Yeah."

They watched a few more minutes, entranced by the ability and the innocence embodied in their daughter.

Tarian leaned into Daric, enjoying the warmth of his body against hers. She covered a yawn.

"Still tired? I can help with that." Daric pulled Tarian away and led her back to the bedroom. When they reached it, he pulled her gently to him and slipped her shirt up and over her head.

"We don't have time."

Daric kissed her neck.

"We should get back."

He kissed the little dip at the base of her throat.

"They're all probably really worried."

He kissed the corner of her mouth. Her nose. Her cheek. He rained kisses down on her face and chest in rapid succession until she giggled and pushed him away.

"Seriously," Tarian murmured. She was having a little trouble breathing, but this time it had nothing to do with elemental energy. "We should...get..." His lips touched hers and obliterated the thought.

He tasted like sweet cream and hot coffee. She rolled her

tongue over his, enjoying the flavor and the feel of him. He probed deeper, and she sank into it. When he pushed her onto the bed, she didn't offer any more arguments. Instead, she helped him get his shirt off and kneaded the muscles along his shoulders and neck while he paid more attention to her breasts.

Daric took his time getting the rest of her clothes off. He massaged along the way, gently teasing a nipple here, a butt dimple there. He paid special attention to the little nook behind her ear that made her whole body quiver.

They'd had sex here before, usually in a hurried frenzy because they squeezed a session in while Ember napped or in between meetings or training sessions or any number of other interruptions.

This time was sweet and unhurried, but also more intense. As if they might not have another chance to taste each other. Each kiss lasted a bit longer, went a bit deeper. When he entered her, he moved in a slow and steady rhythm that made her body vibrate.

She opened herself to him, setting the elements she controlled free to roam through his body. Daric uttered a soft groan of pleasure. She coaxed him to move faster, but he refused. He kept the pace steady and the rhythm slow, and the heat built toward a crescendo that she craved.

Daric released his own elements. A heavy dose of Air met her Water and created a cinnamon-filled steam that lifted her spirits and soothed fatigue. She pushed her energy into him. He took it, breathing it in like it was the most expensive perfume, then pushed it back to her.

Tarian wrapped her legs around his butt and pulled, urging him deeper. Coaxing him to go faster and faster. They melted into each other and into the climax that sent fireworks through her body and mind and soul.

They clung to each other, riding the wave, enjoying the high of magic and intimacy and precious moments alone together. Nobody existed in that moment except the two of them.

"I love you," Daric whispered.

"I love you more."

After a few more delicious moments, they uncoupled and lay side by side. Sweat glistened off Daric's bare chest. She traced his name in it. "We're gonna need another shower."

"Oh darn. I hate showering. Especially with you." He put his arm around her and pulled her close.

Tarian snuggled against his chest, enjoying the feel of his skin on hers. Somehow, his arms always made her feel safe. As if any problem could be solved. Any obstacle overcome. He made her feel like they could do anything.

She wished she could bottle that feeling and drink it when she really needed it. Like when she was fighting bubbles of power or yelling at Ruarc.

She traced the muscles along his ribs and teased the hair on his chest. "What happens the next time she goes to see Ruarc?"

"Ah, so that's what's really bothering you. It's not the Agreement itself. It's the change in Ember."

"It doesn't bother you?" She lifted her head enough to look him in the eye. "You telling me you're okay losing a year of her childhood every time she sees that daemon?"

Daric caressed her back, sending little waves of pleasure down her spine. "Won't change the fact she's my daughter. We have a bond he can't break, Tari. All of us. You more than the rest of us now. No matter how fast she grows or how long she's away, she'll always be your daughter. *Our* daughter. She'll always carry you with her, wherever she goes."

Tears formed in her eyes, but she refused to acknowledge

them. "It's not the same as being with her."

"Think about it. You spent half your childhood wanting to get out on your own. Defy your mother. Do your own thing. But even when you did, tell me you didn't think about how your mother would handle things. What she'd say. Tell me you couldn't feel her there, in your mind and heart."

Tarian looked up at the ceiling and blinked furiously. "Still do. Can't get her damn voice out of my head."

"See? It will be the same for Ember." Daric grinned. "Literally. With the connection you described, she won't be able to get rid of you. She's your daughter, Tari. Always. The rest, we'll figure out as we go. Now that you know it'll happen, we can plan for it. We'll come up with something."

"Like how to get out of this Agreement?"

He looked doubtful.

"Don't tell me it can't be done. I don't want to hear that."

Daric pulled her back into his arms, tucking her head under his chin. "It'll be okay. I promise."

She rested there for a minute, enjoying the warmth and the knowledge she could tell this man her true feelings and he wouldn't judge her or condemn her for being weak. Here, it was as safe as the ocean. She looked up at him. "I still love you more."

Daric chuckled and pulled her closer for another exchange of power.

—10—

A hazy amount of time later, Tarian rested her head against Daric's chest. The steady beat of his heart in her ear, and the deep rumble of his laugh, left her feeling safe, loved, happy, and content. An island of safety in an ocean of chaos. Their joining brought healing and renewal when she needed it desperately. The second shower hadn't hurt either. "I want to stay here forever."

She rubbed her hand softly over his stomach, savoring the feel of him. He tightened his arm around her shoulder and kissed the top of her head. "Wish we could."

"She'll probably sleep another couple hours." Tarian kissed his chest, moving against him with a suggestive wriggle.

Daric chuckled and squeezed her again. "She needs food, and you need to check in. It's been long enough, I think. They should have everything cleared off the beach by now. Ruarc is probably fuming. You realize he's stuck there until you talk?"

"I don't want to think about *him*." She squirmed around so she could kiss his lips. Just as their bodies responded and power swirled, Daric broke the embrace.

"She'll feel it this time for sure, Tari. We gotta learn how to block the joining or Ember may never have a sibling."

Tarian groaned. "Don't remind me. I don't even want to know what would happen if she absorbed that. No telling what a toddler interpretation of *that* would turn out like. Everyone for miles would be in orgasms. Though, come to think of it..." She ran her hand down Daric's stomach, coming perilously close to more sensitive regions. "Not sure that'd be a bad thing."

Daric grabbed her hand to stop it from wandering. His lips twitched. "She magnifies power, you know."

Tarian giggled at the thought. She pictured downtown Philly, everyone locked in an explosion of pleasure. It was amusing, no doubt about it. But too much of anything was bad. Very bad. Pleasure could become pain in a blink of an eye. That thought killed the giggles.

Tarian moved reluctantly out of Daric's embrace and off the bed, tugging on underwear and pants while she spoke. "Back to reality."

Daric propped himself up on one elbow, clearly enjoying the show of her striptease-in-reverse.

"What now?" She struggled with the button on her jeans, her fingers suddenly shaking. "I have no idea what the next move is. We don't even know what, or who, is causing these bubble things. I can't shake the feeling that it's somehow connected to the Stulos."

Daric wrinkled his forehead. "But you destroyed those."

"I destroyed the constructs. But what happened to the energy they held? You heard Kia. Power can't be destroyed. It didn't just disappear. These bubbles seem kinda like the Stulos, but without the boundaries. I've never felt anything so powerful. What happened to downtown Fort Worth could happen anywhere. And what about the people inside the buildings? What happened to them?"

Daric frowned. "I don't know. We have to assume they...that they're gone."

"They evaporated with the buildings. Without a trace. I can't wrap my head around it. And that's just one spot. One bubble. What if there are more?"

"The ones on the beach didn't level anything."

"They didn't get a chance. We were all right there." She swallowed, hard. "We can't be everywhere."

Daric rose from the bed and caressed one of her bare breasts.

She glanced down at his fully exposed body and raised an eyebrow. "Thought you said we should get back."

"I did. Doesn't mean my body listened." Daric took the shirt Tarian handed him and pulled it on.

"You're trying to distract me."

"And it's working." Daric popped his head out the top of the T-shirt and grinned at her.

«Jerk.»

"You love it." Daric held out her shirt. She put her arms up and let him slip it on, enjoying the way his hands played along her body. He patted her arm. "Let's get PJs and plan the steps."

"That's always your answer. Coffee and plan. You love planning."

They left the bedroom still tugging clothes into place. "And you don't. But it needs to be done. And planning always goes better with caffeine. You still look beat." Daric gently scooped Ember off the couch. She yawned, stretched, and blinked sleepily before snuggling into his chest and closing her eyes again.

Tarian smiled at the picture of domesticity they created. Ember looked so cute and sweet. Her dark hair stuck out every which way. Bits of seaweed entwined in her hair and sand on her face made her look like a miniature mermaid. The tender look in Daric's eyes as he gazed at his daughter was the hottest thing she'd ever seen. She followed them to the front door, wishing they could just freeze this moment and live in it forever.

Daric paused at the doorway to release the shield he'd placed over the door. Ember blinked sleepily at that small use of power, but as far as Tarian could tell she didn't react in any other way. Tarian plucked a strand of seaweed from Ember's hair and leaned in to give her daughter a kiss. Her lips brushed the soft flesh of Ember's forehead, and a jolt of electricity shocked her. The bond that Ember had fortified between them whipped pulses through Tarian's body, into Ember's, and back again. She could feel the blows within the bond. It was like a ping-pong match, and she was both paddles and the net.

Images and thoughts flooded Tarian's mind. Most were simple, full of sparkling wishes and sleepy daydreams. They showed Tarian a world seen from a very young point of view.

It was foreign and familiar at the same time. Like a half-remembered daydream.

Tarian pulled back, breaking the physical connection. The bonding faded to the background, and her thoughts became her own again. She touched her lips where the electricity had passed between her and Ember. It'd left a blood blister behind as a reminder.

"Tari?" Daric's voice next to her sounded concerned and reassuringly *real*. "Tari! Are you okay?"

Tarian looked from Daric to Ember and back again. The sudden intensity of the bond left her feeling fuzzy and confused. But the apartment remained reassuringly normal. Tarian searched Ember for signs of the connection they'd shared. Ember smiled sleepily, looking the picture of innocence.

Daric squeezed her arm gently, his face a map of concern lines. "Tari, look at me. What happened?"

"I don't know. I...we..." She stared at the child in his arms, confusion twisting her already tortured thoughts. "We connected again. She was there, in my thoughts. It's an odd sensation."

She glanced down. Ember blinked at her, sleepy but content in Daric's arms. Tarian tried to smile for her daughter, but only managed a weak half-grin. "It's okay. Let's go."

They left the apartment and walked down the stairs to the alley that ran along the side of PJs Coffee. The spot gave Tarian flashbacks every time she stood in it. She'd been attacked by a laghairtine here. A half-lizard, half-man, all-demon creature who'd snatched her blood and tried to steal her power.

It was a very bad memory, and if she was honest, it was the beginning of the chaos they currently experienced. But she'd also met Daric that day. And later, she'd completed the ritual that left her pregnant with Ember. She couldn't imagine the world without her daughter.

Daric stepped quickly out of the alley into full morning sun. Tarian paused, soaking it in, a little startled. It'd been late afternoon when the bubbles invaded the beach at Xannon. A full night and part of the following day had passed by while she wasn't paying attention. "Damn, I didn't realize I slept so long."

Daric winked. "You needed it. And it wasn't all sleep."

"True." She rushed ahead and opened the door for Daric since he had his arms full. The bell on the door chimed cheerfully as they entered. The room greeted them with conversations and coffee and comfort.

Tarian ordered their usual—plain black coffee with a splash of cream for herself and a vanilla latte for Daric—and added a cup of fruit and a bar of chocolate for Ember. It wasn't exactly nutrition, but it would refresh and rejuvenate faster than something with more protein. She carried it all to the table Daric had chosen near the back of the shop and sat down.

"Looks like there's more now." Daric nodded at the TV near the counter. Several stood around it, absorbing the news.

Tarian took a piece of melon and tempted Ember with it while she listened.

"While Fort Worth reels from the vicious attack that left the downtown area drenched and flattened, authorities in Philadelphia report several locations with odd disturbances that are considered extremely dangerous. Reports of more of the strange phenomena have come in from Los Angeles, Seattle, Chicago, and Detroit as well as rural areas in Vermont and Upstate New York.

"Government officials informed us moments ago that the president is considering an executive order to ban all travel in or out of the country. He's also considering a move to declare martial law anywhere the strange bubbles are found. One official likened them to nuclear bombs. It's not clear who put them in place, but one thing is certain...no one is safe. Authorities advise everyone to keep their distance and to report any sightings to your local police immediately. For more on the terrorist attack in Fort Worth, we take you to Jeb Branch. Jeb?"

Tarian blinked. Took a deep breath. Then continued to feed Ember. She couldn't afford to get upset. Not here. Not with her daughter so close.

"I really need to learn to block my emotions." Tarian smiled as she said the words, hoping a cheerful expression would force cheerful feelings through her body. It sort of worked.

Ember grabbed the piece of melon Tarian offered and shoved

it into her mouth. Her face and hands were shiny and sticky, and she seemed thoroughly pleased with herself.

"Maybe Macari can help with that." Daric shifted Ember to his other knee and picked up his coffee. "We need to get back. I hope Calli got an answer from the archivists. We need more to go on."

"We need to know what's causing them. Or who. Or both." Tarian couldn't shake the lurking suspicion that she'd brought this all on the world herself.

Tarian handed Ember a strawberry. Ember took it, shook her head, and tossed it aside. "No, Mama."

Tarian looked at Daric, stunned at the rejection. They both burst out laughing at the same time.

"Well, I guess you've been told," Daric said.

"Okay then, no more strawberries for sparkly girls." Tarian grinned.

They were enjoying the moment so much, neither of them noticed the noise level in the coffee shop had died away until Ember cried out for another piece of fruit. "Bite, Mama! Bite!" The sound was unnaturally loud in the suddenly still shop.

Tarian handed another melon piece to Ember, then slowly turned to take in her surroundings. The only other sound was the reporter on the TV. But it wasn't the reporter that made every hair on the back of her neck stand on end.

A photo was being displayed as part of the newscast. It was grainy, obviously taken from a security camera blocks away. It showed two people in the middle of the empty square in Fort Worth. A woman, short, with long black hair, held out a hand toward something. A man looked to be running up to her.

The image was replaced with another. This one much clearer. Much more in focus. Much more damning.

It looked like a cell phone image, and although it was blocks away as well, the reporter zoomed in on the face of the woman. Tarian stared at her own face, looking determined and manic with wide eyes and grim mouth. The image moved and video played of her, the lightning sparks, and the flood waters. It looked as though Daric had tried to stop her, not save her. In this scenario, he was a hero trying to stop a terrorist. And she was the villain.

Tarian swallowed. The reporter filled in with words that damned her, and all of them.

"This is the face of the suspected terrorist. Our source within the police department tells us she is to be considered armed and dangerous. They suspect her of a dozen or more other bombings and attacks, including one in the Philadelphia mansion district a year ago. If anyone knows her whereabouts, they should contact their local authorities immediately.

"Do not, and we repeat, do not approach this woman under any circumstances. With all the recent...well, let's just call it what it looks like...magic...running rampant, she is considered to be both the leader and the instigator. For more on this developing story..."

The words jumbled together until she couldn't make sense of them. Terrorist. They'd called her...terrorist? Though her heart immediately balked at the idea, something in the back of her mind taunted and teased and tortured her with the simple truth. It *was* her fault. She *had* instigated this. She'd destroyed the Stulos. She'd unleashed all that elemental power on the world.

She'd never intended for this to happen.

Her inner voice replied. *You never do, do you? Yet it always does, doesn't it? You always destroy things around you. It's in your nature.*

Tarian shook her head in denial but the voice continued,

unstoppable.

You always act before you think. Without considering the consequences. And now look at you. Running from bombs of your own making. Your daughter at risk. She'll die, because of you.

The voice rose an octave. *She'll die. And it'll be your fault. Yours.*

«Tarian.» Daric's voice was low and guarded. "We need to go."

She couldn't stop the sob that escaped.

"Mama, bite!" Ember's demand didn't really penetrate. Tarian's attention now focused on the crowd in the shop. Every eye in the place turned in her direction. Some looked from the TV to her. She could see them assessing. Recognition dawned like the sun on a horizon until it blazed in every eye in the place.

Behind the recognition, fear took root and grew anger, then hate.

A man nearby on the left shuffled his feet. "It's her. It's her!"

Fear spiked. Adrenaline surged. They had to get out. Now. Tarian turned to Daric. He already had a protesting Ember in his arms.

"Go!" Tarian held out her hand and let Air flow hot and fast through her body. The travel portal leapt into life, shimmering like heat above pavement on a hot summer day. The outline of Daric's mother's front door could be seen within it.

Ember's face crumbled, and slow tears began to fall.

Daric shook his head to protest. They didn't have time to argue. She moved closer to him, intending to shove him through if she had to. Anything to keep Ember safe. That was all that mattered.

"Take her!" Tarian raised her hand, but something in the atmosphere made her hesitate. The people behind them grew louder, their anger palpable. But it wasn't that. She'd been around angry crowds before.

This was something more. Something that made her feet turn to lead and her heart turn to bongo drums so loud it was all she could hear. The scent of charcoal and dead fish filled her nose.

Tarian turned.

Flicker.

She blinked. It couldn't be. Not here.

Flicker.

She blinked again.

The air next to the counter rippled and melted. The flicker flashed, then erupted into a bubble the size of two large men. It swirled green and red tendrils. A manic holiday decoration on steroids.

Those standing nearest screamed and ran.

"Witch! She's setting another bomb! Someone stop her!"

Those further away reacted, without any further prodding. They surged toward Tarian, an angry mob without the pitchforks.

Tarian spun and lunged toward Daric. He half-turned, shielding Ember, though Tarian could see her daughter kicking in protest. Ember could sense emotions. They had seconds. Fractions of a second before her daughter erupted in all her two-year-old glory. And then…the bubble.

The portal remained open just ahead. Tarian stumbled over a chair leg. She fell against the table, her hip smacking the edge of it, then lurched forward again.

"Come on." Daric gestured for her to go first through the portal.

The crowd pressed in on them. They stank of sweat and fear and a jumble of elemental signatures. Everything from wet moldy sponges to something like grape juice to dog shit. Though that could have just been on someone's shoe. Over half of them had magical ability, but none of them would admit it. Not here. Not now. Not with an easy target to blame in their midst.

"Go!" Tarian pushed Daric, and he tripped sideways. His momentum carried him the rest of the way into the portal. She watched them step into it, then half-turned to shoot a volley of Water and Air at the abereil. Better to pop it now, while it was so small. Anyone with elemental ability could overload one. That left a dozen or more people in the shop as possible unwitting terrorists.

Her blow struck the center of the abereil. Thunder shook the walls, the floor, and the people. Screams of terror filled her ears. The bubble buckled, then bulged outward.

Tarian leapt at the portal. She knew the second her feet left the ground that it was too late. Her attention wavered a bit too long. The portal collapsed.

The bubble burst.

—11—

The explosion tossed Tarian across the room and slammed her against the wall between a framed picture of coffee beans and a poster for a local band. She slid down to the floor. The wall cracked on impact, and the split followed her to the ground. The coffee beans landed on her head, then toppled to the floor with the clatter of shattering glass.

She sat stunned for a second, half-covered in drywall and dust. Energy raced through the floor, shaking the foundation and her body like a vibrating bed with too many quarters. The ceiling groaned and made an odd popping noise. She looked up in time to see cracks spread across it like varicose veins.

Tarian curled inward, arms over her head, eyes closed, focused entirely on the power rampaging through and around her. She scrapped together a small amount of Air energy and wove it into a feeble shield. The first impact of concrete pushed the shield inward and thumped her on the head, jarring her senses. She struggled to find more power, drawing on the Water Artifact for support. It responded with a trickle. Or what she thought was a trickle. She couldn't be sure, anymore. The bubble had released so much energy into the atmosphere that she wasn't sure where hers ended and it began.

Lights from an instant migraine jabbed at her eyeballs with vicious sharp thrusts of pain. Her breath came in quick, panted gasps. She struggled through it, grappling with the wet, slippery snake her own energy had become as the ceiling and the building crumbled on her and around her. Her shield solidified, then bent. Strengthened, then shrunk. She crouched inside it with barely an inch to spare between her head and the falling stones, drywall, furniture, and random bits of life. She screamed and pushed Fire into the shield. It felt hot and prickly and wrong, but she pressed it up against the Water. It was like trying to shove two opposing magnets together.

Then it gave in and bonded, and the shield solidified. The building beat against her, and the ground shook beneath her, and the sky fell apart over head. But the shield held just enough to protect her from the worst of it.

It was the only thing saving her from becoming flat as roadkill run over by a thousand cars on the highway. She had a fleeting thought that she now knew what it was like to be buried alive. Then another thought that she might not even be alive anymore. She might be dead. Others definitely were. She couldn't hear screams anymore. All she could hear was the rush of blood in her ears and the frantic pounding of her heart.

All she could do was wait for the rocks to stop falling.

It lasted a lifetime. An eternity. More than that even. She waited and waited and waited.

It got very dark. Very still. Dust filled her nose and mouth and coated her lungs. She coughed, and wished she hadn't. Bruised ribs. Maybe broken. She couldn't be sure.

She drifted in the darkness, wondering if this was really what it was like to die. If it was, it hurt like hell.

She wasn't sure how long she lay there, huddled under a mountain of building material and dirt. The shield had vanished somewhere in the darkness and the stillness. She couldn't keep focus long enough to maintain it. Couldn't tie it off so it would last. Couldn't do much of anything, lying underneath a building. She'd never given any thought to how it must feel to be in an earthquake. Now she wouldn't have to. She knew firsthand. The filth of an entire city infiltrated every pore. Every muscle. It covered parts of her body that sand usually didn't reach. If she moved, she was sure she'd make sandpaper-on-stone noises with her thighs.

At least Ember was safe. At least Daric was with her. And his mother. She'd be okay, sequestered in that underground bunker his mother owned. Surely no bubble could reach her there. The place had more security than a bank vault full of gold bars and jewels and billions of dollars. It guarded something far more precious.

A wave of nausea rippled through her stomach. She groaned and blew out a deliberate breath to force the gorge back down her esophagus. Damn migraines. Why'd they always have to turn her stomach too? Weren't flashing lights and throbbing, pounding, cascading pain enough?

The sick feeling subsided, and she let herself drift again, relieved. She just needed to regain her strength. She could travel out as soon as she could focus her mind on the task. At the moment her brain hurt far too much to even picture a destination, much less channel the energy.

Somewhere in the nightmarish merry-go-round of pain and dirt, Tarian thought she heard sounds. Wrenching sounds. Scraping sounds. And voices. Lots and lots of voices.

At first they just caused more pounding pain in her brain.

She wished they wouldn't. She wished they'd go away. She half thought it was the angry mob, back for vengeance. They knew she did it after all. They saw her standing right there when the bubble exploded. She could imagine the news reports.

It was a long time before she could take a full breath. It hurt like hell, but it made her lungs and head feel better. As the pounding in her brain eased, sounds of the city returned, muffled and distant. A car honked nearby, startling her enough that her body twitched in response. Sirens sounded somewhere in the distance. Pain stabbed her with every breath. She'd probably broken a rib. Or three.

Moans from nearby. Shouts from outside. Bits of things crumbling.

The aroma of coffee mixed with dirt triggered waves of nausea. She tried to lift her head, but ended up scooting her cheek along a piece of drywall. It burned like sandpaper on fire. She pushed with her hands, managing to roll over onto her back. The effort left her completely winded and her brain whirling with a chorus of jackhammers. She retched, turning to her side in time to vomit. The smell made her stomach heave harder.

A muffled, deep male voice infiltrated the rubble from somewhere off to the right. "We need...one...no....three ambulances? Hell, just send everything they got. Get started on that fire over there. You, block this area. Get the onlookers back outta here. Section off this block. It's all unstable. More might come down. Get those people back outta here!"

The shout pounded nails into Tarian's skull. She wished they'd stop shouting. It'd all be fine if everything just stayed quiet.

The stench of vomit made her stomach boil. She shifted away from it and rammed into something hard with jagged edges that cut like razors. She stopped moving. Focused on breathing. On pulling in dust-filled oxygen. On trying not to notice how her hair smelled like puke. On ignoring the way everything remained pitch black with jagged white lightning flickering through the darkness.

"Hey, got a live one over here!"

Hands grabbed both of Tarian's arms. She struggled, wincing at the pressure on top of bruised muscles and the glaring sunlight as she tried to get a look at who had her.

The blurred face furrowed. "Easy now. Easy. Can you walk? The wall might go any second."

She moaned and tried to wave him away.

"Easy. Easy." The blur lowered, lifted her easily into his arms, and carried her out into even brighter light.

She shut her eyes tight and groaned.

"Get that stretcher over here."

Squeaks. Chatter. Movement.

Something soft.

"Just take it easy, okay? You got quite a bump on your head. The medic will get to you in just a minute. Okay? You hear me, lady? What's your name?"

Tarian waved her hand at him. "Get the others. I'm…fine."

The blur snorted but patted her reassuringly on the arm. "Nah, you ain't. You definitely got a concussion. Maybe some cracked ribs. Broken…well, I can't see nothing broken. But there might be, so just be still. Medic's on the way. We got quite a few injured here, so hang on. We'll get ya."

The blur left. She lay back into the softness and breathed a sigh of relief. No more talking. No explaining. How could she ever explain this? Right now they thought her a victim.

She had to get out of the area before they figured out the truth. What sort of law governed a bubble explosion? She almost laughed. But it hurt too much.

She tried to sit up again. Failed. Focused instead on restoring sight. She blinked furiously. It did nothing but create lightning flashes and tears. Her mind was a live exposed wire. She tentatively reached out with a trickle of power. The effort made her head feel like the inside of an exploding firecracker.

She stopped. Sirens wailed, some nearby and more in the distance. Orders barked by official sounding voices. Water trickling off something. A phone ringing. Cars honking. Angry voices. Clomping feet.

She focused on breathing. In. Out. In.

Out.

Deep.

Each breath seemed a little less painful.

It'd been awhile since she'd had her ass kicked. She'd never had it beaten so soundly by something invisible, nor by something not directed by another person.

Tarian rolled to the side and fell a few feet to the asphalt. She couldn't stop the moan of pain. "Dammit." She winced at how loud her voice sounded to her ears.

Feeling her way, she managed to pull herself upright, using the stretcher she'd been lying on for support.

Wondering if her sight had returned, she put her hands over her eyes and risked a small peek. Blinding light burned the retinas, and she shut them again, wincing. Relief flooded through her, making her stomach feel weak. *Not gone. Not blind. Just... tired. Gotta wait it out.*

She leaned back against a tire attached to an emergency vehicle, trying to ignore the sharp edges of the wheel well digging into bruised flesh. She pushed her palms into her eyes, in the hope that it would miraculously return her eyesight somehow, and wished for the thousandth time she had any sort of healing talent.

Footsteps crunched across the street toward her. She tensed, and her eyes flew open before she could stop them. Light poured buckets of nails into the retinas. She caught a fuzzy, overly bright impression of a small female figure before quickly shutting them again.

"Tari? What the fuck?"

Tarian started at the sound of her name and the familiar voice. "Letta.»

Footsteps quickened their pace. "Shit, what the hell happened? What are you doing out here in the open?"

Hands grabbed one of her arms to help her stand the rest of the way. She hadn't realized until that moment that she'd been hunched over like an old woman. Tarian winced as her ankle bent sideways.

"You can't be out here. There's an APB out on you." Letta's voice was low and tight. She tightened her grip on Tarian's arm and pulled. Muttered a few colorful words under her breath before adding, "I got her. Take care of the man over there—he's in bad shape." Letta spoke with the tone of authority, the kind that expects orders to be followed. After a second of hesitation, footsteps hurried away.

"Damn, girl. Let's get outta here." She supported Tarian in a slow stagger away from the stretcher, ambulance, fire trucks, burnt collapsed building, and official questions. "You did this?"

Tarian shook her head. "Abereil. I need...to check on... Ember."

"You need to sit down is what you need. And you need a healer. Damn. Come on." Letta put Tarian's arm over her shoulder. "You can explain why you ain't opening your eyes after we sit. Step high, big rock."

Tarian allowed Letta to lead her across the street and onto the opposite sidewalk, relying on Letta's sight and trusting her friendship. They walked for what felt like an eternity. She fell twice, hit a wall once, and hissed out every swear word she knew and some she made up on the spot.

"Where…are we going?" She wanted to stop moving. She wanted her head to stop spinning and the world to stop revolving. She wanted a damn cup of coffee. And a donut. A really big, really sugary donut. Her stomach growled at the thought.

"Keep quiet, fool. Almost there." A door opened, followed by the unwelcome aroma of smoke and liquor and mold. Her stomach heaved, but she managed to keep vomit on the inside where it burned a hole in her esophagus, rather than the floor of wherever it was they'd ended up.

Letta maneuvered Tarian around a hard object, then muttered "It's a booth. Sit and slide."

Tarian did as she was told, feeling her way along the seat and table until she found the back corner. She breathed a sigh of relief as she sank into the thick cushions. They crackled like old pleather, and smelled like stale beer, but it was soft enough and she was glad to be sitting still. She pressed her palms once again into her eyelids. White lights danced a jig. She wasn't sure if that was a good thing or not.

She listened to the sounds around her, all of them seeming amplified. Multiple conversations happened all at once. Most of it chattering about the explosion. The building collapse. The cute firefighters. The mess. Laughter in spots. One angry person ranting about his car. Glasses clinked. Heels clicked on tile.

Tarian couldn't help but tense up. Not being able to see danger coming made her jump at every sound.

Letta returned a few minutes later, her boots thumping against the floor. She placed a warm cup in Tarian's hand. "Drink. There's a sandwich too, right in front of you. It looks...edible."

Tarian picked up the cup, sipped, and gagged.

"I know, but you need it." Letta slid onto the seat next to Tarian. Paper rustled. Something squeaked as she slid it across the table. "Sandwich. Eat."

"Thanks." Tarian put the sorry excuse for coffee down, picked up the sandwich, and sniffed. It reeked of old mayonnaise and stale bread. She sighed and took a bite. Sand encased in cardboard. She chewed. Gagged. Swallowed.

She forced herself to take another bite and go through the motions.

"What's with your eyes?"

Tarian caressed the coffee cup with her thumbs. It might not taste good, but it had ended the flashing light show behind her eyes. She kept them closed, not wanting to risk any forward progress when she didn't need to.

"Nearly overloaded myself."

"Overload. Been there. I didn't go blind."

Tarian took another sip, shuddered, then put the cup down. "It's happened before. I get headaches now, if I draw too much. Calli says they're migraines."

"My mom got those. It should go away. You sense any light yet?"

Tarian moved her head around. "Yeah. But it hurts to open my eyes. A lot. Everything hurts right now. Shit. PJs." She moaned and put her head in her hands in mourning. That place had been more than a coffee shop. She'd met Daric there. They hid away from the world there. It was a sanctuary in a world of chaos. "Was" being the key word.

She heard rustling of fabric, then Letta pressed something into her hand. "Try these."

Tarian risked opening her eyes a sliver. She caught a flash of something dark and closed them again.

«Shades. Put 'em on, then open your eyes."

«Pushy.»

«Yep.»

Tarian did as she was told. The dim light of the bar, from behind the sunglasses, made her squint, but it wasn't painful. Everything was a bit blurry and out of focus, but she could make out shapes and some details. She could definitely see the smirk on Letta's face.

"Nice. Thanks." Tarian leaned back into the worn pleather of the booth, then winced as pain shot through her ribcage. It felt like someone stabbed her lung.

"Hey, you hurt?" Letta poked Tarian's side.

Tarian yelped and cringed away, then moaned. "Watch it!"

"You are! Fool. Why didn't ya say? You trying to be a hero or something?" Letta cursed and slid back out of the booth.

Tarian listened to her go, the clack of her boots on the floor oddly comforting. She'd noticed something else in between the stabbing throbs of pain. Signatures. Lots of them. Everyone in the place had magical ability.

She listened more closely to the conversations around the room. All were discussing the odd pulsing power they'd felt an hour ago. The collapse of the building. The reaction of the emergency responders. She caught one mention of a special squad that had been formed to handle the injured with elemental abilities.

Clomping footsteps announced Letta's return. She was followed by an extraordinarily tall, thin man. Tarian looked up at him, squinting through the sunglasses to make out facial features. He looked like a really tall, pale, super thin, elf, with deep purple hair standing straight up in spikes and slightly pointy ears, a pink goatee, long nose with a hoop through it, and shocking light blue eyes. They were so pale, they were almost white.

Letta pointed at Tarian. "She was in PJs when it blew. Think maybe ribs, definitely head."

"Well, well well. So you're the one we have to thank for all this?" The man slid onto the bench beside her and tapped her forearm in a comforting, soothing sort of way. His voice was deep and smooth and completely at odds with his physical appearance. He could have made a fantastic living as a radio DJ. Or a hypnotist. "I haven't seen a blast that big since New Year's Eve. And let me tell you, that was some party."

Tarian frowned at him. "I didn't do it. I was just...in the wrong place."

"At the right time, I'd say." He winked. "I'm Joel, by the way. Joel Fishbinder. I've been on the healing circuit in Philly for the past ten years. But I only really got good after the storm. I have you to thank for that. We all do. Don't you listen to the news. We don't all think you're a terrorist."

Joel took her by the shoulders and turned her to face him. She winced, and fought the urge to backhand him. He was trying to help. She knew that. But she felt vulnerable, and more than a little irritated. And weak. Too weak to do much more than groan.

Joel took her face in his hands. "Yes yes, I see it. Oh my that's a nasty little bump you got there. Yes, yes. Good. Oh yes." As he spoke, Joel emitted the most heavenly scent Tarian had ever smelled, next to Daric's cinnamon. It was almost, but not exactly, like roasting coffee beans. Lighter than real ones, with notes of some sort of flower she couldn't name. It was an odd combination but it worked. It left her light-headed and relaxed, like she'd been to a spa retreat instead of a building collapse. The light show in her eyes faded away, taking the pain with it. Several scratches and scrapes mended. She felt them itch, and then even that was gone as the scabs disappeared.

Joel's healing heat traveled from her face, down her neck, and stopped somewhere south of her boobs. He took his hands away and tsk'd. She didn't think she'd ever heard someone actually make that sound before.

"I'll need to get closer for the next part. So sorry, love, but I have to get a little handsy. I'm a handsy kinda guy." He winked again and shifted close enough their butts touched. "Don't worry. Nobody around here will care. They're used to me."

"Used to you doing..." Tarian jumped as Joel shoved his hands up her shirt. He shifted her bra aside, and placed them directly under her boobs. His fingers were cold, like little ice cubes on sticks of ice, but an odd warmth infiltrated her chest, and ribs. The scent of coffee intensified. "Oh my my my yes yes yes yes yes."

She felt something crack and heard a pop as something inside shifted back into place. She couldn't stop the gasp of pain.

"There there there now. One more. Hang tight, lovey."

She was about to protest when another rib cracked and popped. But before she could get a word out, it was over. Soothing warmth penetrated the painful parts, and then something hot flooded through her body. It brought pure bliss along for the ride. She relaxed back into the seat. "Oh...damn."

Joel laughed, a high-pitched giggle that made her want to giggle in response. "Now don't go driving for at least an hour. I'm like morphine, honey—I soothe all the right bits."

He pulled her shirt back down and shifted off the seat. Tarian looked up at him. He winked. "Take care now, sweet cheeks. You need healing, you just come on back and see me. I'm always here." He patted Letta on the behind and sashayed back to the bar, purple hair waving as he went like a proud flying flag.

Letta plopped down onto the seat beside her. "Better?"

"Oh yeah." Tarian took the sunglasses off and handed them back to Letta. She looked around and blinked. No more lightning show. They sat in what probably started out as an ordinary dive bar. Dark wood trimmed the walls and doors, and the floor had probably been the same wood once upon a long time ago. Now it was painted a vibrant purple. Every wall was a different color ranging from reds to yellows to greens and blues. Instead of a pool table, there was ping-pong. Instead of TVs blaring sports channels, there were lava lamps and electric balls of lightning. It looked like the 70s had come for a visit, spawned 80s children, then morphed into a blend of disco. She glanced up and saw an actual disco ball.

The place was an explosion of colors and smells and sounds and comfortable furniture. Puffy poofs, fluffy stools, and padded benches dotted the floor. Tables lurked everywhere, every one of them different. One looked like a giraffe with long legs. She took it all in, astonished. "Um, where the hell are we?"

Letta laughed. "Officially? We're in the Pot of Gold. It's a gay bar. Unofficially? We're in a club for those with magic. There's several cropped up over the city in the last year. This one was here before, but a lot more hush-hush back then. I never knew about the magic part. Just the gay part. And I never came in here. Now it's a place we all come to get healed up and other stuff."

Tarian watched Joel as he poured a drink behind the bar. "I think he got a triple dose from that storm."

Letta nodded. "Like me."

Tarian looked at her. "You got more than triple."

"Whatever. So." Letta nodded toward the door. "How many bubbles?"

"One. In PJs. How'd you know I was here?"

"Don't take a genius to put these pieces together. An APB on you, an explosion just like the one on the beach, in PJs, your favorite place. It has you written all over it."

Someone nearby screamed a laugh. Tarian winced. "APB?»

"They think you blew up Fort Worth. With PJs and the bubbles in Mission Park, every cop in the city is looking for the Keeper."

Tarian put her head back down on the table. "This can't be happening."

"Least you don't look like you at the moment. You look more like a homeless prostitute." Letta slid out of the seat, returning a couple of minutes later with a hat. She handed it to Tarian looking amused. "This'll do for now."

Tarian looked at it. "Jesus Loves Everybody But You." She gave Letta a you-can't-be-serious look but put it on anyway. It felt grimy, like it'd been dipped in oil. It smelled of unmentionable body fluids. And it was a little too tight. She decided she didn't want to know where this thing had been. Probably up someone's ass. "So Daric wasn't there when you left?"

"No. Should he be?"

"No. Maybe. I sent them to Boston. Hope he stays there."

"Any idea what's causing these things?"

«No.»

"Any idea how to get rid of 'em without blowing shit up?"

«No.»

Letta drummed her fingers on the table. "Maybe we contain them. You know, like the bomb squad does." She stuffed her hand into her jacket pocket and, after several hard tugs, brought out a towel.

Tarian feigned excitement. "Oh that solves everything! A towel! Why didn't I think of that?"

Letta rolled her eyes. "It ain't like I can go around flashing prisms, ya know. This is Philly. This one's a bit bigger." She placed the bundle on the seat between them and unwrapped enough for Tarian to see it. Baseball sized brilliance sparkled at her.

She nodded in appreciation. "Gorgeous. But is it big enough?"

"Dunno. Just have to find out, right?"

"Right." Tarian stood too fast, and the room swam. She grabbed the back of the seat for support.

"He told ya not to drive. Joel's healing has side effects sometimes. He healed me once, and I couldn't walk straight for two hours."

"Can't wait two hours." Tarian gingerly felt for stirrings of energy within. Every nerve was taut as a bowstring. It didn't hurt to simply touch it, but she had a feeling if she sounded even one note, the string would break. "We have to figure this out. We just need to do a quick test. We won't try to destroy the bubbles. Just get close enough to see if it'll work."

"Fine. But you need another sandwich. You look like shit. Joel heals physical. Not magical."

Tarian started to argue, saw the look on Letta's face, and stopped. She knew that look. Her mother made that look. "Fine. But not that sandwich. Cardboard would work better."

Letta laughed. "Tough it up, Keeper. I'll be right back." Letta stepped up to the bar to talk to a goth girl with giant black eyes and tattoo sleeves. She pointed at Tarian, then said something that made the girl laugh.

Letta slid into the booth beside Tarian with a packet of M&Ms, another sandwich, and coffee. It reminded her so much of Joel's signature that she glanced back at the bar. He winked at her, then continued pouring drinks.

Tarian pulled the plate close and examined the sandwich. It looked like a meatball sub and smelled wonderful. "Wow, thanks."

"No problem," Letta said.

By the time Tarian finished, the familiar surge of power through her veins had returned. "Let's get out of here."

Tarian stopped at the bar and waved to get Joel's attention. When he got close, she leaned across to whisper, "Anything you need for this place, you let Frankie know, okay? Just get to Xannon, and tell him I sent ya. Anything. Got it?" She glanced around. "You do good work here. Keep it up."

"Oh honey, I always got it up." Joel grinned.

Tarian followed Letta out of the bar and into the street, grateful that the sun was thinking about setting. It would be easier to hide what they were doing in the dark. "So how far is the park from here?"

«'Bout twenty minutes by train." Letta glanced behind them, then picked up the pace. "Keep that hat down over your face. Try not to stand out so much."

Tarian didn't need to look to know there must be police behind her. She did her best to look like a homeless street rat and resisted the urge to use a shield. She needed to save her power reserves. Just in case.

The street to the right blocked off because of the explosion, so they turned left and head around the corner. Letta pointed at a side street. "It ain't an alley, but it should do for travel."

Tarian hesitated.

Letta looked at her questioningly.

Tarian tried to gather a small amount of power. The headache instantly returned. She stopped and winced. "I don't think I should make a portal right now. And you never learned how, did you?"

Letta shrugged. "Nah. I go a different way. But I don't know if that's such a good idea right now either. You still look hungover." Letta turned and walked back down the street. "Time to slum it. Subway's right over here."

Tarian followed, feeling like an outsider in a city she would have labeled her second home. She'd never depended on any sort of human transportation. Cars were nothing more than clever ways to die. They didn't leave you free to fight or escape. She'd never even looked at the rolling underground prisons so many willingly took on a daily basis. She stared doubtfully into the abyss of the stairwell. "You sure it's safe?"

Letta barked a laugh. "Hell no. This is Philly. But it's what we got. Plus, nobody looks at nobody on the train. Come on."

—12—

Tarian pressed against the exit door of the train as it sank underground into a dark, damp, smelly tunnel. It slowed to a crawl, inching forward at the breakneck pace of a snail. She took a breath, but her throat suddenly seemed too constricted for something as thick as oxygen.

"Why does anyone ever allow themselves to be boxed up in this thing? It's falling apart, and it smells." Tarian put her hand over her nose, but it did little to mask the competing power signatures and body odor. "You do realize I was just buried alive, right?"

Letta leaned casually against a dirty metal pole nearby. "Don't whine. You lived. Besides, how else ya gonna get someplace in your condition? We ain't all got a car."

"You don't have to do this anymore. There are...other ways."

Letta raised an eyebrow. "I don't know your way. I only know my way, and *my way* would freak you the hell out right now. This works just fine for what we need."

The train strolled up to a platform and stopped. To the left, Tarian couldn't see anything but a dark wall with a dim light desperately trying to cheer the place. On the right, the door scraped open. People shoved her on their way out of the contraption, obviously eager to be anywhere else. She watched them go, envious. Her foot inched toward the door. It slid closed, oblivious. The train sauntered away from the platform and back into a long, dark, hellish hole.

"Why is it so hot in here?" Tarian brushed sweat off her forehead and tugged at the neck of her shirt. "How do you live like this?"

Letta looked away, hiding the grin Tarian knew was on her face.

"This is not funny."

"It's a little funny." Letta peeked at her from underneath her lashes and grinned. Her teeth glowed in the surreal lighting of the train.

"You're actually enjoying this."

"You bet your ass." Letta glanced out the window as the train finally crawled out from under the rocks and into the hazy afternoon light. "We're almost there."

The train wheezed up to a platform, stopped, inched forward, stopped, inched, stopped, coughed a final breath, and died. The door whined open, and Tarian bolted out.

"Ugh. It's like being digested by a giant worm that regurgitates out of both ends at the same time."

Cold air slapped her face, and she sucked it in eagerly. It smelled a bit like industrial waste but relieved tension all the same. She drank in the surprisingly cloud-free sky, resisting the urge to hug herself or rock like an infant.

"Damn, girl, you really gotta get a grip. It's just a train." Letta slapped Tarian on the shoulder as she led the way from the station to the street. "You claustrophobic?"

Tarian focused on unclenching her fists. "I just don't like

mechanical transport. It's unreliable."

Letta coughed "bullshit" behind her hand before turning to lead the way. "We got about six blocks on foot to enjoy the wide open space of the 'hood."

Tarian fell into step beside her, assessing the scenery as they went. The street was like an empty field compared to the train. "I'd rather have walked the whole way."

"Not in this neighborhood you wouldn't." Letta strolled forward, altering her gait into a panther-like stalk that shouted get-the-hell-away-from-me. Tarian did her best to duplicate it. It seemed to work. They passed a few homeless, some people obviously heading home from work, and a patrol officer who nodded ever so slightly at Letta as he slowly drove past. Nobody really made eye contact, let alone harassed them in any way. After the scene in PJs, Tarian appreciated being left alone.

They'd traveled a few blocks when she first smelled it. A hint of cold. A whiff of frigid metal. Like a frozen metal pole. It was twilight in winter, in Philadelphia, so cold air was to be expected. But this particular cold air smelled familiar. Too familiar. Tarian grabbed Letta's arm to stop her. "Shit."

Letta glanced at Tarian, then around at the street. "What?"

Tarian sniffed. Someone nearby, several someones, actively channeled Air. Lots and lots of Air. For her to smell it this far away, it was being done at a level humans weren't capable of creating. At least, not without an artifact. And she knew exactly where two of the artifacts were. She'd bet anything the third, Macari's Fire, wasn't anywhere near Philadelphia. That only left one unaccounted for. Air.

"Shit. Shit. Shit."

"What?" Letta yanked her arm away and punched Tarian's shoulder. "What's wrong with you?"

"We have company. Lots of it."

She looked at Letta, Letta looked at her, and realization dawned in both their eyes.

"Is it who I think it is?"

"If you think it's First Mother, then yeah."

Letta swore. "There's cops in that park. Before I went looking for you, they were setting up a perimeter."

A disruption of energy raced down the street like an ocean wave. It brought several signatures with it, but one dominated—frigid cold bitch. Tarian started down the street at a fast pace.

Letta raced to keep up. "What was that? My artifact just twinged."

Tarian wrinkled her nose, trying to sort the signatures as they ran. "Felt like something I've used for a fight before. But twisted. How many cops?"

"I don't know. I was consulting on the task force, not leading it. A lot. Plus the peepers."

"Peepers?"

"Yeah, peepers. Folks who refuse to leave, who like to watch the drama. We were trying to clear the neighborhoods around that park but some won't go."

"Great."

They raced down the next two blocks, turned a corner, and stopped when they saw the first squad car blocking off the street in front of them.

Letta held out a hand to stop Tarian and motioned for her to wait. She walked up to the car looking casual but stopped a few feet away. Her back went rigid as she looked left, then right. She motioned for Tarian to join her, then sat in the car and picked up the radio handset.

Letta spoke words Tarian didn't really understand. They

sounded like code from a movie. But she understood the gist of the conversation. Letta told them to stand down, get away from the park.

Someone on the other end acknowledged after a brief exchange. Letta got out of the car and flashed a grim look at Tarian. "They stopped responding to hails about five minutes ago."

The dread circling around Tarian's stomach took a leap for her lungs. "If they attacked her..." Tarian let the sentence drop.

Letta looked at her, eyes wide. They both turned from the car and sprinted. At the end of the street, another abandoned patrol car and a fire truck haunted the intersection. They stopped behind the car, using it for cover.

"Look!" Letta pointed.

A large bubble floated near the new fountain in the center of the park. It bobbed up and down as if taking a drink from the cascading water.

Next to it, several daemon in white and silver robes clustered around two obviously more important daemon. One, a male with long white hair and beard, dressed in a robe edged with crimson, stood with a deliberately neutral face, hands clasped under his robes. The other, First Mother herself, in a full white flowing kaftan. She stood tall and stiff and looked more like a judgmental statue than a living, breathing person.

First Mother held something up with one hand. Tarian couldn't quite make out more than a whitish glow from this distance, but she could feel the result. Air energy brushed her skin and tickled her nose as the daemon spun a tight web. Tarian followed the daemon's gaze to see what she targeted.

A group of at least fifty people, maybe more, huddled together inside a large, nearly transparent shield. It looked like a giant snow globe, but instead of snow it was filled with police, firefighters, teens, parents, and a few homeless looking people. The people trapped within it beat and clawed against the sides, their eyes wide with panic. Older ones were already on their knees, clutching their throats or chests.

Tarian recognized the weave. She'd used a shield exactly like it once or twice to put out fires or candles because it sucked out all the oxygen from the inside. But she'd never made one this size, and she'd never put a living thing, human or animal, inside one. It was too cruel. Too final. Too horrible. More effective than a gas chamber. It meant death. Painful, suffocating, excruciating death.

Her stomach roiled. The people inside had a minute left. Maybe two. Tops. She searched the edges of the shield for a weakness. With an active channeling of energy, there was always a weak point where the energy flowed in, then spread to create the shield. But even as she hunted for it, the spot closed. First Mother tied off the channeling, making the shield one solid mass of impenetrable Air.

"What the fuck?" Letta half-rose, trying to get a better look.

"She's suffocating them." Tarian's heart pounded loud enough to lead a band. She searched for a way to fix this. This kind of shield could be shattered or the weave unraveled, given enough time. The one thing they didn't have. Fire would strengthen it. Water would simply bounce or absorb. Earth…

"The fuck she is." Letta stood, anger and determination flooding her face. She started for First Mother, calling on the power in the Earth Artifact she'd bonded with. The ground shook, and the smell of fresh mown grass was so thick, they might as well have been standing in someone's lawn getting showered by glass clippings.

"Wait. Shit, wait. Letta!" Tarian grabbed Letta's shoulders and tugged, hard. They fell. Tarian scrambled to get on top of Letta, to keep her from racing straight toward certain death. Letta kicked and punched and fought to get away. "Wait! You attack her, they die. You die. She doesn't have to...stop kicking! You idiot! She's stronger than both of us. She doesn't have to hold the stream. The shield is set. We have to get around it."

Letta stopped kicking but glared at Tarian as she panted to catch her breath.

Tarian waited long enough to be sure Letta heard and understood, then pointed at the globe. "You're Earth. Use it! The shield doesn't dig. You do. Get them out. Your way. I'll distract her. On three. One...two..."

"Three." Letta almost growled the word. She planted both palms on the ground. It vibrated, and Letta sank down into it, leaving only a small lump of freshly turned dirt to show she'd even been there.

Tarian moved to the right, hoping to draw First Mother's attention away from her targeted victims. She reached through the Water Artifact and pulled as she went, bringing the power forward to mix with her own abilities with Air and Fire. Letta's signature scent of licorice and grass reached Tarian a fraction of a second before the ground bucked. Tarian stumbled a few steps before getting her balance back. It broke her concentration, leaving the untamed power to tangle like loose headphone wires.

First Mother rose into the air, obviously distracted by the earth shake. Her guards clustered around her to form a wall of daemon protection. The one with red trim on his robes remained on the ground next to the bubble. His jaw clenched. His hands remained under the folds of his robe. He watched the abereil, not his leader. He waited for something. Tarian wondered what. She glanced up at First Mother.

The daemon held one hand up slightly, elevating an object big enough to fill the daemon's palm and filled with white and light blue filaments that slithered in seductive undulations, like clouds moving on the breeze.

Tarian gaped at it. First Mother hovered for all to see, in the middle of Philadelphia, near an abereil, holding the Air Artifact.

In the space between one pounding beat and the next, Tarian saw pieces of a puzzle collide and wrestle. The bubbles of elemental energy that suddenly sprang to life in Fort Worth. In Philadelphia. On her own beach. The way one exploded when she'd brought the Water Artifact too close. The way one had obviously destroyed three city blocks. First Mother with an entire squad of guards here, in a park containing two abereil as if she'd known they were there.

Tarian fought for understanding. The pieces didn't quite fit. Some were missing. The puzzle wasn't complete. Time ticked away. First Mother advanced. White vapor swirled from the artifact. Tarian's own Water Artifact stirred in response. The power she'd already called strengthened and tightened and entwined into one band of energy that raged forward and slammed into the vapor volley at supersonic speed.

The elements collided and fountained up up up. Sparks flew. A boom sounded, loud enough to shake windows out of walls and cars and set off alarms.

First Mother's calm exterior shattered for a second. A flash of disbelief raced across her face and was quickly replaced with a flicker of a smile. It was a cruel expression. One filled with superiority, disgust, and triumph. She kept her gaze locked on Tarian, while she raised the Air Artifact out toward the bubble. More white vapor spilled from it and slithered to the bubble. It caressed the surface before plunging inside.

The colors inside the bubble swirled around the white vapor, mixed with it, and turned an angry gray. The bubble bulged, stretching thin and tight. It looked like a balloon ready to pop with the slightest touch of a pin.

The red-trimmed daemon stiffened. He had a resolute, resigned look about him. It was the look of someone used to obeying orders he didn't like.

First Mother inclined her head slightly toward him. He bowed his head in obvious agreement with an unspoken command.

First Mother tucked the Air Artifact away under her robes, then she and her guards vanished.

The remaining daemon shot a quick glance at Tarian, keeping his head tilted down. His lips moved. Tarian couldn't make out what he said, but she understood the message.

Run.

He turned to the bubble and extended his arms. The sleeves fell away to reveal two fists, loaded with power and ready. He opened his hands. Bolts of pure Air energy shot from him and plunged into the abereil. The daemon whirled and vanished in one fluid motion.

Lightning flashed from storm clouds overhead. One struck the bubble. It doubled in size.

Tarian heard the distant sound of dolphin cries. The medallion on her chest heated rapidly, answering the call that she hadn't even voiced.

The bubble engulfed the fountain and part of the street on both sides. It reached for the smaller version of itself and swallowed it, turning violent shades of red and yellow alternating with black and blue.

Tarian watched for only a second. She couldn't think of a

way to contain it. The thing would blow. It would sweep over the park, the buildings, and the city. It would destroy everything in its path.

She glanced toward the end of the park where the cops had been imprisoned. The shield glistened with every lightning flash, empty. A small flash of relief traveled through her gut.

Realization followed close behind it. She was left standing alone in the park. Just her, a massive abereil time bomb and an electric storm about to light the fuse.

Tarian ran for cover. First Mother appeared in the sky near where the cops had been, the glow making her white face look ethereal and almost angelic. Almost. She held the Air Artifact aloft like some sort of trophy or sword. Flashes of light shot toward the abereil.

Tarian reached one of the larger trees and ducked behind it. Curiosity forced her to stop and look back. She had to know what First Mother was up to. The Benata leader wasn't just exploding abereil for the fun of it. If that was all she wanted, she'd have destroyed this one by now. Obliterating part of Fort Worth hardly seemed worth her time. Daemon wielded overwhelming power over their element, and this particular daemon had a stick up her ass. Pestering humans seemed beneath her.

Tarian watched the bubble dip along the top, as if something very heavy stepped on it. It bent until the top met the bottom and split the pregnant bubble into two. The sides pushed away from each other as if shot from a gun. A loud crack sounded, and a wave of energy lifted Tarian and tossed her against the warehouse wall across the street from the park. She hit it hard enough to shove all the air from her lungs.

Tarian fell to the ground along with a shower of bricks and window glass. Dizziness spun the world around her, and her lungs burned as she worked to get oxygen back into them. For a few precious seconds, it was all she could think about. All she could hear was the roar of blood through her ears. The world turned upside down, like a surrealist painting.

Tarian gasped. Rolled to the side. Looked up. First Mother hovered over the park, the Air Artifact held firmly in front of her as she directed a stream of energy from the place where the abereil had been through the artifact and out toward Tarian.

Tarian slapped a hand over the medallion on her chest and yanked power through it. It roared through her body, filled her ears with dolphin screams, and raced out toward the volley of power from First Mother. Water met Air with the force of two runaway trains. The collision thrust both of them backward.

A migraine sprang to life in Tarian's mind, bringing with it a kaleidoscope of colors and pain. She grabbed her head with both hands trying to keep her brains on the inside of her skull.

Mama! A child's voice tap-danced with the migraine against Tarian's skull. Somehow her daughter's signature scent arrived with it. *Mama!*

Tarian froze. *Ember?*

—13—

Mama hurt!

Tarian spun, searching for the source. The voice was so loud, so clear, Ember had to be there in person. She could smell her daughter's signature. She couldn't do that from a distance. But she didn't see Ember anywhere.

"Ember!" Tarian shouted into the element storm, fear pounding through her ears. A pulse of Air shoved her back against what remained of the warehouse wall. She pushed forward, but she was a salmon in a stream of elemental power. She couldn't get enough momentum. Air blasted everything. The bond between her and her daughter was a hot dagger somewhere in her midsection. Ember was close. Very, very close.

Ember?

Mama! Help!

Fear reached into her lungs and squeezed. She tried to search, but all she could make out were two shadows and a blur of debris.

"Letta! Ember!" Tarian heard a return shout. A woman's voice, not a child's.

The debris circled like a tornado. What was random became a pattern, a funnel centered on the location where the abereil had been. Except now, instead of one giant abereil, there were two smaller ones. They moved with the force of the wind around the funnel, making their way slowly down.

Near the bottom of the tornado, Ember sat alone. Daric wasn't with her. A quick check on her bond with him told her he wasn't anywhere near them. The realization of what that meant dug into her gut.

"Oh, sweet heaven. She's come here on her own."

Tarian stared at her daughter. Ember reached her hands up as if she directed the storm. As if it were a child's toy. A top, doing her bidding. Ember squealed and clapped her hands. Lightning flashed, and Ember's eyes danced with delight.

About twenty feet from Ember, a small black woman waved a purple flag. Tarian squinted at it. Not a flag. A towel.

Letta shouted again, but the roar of the storm swallowed the words. Letta held up something large and round and shiny, and Tarian suddenly understood. She was going to try using the prism she'd shown Tarian in the Rainbow Room to absorb the abereil.

First Mother appeared above the tornado. Her white robes against the black sky made her look like an avenging angel in space. Her attention fixated on Ember.

Letta stood like a pitcher on a baseball mound, one hand holding a brilliant diamond baseball. She took aim and threw the object at one of the bubbles. It grabbed the last of the setting sunlight and danced with it as it sailed toward its destination. Tarian watched it arc and land in the middle of the tornado. The tornado took it and flung it around and around and around. It sparked as it sucked in power from the abereil and the storm. Light shot out in a rainbow of colors, which would have been beautiful somewhere else.

The prism glowed with the light of a thousand colorful

suns. It mesmerized. It blinded. It distracted a toddler who loved sparkly things. Ember sat next to the fountain, in the tiny eye of the storm, staring with fascination at the brilliant object floating above her. She held out her hands, and the prism sank through the center of the funnel toward chubby outstretched fingers. It landed softly in Ember's palms. She squealed with happiness and waved it around like the prize it obviously was.

The prism lit up like a firework, sparks shooting off in all directions. It plucked energy from the atmosphere and pulled it toward Ember. Her hands cupped the thing. She gazed down at it as though she held the most beautiful butterfly in the world. Her hands glowed, and her face twitched as she absorbed the elements from the atmosphere.

"Letta!" Tarian tried to move toward her daughter, but the way was blocked by the elemental storm. She couldn't be sure now if it was the bubble, First Mother, or Ember. First Mother hovered a few feet away from her daughter, a thoughtful, calculating, cold expression on her face.

One bubble traveled down the funnel, through the shield, and into the prism. Colors erupted outward, embracing Ember in a rainbow. Her tiny mouth fell open, and her eyes looked wide and unfocused.

"Letta!"

"Here!" Letta's head popped up from a bunker almost behind Tarian. She hadn't noticed it before.

"Letta! She can't stop!" Tarian shouted.

"On it!" Letta shouted her response, crawling toward Ember with obvious effort. Shadows stalked her, looking like evil spirits about to devour their prey. Tarian had seen them before, whenever the Earth Artifact thought Letta needed protection. They were projections of the woman, but far more deadly and completely independent.

The second elemental bubble fell into the center of the storm funnel and dropped like an anchor into the prism. Ember clutched the thing as if it were an electrified fence. Her body shook.

First Mother moved within a foot of the shield. She reached out toward Ember, but Tarian couldn't tell if she was trying to take her little girl, or the prism, or both. The daemon stopped abruptly, and an expression of confusion flashed across her face.

Tarian launched herself at Ember, determined to put her own body between the wretched daemon and the girl. She slammed into an invisible barrier a foot away from her daughter and crumpled to the ground next to Letta. "Shield!"

"Going down." Letta sank into the ground, leaving behind only a slight indentation where her body had been. Tarian touched the barrier. She smelled an overwhelming scent of cinnamon, sea spray, sunshine, and mountain breeze.

Dumbfounded, Tarian looked down at her daughter. Ember had crafted a protective shield around herself. It was a lot like the one First Mother had just used to kill people, but more dense, with all four elements making it a thousand times stronger. But she hadn't tied it off. Tarian could see the weak spot. With all four elements at work, the hole was large and obvious. The elements formed a straw that fed the shield. The center stood open.

She felt a tiny stab of gratitude to all the elements that Ember hadn't yet learned how to tie off a weave.

Ember smiled with delight at the sparkling prism, oblivious to the danger around her. The rainbow colors in the prism moved up Ember's arms and spread across her chest, into her face, then engulfed her body. Ember cried out, but Tarian couldn't tell if it was a sound of pain or triumph.

Tarian pounded on the barrier. "Stop! Ember, stop! You're taking too much. Let me in. Ember, let me in!" Pain pressed her mind, but she pounded again and again. Tears streamed as she fought to get through. She couldn't stop the artifact from spilling more and more. If Ember called to the power, then Ember would have to be the one to send it away.

Ember! Don't hurt me!

Ember turned confused eyes toward Tarian. "Mama?"

Tarian took the moment of distraction to force every ounce of control she possessed through the artifact. She used it to punch at the shield surrounding her daughter. It penetrated through the weak spot and continued forward to strike the prism itself. The thing cracked, and with a loud pop the glow vanished and the rainbows of light disappeared.

Ember looked from Tarian, to the now dead prism in her hands. The girl's face crumpled, and she emitted a wail that magnified a thousand times. She pulsed a wave of energy that swept everything away from her like a broom. Tarian flattened herself on the ground but couldn't stop the momentum that carried her several feet away.

The ground rumbled, surged, and vomited a wall around Ember. Then the earth beneath Tarian wiggled and abruptly sank. She dropped about ten feet into a newly formed hole. The impact when she struck bottom made her feel like she'd become part of a very large bell. Her legs tingled, and her head clanged. She reached for the sides of the vertical tunnel for support, wishing the world would stop spinning. She wanted off this ride.

Bits of crumbling rock pelted her head. Tarian shifted to the side, but she only had a foot to maneuver. No handholds were visible, so climbing wouldn't be an option. She could travel out, if she could focus enough energy through the pain and the raging tempest above. She clenched her teeth and pictured the side of the warehouse. Just as she was about to make the jump, a small side tunnel opened up instead.

"Tari! You okay?" The muffled voice led the way out of the small opening, followed by Letta's face, dark red and covered with dirt.

Tarian held her head to keep her brain from exploding. "Ember! She's overloading." She gasped as another wave of pain stabbed her eyes.

"Shit. Come on. Follow me. I couldn't get past the barrier at first, so I walled her in." Letta backed away into the darkness and disappeared.

Tarian fell to her knees and crawled into the tunnel, biting her lip to mitigate the pain in her head. It didn't work. She felt her way along the ragged awkward path, swearing with every move. The thought of what First Mother might be doing drove her forward against the pain.

The tunnel turned upward. Letta's feet disappeared through the hole above. Then her hand appeared. Tarian took it, crawling up and out with Letta's assistance. She fell to her side next to Ember, warm relief flooding her body.

"Ember?" Tarian took Ember by the shoulders and shook her, but Ember didn't respond. Tarian scooped the girl up. It was like trying to move a tree. One with deep roots, a thick trunk, and immovable branches. Tarian felt Ember drawing power from around her, even though she obviously had passed the point of being able to hold it. She seemed locked in the cycle of her talent. Small pulses sent waves of it back out.

Around them a dark, angry sky raged and threw down bolts of lightning.

Ember still held the dead prism in her hands, her attention

focused on it, though Tarian couldn't be sure she even saw it anymore. Tarian ripped it from her grip, tossed it to the side, and tugged the girl into a tight hug.

"Look out!" Letta landed on all fours next to them, muttering to the ground. It began to shift in answer to her call, sinking rapidly.

First Mother hovered at the top of their makeshift bunker, looking from Ember to Letta to the prism and back. Tarian shifted Ember to shield her from First Mother and grabbed Letta's arm. "Take her." She handed the catatonic toddler to Letta. "Hide."

"What about you?"

"Get help. She needs...release! The Caraigg. Go!"

Letta cuddled Ember into her arms and glanced at First Mother. She touched her stomach, muttering something Tarian couldn't make out. Letta looked back at Tarian. "Meet you at home." Then she and Ember sank into the Earth, vanishing from sight, with nothing to show they'd ever been there.

Tarian stared at the empty place where her daughter had been. Watching her vanish like that ripped a hole somewhere in the pit of her stomach. *She's safe. She's safe.* The words repeated, echoing through her brain.

The storm vanished with Ember, taking the lightning and thunder with it. Water dripped off leaves and crumbled bricks, and the whole place smelled fresh, like air after a rain shower. It was eerily silent.

A tingle raced along Tarian's arms, and she smelled icy cold metal a second before an elemental Air net descended around her. She instinctively reached for her own power, but it fizzled before she could form anything with it.

The net fell to the side and landed on the prism, scooped

it up, and deposited the rock into the open palm of the male daemon with the red trim. He handed it to First Mother. She clutched it in her fist and studied Tarian.

The guards stepped closer to First Mother.

Tarian flexed her hands. Five guards. One lieutenant daemon of some sort and First Mother herself. Her best hope of surviving this fight was to run.

The shadows that usually appeared around Letta emerged from the storm to circle the daemon group with a screaming howl. They formed a ring and emitted a black band that stretched out and over the daemon. First Mother moved back, eyes widening at the intrusion. Her body stiffened, and her fists clenched. Tarian knew that look and that stance. She did the same when she was about to fight.

Tarian reached within for enough power to travel. Even a few feet would help. It felt like trying to pick up ice. She tried again. It slipped out of her grasp.

The lieutenant leaned toward First Mother, holding a hand out to touch his leader's arm. He stopped just short, but the look on his face was intense, his eyes drilling sincerity at his leader.

First Mother worked her jaw as if chewing something bitter. She glared at Tarian, a look filled with the heat of an exploding sun, then vanished.

The lieutenant studied Tarian. His eyes missed nothing, she was sure. She probably looked like a child herself, buried in a hole, weak and defenseless. The Water Artifact sang, but she had nothing left to give. Her daughter had drained her dry. She wondered if the daemon felt the same. Ember surely hadn't been selective in the power she claimed. Anything and anyone nearby was fair game to a toddler.

The daemon flicked his hand, and the guards around him

disappeared one by one. He remained behind but made no move to attack or defend or to pull power of any kind. He simply stared at her with intense eyes.

She stared back at him, holding his gaze with one of her own. She made it as steady as she could, in the circumstances. She took in a deep breath and huffed it out.

"My daughter is off limits."

The daemon didn't answer or acknowledge her words. He looked at her so long she thought he might be injured. She stared up at him, not sure what he wanted or why he'd remained behind. Was he supposed to mop up or kill her? Both?

"What?" She crossed her arms and glared at him. She felt helpless and ridiculous, standing in a hole in the ground, drenched, with a pounding headache and no way to defend herself. "First Mother's the one releasing abereil, isn't she? How? Why?"

The advisor inclined his head slightly, then vanished.

"Oh no, you don't." Tarian clenched her fists and sent her tracking sense out, hunting the prism. The signal returned, a gentle pulse that alternated warm and cold. Distant, but distinct. She turned toward it.

Set her jaw. Opened a portal to a spot halfway to her destination, head roaring in protest, and stepped through.

—14—

Tarian emerged from travel, stumbled forward one step, then two, tripped on a jagged rock, and caught herself on another. The edges, rough as old knives, sliced into her palms. She hissed and snatched her hands back. Blood painted the rough tips of the rocks, making them look like angry vampire teeth. She crouched next to the things, wincing as the pain in her palms and the pain in her head did a little jig.

Pound. Pound. Pound. *Whomp whomp. Whomp whomp.*

Something grabbed her heart and twisted the beat. It felt like being at a really loud rock concert with the base turned up full so the beat beat beat could rip rip rip the breath right out of her body. She forced herself to take a breath after every third beat of whatever it was, but she couldn't stop her heart or the pain in her head from falling in line with the rhythm.

Pound pound. *Whomp whomp.*

She pictured the ocean. The waves rumbling against the shore. The dolphins. Her sister, healing the soreness. Anything to soothe the beast within.

Pound pound. *Whomp whomp.*
Whomp whomp.

Pound.

Whomp whomp.

Whomp whomp.

Pound.

Whomp whomp.

Whomp whomp.

Whomp whomp.

The pain subsided enough to let her take more interest in her surroundings. She'd landed on a platform about ten feet across. Boulders protruded every few inches, leaving very little space to stand but excellent places to hide.

Beyond the rock, three other bumpy peaks stabbed a sky so brilliant and so blue it hurt to look at it. The four platforms outlined a deep, bowl-shaped valley so vast she couldn't see the bottom from where she crouched.

Whomp.

Whomp.

Whomp.

She couldn't see what made the noise. Didn't know if she wanted to see. Something, somewhere, churned with raw, pure, pounding power.

First Mother hovered in the wide open space between peaks. She might as well have been walking on water. Tarian sniffed but caught only a trace of signature from the daemon. Nothing active. Nothing supported her that Tarian could see or sense.

First Mother held the dead prism out in front of her as if offering it to someone. But there was nobody there. No other signatures in evidence.

Tarian waited and watched. No sign of movement from First Mother or anyone else. No daemon guards. No Ancients of any element. No bugs on the rocks. Nothing.

Sun glinted off the prism and fractured into a small rainbow that quickly vanished. Tarian inched forward slightly, positioning for a better viewing angle. She still couldn't see below, but now the prism was in full view.

Another glint, followed by another, and she realized it wasn't the sun causing it. The prism sparked from inside, slowly building to a steady glow. First Mother's chin tilted up slightly, and there was a satisfied gleam in her eyes.

Tarian squinted to get a better look at the prism. She'd thought it dead. She'd shot enough power into it to overload it and heard the crack. Saw the glow vanish. It had to be dead.

Colors flickered outward from the thing, as if calling her out for being a liar. The general hum of power dipped slightly. It was so subtle Tarian almost missed it. The prism pulsed a little brighter, and the colors stretched out a few feet, then dissipated.

First Mother looked from the prism to the open maw below. Tarian tried to follow the daemon's gaze but couldn't. Her vantage point didn't give her any view at all of whatever filled the valley between the ragged peaks. Her graceful entrance might have gone unnoticed, but if she moved from behind the rocks First Mother was sure to see her.

Tarian rested a hand on the Water Artifact and assessed her own status. She was drained, exhausted, and sore in places she'd rather not notice. Trying to channel energy of any sort wasn't a bright idea. She stifled a groan of frustration at her own weakness.

First Mother reached under her robe and pulled out the Air Artifact. She clutched it tightly in one hand. Frowned at the prism. Then pulsed. Blue-white vapor circled First Mother's hand, then jumped from the artifact to the prism. The diamond glowed brighter. The atmosphere crackled, flashed, and flickered. Sparks like fireflies flared around it, then vanished.

First Mother shifted her attention from the Air Artifact and the prism to something below. Tarian half rose to get a look at whatever it was, but she wasn't close enough to the edge to see anything.

Frustrated, she shifted out from behind her rock shield. She kept low and scuttled like a crab from one rock to another. Then another. One more, and she knelt on the edge of the platform next to a small boulder.

She paused to make sure First Mother hadn't noticed her. The daemon remained focused on whatever it was she was trying to do.

Tarian inched closer to the edge and looked down. Her breath caught somewhere in her chest and stayed there.

A gelatinous, pulsating mass the size of a small city filled the valley below. It quivered like jello with each *whomp*. Tentacles of power intertwined, forming a complex rope of energy that surged, ebbed, and flowed to the internal rhythm that pounded the air and squeezed her heart. The surface glistened like slick spots on pavement, oily and luminescent.

It looked like an overgrown abereil on steroids. The mother of all abereil. The source of all the small child abereil everywhere. Tarian licked her lips with a tongue so dry it scratched.

The flickers and flashes made sense now. What disappeared here appeared somewhere else. Fort Worth. The park. The beach.

Tarian looked back at First Mother. For the first time, emotion played on the daemon's face like a child on a merry-go-round. Frustration. Anger. Desperation. Other emotions Tarian couldn't name. The usually carved ice had melted, exhibiting more life than she'd have thought possible for the daemon. Here in what she probably thought of as her own personal haven, First Mother didn't bother to hide her emotions.

First Mother turned the prism in her hands, frowning as she examined the surface with long fingers. She probed with Air. More sparks flared and vanished.

Tarian felt the weave of a net, but it fizzled. She didn't see any kind of shield form.

The daemon screamed in frustration, loud enough to startle Tarian. Tarian jumped reflexively, bumping into the boulder beside her.

First Mother turned toward Tarian and narrowed her eyes.

Tarian scrambled back, struggling to get to her feet without falling off the edge.

"You." First Mother floated forward, stopping just beyond the lip of the platform. "Bring that. Here."

First Mother glared at the space between Tarian's breasts, where the Water Artifact lay embedded in her flesh.

Tarian pointed at the Air Artifact. "I could say the same to you."

"Air does not act without provocation. Air contains. Water is uncontrolled chaos in the hands of someone like you. It should never have been entrusted to *humans*." The word held contempt and scorn and hate, as if it was the worst four-letter word in the history of words. "You have broken a balance as ancient as time itself. You are a child, weak and foolish and ignorant."

Tarian ignored the obvious attempt to get to lose her temper and glanced at the Source abereil below. Sparks still spawned, but slower. "Why are you doing this? Are you trying to destroy the world? Because that's the road you're on."

First Mother's nostrils flared. "This anomaly exists because you took it upon yourself to destroy a system that kept us safe for thousands of years. This…"—First Mother gestured at the valley—"is your creation. Your actions endanger everything."

Tarian frowned. First Mother's words echoed thoughts that had been running around in her own mind for the last year. But she hadn't said them out loud. She'd tried to convince herself that she'd only done what she'd agreed to do, that day they all stood before the Dulra in the Balance Court. She'd promised to break the Stulos and release magic into the world. Combine the planes. It was the first step to restoring balance, and she'd done exactly as they'd asked her to do. But self-doubt was a tricky thing when lying awake in the darkness listening to news reports. A harsh, tricky, insidious thing. She'd heard nothing more from the Dulra. Not when she broke the Stulos. Not when magic fell so unevenly. And not now, nearly a year later. They remained absent as the world fell apart.

Tarian swallowed. Pushed the thoughts aside. "How could this possibly be my fault?"

"Did you think, when the Stulos collapsed, that the power it contained died with it? Life force does not evaporate, Keeper. Power does not vanish. Ever. Power calls to power. Freed from constraints, it pooled here at one of the strongest deposits of natural power on earth, the space below Benata City. The Source readies itself to be born again and when it does, it will consume everything. I am here to clean up your mess, child. Yours, and those who swore to protect and uphold our natural laws. I am here to right the wrong."

Tarian frowned. "Every time you let out a trickle of power, that...Source...spawns an abereil somewhere. Have you seen what happens when they explode?"

First Mother sneered.

Anger flared in Tarian at the obvious scorn and derision. "You're spawning them on purpose. Why?"

"My actions serve the greater good." First Mother brought

the prism in line with the artifact, one next to the other. The prism pulsed faster. "Can you say the same?"

"Who's good? Yours? Every time one of those things explode, they destroy everything around them. You've killed people. Hundreds, maybe thousands by now. How does that serve anything at all?"

"A thousand more humans are worth it, if it means stability can be attained for those who are left."

Tarian stomped her foot. "No deaths are worth it. Of any species. They aren't necessary. That thing wasn't doing anything until you..."

"All I need is a way to harness the natural energy emissions. With that, I can put things right."

"Harness." Realization shone light on exactly what First Mother intended. "You mean steal. You don't want to fix anything. You want to keep power from everyone else. Isn't that right?"

First Mother stared down her nose at Tarian as if she confronted a particularly smelly pile of dog shit. "Power is for those capable of wielding it. It was never intended for humans to reach so high. You should have stayed where you were, in the mud. Crawling in it, like the ants you were meant to be."

Tarian glanced at the Source abereil. It pulsed and jiggled with every *whomp*. "Are you seriously trying to put a net around a giant energy bubble?" Tarian surveyed the flickers that continued to pop in and out of existence. They danced around First Mother like proverbial moths to flames. The Source vibrated with every flicker, as if tickled by an invisible hand.

"It won't work." Tarian flexed her hands and gently gathered energy, ready to push it through the Water Artifact.

"It will, *child*. You have provided exactly what I need to

succeed. Ironic." First Mother half smiled, amused by some private joke.

"The prism?" Tarian's gaze flicked to it. It emitted a dull glow that didn't pulse any longer. "It's done. It can't hold any more and even if it could, you can't extract anything from it. It's a sponge, not a pitcher."

"Capacity will expand given enough Air. You will soon learn that Air is the most vital, the most pure, the most powerful element." First Mother extended both hands in front of her. A wave of energy cascaded over Tarian as the daemon pumped Air through her artifact and into the prism. The prism grew, expanding to twice the size it had been. The atmosphere crackled, filled with the stench of burnt ozone and the tingle of electricity that raced along Tarian's body and into her own artifact.

The Water Artifact reacted before Tarian could stop it. Water energy, full of salt and sea, surged from her chest and raced toward First Mother. First Mother shot back, wrapping Air around Water until the two melded.

Tarian tried to dodge the attack, but couldn't. Her feet were suddenly too heavy to lift. Gravity somehow tripled. It dragged everything down down down. She couldn't lift her hands. Her eyelids wanted to close. Her head dropped, chin to chest. Pressure pressed and pushed on her lungs, skull, spine. She dropped to her knees.

She used the pressure to shove more power through the artifact. Forced it up and out. Poured pure Water into the Air and locked onto it. Used it. Molded it and used her own ability with Air to make it grow. Gravity reversed. She was suddenly light and mobile and energized. Tarian focused on First Mother and pulsed. Air and Water returned to sender, intensified.

First Mother flew backward, the objects in her hands flying

outward in opposite directions. The Air Artifact raced up and out as though shot from a cannon. Tarian lost track of it against the dark blue sky.

The prism arced through the air and then plummeted to the Source. It touched the surface, which bulged inward. It caved further and further as the prism pressed against it. Then the surface folded over and swallowed the diamond.

The Source groaned and bubbled. The surface looked like a pot about to boil. Tarian watched in horror as sparks flickered in the atmosphere above the Source. The flickers merged and resolved into spheres. Bubbles of power formed across the valley as if a child had waved a giant bubble wand.

One formed above the peak where Tarian stood. It loomed above her like a blimp at a football game. She scrambled away, but couldn't go more than a couple of feet before she teetered on the edge of the platform. She struggled to keep her balance, backing off a few inches. She was caught between an abereil and the edge of a cliff, with the Source waiting to catch her below.

Tarian's heart skipped a beat, then two. She couldn't breathe. The Water medallion heated up as it activated. The scent of salt and sea filled her nose as power from it reached out toward the bubble over head.

Tarian stared up at the abereil. Red, green, and silvery-white tendrils twined around one another like a pit of snakes. It didn't look stable. It looked lopsided and agitated.

She watched the way it churned, felt the way the Water Artifact responded, and knew this would be a repeat of Fort Worth. The artifact would strike out at the prism. One hit, and it would blow. One hit would throw a lot of loose elemental power into the atmosphere and start a chain

reaction to all the others, including the Source. One abereil
was devastating. This many would end the world.

—15—

Adrenaline raced around Tarian's body like a caffeinated toddler. She tried to put a shield around the Water Artifact. She tried to stop it from launching a protective strike. It was like hitting her head against a rubbery brick wall that bounced and reformed at will. The artifact ignored her commands and shot a stream of Water.

The water jet plunged into the abereil. The blue Water stream twined around the red, green, and blue tendrils and formed a rope that pulled the bubble closer and closer to Tarian.

Her stomach churned acid and delivered it straight to her mouth. She wanted to run straight off the cliff. Throw herself into the air and fly. Drift high on the wind, far away from this minefield.

That would take power.

She couldn't use more power. It would make things worse. A lot worse.

The abereil expanded, feeding off Tarian's energy. It grew and grew, spilling over the rock, the platform, and Tarian, engulfing her in an embrace that smelled of sulfur, grass, ozone, and sea spray.

Hot, molten jelly oozed over her skin and invaded every pore. Her mind turned somersaults, overwhelmed by all the sensory details and raw, undirected chaos.

Lightning flashed on all sides as the medallion reacted to the bubble. Dolphins cried a warning, but it was faint, far away, and out of place in these mountain peaks.

The edge of the bubble bent inward toward the artifact, which grew hotter and hotter until it felt like someone held a Taser or cattle prod to her chest. She tried to shift away from the edge of the abereil, but couldn't get a grip on anything.

The bottom of the abereil surged upward, pushing Tarian to one side in its quest to reach the artifact.

The two edges met in the middle. Fire flared and scorched. Water baptized. Air cleansed. Earth smothered. The overload pushed through her pores and into her marrow. It burrowed deep, sent shoots of pain and pleasure and power through her bones and veins and into heart and lungs, until it embedded into the artifact. The artifact kept pure Water and let the rest pass through unheeded, back into the abereil.

Where one abereil had been, two bobbed along toward the edge of the mountain peak. The two bumped against each other and rocketed away in opposite directions, leaving a rainbow-hued comet trail of energy in its wake.

Every time the bubble hit something, it shot off in another direction, knocking her off her feet. It was like a giant exercise ball, and she was a gerbil. And the ball was in a giant bathtub filled with elemental power.

The abereil morphed inward from the top and bottom, pushing Tarian to one side.

"No no no no. Not again."

Tendrils of Earth, Air, and Fire touched the Water Artifact

and sparked. Lightning flashed. The jolt of electricity knocked Tarian back against the side of the bubble. The top and bottom of the abereil bent toward the middle and split it into two. Jets of energy pushed Tarian's bubble off in a new direction.

Her abereil bumped into another. Lightning sparked from one to the other, and the two split into four that bounded away to bump into more bubbles.

Nearby, a larger abereil pulsed an odd blue-white light. The center flared, power arching out to touch another abereil. The two raced toward each other. Collided. Flashed brilliant light. Combined. Then began to split.

In the seconds of light, Tarian saw a small glowing object in the middle of the abereil. She shifted in her bubble prison, trying to get a better view.

Excitement raced through her when she realized the Air Artifact now floated encased in an abereil just a few feet away.

She shoved at the side of the bubble, feet scrambling to push forward. But she was too late. The abereil she inhabited bent, split, and zoomed off in a new direction.

«Dammit!»

It took seconds to expand and split. Every new bubble created another and another. They all seemed to be reacting to the artifacts or the instability or something else she couldn't see.

The Air Artifact taunted her from a distance. The bubble carrying it already bulged in from the sides, ready to give birth. Tarian threw herself at the side of her abereil. Momentum tumbled it toward the Air Artifact a short distance. She hit the side again. Slid a bit closer to her target. Once more. Now a few feet away.

So close.

She took a running leap at the side of the bubble. It edged

forward and bumped the one carrying the Air Artifact.

Lightning crackled. Jolts of power lit the atmosphere. Thunder clapped, so loud it reverberated around the inside of her skull. Both abereil split, then the four new bubbles shot away from each other as if propelled from a gun.

Tarian's prison tumbled her like clothes in a dryer. By the time she righted herself and hunted for the Air Artifact, it was so distant she could barely see it.

Tarian's abereil surged inward to split. She leaned against one side, hoping to change directions. When the split happened, she joined the thrust of energy with some of her own, directing it down toward the rocks of a nearby platform. Her bubble ping-ponged off the stone and caught an updraft. The bubble split again and again and again. Flashes of colors and cords of power extended out into the darkness, providing eerie light and shadows that played along the jagged peaks.

The bubble split three more times before she could gather her thoughts. It split five more times before she realized there was no way to block it using the artifact energy. Any she sent out was immediately scooped up by the abereil and only served to speed up the splitting process.

She focused instead on using the excess from each split of the bubble to push toward the Air Artifact. It took ten or fifteen tries, but each took her closer to her goal until finally the Air Artifact dangled, bobbed, and taunted just two feet away.

Split.

Push.

Twelve inches.

Split.

Shove.

Six.

Three.

One inch.

Tarian reached for it, shoving her hands into the gooey edge of the bubble.

First Mother appeared in between Tarian and the Air Artifact, blocking the way. She looked like an angry banshee with her white robes in stark contrast with the dark sky, her hair loose and flying in every direction and her face so angry it'd turned a deep crimson. "Greedy, ignorant fool! You hold an artifact. You cannot hold another."

The daemon flicked one hand in Tarian's direction. The abereil flew backward, taking Tarian with it. She had a fleeting view of First Mother pumping the abereil holding the Air Artifact full of energy. It burst, and power erupted like a volcano to shower everything nearby. First Mother took the Air Artifact and vanished.

Tarian's abereil continued to carry her away until it hit another one, bounced, and zipped off in a new direction. She hit several more before some outside force halted her mid-bounce. The abrupt stop flung her to the side. The bubble bulged outward with the force of her blow, but didn't move and didn't break.

First Mother reappeared near Tarian. She looked down her nose at Tarian with a triumphant expression. Tarian pounded the side of her prison, but it was like hitting a sponge—extremely ineffective and unsatisfying. "Why are you doing this? You're going to destroy the world! The prism is gone. It's done. Whatever you're planning, it won't work."

First Mother smiled. A cold smile that snaked across her cheeks but didn't reach her eyes. "From what I witnessed, I do not need the trinket. It seems, Keeper, that your offspring has a use after all. With her, and this"—First Mother jiggled the Air artifact like a bell—"field of abereil you have so conveniently provided, I'll be able to finish the mission after all."

"What mission?"

First Mother tucked the artifact into a fold of her robe. "To take back what is ours. Magic belongs to daemon. Not humans. Once I have it in my control, your kind will be what it once was...inconsequential. There to serve the greater good." She raised a hand toward Tarian. "All I need is the Scion." First Mother nodded, smiling to herself. "Most helpful. See that you create more abereil while I'm gone? The energy they provide is vital."

First Mother vanished, leaving Tarian to drift inside an abereil that continued to create more and more and more.

—16—

Tarian raged against the walls of her prison. The abereil continued to split and multiply, oblivious. Every split brought a wave of cries, like the plaintive wail of a small child, muffled but insistent.

Mama?

The weak whisper was a slice of ice through her veins. Tarian stilled.

Ember?

Want...Maaamaaaaaa!

Tears of frustration streamed down Tarian's face. *Ember, stay with Letta, sweetie. I'm okay. You're okay. It's all going to be okay. Hush, sweetie...hush now. It's okay.*

She continued to soothe Ember with her thoughts, not knowing if her daughter could hear them or not.

The cries silenced, sending a new kind of worry rocketing through Tarian's mind. She imagined First Mother finding Ember. Doing unspeakable things to her. Turning her into a tiny human battery that she then used to destroy the world.

Surely it wasn't possible. The Caraigg and Letta guarded her daughter deep in the bowels of the earth. They'd keep her safe.

They were sworn to it. She trusted them. And there was no way First Mother could penetrate that far beneath the surface, that deep into the ground and rock. The daemon was pure Air. She couldn't do it. She couldn't. Surely not. Surely.

"Ember?"

No answering cry. No soft whisper. Nothing. No response was a good thing. She didn't want Ember rushing to her side. Not here. At the same time, when no response came...her stomach flopped and churned and threatened to spill over. She felt feverish and slow. She couldn't take much more. She needed rest. Food. A hundred years of sleep.

She needed to get to her daughter before First Mother found her.

She closed her eyes and tried to focus. She needed a way to get home. Any way. Anything to get out of this prison.

She tried a thin, light shield. Barely using Air. It fizzled, encased by the abereil prison.

She tried a travel portal.

The abereil split once, then again, then a third time so rapidly she was thrown upside down.

Tarian sagged against the side of her prison. She looked out over the valley while she caught her breath. An enormous, effervescent, bubble bath of sparkling beacons of death, doom, and raw power, as potent as nuclear weapons with no guidance systems, extended as far as she could see.

She caught a glimpse of the giant Source abereil below in between the multitudes of abereil she'd spawned over the last few minutes—days?—she couldn't be sure of the time. The sight of it overwhelmed. If one small bubble could flatten Fort Worth, she had no doubt the Source was capable of annihilating the planet. Maybe even more than one. It might reach to the moon and beyond. It might eat the sun and then look around for dessert. Without First Mother bombarding the abereil with shots of Air, the mass looked dormant and stable. Anger flared, hot and quick. The damn daemon had done it all on purpose. She'd fed the Source, a bomb capable of wiping them all out. She'd released abereil into the world on purpose. Three city blocks vaporized... on purpose.

Tarian quenched the thoughts. They led to emotions. Ember would feel them and react.

She pictured Ember popping up over the valley of bubbles, the way she'd done in the park. Just materializing out of nowhere. She'd obviously escaped Daric's arms, from his mother's underground bunker, to run to her mother's rescue. Ember already showed more courage, more protective instincts, than most adults. A that's-my-girl pride swelled at the thought.

But if Ember showed up here, above the Source abereil, with multitudes of abereil bursting with elemental energy around her, the results would be...catastrophic.

She imagined First Mother's manic glee as Ember absorbed bubble after bubble until she glowed purple with overloaded energy.

She imagined Ember exploding from the sheer force of carrying too much magical power.

She imagined how Ember's talent for magnifying the energy around her would act on the Source, an object strong enough to destroy the planet all by itself.

She imagined Ember, the tiny toddler turned terrorist equipped with enough nuclear bombs to scramble the universe, and the world began to spin.

Tarian closed her eyes. She blocked the landscape and the daydream from her mind and ignored the rising tide of panic. She had one simple task. Just one.

Figure out a way home.

She'd tried a travel portal, but that'd just spawned more abereil. But she hadn't tried the daemon way. Daemon didn't create outward portals—they kept theirs internal. She'd done it before, when she'd followed First Mother into this hellscape. She just needed to focus. Clear her mind. Soothe her frantic thoughts. Ignore the headache, the exhaustion, and the fear.

Picture one place.

Focus.

Time to go home.

—17—

Tarian landed on the hard stone floor in the House of Xannon entry and slid into the wall, hitting her head against the rock. It was like ringing a bell inside her skull with a hammer of steel and stone and electric bug zappers. Tears ran and curses flew. She gripped her head with both hands and winced. The kaleidoscope of lights was back, only now it brought friends. Her eyeballs ached. Her head reverberated with each wave of the ocean outside.

«Keeper!»

«Shhhhh. Shit.»

The Sentinel guarding the entry obliged, lowering his voice to a whisper. She heard a few words: "Healer" and "Calliope."

Tarian lay down and rolled her forehead back and forth on the cold floor. It struck her that this wasn't the first time she'd arrived home exactly like this, writhing in pain on the floor.

Footsteps pounded. She wished they wouldn't do that.

«Ember.»

"Pardon?" The Sentinel sounded confused and more than a little worried.

"She here?" Tarian cleared her throat. "Letta. Ember. Here?"

"No, Keeper. The Scion is not here. We thought…»

"Shhhhh. Damn."

The Sentinel lowered his voice and continued. "We thought she was with you. Letta disappeared three days ago. A search is ongoing for...all three of you. There's been no word. Keeper, you've been missing for three days."

"Not with me." Tarian put an arm over her face, shielding her eyes from the glare. "Three?"

«Tari?» Footsteps *click-clacked* across the floor. They sounded like a thousand cymbals from a marching band. The scent of fresh clean breeze and cool river water wafted before them like a banner.

"Calli." Tarian kept her arm where it was. "Please…don't… shout."

Calliope knelt beside her. Her voice remained loud and hyper. "Where have you been? We've been frantic. The Carraigg would only say Ember was safe. They wouldn't give details. They... What happened?"

"Bubble. Ember overloaded." She couldn't put urgency behind the words. Every breath hurt. Every whisper. Every thought. Traveling like a daemon out of a pot boiling over with elemental energy had felt like ripping her skin off with her teeth. It created quite a hangover. The kind that went along with tequila and one-night stands and regrets.

Calliope made a shushing sound. "Never mind. Tell me later."

Tarian whispered. "Head. Hurts."

Calliope gently moved Tarian's arm aside. "I'm not great with headaches, but let me see what I can do." She hummed softly, healing warmth flooding into Tarian's head. The pain lessened somewhat but didn't go away. The lightning didn't seem as bright.

The humming intensified. Her head spun with the energy

Calliope shot through her skull. She tried to pull away but Calli's strong hands held her in place. The pressure reached unbearable. Tarian squeaked in protest.

Calliope removed her hands. "How's that?"

"Ugh." Tarian grunted and tried to sit up again. Halfway to sitting, her stomach heaved and she lay back down.

"Just stay still for a bit. Healer Chloe will be right here."

She reached for her sister's hand and squeezed it. "First Mother is coming."

"First Mother? Here?" Calliope leaned closer, smoothing hair away from Tarian's forehead just like her mother used to do. "Is that even possible?"

"Is now." Tarian pushed against her.

Calliope held her down. "Rest, Tari. It's hard to protect anyone or anything if you don't take care of yourself first. Tell me what happened."

"Overloaded."

"You said that before. Ember? Or you?"

«Both. Daric? Alex?»

"They're leading the search for you, Tari. Ember disappeared. Daric told us what happened. We saw the damage to PJs. The news. You don't know...we thought you might be...the building..." Calliope swallowed hard. "I didn't think you were. I knew you weren't. The symbol didn't glow. The dolphins...everything felt normal. So I knew the artifact couldn't have transferred. But all three of you missing...it couldn't be coincidence. The Caraigg told me Letta and Ember were okay, but they refused to say where or what happened and refused to say when or if they'd come home. And they had no news of you. Nothing. I just...we didn't know what else to do."

"Great." Tarian winced. Three days. Ember and Letta, in

the ground, for three days. That the Caraigg assured her sister everything was okay was a small comfort. Very small. That they weren't here, though, kept her from feeling happy about it.

"Tell Frankie to call everyone back," Calliope said to the Sentinel standing nearest. He nodded and hurried away, boots pounding on the stone floor in a syncopated, obnoxious rhythm.

Tarian sent a tentative feeler out for Ember's signature and instantly regretted it. The jackhammer in her head reminded her she wasn't ready for that sort of thing. Her stomach insisted she had better things to do, like vomit.

Quick footsteps announced more people. The slap of flip-flops announced one in particular.

"Keeper." The disapproving tone said everything Chloe would never verbalize. Healer Chloe knelt on one side of her while Calli continued to prop up her head on her lap. She wanted to protest that they made her feel like an infant, but gave it up. She was too weak to do much about it.

Hot and cold followed Chloe's fingertips as she traced Tarian's body, probing for injuries. Calliope's hum joined in. Gentle taps. Pokes. Mutters. Whispered discussions. Tarian let herself drift, knowing it was useless to argue and better for healing if she just rolled with it.

Chloe's healing talent joined Calliope's and waltzed through Tarian's brain. It made her skin itch, but the headache eased. The exhaustion receded to a need for two full days of sleep instead of three weeks. Her stomach roared a protest at the starvation it endured.

Chloe moved back, making disapproving noises. "Where've you been, Keeper? You feel different. As if you took a bath in all the elements. Your skin drips with them."

"That's basically what I did."

"Well, it's interfering, but I think I got most of it. How is your head now?"

Tarian moved her head back and forth to test. "A lot better. Thanks." Tarian squeezed Calliope's hand. "Both of you. Much better."

"Keeper. I see you've returned." Ruarc's usual arrogant lilt had been replaced with heavy sarcasm.

Tarian squinted up at him. "Pissed?"

The Mayfanata leader stared back with cold hard eyes. "We had an Agreement. I honor my Agreements, Keeper."

"Right. You have to stay until we talk about Ember. Sorry. Wait, no, I'm not." Giggles rushed up from somewhere and spilled out before she could stop them.

Ruarc's eyes narrowed with suspicion. Calliope and Chloe stared.

"Hysteria?" Calliope whispered to Chloe.

"Shock more like," Chloe answered.

Tarian covered her mouth to stifle the misplaced mirth. She hadn't meant it. Nothing about this was the least bit funny. "Sorry," she mumbled through her fist.

She shifted until she could lean against the wall. Chloe shook her head and backed away, muttering something about food. Two Sentinels ran from the room at her instructions.

Tarian sent out gentle feelers for Ember, Daric, and First Mother. This time, the headache remained distant. She breathed a soft sigh of relief, both at the lack of pain and the lack of First Mother's presence anywhere nearby. She couldn't feel the daemon at all. Or the Air Artifact. Odd.

"Not a good time, Ruarc."

"Did I understand correctly that our daughter has overloaded again?"

Tarian nodded. Ember felt insulated, somehow, but not far away. Moving fast.

"She is far too young. She has not learned how to shield properly."

Tarian held up a hand. "Save the lecture." She caught Daric's signature just as it shifted. He was on the move.

"Our daughter..."

"Mine." Tarian glared up at him. "You aren't even a sperm donor."

"I 'donated' far more than that."

"You tricked me." Anger welled up in her stomach, arguing with her headache for attention.

"Careful, Keeper. It's quite obvious Ember will react to your mood no matter where you are in this domain."

"In *this* domain? You mean there's a place she won't feel me?"

"That is what I wish to discuss."

"Not now." Tarian hesitated, debating whether she should tell him about how Ember had somehow teleported herself to the middle of the park. How she'd absorbed even more power. And what she feared was about to happen with First Mother. If she told him, she'd have to admit just how badly she'd bungled things, and how much she needed help. It would give him the upper hand. He'd lord it over her worse than Alex when he'd finally beat her in the arena.

It irritated. To admit weakness to Ruarc of all people...she'd almost rather have the headache back. But she needed his help. As much as it stung to admit. She looked at Calliope as she spoke, which made it easier to get the words out. "First Mother is hunting Ember. She'll come here."

Calliope gasped. Mutters filled the alcove as Sentinels reacted to her words. Tarian held up a hand. "The Caraigg guard her. First

Mother can't dive into the ground. But when Ember surfaces...we should be ready."

"All the more reason for us to talk, Keeper." Ruarc knelt in front of her. "How solid is this Agreement with the Ancient Ones?"

"Very." She glared at him. "They don't try to trick people. Unlike you."

Ruarc's eye twitched once. It lasted a fraction of a second, which said a lot about his irritation level. Off the charts, she'd guess. "Ember inherited a great deal of daemon essence. Not just mine, but yours as well."

Tarian frowned. "I'm not daemon."

"I assure you, somewhere in your lineage, quite recently in fact, there is daemon essence. Perhaps something stronger."

"Not possible."

"Which? That you're part daemon, or that you're part something else, something stronger?"

"Either. Both."

Calliope coughed. "It could be. I've studied our family history...it could be. The way the rituals played out for Mother and Grandmother...it could be. That doesn't even begin to cover what might have happened a few more generations back. They didn't keep good records back then."

"Stronger than daemon? That'd mean Ancient. That's just..."

Calliope raised an eyebrow. Her mouth opened to expand on the idea, a sure sign they'd all be there awhile as she explained.

Tarian held up a hand to stop her. "Whatever. So?"

"Ember's power can be shielded so that she does not react to your mood swings, but she'd need to be in an Air domain. There, she could be taught as daemon children are. The basics of how and when to manifest her unique gifts, how to shield them from others, and how to guard herself from attack. Things all Mayfanata children are taught. And she would be protected against the Benata. They, specifically First Mother, are not able to cross into our domain. Such an attack triggers ancient protections and Agreements. She'd be foolish to the extreme to risk it. To do so would mean death."

"Daemon teach how to bottle talent and emotions. How to never let it out," Macari said from the hallway. "Ember doesn't need your sort of education, Mayfanata."

Tarian shielded her eyes to stare at Macari as she entered the entry. She wore a vibrant yellow sundress, bare feet, and a steely attitude. It wasn't like her. Usually the daemon was chipper and full of sorority type energy.

Ruarc stood and turned a cold gaze toward Macari. "Mayfanata do not teach such things. That is a Benata tradition. One First Mother obviously embraced. Though with your particular talents, perhaps it was warranted."

A blast of anger from Macari hit like a battering ram, with enough physical pressure to drive Tarian into a crouch before she realized what she was doing.

"Warranted?" Macari glowered, her anger toward her mother spilling out onto everyone in the room. "You're saying I *deserved* to be treated like that?" The emotion was so intense it burned flesh and bone as if they all stood in the middle of a furnace. Everyone in the room, from Sentinels to Ruarc, reacted. Some turned their heads and raised their arms in defense while others left the room altogether.

"Macari! Please." Tarian covered her head with her arms in an effort to fend off the attack. Not that it did any good. It wasn't really fire, although Macari *did* hold the Fire Artifact. But it might turn into real fire any second if she lost control. "Shit, turn it down! You're burning us up!"

"Sorry." The emotion vanished, as though she'd simply shut a door. It felt odd, like a rock concert after the last song when the invasive beat suddenly stopped, leaving nothing but a roar in the ears. "See? That's how well I learned. I can teach her how to shield like that, Tari. I can show her how to contain her power and how to control it."

Macari stood her ground, squaring off with Ruarc with a set jaw and determined shoulders. She looked like a barefoot fairy princess in that sundress, but her face said pissed-off warrior.

Ruarc leaned against the opposite wall and stuck his hands in his pockets, the picture of casual. Only his clenched jaw gave away his real mood. "You could teach her, but not here. You would need to be at her side constantly. And you would need to teach her mother how to do it as well."

Macari flashed an uncertain look toward Tarian.

"I am suggesting that the best way to keep Ember safe, at least until she's learned to guard her own power, is to remove her from the volatile surroundings she currently inhabits. Her strength intensifies exponentially with each passing day. Each day she becomes more attractive as a tool for First Mother. And soon she will be far too strong for anyone in Xannon to handle, even someone as strong as I. Even"—he pointed at Macari—"a daemon supplied with an artifact might find Ember a handful before she's four turns if she's not within the confines of a daemon environment, particularly with her unique talent of absorption."

Macari grumbled. "There's more than one place like that."

Ruarc raised an eyebrow. "I am certain the Keeper would prefer to keep the Scion away from Benata City, aren't you?"

Macari scowled.

Tarian took that as a sign Macari agreed with his assessment.

"So, to keep her safe from the abereil and First Mother, and to keep her from reacting to my least mood change, she needs to be sequestered at your place or at Benata City?" Tarian kept her tone light. Her stomach churned. The walls revolved slowly. She rubbed her temples, willing everything to just stop and leave her alone. The walls listened. Her stomach didn't. "There's no other safe place? You're sure?"

Ruarc met her gaze with a steady one of his own, but didn't answer. She looked to Macari. The girl's face looked impassive. Emotionless.

"Well, you both certainly learned well enough. Neat trick. Would come in handy at poker tables."

Tarian leaned back against the wall and closed her eyes. She fished for Ember's signature. It was blurred, distant, and spongy. She tried for Letta and found a similar spongy feel to the woman's signature.

«Keeper?»

Tarian glanced up at him, shocked at the concern in Ruarc's voice. He never let emotion show.

"Are you all right?"

"No. Everything is very much not all right." She stared at him. His suggestion made sense. Logically, it was a good plan. Ruarc was already sworn to protect Ember with his life. She had no doubt he would fulfill the promise. But something made her stomach churn and her heart ache as though she'd lost her best friend. Something didn't sit right. Realization dawned. "If she goes with you, she'll grow up too fast."

"In your eyes, perhaps."

"It won't seem fast to her, Tari," Macari whispered. "But I'd try it here, first. She has a lot of people, *strong* people, who care about her. The House of Xannon has a lot of safeguards too. My mother will find this a difficult place to breach. Impossible, I would say."

Tarian eyed Macari. "It wasn't for you. You waltzed right onto the beach."

Macari flushed. "The beach, yes. Your protections didn't extend to the beach. The house, no. Although..." Macari paused, looking thoughtful.

"Those bubbles had no trouble showing up on the beach," Calliope said softly. "Would the walls really stop them?"

Tarian hit the wall with her fist. "Damn her. Why can't First Mother just leave us alone?"

A gong sounded, announcing the arrival of someone through the travel portal alcoves. Tarian knew who it was even before he materialized. Her connection to him remained a constant, warm blanket.

"Tari!" Daric raced through the portal and to her side before she could say, "I'm fine."

"Where the hell have you been? Where's Ember?" He knelt by her side. "She screamed and disappeared, right out of my mother's den and you know how secured that place is. She didn't portal— she just vanished. Ma and I searched. We found traces of both of you at the park. But the traces ran cold. Like you vanished into thin air. The Caraigg couldn't find you. Damn, Tari." Daric ran a hand through his hair, relief and frustration warring for attention on his face.

"Head. Head. Don't shout." Tarian grimaced at the flash of pain the added volume in his voice caused. "I'm here now. Ember traveled."

"Traveled? She can't..." Daric sat back on his heels. "Where?"

"To me. At the park. She thought I was in danger. She came to...well, to rescue me I suppose."

Daric grimaced. "What happened? Is she okay? Where is she now?"

"Letta." Tarian leaned into him and closed her eyes. She just wanted a minute to sleep. And a sandwich. A really big sandwich. Her stomach growled at the mere suggestion.

"Letta?" Daric smoothed her hair as he spoke. "She did this to you?"

"No." Her voice muffled as she spoke into his shirt. "Short version. Bubble in the park. Ember popped it, overloaded. First Mother showed up. Tried to take Ember. Letta took Ember into the ground, to get her away. First Mother took the prism. I chased her. Wanted to see..." Tarian yawned. "What she was up to. She's found the Stulos. What's left of them. Using it to create abereil. Thinks it'll save the world." Her eyes drooped, but she managed to get one more sentence out. "It won't."

Blissful silence reigned for several seconds, a welcome relief. She rested against Daric, contemplating the situation and dreaming of lunch. She was just about to suggest they go to the kitchen when a loud screeching alarm announced an arrival on the beach.

Tarian felt suddenly wide awake. The alarm spiked an adrenaline rush, but that wasn't the reason. Following just behind the alarm was the snap of her bond with Ember falling into place. It wrapped her in tiny toddler arms and squeezed. Her heart pounded with excitement so loud she couldn't hear the alarm anymore. Or anything else for that matter.

"Ember!" Tarian ran toward the front door, elated and overwhelmed with the feeling coursing through her bond. "She's home! She's home!"

Daric, Calliope, and Macari ran with her to the beach. They were like a circus act trying to get through the front door. Tarian raced down the path and reached Letta and Ember first with the others just steps behind. Ember seemed unharmed, happy, and encased in a layer of dirt.

"Ember!" Tarian beamed at her giggling daughter and held out her arms. "I missed you! Come here, girl!"

Ember threw her arms wide, reacting to Tarian's elation with a joy only children can create.

Letta handed Ember over to Tarian with a raised eyebrow at Tarian's ragged appearance. "About time. Didn't think you were ever gonna come home."

"Me either." Tarian gave Ember a long hug, her eyes closed against tears. It was the reunion they should have had before, when Ruarc first brought Ember home. All the fear, worry, insecurity, anger, pain...all of it melted in the arms of her two-year-old daughter. "Where were you? You were moving so fast I couldn't lock on."

"The Earth stream. I took her to the cave, you know the one where I first met the Caraigg? Anyway, I go there sometimes to work on the prisms. Lots of stone down there, so Ember had no trouble using it for the excess. She cleared it pretty quick, like she knew how. The Caraigg helped of course, but still."

The implications caused a surge of pride through Tarian. Her daughter picked things up so fast.

"Anyway, we tried hanging out there for a bit, but a bubble popped in so we left. I swear that girl is a magnet or something. Every time I paused somewhere, I saw a flicker. We ended up staying in the stream, constantly moving, to make sure they didn't catch up. The Caraigg stayed alongside us like a guard, but they couldn't hold on to her so I did. You know, she's not as light as she looks."

Tarian hugged and rocked Ember, hoping it would hide her

unease at the information. "Every time you stopped?" She glanced around the beach. No flickers. Yet.

"Mama! Too tight!" Ember pushed against Tarian's chest in protest.

Tarian laughed and loosened her grip, which allowed the others to welcome Ember home as well. Ember traveled from Tarian's arms to Daric's, who gave her a quick look of concern before he administered kisses all over the child's face. She giggled with delight. Daric handed her to Calliope, then turned to Tarian and leaned in close to whisper in her ear. "Trouble?"

"Maybe," Tarian whispered in return. If Letta was right, it was only a matter of time. Minutes, maybe. First the beach, then the ocean, and PJs, then so far under the surface of the earth Tarian didn't want to contemplate it, and now back here on the beach. If another abereil appeared here, she'd believe Ember really was attracting the things. A thought struck her, the truth of it burrowing in deep like a sand flea. "Power calls to power."

She looked into Daric's eyes. "She's already so strong. What if…"

They both looked at Ember. Calliope sat with the girl on the sand, helping her build a castle or a moat or something. Ember seemed unaware of the shifting mood, thank the stars. Then Tarian realized why. Macari knelt on one side of Ember, and Calliope on the other. Both their signatures wafted on the afternoon breeze to mingle with the sea salt and ocean spray. They both used their talents to suppress anything Tarian was sending out.

Tarian noticed Sentinels clustering around the beach and another welcome party of Sentinels descending the path with Alex leading the way. He looked exasperated and frazzled, with his thick black hair standing up in all directions like he'd raked his fingers through it a thousand times.

"Tari!" Alex's voice thundered. He pounded down the pathway. "Freaking hell, Tari. You okay? Ember okay? What happened? What the f…" He stopped mid-word and flashed a glance at Ember. She thought he might have even bit his tongue trying to stop that particular word from escaping.

"We're fine, Alex." She patted him on the arm. "She's okay. Letta kept her safe."

"You can't just go disappearing like that. *Tú probaría la paciencia de un santo. Me haces loco, mujer.*"

Alex rarely launched into Spanish. It showed just how upset he'd been. Tarian didn't know exactly what he said, but she caught the word "loco" and could figure out the basic sentiment. Since she'd become Keeper she seemed to make a habit of driving him crazy.

She offered him an abashed look and squeezed his arm for an apology.

"Alex!" Ember thrust her arms and body out toward him, ready for another round of hugs.

Alex pushed past Tarian, gave her a you're-going-to-be-the-death-of-me glare, then took Ember from Calliope and spun her around. "Hey baby girl! How are you? Are you feeling okay? Do I need to fight someone for you?"

Ember laughed as he continued to spin. Watching the two of them lightened her mood a thousand times. The joy one little person could bring with just a laugh…it was contagious. She noticed silly grins on everyone's face.

Ruarc leaned against the doorway of the house, watching the scene. His face was an impassive mask of calm, but she knew he studied and calculated and catalogued. Every move, every word, would figure into some plan—she was sure of it.

Except.

She saw how he looked at Ember. He had eyes only for his daughter, and those eyes were filled with love and pride. When Ruarc noticed her watching, Tarian gestured for him to join them. He took his time, making sure to wave at Ember and offer her a quick kiss as he passed by.

"You're still here," Tarian said when he finally joined them.

"We haven't finished our discussion. Per our Agreement, I'm required to stay."

"Right." Tarian glanced at Daric. He shrugged as if to say, "Hey, you're the one with the problem."

The silence stretched out between them, punctuated by the ocean tide's soothing rhythm as it washed the beach.

She thought of all the crap he'd put her through. Their stupid deal with the stupid loophole she'd been too blind to see. The way her heart broke when she thought of Ember growing up with Ruarc. Learning daemon ways. Mayfanata ways. She thought of the ulterior motives he might have for such a move.

Then she looked past the pain and thought of the expression on his face when he'd arrived. The pride in his eyes as he looked at Ember. The lift to his mouth every time he spoke of her. It was subtle, but she couldn't deny the fact that the daemon loved her daughter.

He stood there waiting for her assessment, not moving. Barely blinking. He waited with the patience of stone. It'd been three days, and he remained right where she'd left him. He'd agreed to remain until he explained himself, but she had to admit it'd gone further than she'd intended.

She bit her lip. Then made up her mind. "Tell me, straight up. Why did you want to make that deal?"

Ruarc lifted his chin, but it wasn't in defiance. It was almost a nod of approval. "I wanted to know the child I helped create." And there it was. Simple. Direct. Finally. A real honest answer. And one she could live with. Like any parent, he wanted to know his child. Their circumstances might have been strange and their family an odd mix of people and power, but when she thought about it, the motive was very simple. Selfish, maybe. But no more than she'd been. Was it really selfish to want to know your own child, no matter what the circumstances of her birth? She didn't have an answer to that. But she'd heard enough from Ruarc. "Okay, then."

Ruarc looked as if he couldn't believe what he heard. "Okay?"

Tarian nodded. "Yeah. Okay. I'm satisfied."

A breeze brushed past as the Agreement lifted, complete.

They all played with Ember on the beach for another few minutes, but they weren't happy minutes. They were filled with tension and unvoiced worries. Tarian couldn't keep her mind off the memory of those abereil and the thought that Ember might attract them. She jumped at every flash of light. Saw flickers in every shadow.

She noticed a storm gathering on the horizon. Just a few dark clouds in the distance at first. But it quickly built up, as storms often did in the Pacific. Rain didn't usually bother her. Water was her element after all. But still, it had been a long few days. She was tired. Ember had to be tired too, although the way she giggled, it sure didn't show.

But surely as a mother, she should order her child in out of the rain. That's what good mothers did. She'd read that somewhere.

Ruarc rose from where he'd been helping build a sand castle to join Tarian.

"I know we should go in. I just like to watch the storms come in. It's relaxing." She glanced at Ruarc. "Well, maybe not to an Air daemon."

Ruarc frowned at the storm. It loomed much larger now. The clouds were an odd brownish green. "This is no thunderstorm." He turned, his face tight with tension. "Get the child inside. Now."

Tarian was about to protest his rough treatment when Macari pointed, a strangled noise coming out of her mouth before she cleared her throat and shouted. "Ercklings!"

Ruarc gave Tarian a shove. ""Now, Keeper."

Adrenaline shot through Tarian like a drug. Fatigue vanished. Senses heightened. Fear chased it, fed it, encouraged her to her feet. She swept Ember up into a tight hug, prepared to run. Daric pointed toward the house. "Go."

She hesitated only for a second. The ocean might be better. She half-turned toward it. The dolphins would...

"Tari! They swim!" Macari grabbed her arm. "Get to the safe room!"

Calliope ran past them, shouting for the guards.

Alex called out to the ones already positioned around the beach, giving directions and orders for formations.

The sky darkened. An alarm sounded, screeching an announcement of something arriving through the barrier to the island. Tarian froze, her gaze fixated on the incoming storm that wasn't a storm at all. This storm had insect-like bodies and large wings.

Her heart pounded so loud everything else faded into the background. Her breath caught. Her lungs wouldn't work. Her brain wouldn't think. Ercklings hunted and killed. They never deviated. They never stopped. They poisoned anyone in their way until they reached their objective. They'd chased her into the ocean. They killed with one touch. She had no idea how to stop them, and they had never been able to test the safe room against them.

Ember began to cry. Softly at first. Like a kitten.

Ruarc held out a hand, shooting a stream of white toward a spot on the horizon. It struck something that flared bright white. There was a loud popping sound. He turned to Tarian. "Go, woman. Go! Save the child!"

Tarian clutched Ember tightly and ran up the path. She'd gone halfway to the house, sheer terror making her feet light and quick, when she heard her sister scream. The sound cut through her heart. She turned back.

An erckling beat at her sister's body where it lay sprawled on the beach, half-covered in sand. It had struck true. The thing had stung Calliope. She couldn't remember if these were the smaller scouts or the larger hunters or the largest, meant for death. She'd seen them before, once. The scouts had been looking for her at the time, to mark her for the hunters. The hunters in turn would take her to First Mother, who'd wanted nothing more than to kill Ember before she was born.

And now? In one vicious thrust, the thing had killed her sister. But her sister was not who they sought. They continued to attack. Wave after wave of them filled the sky with black wings and brownish green bodies covered in small claw-like limbs. They resembled cruel wasps, with large stingers that carried venom so potent it would wipe out their target with one single hit.

These things didn't stop until they found their target. Between one painful heartbeat and the next, Tarian knew who they sought. She knew why First Mother would send them. What she was so desperate to have.

Ember.

They wanted Ember. Not to kill. Not this time. They were here to mark her daughter for something, someone, else.

A group of three zeroed in on Tarian and Ember where they stood near the door to the house. She could run inside, but they'd catch up before she got to the panic room. It was too far away. Too many halls. They were too fast.

Letta and a Caraigg appeared beside Tarian. "We should go under. They can't burrow. Can they? What they fuck *are* these things?" Letta grabbed Tarian's arm.

Flicker. Flicker.

Tarian swore. Between her and the house, another flicker. Two more on the beach. All of them far too close to Ember. Ember, who was now wailing with a sound only a toddler could make.

"Abereil!" Tarian turned from the one behind them to the ercklings headed straight for them. Nowhere to go. Rock and a hard place.

—19—

Tarian huddled on the sand next to Letta, shielding Ember from the swarm of ercklings with her body. "Take us down."

Letta nodded, but instead of sinking into the ground, Letta released Tarian's arm and doubled over, as if punched in the gut.

"What's wrong?" Tarian shook Letta's shoulder. "Letta?"

Three shadows erupted from the woman's stomach. They popped out one after the other, dark, deadly, and pissed off. They made other worldly screaming howls as they attacked three incoming ercklings, leaving a black trail of vapor in their wake.

The three ercklings fell one by one, like they'd been swatted by a giant newspaper. Or sprayed with a big can of Raid. But there were more behind them. Hundreds more. Thousands.

Ruarc shot down one after the other, using some sort of Air bullets. Macari protected another part of the beach. She danced, her movements fluid and mesmerizing. Deadly bolts of red and orange fire raced from her body toward the nearest ercklings. They dropped, black and smoldering, to the ground. The scent of burnt bugs and charcoal swept past Tarian, along with the heat of the blast. It was like standing in front of an active volcano.

"Bubble!" Letta panted. "Gotta move. Come on."

Tarian tightened her grip on Ember and reached for Letta. Just as their fingers touched, an erckling struck Letta's arm, and she crumpled to the ground, lifeless. The erckling fell to the ground next to her, the stinger gone. It twitched a few times, then stopped.

Tarian stared at her friend, horror building a hard knot in her chest. She couldn't be dead. These had to be scouts. Not hunters. "Letta!" Tarian lunged toward the fallen woman but found her way blocked by an invisible force. "Letta!"

Panic and fear made her feel sluggish and slow. Ember shook in her arms. A wail started low in her daughter's throat and grew until it became a counterpoint to the erckling hum.

Tarian patted her on the back, harder than she should have, desperate to soothe the girl. She had to get her daughter out of here. But the way to the house and the safe room was blocked by a shield Tarian hadn't put in place. She couldn't see how it was created, so she could dismantle it. Didn't have the time. More ercklings advanced up the beach, and they didn't have enough people, or enough power, to stop them all. Even if they did, more would follow. Macari had explained it before…ercklings didn't stop. Not until they reached their objective. They'd find Ember. Sooner or later, they'd find her.

Panic swelled to a crescendo.

Ember's cry punctuated like a fire alarm.

The Water medallion surged within Tarian's chest, and power pounded outward. She hadn't called it. Hadn't reached for it. Something outside her body did that. Something else used the Water Artifact.

Tarian shifted Ember from one arm to the other, trying to put some distance between her daughter and the object embedded in her chest. She couldn't stop the swirl of emotions or the fear that constricted her throat and lungs. Letta lay still on the ground. Dead or knocked out, she wasn't sure which. They wanted Ember. And they couldn't have her. She refused to let them have her daughter.

Ember screamed. The tug on Tarian's artifact turned stronger and more violent.

Tarian hugged Ember tight and tried her best to reassure the girl. "It's okay, Ember, it's okay." Stupid thing to say. Things were obviously not okay. She didn't believe her own words, and Ember ignored them. Her daughter's terrified cries filled Tarian's ears.

One of the abereil quivered and bobbed, shifting toward Tarian and Ember a foot, then two.

Two ercklings buzzed by the shield and circled behind it. Tarian spun to keep them in front of her. She grappled for control of the artifact, but it slipped through her grasp.

One erckling honed in on Ember and shot straight toward her. It struck the shield and fractured on contact into tiny specs of black dust.

Tarian gaped at the spot where the erckling had been a fraction of a second before. No evidence remained. The ash dissipated on the wind and into the sand as if it'd never existed. She'd never seen a shield do that. Shields blocked. They weren't electric fences. They didn't burn. They weren't formed with Fire at all. Not usually.

The abereil moved a fraction closer. The second abereil shifted toward them, falling in line behind the first. Like flies to Ember's Fire.

Tarian clutched her daughter. "Power calls to power." She looked down at the upset toddler in her arms and felt utterly helpless.

Another erckling zoomed into the shield and exploded into

a cloud of dust. Tarian gaped at it, then at her daughter. Ember's face as red and angry and scrunched. Her daughter wasn't afraid. She had the look of a toddler in the midst of an epic temper tantrum.

Tarian shifted again to get a better look at the beach. Two Caraigg huddled a foot away, just on the other side of the shield. They shifted around it, but didn't advance. She had a feeling if she could take one by the hand, she'd hear a million very upset voices. They couldn't reach the Keeper they were sworn to protect.

Another erckling struck the shield, then another. Both evaporated into ash. Tarian froze in place, not sure if it worked the same from the inside and not wanting to find out the hard way.

The abereil inched closer and closer.

"Daric! Alex!" Tarian shouted but couldn't tell how loud her voice really was. So much noise competed. So many ercklings in one place sounded like a hundred motorcycles on the freeway.

"Tari! What…" Daric ran toward her but stopped when he saw another erckling hit the shield and dissolve. He blinked and looked at her. "You?"

Tarian shook her head and shifted Ember to free up a hand. She pointed. "Bubbles!"

Daric looked where she pointed. His lips tightened, then he turned and shouted. "Alex! Guards!"

He ducked an erckling, then another, as he picked his way past Letta and the Caraigg. Tarian waved at him to stop when he got too close.

"I can't move. I can't break the shield."

Another wave of ercklings approached.

Ruarc's hands flashed so fast they became a blur. Macari's dance became a rotating beacon of light that scorched hornet after hornet.

Daric and Alex placed themselves between the advance of ercklings and Tarian and Ember. Several ercklings zoomed toward their group. Alex shoved Daric aside. "Look out!" Daric fell to his knees, and the ercklings aimed at him zipped harmlessly over his head, slammed into the shield, and fizzled.

Alex turned toward Tarian and opened his mouth to say something, but before he could get the words out, another erckling turned a sharp, pointy needle of a stinger forward and struck him in the back. Alex dropped to his knees, a stunned expression on his face. Then he collapsed.

"Alex!" Tarian screamed.

Daric thrust both hands out in front of him to form a shield of his own. It knocked an erckling aside and gave him enough space to get to his feet. He stumbled toward Alex. Knelt beside the fallen warrior and put two fingers on the side of his neck, checking for a pulse. Tarian smelled the wave of cinnamon as Daric activated his healing talent.

He glanced up at Tarian. "Knocked out."

Movement caught Tarian's eye. She pointed at the rapidly expanding abereil. "Behind you!"

Daric turned toward it.

An erckling circled from behind a rock and struck Daric in the neck. Daric collapsed awkwardly to the side. The abereil hovered a few feet away from him.

"Daric!" Tarian wanted to run him. She wanted to travel to safety. She wanted a lot of things. But her body was locked in position, her magic siphoned by a toddler with no real communication skills and a lot of fury who now called the shots with the Water Artifact. Power raged out of Tarian's body. She focused on it, traced the path of the stream from her own body to Ember's.

This close to her daughter, with her tracking ability active and the artifact bonding them like magnets, Tarian felt the churning of energy within the tiny body she held in her arms. The swirl of it, the way it mingled and merged and magnified. The surge as what once was four distinctive elements became one. It was a joining, of sorts, but more than that. It was...synergy. For a few seconds, the rest of the world dropped away as Tarian was swept up in the miracle her daughter performed instinctively.

She squeezed Ember tighter. She couldn't think. Couldn't do anything but wait to see what her daughter created. She'd been locked into a dance with her daughter that neither could diminish.

Ember continued to cry, her tiny face screwed up in purple anguish.

Tarian looked for help, but others were worse off than she was. Most of the Sentinels had collapsed. They lay in heaps across the beach, some lying on top of each other. Like discarded toys. Even more ercklings littered the sand, their wings wet and glinting like evil gems.

Tarian gasped when an erckling struck Macari. Macari stopped whirling, and stumbled through the air like a drunk bee. Ruarc moved closer to her, grasped her arm, and steadied the daemon girl while he continued to shoot bolts at ercklings.

She was running out of options. They had nowhere to run. She couldn't burrow into the ground like Letta or Alex. Ercklings would follow them into the ocean. She couldn't get through the shield anyway, not while Ember actively used all available energy to power it. Panic made it impossible to catch her breath. She panted and searched her mind for an answer. Any answer.

"Baby. You have to stop this. You have to drop the shield. I can't get us out of here. I can't save us. The bubbles...the ercklings...we have to get out of here. Ember...please..."

Ember looked up at Tarian's face, and the angry tantrum melted from her eyes to be replaced with the saddest, most forlorn expression Tarian had ever seen. Something flickered through her expression. Understanding? Concern? Something more? Tarian couldn't be sure. Ember wasn't old enough to understand. She didn't know the danger they were in. She only knew Tarian's mood. And yet...there was something more in her daughter's eyes than just a little girl upset about her mother.

Ember's eyes darkened, turning from deep sapphire to almost black. She twisted her body until she could see the beach and shouted at it. "No!"

Something reached inside Tarian and grabbed every element she controlled into a giant fist. The fist punched out through her ribcage. Her body convulsed with the force of it, and she staggered back a step, then two.

Dolphins screamed. She couldn't be sure if they were coming from the medallion or from the ocean itself or both. The energy Ember gathered burrowed into her daughter, gathered itself, and then punched outward from Ember like a sonic boom. It traveled across the beach, dropping everything and everyone in its path. Ercklings fell, swatted by the invisible hand. Ruarc and Macari dropped to the ground in a heap.

In the distance, the next wave of ercklings fell to the ocean, leaving blue sky and a bright sun to deny anything had happened.

—20—

Tarian panted and gaped at the scene in front of them. She and Ember stood alone, surrounded by motionless ercklings, Sentinels, Caraigg, and all of her friends. Her sister. Everyone. Energy buzzed and snapped, but the only thing that moved were the two abereil. They'd expanded more than triple their size, fed by the power Ember had rocketed into the atmosphere. They bulged outward, pregnant with potential. After so much action and so much stress, the stillness was even more unnerving. It was like what she imagined life would be like after a war ended. Eerily quiet.

Ember sobbed, a heart wrenching sound that made Tarian's chest hurt. The grief was profound and absolutely inconsolable.

"Shhh, Ember. It's okay. It's okay." Tarian rocked her daughter, thoughts racing, plans formed and discarded for more discarded plans.

Ember continued to absorb power, creating a raging torrent of elements. The stream of energy pulled the abereil along with it. They turned dark and angry and forbidding. She knew now what that meant. They were ready to pop.

Tarian backed up a step, then stopped. The shield still held.

She couldn't risk touching it. She pictured them both dissolving into a pile of ash and shuddered.

"Ember." Tarian searched her mind desperate for any idea that might break the shield. If she could get past it, then maybe they could travel. "Baby, let the shield go. Let it drop, sparky. We don't need it anymore. See? They're gone. The bad things are gone. Let it go."

She kept her eye on the abereil. They'd explode any moment. At the size they'd grown to, she was certain part of the house would go with them. Everyone on the beach would too. She remembered the result in Fort Worth and shivered.

Scuffling sounds behind her made Tarian spin around. Kia ran down the path toward them, heedless of the erckling bodies that decorated the rocks and sand and every available surface.

"Now, Ember girl, you don't need to be doin' that." Kia looked determined and serious but confident as she raced toward them. "Sorry, Ms. Tari, I couldn't get past the swarm. Had to wait 'til it died to get through. Like I said, I work best up close."

"Wait!" Tarian waved a hand, frantic. "Stop! The shield..."

Kia walked through as though it didn't exist, her attention focused on Ember. Tarian stared at her as she took Ember's hands into her own as if it were an ordinary day and she hadn't walked through a wall of death and there weren't two nuclear bombs about to blow nearby. "Can I get me some sweetness?"

Ember grasped Kia's hands.

It was as if a cleaver severed the power flow with one heavy blow. The pressure and pull on her power stopped, and Tarian stumbled backward. Kia took Ember into her arms just before Tarian fell, landing hard on her butt on the sand.

The abereil stopped advancing. They hovered a few feet away, large and pregnant but docile.

"Kia!" Ember hiccuped.

Kia hugged Ember, rocking the girl gently, speaking with a light tone that denied the destruction surrounding them. "There's my girl! What're you up to, sparky? Seems like mischief." Kia kissed Ember's forehead before surveying the devastation. She fixated on the abereil. "Best get her away from those. She be plump full of energy. Not sure I can stop all that. Least not yet."

«Yet?»

Kia gave her a look full of enigmatic meaning.

"Damn, Kia. You just...damn." Tarian turned to the bubbles. The sea crashed against the shore nearby, beating a steady rhythm that gave her an idea. Ocean waves could dissipate a lot of energy, with little side effect. And she'd seen First Mother's way of handling the abereil.

She glanced at Kia and Ember. "You got her? I want to give these bubbles a nudge."

Kia nodded.

Tarian turned back to the abereil and raised her hands, letting a small steady stream of Water and Air wind its way across the sand. It brushed past motionless ercklings and Sentinels. When it reached the bubble, she crafted a net and gently nudged the abereil as she'd seen First Mother do. Just enough to shift the bubble away, toward open water. She focused on one, getting it as far out as she could, before changing the direction of the stream. She added a little more Water for weight, then released. The net dropped onto the abereil. It bulged to the sides. Tarian held her breath, hoping it wouldn't break.

The abereil squished, then slowly dropped. It sank into the ocean, buffeted by waves, but carried down by the weighted net until the ocean consumed it. Seconds passed like hours. She glanced at Kia and Ember. Kia wore an unconcerned expression.

Ember had calmed enough to suck her thumb, with only mild hiccups and damp cheeks to suggest the storm that had just passed. Her face looked red, rather than purple.

A muffled concussion shook the ground. Tarian snapped back to the ocean in time to see a geyser rush up up up up. The fountain spread out like an umbrella, then crashed back to the sea with a roar. Tarian turned away, shielding herself from the wave that rushed the shore. Backwash flooded the beach, rushing over sand, ercklings, Sentinels, daemon. She put another layer of shielding between Kia and Ember, noticing how intently Ember watched. Her thumb hung half-forgotten out of her open mouth.

At the far end of the beach, Ruarc struggled to sit up, followed by Macari, who coughed as though drowning. Sentinels nearby stirred.

Tarian breathed a sigh of relief. Not dead. Stunned.

She turned her attention to the second bubble, giving it the same treatment as the first. The second backwash reached the entrance to the house itself. It receded, leaving everything soaked and bedraggled but alive.

An erckling nearby twitched. Several more followed.

Soon they'd all be awake and ready to hunt.

—21—

Tarian muttered, "How can I protect her if there's nowhere to hide?"

"She be her own protection soon, Ms. Tarian. She just needs time to grow into it. That's all." Kia continued to rock Ember, who hiccuped before turning her attention once again to the well-soaked thumb. Kia nodded meaningfully toward Ruarc.

Tarian watched the daemon get to his feet, then extend a hand to Macari. He'd shielded the daemon girl from brunt of the attack at the end with his own body. Mayfanata helping a Benata. She never thought she'd see it. Nor the flash of gratitude from Benata to Mayfanata. Whatever reason for the original hatred, she suspected that reason no longer mattered.

"He's not a bad man," Tarian whispered to herself.

"His ways be different, but he be honorable. Where you and this sweetness be concerned anyways." Kia half-smiled but didn't look at Tarian.

Tarian had no idea what the girl meant. Kia had always been an enigma. Excellent with Ember. She possessed a talent nobody had ever seen before. She could quell any use of power with a single touch. She acted much like insulation did for electrical current. Tarian still didn't understand the depths of it. Kia had blocked Ember and Tarian and the bubbles, all without any apparent effort, though she hadn't used any active power of her own. Whatever she did, her power remained completely passive and incredibly strong. She was a fascinating match for someone like Ember, who absorbed energy around her and magnified it. No matter how strong Ember became, Kia would probably be able to block her from sending that magnified energy back out.

At least, Tarian hoped she would. A plan began to form in her mind, one that would cut her heart in a million pieces but hopefully would allow Ember to grow up. Too fast. But Ember's safety was worth the cost of a lost childhood.

An erckling wiggled nearby, clearly awake and about ready to rise. Tarian sucked in a breath.

"Will she be safe?" She faced Kia. "Will you go with Ember? Will you stay with her? She'll need a friend. Someone to remind her of…well, she'll need you."

Kia nodded, her eyes round and solemn. "She be like my own sister. I'd be happy to go."

"You'll age. You know that, right?"

Kia smiled. "Age be just a number, Ms. Tarian. I ain't got no worry 'bout that."

Daric rose to unsteady feet, looking dazed. Calliope clutched her head with a low moan. Alex leaned against a nearby rock. He made a guttural noise. "They're waking up."

Ruarc stepped over twitching ercklings to join them.

"Keeper, the safe room?" Ruarc's jaw tightened, his face darkening with an emotion Tarian had never seen on his face before. Anger. Raw, hot, anger. But it wasn't directed at her. He flexed a hand, and the nearest erckling turned black and dried into dust.

Something in that expression made the decision for her. Tarian put a hand on his arm to stop whatever he'd been planning. "You can keep her safe. From abereil. First Mother. My...you can shield her from me? Keep her from traveling?"

Ruarc's eyes turned solemn. "Yes." It held promise, a vow unspoken, but no less potent.

Alex cleared his throat. "*Chica*, Frankie's bringing backup, but you and Ember gotta run. There's too many." Alex cupped his hands, and sand rose to swallow two ercklings. The beach lay thick with them, their dark brown bodies obliterating the black sand. They struggled to wake, making the island look like a quivering mass of worms. So many would take all of them hours, or days, to destroy.

Tarian knew what she should do. What she *had* to do. It broke her heart into pieces that might not ever heal. She couldn't quite say the words. They clung to her lips like miniature vises, sealing them shut.

"She'll always be your daughter," Daric said in a low voice, for her ears only. "No matter what."

Tarian nodded, pressing her lips together so they wouldn't quiver. She glanced out to sea, to keep tears from falling. When she spoke, the words were a whisper that wrenched away pieces of her heart. "Take Ember and Kia. Keep them safe, Ruarc. Just promise you'll do that, and return them when we're done with this."

"You sure?" Macari shot a bolt of Air at a nearby stunned erckling, and it exploded up in a fountain of sand and body parts. "There's no way to keep ercklings out of Benata City. Why would Mayfanata be any different?"

Ruarc flashed her a cold smile. "Because ercklings are a Benata construct. The Agreements prohibit such an encroachment. She'd be a fool to send them on an attack. She'd lose her standing. Her power. Everything."

Macari frowned. "Benata construct?" She glanced down, thoughtful. Or embarrassed, Tarian wasn't sure which.

"If his guards can't keep them at bay, we'll come up with another plan. It's this, or Letta and the Earth Stream." Tarian glanced at Letta, who leaned heavily against a boulder near the house looking pale and worn. "I don't think Letta could keep that kind of movement up long enough. Not right now. It's a good backup, but...Ember's better off with the Mayfanata right now." It hurt somewhere deep in her gut to admit that out loud, but once said, she straightened her shoulders and faced the group. Her team. Her friends. Her family. All would give their lives for her, and for Ember.

Tarian buried her face in Ember's neck. "I love you, sparky. You be a good girl for me, okay? Go with Ruarc. Learn lots. I'll see you..." She swallowed, unable to finish the sentence.

"Do you wish a new Agreement?" Ruarc's voice was soft as if he were afraid of disturbing her decision.

Tarian shook her head.

Ember began to cry softly, her sadness echoing Tarian's. Calliope joined them and put a comforting arm around Tarian. Her talent leached into Tarian's heart and softened the hurt. Ember sniffled.

"Wuv you, Mama." Ember's lower lip quivered.

Tarian pulled her in tight against her chest and kissed the soft hair. "I love you more than anything in the world. More than anything in the universe. Now, don't be sad. You'll be with Ruarc and Kia, and you'll be having so much fun you won't miss me at all. Okay?" She kissed Ember on the cheek, relishing the soft sweet warmth of her. "No matter what you feel from me, you stay with Kia and Ruarc. Okay? No running after Mama. No matter what."

Ember stuck her chin out again but didn't answer either to agree or disagree. She's learned too much from Ruarc already.

Or maybe she learned it from me.

She gave Ember another kiss, then handed her to Kia. "I owe you my life. More."

"She'll be okay, Ms. Tarian. She got a bright future ahead." Kia snuggled the little girl close to her. "I'll look after her like she was my own." Daric leaned in to give Ember a kiss. Tarian kissed her opposite cheek.

Alex gave her a pat on the back. "You get going, chiclet."

Ruarc created a portal, then turned to Kia. "Hold Ember tightly. I can guide you through the travel, but you will feel some resistance, and if our bond is broken, it will be difficult to locate you."

Kia put both arms tightly around Ember. Ruarc took them both into his arms and stepped through the portal, which snapped immediately closed.

Tarian stared at the now child-free spot.

Her heart weighed a thousand pounds. It sank through her body and buried itself in the sand beneath her feet.

It was as if a piece of her flesh had just been torn out of her body. Now that she knew the consequences, watching her daughter leave in the arms of Ruarc, not knowing when she'd see her again, hurt more than anything she'd ever experienced or imagined. Daric slid his arm around her shoulders. She pressed her body into his.

A soft hand on her arm brought warmth and eased the pain. A little. Tarian leaned her head toward her sister until their foreheads touched.

"They'll be okay, Tari," Calliope whispered.

«Yes.»

"What worries you?"

"Was that the last time I'll see her? If I do see her again, will she know me?"

Calliope's eyes glistened with unshed tears. For an answer, she pulled Tarian into a hug. Warmth and empathy spread through the touch. A burden shared, halved by their sister bond.

Their moment of Zen broke when Alex shouted, "Incoming."

A nearby group of ercklings rose like inebriated mosquitoes, unsteady but determined. Across the beach, more began to wake.

Ercklings all around began to rise. Macari spun, gathering energy with her movements. The level of power in the atmosphere rose exponentially as she continued faster, faster, faster. Her movement created a buzzing sound like high line wires the revved the nerves and ratcheted the tension up tenfold. As it reached an intolerable pitch, one by one, ercklings disappeared. Like popcorn in reverse. Like they'd never existed.

The sky brightened. The beach cleared.

They stared around them, confused.

"Sneak attack?" Alex kicked at the sand. "They hiding?"

"No," Macari answered.

"Where'd they go?" Calliope asked. She still held the side of her head, and the words came out more like a whisper.

"Hunting." Macari pressed her lips together. "We were not their target. They never deviate from the designated target. I hope Ruarc is right about the Agreements."

Tarian shivered and silently agreed.

"What if he isn't?" Calliope asked.

Tarian took Daric's hand in her own and squeezed it hard. "We stop First Mother. Now."

"How?" Alex said.

Tarian turned to Letta. "How big are those prisms you have?"

Letta grinned.

—22—

Tarian followed Letta down a tunnel that decreased in size the further they went until she was almost bent double in the tight space. "Did I tell you I was recently buried by a collapsed building? Did I mention how horrific it was?"

Letta laughed. "You're still alive."

"You sure about that?" Tarian put her hands on both sides of the tunnel, mostly to keep herself from falling down. It was dark, cramped, and made her head spin. Too tight. Too small. Too rocky.

Daric patted her ass as if to comfort her. Or distract her, she wasn't sure which. The cave they'd arrived in had been large enough to host a Baptist church for Sunday dinner and filled with light from phosphorescent rocks or plants or protrusions of some kind. She'd liked that cave. It was easy to forget how far under the surface they were in that cave. But this tunnel reminded her every single inch exactly how much dirt lay directly above their heads. It gave new meaning to the phrase "buried alive."

"This is worse than that damn train. So much worse. This better be worth it." Tarian wiped sweat off her face. Then realized she'd created a mud trail since her hands were covered in filth from the walls of the tunnel.

She hadn't heard Macari speak in quite some time. "Macari? You okay?"

She thought she heard a low moan in response. Or it could have been the tunnel caving in. "Alex? She okay?"

Alex chuckled softly. "Yeah, she's good. She don't think she is, but she is."

"We're here, you big babies," Letta said. She moved away from the mouth of the tunnel to make room for Tarian to crawl out.

Light spilled into the tunnel and enticed her forward. She gratefully scrambled out of the dark hole of death. She glanced up, ready to get off her hands and knees, then froze. "Holy... mother..." Tarian said.

"What? Tari, move over." Daric gave her a gentle nudge on the behind.

She crawled to the right, then realized the space she was now in had plenty of headroom and got to her feet. Daric paused and stared at the same thing she stared at.

"Hey, shove over," Alex called out.

Daric shook himself, took Tarian's hand in his, and led her to the side, leaving enough room for the rest to crawl through the opening.

Macari and Alex emerged, then stopped short just outside the tunnel.

"What's wrong?" Calliope pushed Alex aside and scrambled to her feet. Then she, too, stopped moving and gaped at the sight that greeted them.

Alex whistled and muttered something in Spanish before crossing himself.

Two diamond pyramids, each over eight feet tall, with a base over eight feet square, dominated the center of the cave. They gathered the bluish green glow of the phosphorescent rocks in the walls and reveled in it, broke it up into a million shades of a billion colors, and then returned it magnified a hundred times. The result blinded them with brilliance and mesmerized them with colors. It was the most awe-inspiring thing Tarian had ever seen.

The more she stared at the prisms, the more she saw in their depths. She saw their faces reflected back at them. She saw angles and curves that refracted the light. She touched the cool smooth, slick surface, and shivers raced through her body. The prism—diamond—exuded raw, bottomless, fathomless potential.

Tarian noticed the others doing the same. They all wore the same dumbfounded look she knew was on her own face.

"Damn," Alex said. "Now that's a rock."

It was such an understatement that they all laughed.

Tarian glanced at Letta where she sat on a boulder off to the side. "I don't know what I expected. I never pictured this."

Letta shrugged, then rubbed the back of her neck and looked sheepish. "You said bigger."

"Yeah, but…damn." Tarian took her time walking all the way around both prisms, evaluating their potential, and imagining the possibilities.

"Can we leave now?" Macari asked. "It's hard to breathe." Every muscle in her neck and jaw tensed as she struggled to take a breath.

Alex put his arm around her shoulders and squeezed. "You need to relax. Do some of that voodoo emotional stuff on yourself."

"It doesn't…work that way." Macari panted, her breath becoming more shallow by the second.

Calliope slid an arm around the daemon's shoulders and began to hum softly.

Tarian gave Macari a sympathetic look. "We won't stay long. At least we know First Mother won't show up here."

"What're we gonna do with these things?" Alex asked. "They're freakin' huge. Too big to be much good."

"I don't think so. I think they're exactly right." Tarian faced Letta. "Why the pyramid shape? The one you brought for Ember was oval."

Mentioning her daughter's name reminded her that it'd been a full day since Ruarc had carried her away to Mayfanata City. She didn't have time to wonder how her daughter was doing or worry over how much older she must be. No time to feel guilty or sad. No time to feel anything. She cleared her throat and focused on Letta's answer.

"When that one broke, I wondered why, so I came here to ask the Caraigg. There are always some hanging out here," Letta said.

When she mentioned Caraigg, Tarian realized Letta was right. There were a dozen, at least, stationed in this cave alone. She hadn't even noticed them before, not that anyone would blame her with two larger-than-life diamonds stealing the show.

"Anyway, when I brought your girl here to chill out, she got bored. And she likes things that sparkle. One thing led to another, and here we are."

"One thing led to another?"

"Yeah." Letta looked around and picked up a palm-sized round diamond. "This one ain't the right shape. It don't hold much. Neither did the oval. And the other…hang on."

Letta popped up and jogged to the other side of the cave, rummaged in a pile of diamonds, and returned with a cylinder shape. "This one don't absorb at all. And the square ones, they don't do nothing other than look good." She tossed the cylinder onto a pile nearby. "Pyramid worked the best. Especially when Ember put her hands on it."

They all gathered around Letta, except for Macari. Macari clasped her hands tightly in front of her and stared at them as if they offered an escape from prison.

"A two-year-old made these things?" Alex asked.

Letta laughed. "No. I made them. She enhanced them."

"What happened when she put her hands on it?" Calliope asked.

"She made 'em bigger. Spread 'em out a bit and somehow made 'em harder at the same time. These big ones don't absorb until they're primed. They gotta be turned on."

"When did the abereil show up?" Tarian held her hand up to stop the flow of questions.

"After we made four of these and she got bored," Letta said. "She started crying for you and that's when the first bubble popped up."

"She really is attracting them, isn't she?" Calliope asked. "Not the one in Fort Worth. But two on the beach right after she got home can't be a coincidence."

"The one in PJs too," Daric said.

"And in the ocean." Tarian glanced around, but she didn't see any sign of elemental explosions. Just piles of sparkling diamonds. "What happened to the abereil that popped up in here?"

Letta pointed to the far corner of the cave, where a larger pile of cast-off diamond experiments lay discarded. "Those basically absorbed it before it got very big. But they filled up. Took all of 'em to catch just that one bubble, and I knew I couldn't make more fast enough if another popped up. Didn't wanna waste my big ones so we took off."

"Can they get into Mayfanata City?"

Macari shook her head. She kept her gaze firmly fixed on her hands. "If what Ruarc said is true, no. They have the same sort of shields that Benata City has. No hostile element passes through the barrier. Air judges intent. They might form along the border. But not inside."

Tarian strode over to the pile and picked up a baseball-sized prism. Her fingers tingled on contact, ever so slightly, as if her hand had been asleep. It glowed a soft, steady light blue. She looked at the others. All glowed with hints of various colors ranging from blue to red to green to white. They were beautiful and powerful and beyond amazing.

"I still don't get what you expect to do with these things," Alex said. "If that Source is as big as you say, they ain't big enough to absorb it. Not even if you use all four."

Tarian contemplated the pile of cast-off stones, an idea tickling her thoughts. She looked from a small pyramid-shaped version to the big ones in the center of the cave and back. "She used Air."

"What?" Daric said.

Tarian turned back to the group. "Ember used Air to make them bigger." She pictured the field of abereil, and the Source below. She imagined the four large prisms in place, and then suddenly the plan fell into place in her mind. It would work. It was a good plan. A solid one. More than she usually ran with. "We don't have to absorb it. We just have to contain it. Shield it. If we get the Air Artifact, we can do that. We can put the four pyramids at the corners of the Source. Then use Air and Water to make them grow until they join into one large prism. Then use Earth and Fire to harden and *voila!* Nobody will be able to get to the Source or use the energy. First Mother will be cut off."

Tarian nodded at the pyramid. "And we already have everything we need. Except for the Air Artifact."

Protests and arguments erupted behind her.

"How the hell we gonna shift these?" Alex gestured with both hands. "We ain't anywhere near that Source. Are we? We can't just drag them through a portal."

"First Mother has the Air Artifact," Calliope said. "You can't just walk up to her and take it away. There's no way she lets you anywhere near it."

"Yeah, and what makes you think First Mother will just sit around while we activate four prisms?" Letta added. "She ain't gonna let us cut the Source off."

"It's true, Tari," Daric said. "First Mother is bound to have plans in place. She knows you're coming."

"If we do something she least expects, we'll get a step ahead of her." Tarian ran a hand over the pyramid's slick surface, appreciating the work and the potential buried inside the thing. "We have to get a step ahead. The longer we wait, the more abereil will form. The more that form, the more they'll spread. By now who knows how many are popping up in cities around the world. How many people have been killed so far? How many more? We have to get moving. We have to."

Tarian paused to take a calming breath. Then two. "She doesn't know how these work. She doesn't know we have them. She won't expect us to be in that field placing things like this. She's busy with something else."

"What?" Alex asked.

"The thing she's always wanted. Ember." Tarian watched their reflections in the pyramid. She saw the looks exchanged between Alex and Daric. Calliope covered her mouth with a hand as if to stifle a scream. Macari stared at the ground. Letta leaned back to take it all in. From the body language, she'd guess they all thought she was right, and foolish at the same time. "We'll get these in place. We'll get the Air Artifact. And we'll trap the abereil."

"And Ember?" Daric asked softly.

"I'm trusting Ruarc. I have to." The thought chilled her in the recesses of her heart. She didn't have a choice. But that didn't make the decision any easier to live with. She had to believe that the daemon who'd tricked her could also be the daemon who'd save her daughter. She had to believe he would protect Ember with his own life. She had to believe that Mayfanata City was the impenetrable fortress he'd claimed it to be. She had to believe, because there was nothing else she could do. They were running out of time. The faster they moved, the faster they solved the problem, the safer everyone would be. Including Ember.

"Tari, you can't just take the artifact from someone who's bonded with it." Calliope stepped up to Tarian and touched her shoulder. "They have to die first. Don't they? That's how the Water Artifact works. Are you saying you want to kill First Mother?"

Silence descended as they all waited for her answer.

She wanted to say yes. She wanted to say they should do that first, before anything else. Their problems would be solved if only First Mother were no longer the cancer destroying the world.

But she remembered the people in Fort Worth. The ones with the camera phones. The cop who hated them simply because they could harness elemental energy. She remembered the people in Philadelphia, both the ones who attacked and the ones who helped. They were so desperately afraid, because it was all so new. So different.

Fear led to hate. First Mother hated humans, but more than that, she hated Tarian and the House of Xannon for what it represented. Humans with power.

Tarian thought of her life before the Water Artifact. Before her mother died. She'd spent it catching those who would harm others with power. But she'd never killed someone. Not until the laghairtine attacked her and her family. He'd killed her mother. He'd have killed them all. It was self-defense, pure and simple.

Could she say the same about First Mother? Would that justify killing her? The daemon wouldn't blink before wiping out all humans. Her idea of greater good included daemon. Benata daemon, specifically. No one else. She was a cold sociopath who seemed bent on destroying the Earth. But...to hunt her down and assassinate her just seemed wrong. It struck something deep inside, a core fundamental belief that Tarian couldn't shake. Didn't *want* to shake.

She despised First Mother for what she intended. She hated her for hunting her daughter. More than anything, she wanted to put an end to First Mother. But not this way. She'd lock her away for all eternity first.

Tarian shook her head. "No." She turned to face her friends. "That's not who we are. I want to stop her plan. Let's focus on that."

Macari lifted her head, her face determined. "She has not bonded with the artifact."

Excitement surged through Tarian at the statement. "How do you know?"

"The Air Artifact was split along with the planes of existence and remained that way for thousands of years. It was displayed in the Rotunda in a stasis field. None could have bonded with a broken artifact." Macari glanced at Tarian. "Once you provided the key and the artifact was restored, none would have attempted to bond without First Mother's permission. A thing she would not give."

"Are you sure she didn't bond with it herself?" Tarian said.

"She's my mother. She's not capable of bonding with anything. Or anyone." Pain flashed across Macari's face so fast Tarian might have missed it if she hadn't been watching so closely. "And you said yourself the artifact was separated from her for a time. That is not possible with a bonded object."

"She's right!" Calliope said. "Look at the rest of you. Have you ever been apart from your artifact once it bonded? Even for a second?"

Letta, Macari, and Tarian all looked at each other. All shook their heads.

"So it's up for grabs." Tarian tapped the Water Artifact. "For someone who doesn't already have one."

"I could try," Daric said.

"No," Calliope said. "It should be a female. Women are able to use more elemental energy than men. It's part of the biology that goes along with giving birth."

"So we need a woman who don't already have an artifact," Alex said.

They all stared at Calliope. She looked startled. "Me? I can't hold an artifact. I'm Xannon. I'm in line for Water."

Tarian shook her head. "Not any more. Ember's the Scion now."

"Oh." Calliope's eyes widened. "Oh."

"I'll help," Tarian assured her sister. "I'll distract her. You grab it and bond with it if you can. The rest of you can work on getting the prisms in place. Once we have Air, we'll meet you at the bubble field and activate the prisms. The Source will be contained before First Mother knows it's happening."

Everyone spoke at once, debating the plan, offering their opinions. A hand around her ankle got Tarian's attention. She knelt next to the Caraigg and took his hand in hers. "What's up?"

Keeper must hurry. Abereil appear.

Tarian's heart stopped when she heard the voices and saw the images they projected. Hundreds, maybe thousands, of abereil in city after city. Collapsed buildings. Panic.

Tarian stood, breaking the connection. She'd seen enough. "We need to move."

—23—

After another hour lost to planning, arguments, and negotiations involving who would go where, with what and whom, Tarian finally had enough of strategy by committee. They couldn't reach any kind of agreement.

"I guess this is why there's only one Keeper." Tarian tugged on her hair, frustrated. "So the Keeper can call the shots when her team doesn't agree."

They all quieted down and waited for her to continue, but she could tell none of them were happy about it. "Look, I know you all want to make sure I'm safe. That Ember's safe. I get it. I appreciate it. But nobody is safe right now. Nobody. I will not sit back while all of you are at risk. We need all four artifacts for my plan to work, and since none of you have come up with anything better…it's the plan we're sticking with. So."

Tarian crouched next to the Caraigg waiting nearby and took his hand. *Can you help my friends take the prisms to the Source?* She showed them an image of the place, picturing it as clearly as she could manage. The blue sky. The four flat-topped peaks, jagged with boulders. The giant abereil filling the valley below.

Their voices filled her head, and the image shifted in her

mind to show different angles. They picked out details she hadn't really noticed. Discussed distance and stability issues. All one on top of each other in a jumbled mass of sound and images and thoughts.

She cringed at the noise and infiltration of her mind and waited until finally, one voice rose among the rest.

Caraigg can help. Caraigg can move prisms. Caraigg need time and Earth human Letta. She must use artifact to place.

"How much time?" Tarian asked out loud.

The voices rumbled and tumbled and emerged with an answer. *Prisms must move one at a time. One human hour for each.*

"Okay." Tarian stood. "Four hours. They need Letta and her artifact to shift the prisms, and they have to move one at a time. Alex, we'll need backup. Can you get the Sentinels together? Use the Caraigg to get them to the bubble field? Keep the numbers down—those platforms don't have much space."

Alex looked as if he were going to argue, then thought better of it. "Yeah, okay."

"That leaves the rest of us to find the Air Artifact." Tarian closed her eyes and tried to track it, but the connection was fuzzy and out of focus. The artifact was too distant or there was too much interference to get even a vague direction.

She tried tracking First Mother but found no connection. They'd never touched physically, and she'd never formed any kind of relationship with the daemon. There was no bond to use as a focus.

"We're too far away to get a lock on the artifact. We'll have to do this the hard way. We'll have to start somewhere and triangulate."

"Would it help to start where the artifact was last seen?" Macari asked.

"Normally, yes." Tarian thought about it. "But that was in the bubble field. There's a lot of power in the atmosphere there. I'm not sure I could get a good signal."

"Maybe that's why you can't get one now," Calliope said. "Maybe it's still there."

Tarian checked again, this time focusing on the bubble field first in her mind. The connection remained fuzzy and soft. "I can't tell. There's too much in the way."

"We're way underground here," Alex said. "Maybe you gotta be up top to get a good read?"

Tarian looked up at the solid granite that formed the ceiling of the cave they stood in. It was jagged and bumpy and glittered with something phosphorescent. She thought about how fuzzy her connection with Ember had felt, when her daughter was traveling the Earth stream, and nodded. "You're probably right. Let's try it. Macari, Calli, Daric, and I will jump to the bubble field. Alex, Letta, and the Caraigg will follow with the prisms."

"What if First Mother is waiting? What if she's there holding the Air Artifact?" Calliope asked.

"She won't be. She's after Ember. That's the last place she'd think Ember would be."

"You sure?" Calliope looked around.

Tarian glanced at Daric. She relied on her sister and Daric for strategy. Her first thought was always barge on in and sort it out after.

Daric considered, his head tilting slightly to the side in a way she found utterly adorable. He looked like a puppy when he did that. "Can the Caraigg scout it out? Just check to see if she's there?"

"Good idea!" Tarian knelt and held out her hand to one of the Caraigg.

"Can you give us a scouting report? Is First Mother there?" Tarian pictured the bubble field.

They returned a similar image almost immediately. *Caraigg wait for prisms. Caraigg may not breach the surface, but Caraigg detect no daemon presence.*

"Can you see the Air Artifact?"

Caraigg cannot breach the surface. Caraigg would create instability for abereil. Caraigg must remain insulated by Earth.

Tarian glanced up at the others and relayed the information. "It's a good place to start. I might be able to get a better signal, and Macari could use it as a jumping off point to check the Corsaerie. Agreed?"

They all nodded, though they didn't look happy about it. She had to admit, there wasn't much to be happy about. The plan might work, it might not. The ercklings might find Ember, they might not. They might save the world, and they might not.

"Remember, when we get there, don't use any power at all. If a bubble gets too close, we pop right back out. Macari, especially you. Just go, and don't look back. We'll regroup at Xannon if something happens. Got it?"

She waited until everyone nodded their agreement. "Alex, Letta…see you on the other side." She and Alex bumped fists.

"Yep." Letta knelt to talk with the Caraigg.

"Okay. Let's get outta here." She held out her hands. Daric took one of them, Calliope grasped the other, and Macari wrapped her arms around Tarian's neck so tight she nearly choked.

Tarian focused on the image of the platform where she'd stood above the Source abereil. She pictured every detail of the boulder she'd hidden behind, down to the bits of blood she'd garnished it with. When she had it as clear as she could make it, she gave a giant push of Air and traveled.

She deposited her passengers on the small mesa pockmarked with boulders without any stumbling or falling over rocks. Daric, Calliope, and Macari released their hold on Tarian and looked out over a city-sized valley full of bubbles.

Despite what the Caraigg had told her, she'd half expected First Mother to be hovering in the center of the valley, sending the abereil off into the world with glee. But a quick glance showed her nothing but bubbles.

The atmosphere still thrummed with elemental energy that pushed at her heart and brain and bent her pulse. *Whomp. Whomp. Whomp.* Calliope put both hands on her chest as if she could stop invasive rhythm. Daric looked uncomfortable as he shifted from one foot to another. Macari seemed unaffected.

"Mac…can you hear it? The heartbeat?"

Macari nodded but didn't say anything. Her attention focused on something in the distance. Tarian followed her gaze but saw nothing other than abereil. Lots and lots of abereil.

The number of them had grown since she'd left. Every now and then, two sped away from each other with a loud crack, which Tarian knew meant the birth of a new abereil. Every now and then, one flickered and vanished.

She swallowed, hard.

Daric took a few cautious steps forward to peer over the side of the cliff. "That's the Source?"

Tarian joined him. "Yeah." Something in the atmosphere made her skin crawl. She sniffed, hunting for any signature or sign that shouldn't be there. The *whomp* of the Source abereil added to the general sense of unease, but she didn't detect any human or daemon signatures.

"Something doesn't feel right." Tarian rubbed her arms, trying to make the creepy crawly sensation go away.

"It feels like someone is watching," Calliope said.

Daric turned to survey the landscape behind them. "Anything changed? Anyone here?"

Tarian sniffed again. Shook her head. "Looks the same. Exactly the same."

«But...»

She shrugged. "Macari? What're you staring at?" Tarian waved a hand in front of Macari's eyes. The daemon finally noticed Tarian standing there and looked sheepish. "Nothing. I guess. This place feels like a reilig."

"A what?" Tarian asked.

"A reilig. The place where souls collect. You know, energy never dissipates. When the body dies, the energy stored within goes there to wait for a new vessel."

"She means a cemetery," Calliope offered.

Macari pointed. "You can almost see the pathways, there is so much raw energy. See? The faint white vapor trails? They're paths. You can use them to travel, instead of the usual way. They're natural and easy to find if you have eyes for Air. If you saw First Mother floating out there, she wasn't actually floating at all. She stood on a pathway."

"So when she went flying..."

"She fell off," Macari said. "She might have fallen onto another pathway. They aren't all static. Some move very fast. They aren't very reliable. Most daemon won't use them. But in this place, with so much energy, I can see why she did. It would have been safer." Macari's lips twitched. "Until you knocked her off."

Daric pointed at the opposite platform. "Hey, I think Alex made it."

Tarian sensed her friend's signature, as comfortable and familiar as her own. She waved, and Alex waved back.

Alex gestured to the ground, and Sentinels crawled up through the dirt like ants. By the time they all arrived, there was no room for more on the small platform.

"I thought I said a few. That looks like more than fifty." Tarian looked with amusement at the platform on the right. "And there's more coming out over there. His idea of a few is a lot different from mine."

Daric nudged Tarian. "You know, that Source bubble seems stable enough."

Tarian joined him, taking his hand as they studied the Source. "It is. Until someone like First Mother shoots at it."

"It doesn't feel stable, though, does it?" Macari once again stared at what looked like empty space above the Source bubble. "The paths avoid the center. So do the abereil."

Tarian looked from Macari's serious expression to center space. She blinked. Squinted. Frowned. "I see plenty of bubbles in the middle."

"The angle is wrong." Macari looked down as if she were following something, tracing it to wherever it originated. Her eyes fixated on the Source. "That's not...that looks...I need to get closer."

Before Tarian could stop her, Macari danced off the edge of the platform and vanished in a whirl of yellow and white. Tarian watched the spinning top twirl and teeter along a trail of white vapor until it was lost in the sea of bubbles.

Tarian surveyed the Source, wondering what it was Macari saw. She traced the surface of it, looking at every detail that she could from her vantage point. It huddled between the peaks like gelatin, a white, luminescent pearl in a dark tub full of abereil bubbles. Her gaze traveled along, noticing how perfect it was. Smooth. Shiny. Sleek. Until it wasn't. A nearly imperceptible shadow marred the surface. A dark gray scar on an otherwise perfect white landscape. It seemed small, but size was hard to gauge from this far away. "Hey, do you guys see that?"

"What is it?" Daric asked.

"I don't know. It wasn't there before."

"It's hard to see anything with all these bubbles floating around," Calliope said. "You mean that shadow?"

"It's not a shadow. There's nothing to cast a shadow like that. The sun's not right."

The other two platforms were too far away for her to see anything other than shadows and a hint of movement. She squinted at them, abereil bobbing into and out of her view. She swore under her breath and turned back to the one platform she could see.

A low rumbling made them all jump. It sounded eerie and out of place, and combined with the odd atmosphere, it made the hair on Tarian's neck stand up and salute. The ground began to shake, and they all stumbled. Tarian held out her hands to steady herself, latching on to Daric and Calliope.

The ground crumbled beneath her feet. She lunged and managed to tug the others away just in time. A sinkhole rapidly formed where they'd been standing. They all backed away as the hole grew larger and larger. Tarian readied herself to fight, but relaxed when she saw Letta's head pop out from the shadows.

Letta leaned her elbows on the edge and wiped dirt off her face. "Prism one, locked and loaded. Wait, not loaded. Just locked. It's here, but ya need to back up. Far as you can get. The Caraigg will push from underneath and stay to guard them, but they can't surface. Too many abereil."

The three of them moved as close to the edge as they dared. Letta sank into the hold, which re-filled behind her to leave no trace it had ever existed. Tarian blinked. She'd never get over how a street girl from Philadelphia had turned into a mole.

After a few seconds, the ground jiggled. Dirt and loose rocks bounced along the surface and fell off the edge. Tarian grabbed Daric's arm for support. The ground shook harder as it woke up and dusted off years of inactivity with a vengeance, shuddering and shifting until a gap appeared in the center of the platform. Rocks crumbled and fell into the void below.

Tarian looked at the field of bubbles, expecting to see them start multiplying, but they remained stable.

The ground moaned and pushed a small pyramid of glass up through the hole. It glinted in the afternoon sun, refracting the light into a small rainbow. It sliced through the air and bent at an awkward angle.

Tarian stepped toward it, apprehension growing. Rainbows didn't bend.

"Letta! Tari! It's a trap! Stop!" Macari's shouts came a second too late.

The rainbow continued, becoming more fluid as it spread across the platform. It turned the air thick with multicolored fog that stung the second it touched her skin.

Daric grabbed Tarian's arm, and they tried to back away from odd mist. But there was nowhere to go. They teetered on the edge as it was.

"Look out!" Macari zoomed closer. She reached for Calliope, but as she got closer, the rainbow fog struck. A shot of red fire leapt from Macari's artifact, traveled along the fog to the prism, struck with a clang, and rebounded back toward Tarian.

The Water Artifact responded. Tarian screamed as scalding hot water lashed out through the medallion and met the fire head-on.

Water met Fire halfway between Macari and Tarian and erupted into a column that shot up and out, spilling furious power onto every abereil close by. Tarian grappled with the Water Artifact. But it was like wrestling with something hot and slimy.

"Shield!" Calliope reached for her, hit the beam of power, and was thrust backward. She slid across the platform, leaving a trail of flames.

Something hit Tarian hard in the back and knocked her to the ground. Daric landed on top of her. His heat traveled along her back, and his talent with Air tried to block the Water Artifact. It didn't help. The connection between Fire and Water was too strong. Abereil split and split again as the cast-off power struck home and lit them like fireworks.

It took Tarian a second to register what happened. Another second to realize how badly she'd underestimated her enemy.

One more second to realize she should have listened to her instincts and jumped away from this place when they first arrived. She'd known something was wrong. She'd felt it. She'd just ignored it.

Energy pushed, squeezed, ripped, and boiled until she thought her brain would burst.

Daric shook her and shouted something she couldn't hear.

She turned her head to shout in his ear. "What?"

He grimaced and then rolled with her, away from Macari. It stretched the tension of their connection tight tight tight until something broke. They flew away from each other. Macari toppled head over heels into the valley. Calliope rolled toward the edge of the cliff, grappling for a handhold. Just before she went over the edge, a hand reached through the ground and grabbed her wrist. It dragged Calliope down into the stone. Her body melted into it, leaving no trace her sister had ever been there.

Daric's grip on Tarian loosened. He struggled to hold on to her, but something pulled him away. He flew backward, out into the open air.

"Daric!" Tarian reached for him, stretching her hand out because her body refused to respond. The space he'd occupied... empty. Gone.

Gone.

"Daric!" She pushed herself to her knees. Forced herself to crawl forward. "Daric!"

Abereil exploded around them like fireworks, creating more and still more bubbles of energy.

"Daric!" Tarian reached the edge. Daric flailed, already a small figure against the large expanse of murky white. "Daric!" Tarian scrambled to her feet, everything forgotten but her need to get to him. She ran and jumped off the edge of the platform, eyes fixed on Daric.

He wrestled the air, his face contorted. His gaze found hers. They fell together, miles apart but locked in a dance of recognition and resignation. This was how it would end.

Tarian fought against it. She refused to accept it. She dragged energy from her deepest core through the medallion and shot it outward, a tether to tie the two of them together. It reached for Daric but diverted away at the last minute.

Time suspended. For an eternity, they were the only two in existence in an endless free fall. They revolved around each other, both reaching out. Lightning flashed. Energy bolts decorated the landscape. Fireworks at a cosmic celebration.

Whomp Whomp Whomp.

Daric's face froze with horror.

Someone screamed her name.

She ignored it.

Nothing existed but Daric.

She had to get to Daric.

The Source loomed, a gleaming palace of white. Daric struck and sank into the gelatinous surface, which caved and dipped, and then swallowed him. The surface bounced back into place as if it had never been breached.

"Nooooo!" Tarian shot a bolt of Air blended with Water. A shield and a web, meant to haul him up. It reached the Source and evaporated. The bubble didn't register the intrusion. Within it she saw flashes of light and colors that flared and vanished.

She was seconds away. He was gone. She had seconds.

«Tari!»

The voice sounded distant. She ignored it. One more second she'd hit the Source and join Daric. She closed her eyes and braced for impact.

Arms went around her. They twirled with her, spinning her body around and around in some sort of dance. Wind howled a greeting. Something deep in Tarian's chest echoed the sound.

"No! Let me go!" She struggled against the arms. She didn't want them. She didn't need them. She needed Daric. She had to get to Daric.

Bands of steel wrapped around her. She pushed against them, but they only tightened further. She wanted to get free. She wanted to get to the Source. To Daric. She wanted...

"Tari. Stop fighting. If I lose my grip, you'll be lost here." Macari's voice sounded breathless and high-pitched. "It's the Corsaerie. I can't let go.»

Tarian thrust her elbow backward. Macari grunted, but held on.

"Let me go. Let me go. Let me go." Tarian raged against the daemon girl. Against the Wind. Against fate. "Daric! Get Daric!"

"We can't. Tari. We can't."

Waves of comfort slammed into Tarian. They weren't welcome. She tried to ignore them, to see past them, but couldn't. Her anguish and anxiety drifted away, as if she'd been given a some powerful drug that dulled thought and reflexes and mood all at once. "He's gone. He's gone. He's gone." She repeated the phrase like a macabre mantra. But she stopped struggling. She couldn't get the strength to push against her captor any more. "Please. Please, let me go."

She'd never begged for anything in her life.

"No, Tari. I won't let you go. We need you. Ember needs you." Macari rocked Tarian in her arms. The wind raged around them, expressing the anger Tarian couldn't.

"Tari!" Macari sounded distant now. As if she spoke from behind sound-proof glass.

Tarian curled inward.

"Stars. Hold on! I'm going to get you out." Macari shoved, hard. Tarian tumbled forward, then down down down.

—24—

Tarian dangled, a mote of dust kept aloft by the mercy of the wind. Between one heartbeat and the next, mercy vanished.

Nothing.

Tarian screamed, a primal sound that connected with something nearby and echoed back to her, over and over. Rocks. She couldn't see them. But they saw her. Mocked her. Waited to kill her. And for half a heartbeat, she wanted them to kill her and be done with it. Daric...

"Tari!" Macari shouted from a good distance away, the sound tinny and small.

Energy, soft and seductive, wrapped around her and eased her descent, cocooning her in cool mist. It kept her body from falling but not her heart.

"Daric." The word wrenched from somewhere deep. She could see his face. His horrified, terrified, face. His eyes begged her to save him, and she couldn't. He was her friend. He was her lover. He was her rock. Her anchor. Her partner in every way she could imagine. He brought her comfort and happiness and peace. And he was gone gone gone gone gone.

The hurt was sharp and deep and intense. It took her heart

and squeezed, squeezed, squeezed until she couldn't breathe.

«*Mama?*» Ember's voice in her mind was distant, but solid. Older. Frightened.

«*S'lan che!*» Macari's voice sounded annoyed and frightened. "Brace."

Tarian hit something hard. The air left her chest in a swift rush. "Oof!" For a few seconds all she could do was try to coax her lungs to work.

"Oh stars. Tari, are you okay? I'm so sorry. I didn't know. They must have moved the shields after I left. They cut off all external forces, not just hostile ones. This hill used to be outside... Tari?" Macari paused. "What's wrong?"

«Daric.» Tarian sobbed.

Mama? Are you sad? Ember sounded clear, strong, and confused. *Ma...* Her voice cut off abruptly.

"I know. I saw." Macari touched Tarian's face with soft fingers as if she might break. "Look at me. Are you all right? Stars. Is anything broken? We need Calli. I can't...oh..." The sudden stiffness in the girl's fingers said more than her words.

Tarian tensed and tried to sit up. Her ribs screamed a protest. She rolled to her side instead, intending to leap to her feet but only managing to get to all fours. "Ember. I can hear her. Ember!"

"Tari. The guard is coming. We have to hide," Macari whispered. "We can't travel from here. Can you walk?"

A stone tinked nearby. Footsteps on pavement, not far away to the left.

"Stars. Tari...I'm sorry. We're inside Benata City. There's detection and dampening effects, and...I'm banished. I have to get out of here. If I go any further...I'll be...we can't be seen. I can't... stars." Every word, a higher pitch than the one before. Macari grabbed Tarian's arms and hauled her to her feet. She fumbled to get her balance, grateful for Macari's steady grip.

In the distance, footsteps continued toward them. They stirred a protective instinct inside Tarian. Her friend needed help. Ember needed help. She could do that. Then join Daric.

"Hide." Tarian tugged her hand away from Macari's grip.

"Here, I'll help you."

"Dammit." Tarian shoved at Macari's hand. "I can hear Ember in my head. Hide my feelings? Block Ember? She can't come here."

"Ember?" Macari tugged on Tarian's arm. "She's not here. She can't be. I don't hear her in the mind net. Come on, we have to get out of the city."

More footsteps joined the others. Closer now. Muffled by a building. Maybe two. Tarian pushed Macari away.

"Get help." She spun away from Macari and stumbled toward the footsteps.

"*S'lan Che Fu!*" Macari's voice trailed away.

Tarian ran forward, trying to put as much distance between them as possible. Her ribs protested, but she pushed forward until her feet hit something and she stumbled, landing hard on her hands and knees.

Seconds later, two Benata guards appeared. Air swirled around her and clamped down, binding her hands together. A tight band wound around her head. It pressed against her brain until she couldn't think, and more importantly, she couldn't focus on using elemental energy. The Water Artifact lay dormant. She suspected a shield surrounded it too. Or it might be the protections around the city itself.

The guards hauled her to her feet and pulled her along with embarrassingly little effort. The more she struggled, the tighter the band on her head squeezed. She stopped fighting.

Her stomach sank with each step. Benata City. She'd been delivered directly into the hands of her enemy. Her head pounded from the recent clash of artifacts. Her heart ached like a million tiny daggers had plunged into it and stayed there, slowly twisting and turning and gnawing away at the leftover pieces. She still saw Daric's face. His eyes. Every step took her further away from him. Every step sounded so final. He was gone. She was trapped, and he was gone.

If she managed to get out of this, he'd still be gone. And the abereil kept on breeding. First Mother was winning, and she wasn't sure if she was even capable of stopping the daemon anymore. She'd thought so, before. But now…she'd let Daric die. She couldn't save him. How could she possibly save anyone else?

Exhaustion made each step seem like a trudge through quicksand, uphill. If it weren't for the hands and magic supporting her, she wasn't sure she could have managed to stand at all.

She waited for panic to settle in to the empty, hollow, numb place that used to be her heart. The look on Daric's face burned an accusation into her soul. She swallowed hard.

They paraded her through the city like a prize trophy presented to a cheering crowd, except there were no cheers and no crowd. But she had the feeling everyone in the city knew she was there. She had the creepy being-watched feeling along the back of her neck.

Their threesome slowed when they reached a set of steps leading up to a raised gazebo of epic proportions. If she'd been wandering in a garden, she'd have found this to be the perfect spot to hang out for an hour or two. Flowers crawled up trellises and columns. Water splashed in a large fountain nearby. Birds sang, and a soft breeze played with Tarian's hair.

She'd expected Benata City to be made of billowing clouds or something. Even though the daemon themselves always seemed quite solid and humanoid, she'd imagined them more as angels when she was a child. The reality was a normal, if a bit archaic, town formed of small houses and paths and serenity.

The whole thing would have been relaxing on any other day. But not today. Today was so far removed from relaxing that she couldn't remember what relaxed felt like.

Her captors forced her to the steps. They ascended one at a time, almost in slow motion. With each step, power settled around her like a down blanket. When they reached the top step and entered the gazebo, voices, one on top of the other, high-pitched and low-pitched, soft and loud, filled her mind and fought for attention. Hundreds of daemon voices held multiple conversations in her thoughts. It was as though an entire country full of pushy, inquisitive teenagers suddenly leapt into her brain.

Breach of protocol!

I thought the shields would stop...

First Mother seems most...

A human, here? Who invited her? How did she...

Extremely troubling. The Shee...

I thought I heard First Daughter...

The guards saw...

Did you hear a child in her thoughts?

I caught a glimpse of...

Are we allowed to keep a human?

"Tarian Xannon. Keeper of the Water Artifact. Interesting." The voices in her head stilled. The silence provided a platform for the daemon who spoke out loud in a voice sculpted from ice and daggers.

Tarian lifted her chin and forced herself to make eye contact. She pushed words out through gritted teeth. "First Mother of the Benata."

—52—

First Mother stood on a round dais that placed her towering above the rest of the assembled crowd. She wore white robes, like someone in a church choir, and her white hair was up in an intricate, perfectly done knot. With her porcelain skin, she looked like a statue, crafted by a master artisan. She was regal and cold and absolutely evil.

Another daemon stood on an elevated platform to the right. Tarian recognized him as the one who'd been in the park in Philly. He also wore the official white robes, but his were edged in crimson. He studied Tarian with an impassive face. But she thought she saw a flash of something in his eyes. Apprehension? Concern? She couldn't be sure. His body language told her nothing.

Tarian's captors released their grip and backed away. Invisible chains wrapped around her wrists and ankles and lifted her body until she hung suspended above the heads of the crowd. Now that she had the higher vantage point, Tarian could see the space and the faces staring up at her. They all wore white robes, most trimmed in green, though she also saw a few blue, a few orange, and one yellow. She'd listened to Macari describe them often enough. It appeared the entire Council and some high-ranking citizens were on hand to witness her torture, or execution, or whatever this was going to be.

The faces looking back at her might as well have been carved from stone. She'd never seen so many poker faces in one place. She couldn't read anything in their eyes. Did they agree with what was happening? Did they believe she deserved it?

Tarian struggled against the bonds that held her aloft, testing for weakness. She couldn't see the chains, but she could feel them. They bit into her flesh every bit as solid as metal and every bit as cold as ice. Her body temperature dropped, and she fought to keep her teeth from chattering.

She tested her own power reserves. She could feel them. Water lapped at her insides, eager to escape. The artifact poked and prodded at the shield binding it. But the shield let nothing through.

"Where is your spawn, Keeper?" First Mother spoke aloud.

Tarian pressed her lips together.

Frozen daggers bit into her body on all sides. She struggled against the chains. They held tighter. She tried to curl into a ball. She tried to get free. The attack continued. Voices, like the hum of a large crowd, filled her ears. She fought the urge to scream.

The assault stopped.

"Where is the child?"

Tarian moaned. She couldn't help it. Cold penetrated her bones and made each wound burn.

A whisper snaked through the darkest recesses of her mind. *Do you really think you can resist me? Here, in my city? Surrounded by Air, the most powerful element?*

Tarian wanted to argue. No element was more powerful than any other. She filled her thoughts with images of the ocean. She pictured a brilliant blue sky and the sun glinting off the waves as they washed the shore. In her mind she plunged into the water and swam through the depths. Schools of fish, colorful coral, and dolphins argued on her behalf.

The scene whirled as if an invisible hand stirred the water. It sifted through a filing cabinet containing every memory she stored there. Each one rocketed ice daggers through her body. Each one increased the pressure in her brain and behind her eyes.

"First Mother!" The distant voice sounded alarmed.

Tarian tried desperately to shield her thoughts. She might as well have tried to stop time.

Memory after memory wrenched from the depths of her mind until one took over everything else. Daric, absorbed into the Source bubble. Tarian gasped as the force of the memory wrenched a sob from deep in her chest.

Voices rose, fevered and frantic. They argued, but she couldn't make out what they wanted. She wished they'd stop. She wished it would all stop. Daric. His face. His eyes. He was gone. Gone and would never come back. Her soul cracked a little more every time the scene played. It repeated, relentless, over and over and over.

Tears filled her eyes and spilled over. They left hot trails down her frozen cheeks.

"Where is the child?" First Mother said.

Daric stared at her. His eyes...she couldn't look away.

Show me what I want to know.

Tarian held onto Daric. A lifeline in the midst of tumult.

The chains shook Tarian like a rag doll in the grip of a two-year-old.

Focus. The child. Where is your daughter?

An army of frozen ants marched across her skin. They took bite after bite after bite of her flesh. Each bite flared white hot.

"First Mother!" The voices rose in protest, more of them than before. Angrier.

The ants stopped. Tarian gasped for air and found none. Her lungs burned. Her body bucked against the restraints.

"You must stop!" Panic made the deep male voice high-pitched and breathless.

Tarian's peripheral awareness drifted away. She'd never come close to drowning, but she thought it must feel like this. Her lungs burned, her body ached, and her mind slowed to sludge. Everything darkened. Her head dropped. Her eyes wanted to close. Just close. Close and rest. Rest forever.

"First Mother! The Agreements will judge. You must stop. Now." The male voice sounded firm, now. No panic. No anger. Simple fact.

The pressure released. Tarian panted, taking advantage of the sudden reprieve. The fog cleared a little. She focused on pushing each breath in and out.

The faces below all turned to watch something outside of Tarian's peripheral vision. She tried to raise her head, but it weighed a hundred pounds. A thousand pounds even. She settled for staring out from under heavy eyelids and waiting.

First Mother rode her dais above the heads of the Council toward Tarian with her hands clasped in front of her. She looked like an angel—a cold bitchy one who'd lost her wings and whose eyes lit up with decidedly unholy intentions.

Tarian had seen that look before. It was the expression of someone who enjoyed torturing. They hurt for the pleasure of it and for a release of some deep-seated need only they knew about. They were usually the ones she found teasing and hurting small animals or children with power. It gave new definition to the phrase "power trip." And here she was, wrapped up in invisible chains, suspended above the entire power structure of Benata City, being tortured by their leader, behind a shield she had no hope of breaking. Her situation gave an entirely new definition to the word "helpless."

Tarian gritted her teeth.

First Mother stopped so close all Tarian could see was white cloth. The heat of First Mother's body burned, completely at odds with the cold of the chains. Tarian shivered. Her arms and legs were blocks of ice.

First Mother lay a hand against Tarian's cheek. Air energy prickled along First Mother's fingers. It sank through the pores and drove a path straight into Tarian's skull. Tarian screamed and tried to pull away. The torturous hand held her head in place.

It burned like she'd been frozen a thousand years and then someone had thrown hot water all over her body. The pain drove her out of her mind and into a basting furnace of white, cold fire.

«*Mama!*»

Tarian trembled. *No!*

First Mother emitted a guttural, primitive sound. Ice daggers stabbed, poked, ripped, tore into her mind, leaving wounds that bled memories and images. Ember as a baby, playing on the black sand. Bubbles exploding. Fort Worth engulfed in flames. Ruarc.

Tarian struggled against the chains. She could barely move them. Her shoulders hurt like they'd been dislocated. She couldn't reach any power. The artifact remained blocked.

Mama! Ember's voice, loud and clear, then suddenly silent, hurt worse than the assault on her body.

«Guards! Link!»

Fabric brushed Tarian's face as First Mother gestured. The scent of frigid mountain air and cold bitch shifted and grew. Subtle hints of other smells joined. Flowers. Summer rain. Snow.

Dandelion. Too many to pinpoint. They merged and blended and coalesced.

Voices blasted through her thoughts. Startled voices. Angry voices.

"First Mother! The Agreements!" The male voice shouted from a distance. It might as well have been vapor. First Mother ignored it. Energy thickened and crackled and sparked as she called more and more.

The hair along Tarian's skin stood just before the blast struck.

She convulsed against it. Her body shook so hard the restraints loosened, and she slipped down an inch. Then two. A thousand hands slapped her face over and over and over.

Mama! Ember's wail echoed loud and strong.

More voices penetrated her mind and sliced through the pain. Astonished voices. Confused voices.

No! Tarian moaned. Her mind drifted. The world darkened.

Mama NEEDS me! The determined voice of a very angry little girl silenced the cacophony in her mind. Stunned daemon faces stared up at Tarian.

No no no no no!

First Mother raised Tarian's head in her hands. She stared unblinking into Tarian's eyes. Tarian stared back. The irises were light blue, so pale they were almost white. Her pupils dilated, and the black of them expanded and filled the blue, then reached beyond until it filled her eye socket all the way to the white lashes. Tarian could see nothing but the deep, dark recesses of those black, evil eyes.

Glimmers of colors radiated out from the center. They shifted and swirled and became pictures. Tarian saw beyond the platform, beyond the city, out into the world beyond. Her vision zoomed past houses, mountains, cities, forests.

Mama NEEDS me! Ember sounded frantic and out of breath, as if she struggled against someone or ran away from something. Tarian shook. *Ember. No! Stay away. Stay!*

Mama! Kia won't let me help. I want to help! The complaint was palpable. The wrongness of the situation obviously hurt her daughter's feelings.

The connection between Tarian and First Mother strengthened and reached out for Ember.

It latched on, opening a pathway that flooded Tarian with emotions. Anger. Hurt. Frustration. Ember fought against someone. The connection sputtered, disappeared, then flared again.

Tarian knew Kia must be trying to hold Ember. She must be trying to break the connection. But Ember sounded older. Much older. Tarian wondered how long Ember had been there. She'd lost track of time. Had it been a day? Two days? Weeks? How old was her daughter now? The thought flashed through her mind so fast it was barely there at all, but she heard the sharp intake of breath from First Mother and knew the daemon had heard it.

They formed an absurd triangle, a merge stronger than anything Tarian had ever experienced. Her thoughts raced forward along the bond, like a movie camera racing through landscapes. The camera followed a bright white light like a beacon pointing straight to Ember. It zoomed into a city, toward a building, through a large window, past white sofas and Mayfanata guards.

Tarian's stomach lurched. She wanted to pull back. Look away. Stop the movie. She couldn't.

Ruarc stood in the center, alert, ready for battle. The camera brushed past him, down a hallway, to a room with a purple door. It pushed through the door and focused in on the occupants. In the vision, Kia reached out for a child about six years old, with long black hair, deep sapphire eyes, and a red angry face. She wore a blue dress, but no shoes or socks. "Ember," she whispered out loud. But when the name left her lips, both girls in the vision turned their head.

Ember's gaze connected with Tarian's as if they didn't stand a continent, a world, a universe apart. As if they were right next to each other, a breath away.

Ember's lips moved, and in Tarian's thoughts she heard her daughter's voice. *Mama.*

First Mother reached through the connection with Air, weaving a net. Ember's eyes widened, and her focus shifted as if she could see First Mother and feel the weaving of elemental power. The net traveled through the connection faster than light.

"Look out!" Tarian tried to shout, but the words came out more like a whimper. She had to do something. She couldn't get control of her thoughts. The vision remained firm.

Kia lunged for Ember. Her hands grasped the child's arm. The vision faded, but didn't vanish.

Tarian lifted her head back as far as she could. It was like trying to bend an old two-by-four, but she managed. She thrust herself forward and slammed her forehead into First Mother's face. The impact sent shock waves of pain through her face.

First Mother fell backward. The connection between the three of them severed.

First Mother put a hand on her forehead where Tarian had struck. A bright pink spot bloomed, vivid against the white of her face. She looked stunned, not from the blow itself but from the audacity. As if no one had ever physically struck her before.

"Stay away from my daughter." Tarian's voice came out hoarse and low. Dangerous. "Bitch."

The chains that imprisoned Tarian loosened a bit further. Her body dropped several more inches. She dangled only a few feet above the ground now. It taunted her with how close it was. The Water Artifact stirred, as if it woke after a long night and wasn't a morning person. It stretched and grumbled, pissed off.

Tarian watched First Mother from underneath her lashes. Her head pounded, and blood dripped across one eye and down her nose. She'd hit harder than she thought. Satisfaction surged.

First Mother glared, blood running across the lines in her forehead like battle paint. She cleared her throat and spoke out loud in a forceful tone, but also within the mind net. It created a weird echo, like the announcer at a baseball game. "First Advisor. Make note that the Keeper of the Water Artifact and Leader of the House of Xannon breaks an Agreement so ancient it goes back to the very first of their kind. No leader may attack another." She paused and leaned in closer. When she spoke it was barely above a whisper and didn't echo within Tarian's thoughts. This message was for Tarian, and her alone. "You will die for this."

"You first." Tarian spit blood that had pooled on her lips. Her head lolled to the side, it was so damn heavy.

The daemon with the red trim moved closer to the two of them. Now Tarian knew what the red trim indicated. He was the First Advisor she'd told to make note of the situation. Record the offense. Proffer judgment. He was to First Mother as Alex was to Tarian. Though she seriously doubted they had ever had any sort of friendship.

"First Mother, if she breached Agreement, the penalty would have already been invoked." The First Advisor sounded desperate, his voice a little high-pitched, like a man who'd been suffering a long time with the weight of an out-of-control leader. One who'd long ago stop taking his advice.

First Mother reached beneath the folds of her robes and brought out a small blue-white orb. She held the artifact in the palm of one hand, arm extended, eyes blazing with fury. More emotion splayed across her face and body than Tarian had ever seen on anyone, ever. Whatever First Mother used to keep her emotions in check, it was quite clearly broken.

White vapor billowed from the Air Artifact, thick and hungry. It obscured First Mother's hand and slithered around her arm, tendrils licking and testing like tongues. Her pupils receded until her eyes blazed pure white light.

Tarian reached for the Water Artifact, but the chains held. She couldn't bring her arms down, much less touch her chest. She tried instead to call power from within, but it remained distant, sequestered behind a barrier. Whether it was the protections of the city, something First Mother had constructed, or part of the magic of the chain itself, she didn't know. It was effective. She was cut off from any elemental power use. Here in Benata City, at this moment, she was completely human and nothing more.

The Advisor leapt off his dais to rush toward his leader. He pushed the sleeves of his robe back as he went, and his hands glowed with unspent energy. "First Mother! The Agreements!"

Tarian looked from him to First Mother. The daemon kept her gaze trained on Tarian. Hatred burned in her eyes, white hot and beyond reason. Wrinkles spread like spiderwebs from the edges of her eyes toward the side of her face.

Tarian struggled against the chains. She was too weak to do more than give them a slight jiggle.

First Mother held the Air Artifact high. The white snake uncurled from her arm and slithered toward Tarian. It flicked the atmosphere with its tongue along the way, as if it savored the taste of it.

Tarian jerked back as it drew close. It circled her head, the body elongating as it went around and around and around. It blocked Tarian's view until she could see nothing but white mist with flecks of gray.

The snake began to squeeze.

Tarian gagged. Her lungs pumped. Her body convulsed with the aching burning need for life-giving oxygen. She bucked against the restraints in a last ditch effort to live.

THE AGREEMENT HAS BEEN BREACHED

The words reverberated through her skull, through her body, through the space around her. They didn't make sense. She couldn't grasp the meaning. Didn't care. The white snake turned black. Her vision dimmed. Darkness called, seductive and sweet.

THE AGREEMENT HAS BEEN BREACHED

A low rumble sounded, as though a giant struggled to wake from a long nap.

THE AGREEMENT HAS BEEN BREACHED

The white misty snake enveloping Tarian dissipated with a long hiss. Air flooded in. Sweet, cool, delicious, life-giving air. Tarian gasped. Drew in a breath. Choked. Took another.

THE AGREEMENT HAS BEEN BREACHED

The chains binding Tarian to the space released, and she fell to the ground. Her knees buckled on impact, and she crumpled.

THE AGREEMENT HAS BEEN BREACHED

First Mother screamed a **guttural**, inhuman sound. "Guards! To me!"

Tarian looked up to find the daemon towering over her. She glowered down at Tarian. The white in her eyes had receded. Her hair had escaped the careful knots, and the wrinkles looked more like crevices. She looked old, like one of those apple dolls Tarian had seen once at a festival. First Mother clutched the Air Artifact with both hands. They'd turned pockmarked and freckled, as if a thousand years in the sun had finally caught up with her.

Tarian put a hand over the Water Artifact, not sure what it would do or what she *should* do. She didn't know the Agreement. She'd never been told. Her mother died too soon to give her all the details of daemon-human interactions. And she'd never been a history buff.

First Mother brought the Air Artifact closer to Tarian.

"Die! You and your spawn and the rest of the vermin. You will all die! I will protect the good...of the many!"

First Mother shook the Air Artifact. It looked almost black. The clouds within it stormed and raged. But instead of the attack Tarian expected, instead of one last lethal blow, the Air Artifact moved violently back and forth. Tarian realized it wasn't First Mother shaking the thing—it was the artifact itself struggling to get free of the daemon.

Finally, with one last violent tug, the artifact sailed out of First Mother's hands, up into the sky, and buried itself in a cloud that turned dark and ominous. The cloud evolved into a storm that broke over the top of Benata City.

The ground quaked. First Mother stumbled backward, unable to keep her footing. The Rotunda columns crumbled. Chunks of stone flew off and swirled as if swept up in a tornado. The storm picked up benches and threw rocks like a petulant child.

The daemon Council scattered. Some shouted orders, others attempted to secure the Rotunda. None had enough power to stop the storm.

Tarian ducked debris and searched for shelter. Her muscles screamed from the abuse, and her shoulders burned. She thought they might be dislocated. She'd hung suspended for so long, and at such an awkward angle. It had left her weak and disoriented.

The Rotunda didn't have much in the way of furniture or overhangs or anything else to hide under. What she could see of the city beyond the Rotunda was just as bad. The entire city looked caught up in a hurricane. Buildings toppled. Daemon ran.

Tarian caught a glimpse of First Mother. Several guards clustered around their leader, protecting her from the brunt of the storm. The air was thick with the power they used just to keep themselves steady. First Mother locked her gaze on Tarian. If looks could kill, First Mother would be a very happy daemon.

Tarian blinked. First Mother and the entire group of guards vanished. Tarian looked around, but they were gone. She couldn't tell how many of the Court went with the First Mother. Plenty were left to deal with the fallout of a very angry, ancient magical object and the ire of an Agreement breached.

Tarian ducked lower, covered her head with her arms, and waited for the storm to burn itself out.

—27—

Tarian lay curled in a fetal position, head tucked under her arms, while the storm raged around her. She basked in the return of her own power and that of the Water Artifact. It flooded her veins and filled her senses with vitality and warmth. She shivered as heat pushed cold out of her body. She went from exhausted and near death to the energy of someone on ten cups of coffee and maybe some crack cocaine on the side.

She thought about leaving. She remained in enemy territory, and even though First Mother had vanished, plenty of daemon remained behind. She had no idea what their intentions would be, once they stopped dealing with the storm.

She also had no idea where Macari had gone, or what had happened to the rest of her friends and family...except for Daric. His face haunted her memory, a constant reminder of what she'd just lost. The pain was a knife that picked away at her heart. She shied away from it, tried to put the feeling in a box inside herself with a label that said "do not open." She couldn't afford to even think about it right now. She lay in Benata City. Surrounded by daemon. Thousands of abereil roamed the country, maybe the world. Her daughter was growing up way too fast and way too far away. Her sister...she didn't know what had happened to Calliope. Or Alex. Or Letta.

Her plan had fallen to shit in a spectacular way. The prisms might be in place. But without Letta and Macari, she had no hope of finishing anything. Even if she found her sister and somehow Calliope managed to bond with the Air Artifact, all four of them had to be there in the end for the plan to work. All four artifacts, and the ones who'd bonded with them.

She curled into a tighter ball and tried to shove all of the thoughts out of her head. Every time she shoved one thought out, a dozen more popped in. All of them finally vacated her brain when a dagger formed of rock and dirt shot up through the cracked stone of the gazebo. Tarian rolled to the side, but stopped when another shot up behind her.

Dagger after dagger of craggy rock shot skyward. They knocked daemon off-balance and added to the stormy chaos. The scent of steel emerged.

Tarian wrinkled her nose and sniffed again, then squinted around her. She knew that smell. It was as familiar and comfortable as Calliope's.

"Alex?" Tarian rose to a crouch, dodged a couple of flying rocks and a bird caught up in the windstorm, and shifted closer to one of the rock daggers. They'd formed a haphazard circle around where Tarian had been laying just seconds before. The ground yawned, and a hole appeared in the center of the circle.

She saw short black hair on a large head emerge, then a dark face streaked with dirt. Alex hauled himself out of the hole and stood like a warrior about to do battle. "Tari!" He squinted into the storm and swatted a flying rock away with irritation. "Tari!"

"Here!"

Alex turned toward the sound of her voice. His face lit up

when he set eyes on her. He walked toward her, hunched over, one arm protecting his head and face.

"Alex!" Tarian staggered toward her friend.

He held out his arms, and she fell into a giant bear-sized hug that made it hard to breathe and felt wonderful.

Alex pulled back and gestured at the hole behind him. "I brought backup!" More Sentinels emerged from the nether regions. They all looked sweaty, filthy, and happy to be out of the ground.

Her relief at seeing Alex alive and well made her feel even weaker than she already was. She checked his body for obvious trauma, but other than rips in his clothes and dirt all over his face, he seemed unharmed. "You're okay, right?"

"I don't go down that easy. Sorry it took so long. I couldn't get through. I kept trying. Nothing worked until suddenly...it all worked." He looked around. "Letta was supposed to be trying the other side of the city. She make it?"

Tarian released him and gestured at the broken city. "The protections are gone. First Mother...never mind. What about Letta?"

Alex frowned. "She was going to do something with the last prism, then follow. Thought she'd be here by now."

The wind continued to rage, but something about it felt different. It brought a hint of jasmine and a tease of ozone. Two more scents she knew. She thought she caught a glimpse of giant white birds. She definitely saw a flash of yellow high up in the cloud. "I think Macari brought friends."

Alex looked up. "She said something about Shee. I didn't catch it all."

Daemon, most of them Council by the look of the green trim on their robes, converged on Tarian and Alex where they stood in the middle of the Rotunda ruins. Tarian pushed her back against one of the rock pillars Alex had placed and readied herself. Alex shouted at the hole he'd just vacated and gestured to someone.

Tarian couldn't read a thing from the daemon expressions. But the way they advanced on her didn't leave much doubt in her mind as to their intentions. She was an intruder, and they were protecting their city.

"Macari!" Tarian struggled to see through the dust, flying rocks, and haze. She caught another flicker of yellow, but it moved too fast to get a fix on it. The storm softened from tornado to more of an angry breeze.

The hole burped and regurgitated more Sentinels. They climbed out one after the other in rapid succession and spread out to form a tight protective layer between Tarian and the daemon. The daemon stopped and formed a tight-knit group. They stared at the Sentinels and at Tarian, but their lips didn't move and their faces gave away nothing.

She saw Sentinels emerging from other holes in the distance and pointed. "Letta must be over there."

Alex looked doubtful. Then alarmed. "Hey! Stop that shit!"

Tarian's stomach flopped and flipped when she saw the Sentinels attacked as they exited their hidey-hole by any daemon standing near. The once peaceful city became a battlefield in seconds as various elements and weapons flashed and shot and fought. "Shit! Stop! Stop fighting! Alex, stop the Sentinels. We can't fight the Benata. We *need* them."

She ran forward waving her arms. "Stop! Stop fighting!"

Those nearby heard, but the protective circle around her refused to budge. They didn't fight, but they weren't about to let anything through to their Keeper either. Tarian shoved at one of them. "Let me through! Stop fighting!" She shouted at the daemon Council still clustered nearby. They watched her, seemingly uninterested in the mayhem behind them.

The storm clouds seemed a lot thinner than they had a minute ago.

She turned her attention back to the Council. "We aren't your enemy. Damn it! Tell them to stop. Please!"

The Council turned toward each other. Some gestured, others remained stoic. They looked like gossiping school kids, except none of them were young, and none of them actually spoke out loud. Tarian wished she'd learned to master the telepathy thing. Her connection to the mind net had severed with the destruction of the Rotunda. She couldn't hear what they said, but she saw some turn toward the outer city and others react as if they'd just been given an order.

"Stand down! Sentinels, stand down!" Tarian shouted as loud as she could, but the sound didn't travel very far above all the other clashing and clanging. The storm didn't help. It was dying, and much quieter than it had been, but the wind still made it hard to hear much of anything.

She cupped her hands around her mouth and shouted again, this time pushing some Air energy along with it to magnify the sound. It worked like a bullhorn and got the attention she wanted from everyone, human and daemon. "Stand the fuck down! Stop fighting! We are not enemies! I mean it! Sentinels, back the hell off!"

The Council all turned toward Tarian as one unit, which made her shiver. The precise movement, the way they spoke without actually speaking, and the way they betrayed nothing on their faces gave her the creeps. Her mother had always had a stoic expression like this, but it was something Tarian had never bothered to learn. She'd never wanted to learn it, or needed to.

But now she'd love to spend time studying how they did that, so she could pick up on their unique body language. It was infuriating, not being able to read signs of emotions or anything else. She had no idea if they were on her side or getting ready to kill her. No idea at all.

Another flash of yellow right next to Tarian made her yelp in surprise. The flash resolved into Macari, with her arms wrapped tight around Calliope. Both looked winded. Calliope's blond hair stuck out like she'd touched a light socket. Macari's silvery white hair looked more like she'd touched lightning itself. They both looked harassed, but unharmed.

"Calli!" Tarian hugged her sister tight. "You're okay. You're okay. Right?"

Calliope sighed, a long exhausted release of breath that dropped her shoulders. "I'm all right. We both are. It was just a fight to get in, that's all."

Tarian turned to Macari. "You saved her. I…thank you. I owe you."

Macari flashed a small smile. "I had help. Letta grabbed her arm before she went over. I just brought her here." Macari looked around. Her face crumpled as she took in the fallen columns, the destroyed Rotunda, and the ruined city. Her hand moved to clutch the artifact embedded in her naval. The air around her shimmered like a lazy summer heatwave.

"Oh…stars." Macari breathed the words. "The city…stars. It's…it's gone. It's really…gone." Macari looked like she might throw up. Tears welled in her eyes as she looked around at the fallen columns, the cracked ground, the collapsed buildings. Bodies littered the once beautiful pathway, crushed by stone and debris or victims to the storm itself. The musical fountain that used to form the center of the city lay in ruins.

Tarian watched the crowd, looking for signs of betrayal, of more fighting, of anything out of place. Sentinels and daemon waited, their expectation hanging thick and heavy. All eyes focused on the center of the Rotunda, on Tarian and Macari, and, to a lesser extent, Alex. Alex rubbed the back of his neck as he, too, searched the crowd.

Tarian couldn't see much beyond the wall of Sentinels still guarding her. She was too short to get a peek over their heads. She looked around for the platforms First Mother had used. They'd shattered into a million pieces. But a couple of benches nearby looked like they missed the worst of the damage. She climbed up on one so she could see more of the crowd.

What she saw filled her heart with an ache she didn't expect. The once beautiful city lay broken like a disjointed doll.

Macari joined her on the bench, and the two of them looked out over the devastation. "I saw this. I didn't want to believe it. I saw this on the Corsaerie. She'll do this to the entire world. She's already started. The visions…oh…stars." She sounded exhausted and defeated and sad.

Tarian assessed the damage. Where stately columns once stood, crumbled piles of white pebbles remained. Water ran down the path nearby, freed from the constraints of the previously beautiful fountain. She pictured downtown Fort Worth and realized the entire world might look like Benata City soon, or worse. It might simply cease to exist. It might be wiped clean like an old chalkboard, with nothing left. No buildings. No magic. No life. She shuddered at the thought. But a spark of something else grew in the pit of her stomach. Determination. She turned to Macari. "Unless we stop her. We can. We can stop her, Macari. We can put it right. All of it."

She shook Macari's arm a little to get her attention. "We can fix this. Together."

Macari bit her lip, as if she highly doubted it but would really like to believe. Then she nodded. She glanced at the Council, then stiffened as if she'd decided something. "I'm going to bring everyone into the net so we can all hear."

Tarian knew the second she'd done it because the Sentinels looked around in confusion or doubled over from the assault of sudden sound. Calliope's mouth fell open, her eyes round with wonder and surprise.

"First Daughter! You've returned!"

"Are you well?"

"The Agreements…"

"Where have you been? What has happened?"

"Have you seen First Mother? Do you know her plans?"

"We need an explanation!"

"Is First Mother…"

"What has…"

«Mayfanata?»

«Why?»

Tarian cringed at the onslaught of voices and questions. Though they didn't speak aloud, the anxiety and fear came across with the force of an angry sea slamming against rocks. She held up both hands to stop them. Alex looked at her in confusion. She grimaced back, then shoved her own thought into the mix.

"Quiet!" Her mind voice echoed louder than all the rest, infiltrating even the distant chaotic noise. A shocked silence fell, heavy as a hammer. Every daemon in range turned to face her, eyes flashing, bodies tense.

Macari looked from her to them and back. She held up her hands, one toward them, one toward Tarian. "Wait. Just…wait. Please. Calm down."

Tarian let her hands fall to her sides. She did her best to relax her posture. The tension pulsed so palpable it could be spread like butter on toast.

For a long, silent, anxious moment, the ruined city teetered on the edge.

Something feathery light brushed across Tarian's skin. The slightest hint of fresh mountain air and sunshine drifted with it. It left in its wake a gentle peace that settled over the anger and confusion. It didn't take anything away. It simply took the edge off.

Tarian looked at Macari. Macari stared back. She looked nervous. Intimidated. She kept clutching at her dress, then releasing it, like a squeeze ball people used to soothe anxiety. Tarian relaxed her shoulders and stared meaningfully at Macari. Macari mimicked her action. Tarian took a deep breath. Macari did the same.

Tarian dipped her head slightly, encouraging Macari to continue with something besides emotion suppression.

Everyone waited.

Macari cleared her throat. Shuffled a foot. One hand fluttered to her stomach, but Tarian wasn't sure if she clutched at the artifact embedded there or if she tried to steady her nerves. Or both. Tarian nodded, offered a tight smile, and muttered, "Explain fast."

"Right." Macari nodded to herself. Shook herself as if to steel her nerves, then turned to face the daemon assembled. "First Advisor, please step forward."

The daemon who had protested Tarian's rough treatment stepped forward from the crowd. He held his head high, his hands clasped in front of him, patience etched in every line of his face. His long silver hair hung disheveled and loose around his shoulders.

Tarian considered the implications of this very important daemon being left behind with the others. It appeared First Mother was perhaps dealing with her own personal betrayal. Or worse. She'd formed her own secret team within the leadership itself, and she'd excluded her own top advisor from the group. There'd been a rift in Benata City. A split. Some did not agree with First Mother's recent actions or approach. Probably all the ones left standing here.

"First Daughter."

"First Advisor, may I present Tarian Xannon, Keeper of the Water Artifact. Tarian, this is the First Advisor to the Court. He...he's like Alex is to you."

Alex raised an eyebrow at that.

Macari smiled, a small hesitant thing, but it seemed to encourage her. "Well, not exactly. You understand, though. There is only one other higher in the Court. He stands next to the First Mother and serves as her ambassador, and he leads the guards who protect the city."

"One other?" Tarian asked. "Who's the other?"

Macari shifted but didn't answer.

First Advisor stared at Macari, his expression neutral. "The First Daughter."

Tarian looked from him to her friend, then back. "Wow. Okay then." She held out her hand. The First Advisor stared at it, looking doubtful.

"We don't greet with physical gestures, Tari," Macari whispered.

Tarian dropped her hand, feeling awkward. "Nice to officially meet you, Advisor. Thank you, for trying to stop things before they got out of hand."

The daemon betrayed no emotion, but he did dip his head slightly in acknowledgment. She wasn't sure if it was for the introduction, or for the thanks, or for something else entirely. She detected a hint of something flash through his eyes, but it left too fast for her to identify.

First Advisor turned toward Macari, hands clasped in front of him. "First Daughter. Do you stand with the city?" His mental tone was deep and sonorous. Dignified. Intelligent. And betrayed no emotion at all.

Tarian tried to picture herself looking that passive and failed. The question carried weight. It was the kind of question that could mean death if answered the wrong way. Tarian wondered which the sea of daemon faces would prefer. On the one hand, their leader just tried to kill someone and then hotfooted out when it went badly, leaving them all to deal with the mess. On the other, they could believe First Mother had been removed for her own safety. They might believe their city was threatened and invaded by a human. They might believe Tarian was not included in the credo "the good of the many." She wasn't many. She was few. She was human. Did that make her a threat or an ally to the daemon left standing here among the ruins of Benata City?

Macari shifted from one foot to the other, as if she too weighed the consequences of her answer.

—28—

Tarian waited for Macari's answer, anxiety growing by the second. Silence took the city and wrapped it in soundproofing. It was as if the entire city held its breath and waited.

Macari raised her head and looked directly at the First Advisor. "I stand now, as before and forever, with Benata City. My city."

Her friend sounded confident. Regal. Tarian watched her take up the mantle of leadership with a sense of pride.

Muttering broke out in Tarian's mind. The thoughts and opinions of hundreds of daemon and humans collided into a low hum of white noise that made individual words impossible to discern. It was like standing in the middle of a cocktail party filled with drunk politicians.

The First Advisor raised a hand, an action that quieted some of the commentary. Some, but not all. He turned to face the Council and spoke aloud, ignoring the conference going on in all their heads. Tarian struggled to follow his words over the noise vibrating her skull.

"First Mother long ago abandoned the Benata Way. She acted with forethought, with malice, and without provocation against the Keeper of the Water Artifact despite numerous objections and against the advice of the Council and in direct opposition to guidelines outline by ancient Agreement. First Mother has been judged to be in violation of that Agreement. The destruction of Benata City is one consequence of her actions. Forfeiture of the title First Mother is another. She will be known henceforth as Anadria Sha'Saorla and banished from the Benata. All who stand with her suffer her fate. So it was agreed. So shall it be."

The First Advisor turned back to Macari. "The law dictates succession. You, Naoise Sha'Macariah, daughter of Anadria Sha'Saorla, are the First Daughter. Saorla banished you for a short time, as was her right, but she did not and could not strip succession from you. Leadership is yours by right and by law. More importantly, leadership is granted willingly by all assembled."

First Advisor leaned toward Macari, his voice low and, for the first time, warm. "We have been waiting for the right moment to assert your ascendance. It seems that moment has arrived. At last." He breathed the last part, as if the words tasted like sweet, sweet water after being in the desert for a hundred years. Or a thousand.

He turned back to the Council and raised his fists to the sky. "We serve at the pleasure of Naoise Sha'Macariah, First Mother of the Benata. She directs our minds and captures our hearts. May she reign long, may we stay strong, may our Way continue in the strength of the wind and by the wisdom of the element gifted to us." The Advisor bowed his head toward Macari, pressing both fists to his chest in salute. A wave passed through the crowd behind him as each daemon bowed their head and put fists to chest in acknowledgment.

Macari watched, stunned. "But..."

Pure Air energy thickened around them. First Advisor's words formed the beginning of an Agreement, a bond that would last a lifetime. Macari would be able to return home. At least, she would once it was rebuilt. Tarian took Macari's hand to squeeze it. "Accept it, Macari. I can't think of anybody who deserves it more. You'll be a great leader. One with compassion. Courage. And really amazing friends." Tarian winked.

Macari nodded, slowly. She glanced at the First Advisor. He waited impassively for his leader's decision. She nodded again, then spoke, her voice high but clear and strong. "I, Naoise Sha'Macariah, daughter of Anadria Sha'Saorla, accept the office of First Mother to Benata City and all the rights and duties that reside within. May the wind grant me wisdom and the city peace."

A gusty breeze swirled through the crowd, bringing with it the barest hint of jasmine. Macari stood a little straighter and lifted her gaze to the sky. Tarian looked up and saw hundreds of large white birds circling overhead. She had the feeling that the Shee were as happy to see Macari in power as the daemon. She knew Jasmine was among them. The scent of the jasmine flower was far too strong for her not to be there. They'd come to see the rise of a new leader, and maybe even a new Way. Macari would bring a joy to her city that hadn't existed there for a long time.

Caught up in the moment, Tarian moved to stand in front of Macari and put fists to chest, the way she'd seen the Benata guards salute. "The House of Xannon stands ready to aid Macari of the Benata should she ever require it. May there forever be allegiance between us and those she leads."

The oath dangled in silence, waiting for a response.

Macari turned to Tarian. "We, the Benata, accept allegiance with the House of Xannon and stand ready to aid them should it ever be required. May all present be allies from this day forth against any force that would stand opposed. By penalty of loss of magic to the one who acts contrary or betrays the trust. Agreed?"

Tarian smiled. "Agreed."

Around them, power grew as each daemon and human added their agreement. When all had given it, the Agreement snapped into place with a thunderclap that shook the ground.

—29—

The crowd erupted into a flurry of discussions, some actually out loud. The Agreement left everyone a bit giddy and excited, despite the dark circumstances. Finally, First Advisor raised a hand and announced, "First Mother, Saorla has constructed a lubach. She spoke of the construction many times when she thought I could not hear. I have seen the location, and if the lubach is complete, we are all in imminent danger."

His words had the effect of ice water on a hot stove. A hiss of protests rose, passionate enough that Tarian saw real emotions on some daemon faces. The humans listening in all looked confused, except for one. Calliope's mouth made a perfect "Oh."

Tarian gave her sister a questioning look.

"Lubach act like funnels basically, or conduits for elemental energy. They're used in areas of natural power, usually to provide protections for the area or to bring energy in where it's lacking. You know, like a place that doesn't have water and they pipe it in from somewhere else?"

"Oh." Tarian pictured a pipe digging into the Source abereil. "She's stealing energy? To do what, split the planes again?"

First Advisor turned slightly toward Tarian. "That is doubtful, as the Stulos required the cooperation of all the Ancients, all the elements, and the Balance Court. Saorla does not have the same support since she is not in possession of several artifacts and the Balance Court remains bound by previous Agreement. Neither does she have the allegiance of at least three Ancient groups. Possibly four now, though that remains to be seen. Her task, then, would be difficult."

"Difficult. But not impossible?" Tarian asked.

He inclined his head. "The unique nature of your daughter might make the impossible, possible. Particularly if she combined the strength of those loyal to her with the Air Artifact. I believe that was her misguided hope."

Excitement rushed through her stomach and chest and made her talk too fast. "But she doesn't have Air. I saw it disappear. If we get our hands on it before she does, then her plan won't work, right?"

First Advisor considered. "Possibly. Again, Keeper, your daughter's unique abilities make our suppositions…insubstantial."

"She can't get to Ember. Ember's heavily guarded."

He inclined his head in acknowledgment. "Yes, I saw that she resides with the Mayfanata. It might provide a small amount of time and some distraction. However, as the Agreement has already been broken, she might not be bound by the consequences. She could, in theory, attempt a breach of the Mayfanata."

Tarian considered everything they'd figured out in the last few minutes. The crowd noise gradually faded into the background and was lost to her own meandering mind. Her thoughts bounced through what she'd been told to what she'd witnessed firsthand. The fires in Fort Worth. The bubble field. The Source abereil. First Mother feeding it, or drawing from it, she wasn't sure which. Forming new bubbles. Sending them around the world to do their worst. Ember and her ability to pull the energy from anything near her and magnify that energy tenfold. Her sweet face determined, purple with effort, as she destroyed two abereil simultaneously.

First Mother wanted to siphon power to recreate a Stulos or something similar.

Siphon.

Absorb.

Illumination flashed through her thoughts as the pieces slid into place. She could picture exactly what First Mother planned. She pictured the daemon hovering over the Source, Ember positioned above it, her unique ability absorbing as much as her tiny body could hold. She pictured First Mother working Air, possibly through the Air Artifact if she could manage to get her hands on it again, to enable Ember to hold even more. And then?

Tarian shook her head, trying to puzzle it out. "She won't want to just gather more energy. She's not building something to split the world apart. Look how well that turned out before. No, she wants more than that. I saw the look in her eyes. She's obsessed. She wants to posses power. All of it. She won't be satisfied until she controls it all. When she does, she'll be the only one with magic. Nobody else. Not humans or daemon or even Ancients. She'll take it all."

A collective gasp rippled. Humans and daemon shifted uncomfortably as they processed the idea. Calliope covered her mouth.

"Why does she hate us so much?" Tarian whispered. She couldn't wrap her head around the idea that First Mother would destroy everything, simply to make sure humans either did not have magic or did not exist. Or both. It was a lot of hate, to want to abolish life on that scale. And the idea was in complete violation of the Benata Way.

"It don't matter why," Alex said. "Not anymore. We gotta stop her."

Tarian looked at her friend. "Yes, we do. The goal remains... seal off the Source abereil. Without it, her plan fails. The prisms are already there, right?"

Alex rubbed the back of his neck. "Letta was finishing up the last one, yeah. But...she shoulda been here by now."

Tarian looked around, thinking Letta might have shown up and they just missed her arrival in the excitement. Tarian didn't see her, but the woman was short. She'd blend in with the crowd. Tarian focused on tracking her. At first she detected nothing. Then, finally, a faint signal reached her. It was distant and cushioned, but it was solid. "She's not here. I don't think she left the field. Maybe she stayed to keep watch?"

Alex looked doubtful. "Maybe."

Something queasy stirred in her stomach. "Did you leave Sentinels with her?"

Alex nodded. "Some. 'Bout a dozen. And some Caraigg. They can't come out in the open, but they were gonna stay below and guard the prisms."

"Maybe she stayed with them." She wished she felt as confident as she sounded. "Maybe you should go check on her? I have a feeling we'll need all the Sentinels in place to finish this. When we find the Air Artifact, First Mother, I mean Saorla, is going to want to snatch it. We'll need to run interference long enough to seal up the Source."

"Keeper, be advised that no seal will hold with a lubach in place," First Advisor said. "It would prevent the shield from sealing. There would be a gap through which the lubach would still operate. The lubach must be destroyed if you hope to contain the Source."

"And you know how to do that?" Tarian asked.

"Overload it with power." First Advisor said so matter-of-factly he might have been giving her the recipe for chocolate chip cookies.

"Great." Tarian shifted her feet, ready to run or fight or...she wasn't sure what. Something. She had to do something. Her fists clenched so hard the nails bit her palms.

Tarian tracked the Air Artifact, and the bond snapped into place. She turned in a slow circle but couldn't pinpoint the direction. Then she realized why and looked up. "I think I know where the Air Artifact went."

Macari looked up where hundreds of gigantic white birds still circled. "You're probably right. An unbound artifact would return to the maker. It would go home."

Tarian, Macari, and Calliope left Alex with the First Advisor to organize and plan for an assault at the bubble field. Macari took Tarian and Calliope by the hand and traveled with them to the hill she'd used to access the Corsaerie every day since she was a child. The city looked like some dystopian future from that vantage point, not the very real present.

Tarian peeked over the edge of the hill at the dagger-like rocks below. "I can't believe I'm even thinking about doing this again."

"If you want an alliance with the Shee, you have to. They won't come to you. You can try to bargain for the artifact as well, but I"m not sure it'll work. Calli will probably have to seek the artifact alone. I'm not sure what that's like. It hasn't been done in a really long time."

Macari looked out over the vista, a hint of sadness playing around her eyes. "I used to love coming here. The Shee were something constant and comforting when I was a child. They were the ones to discover I could walk the wind. They showed me the way. Jasmine was more like a mother to me than..." She stopped speaking and let the words drift on the wind.

"Think they'll give Calli the artifact?" Tarian watched the birds circling overhead. The wingspans were so wide, and there were so many, that it looked like huge fluffy white cloud in constant motion.

"I hope so." Macari sounded doubtful.

The scent of jasmine flowers, soft and delicate, drifted by. A soft breeze, almost like a hand, caressed Tarian's shoulders, and a light sing-song voice filled her thoughts.

Keeper of Water, if you would seek to speak with the Shee, then you must leap, Jasmine sang. *But Keeper and sister, be fairly warned, the Air Artifact has been unduly scorned, and power is not something easily won.*

Tarian glanced at Calliope. "You ready?"

Calliope's eyes shone with far more excitement than they should.

"Oh yes. I never thought I'd ever have the chance to meet the Shee. They have so much knowledge. So much history. I could spend a lifetime with the Shee and not learn enough. They're like a living library." Calliope turned with a small hop to Macari. "How do we get up there?"

Macari giggled. "Just dance." She took Calliope's hands in hers and spun. The two giggled like eight-year-olds in the playground. They twirled and danced and laughed and leapt.

Calliope's startled scream, when she saw they no longer danced on the solid ground, made Tarian giggle. She sobered fast when she realized she had to make the leap on her own.

Macari had been her safety net before, but if Tarian wanted to make a deal with the Shee, she had to go alone. She needed them as allies. She needed their strength, their wisdom, and their protection. If not for herself, for Ember. More importantly, she needed to know they would not ally with the former First Mother.

She was the only one with authority to make an Agreement like that for the House of Xannon. She was the Keeper. Air was her secondary ability. She could do this.

She hoped she could.

She took a quick glance over the edge and wished she hadn't. The angry maw of death stared back at her in the shape of tooth-like jagged rocks. If she leapt and failed, she'd impale herself on them. Not a pleasant thought.

Tarian shook off the image and took a deep breath. She took another for good measure, then backed up a couple of feet. She jumped up and down a couple of times, working up courage.

She took one last look at Macari and her sister, now mere specks against the gigantic wingspans of the Shee Ancients.

"I can do this, I can do this, I can do this." She gathered Air energy around herself, took two running steps, and jumped.

For the first few seconds, she felt weightless. She didn't drift like a feather on the wind—it was more like suspended animation. She tried to remember everything she'd learned from Macari. She tried to let go. She tried to remember she'd done this before.

Then she dropped like a thousand-pound boulder. She sucked in a scream and flailed around with her arms for a second or two. Then instinct and muscle memory kicked in. The energy she'd gathered formed into a shield to block her fall. With that in place, she realized she didn't need it. She twisted her body around and pretended she was in the ocean. She treated the wind and the open air like the vast deep sea and swam.

She wasn't nearly as graceful as Macari. She wasn't a dancer. She didn't feel elegant anywhere but in the water. But a few seconds later, the air wrapped around her like the waves and lifted her body up up up.

Tarian kept her thoughts firmly focused on the ocean. She pictured her dolphin friends in place of the Shee and swam straight for them, sure she looked ridiculous but not really caring.

The longer she swam, the further away the Shee seemed to be. Nothing brought her any closer, though she was now several thousand feet above the ground. Oxygen thinned, and cold gripped her with a frosty hand. She couldn't see Macari or Calliope anymore. Just the constantly moving white wings and the endless blue of the sky.

She formed a bubble around her head to provide oxygen, just as she would in the ocean. It helped, but didn't stop the pressure on her body, especially her lungs. She'd suffocate if she stayed here much longer. She wasn't meant to be up high like this. She was Water. This wasn't natural. Nobody could really fly without wings.

Blood rushed through her ears. Adrenaline had come and gone, leaving her arms and legs feeling weak and her chest tight. Her lungs constricted, and her stomach knotted.

She was a fool to even try this. The Shee wouldn't help. They wouldn't want to help anyone now. They'd been betrayed by the leader of the Benata. Why would they ever seek another alliance?

Keeper of Water, you seek to control that which you may not securely hold. When you let go, then you will see what it truly is to be Shee.

"Let go?" Tarian twisted around, but she saw no one. "Let go of what?"

No voice responded. Just the wind rushing in her ears and the beating of her own heart.

"What the hell do you want from me?" Tarian shouted. Her voice disappeared in the vacuum around her. Her body was compressed like she was a thousand miles under the surface of the ocean. Her skin felt raw. She couldn't get a deep breath. The wings continued to beat, but they were too far away.

Her mouth was so dry she couldn't swallow. The sides of her throat stuck together. She licked her lips, but the salt there just made everything worse.

The idea that salt was coating her lips didn't sit right. Something was out of place. Something was very, very wrong.

Salt.

She slapped her forehead. She'd used Water to protect herself from Air. Water weighed her down. She'd used the wrong element. She brought Water into an Air domain.

No wonder they wouldn't talk to her.

Tarian looked down, and immediately wished she hadn't. She couldn't even see the rocks anymore. Her imagination and instinct had allowed her to rise a lot higher than she should have.

It took several long moments to convince herself to let go of Water. To reach for that side of herself that used Air, and Air alone. She focused on the wings still high above her, on the brilliant white of the feathers, the way the sun glinted off them like they were made of stardust. She pictured the wings wrapped around her. She envisioned the softness of them and the strength. Let herself feel the protection they offered. They wouldn't let her fall. Just as she would never let someone drown in the ocean.

Then she released the bubble and shield she'd formed with it and hoped she was right.

She plunged like an anchor into the sea, through clouds and down down down. But this time, she resisted the urge to form a shield. She didn't make a helmet of oxygen. She tried her best to feel the sheer joy of the wind rushing through her hair.

It didn't work. Even though she could harness Air energy, at the moment Air felt like the enemy. She'd been a fool to trust it. To trust *them*. She couldn't believe Macari would just let her fall like this. After everything they'd been through, and everything they had yet to face. The Source abereil would destroy everything. It had already killed Daric.

The thought of him suffocated her. His face loomed in front of her until it was all she could see. His eyes as he fell, the accusation she knew had to be there. She'd let him fall.

She deserved to go the same way.

Sadness seeped into her chest and made it hard to breathe. The ground rushed to greet her, and she wondered if it mattered. It didn't really. Daric...she choked. Tears pushed into her eyelashes and out.

She couldn't do this without him. Didn't even want to. What did it matter anyway?

«Oh Tari." Macari's voice in her ear barely penetrated. "I'm so sorry."

Something warm and soothing wrapped around her body, but it didn't comfort her tortured soul. She couldn't shake the guilt. Couldn't shake the pain. She wanted to fall.

"No, you don't," Macari whispered in her ear, and it was like the daemon's voice surrounded her in wispy clouds of comfort and compassion. "Your daughter needs you, Tari. We need you too. Daric wouldn't want this for you. I know it hurts. But it won't hurt forever. I promise."

"It should." Tarian choked on the words. "I let him die. I let him go."

"You didn't." Macari hugged her tight. "You couldn't save him. Nobody could."

Tarian couldn't breathe, the grief was so strong. She shook with it and let it all come out in rasping sobs. Everything she'd been trying not to feel, everything she'd been trying not to think about, and everything she'd held back came rushing out. She let it go, and Macari held her until she couldn't cry anymore.

She wasn't sure how long they fell or floated. Gradually she became aware that wind no longer rushed in her ears. That she hadn't hit the ground. She wasn't impaled on rocks.

Air energy circled through her body as if her skin didn't exist. She didn't channel it or control it. It simply existed in and around her without effort or thought. It was wonderful. She could take a deep breath with ease. She shifted away from Macari, embarrassed and humbled by the friendship the daemon had just shown her.

Macari gave her a quick squeeze and released her. "That's what friends are for. Besides, emotions are my thing."

Tarian rubbed her nose. "Yeah, well, wish you'd just suppress them. I could do with a few less."

"No, you couldn't. Trust me, the longer you put that off, the worse it gets."

Tarian looked around, realizing for the first time that they walked on a pale white pathway. Several Shee stood nearby, their wings forming a circle around her. She couldn't see beyond them, but she could see the sky above and through the path below to some clouds. They looked as if they might work their way into storm clouds, with hints of gray that swelled the edges with moisture. "Where are we?"

Exactly where you wished to be, Keeper of Water.

Tarian turned to face the Shee. There were three, though she sensed more just beyond their wings. She sniffed but detected no hint of jasmine.

She didn't see Calliope. Fear stabbed her heart. "Where's my sister?" When they didn't answer, she turned to Macari. "Where's Calli?"

"You are granted an audience, Keeper of Water. Not answers."

The one on the left spoke with a gruff male voice. He looked stern, like a father chastising a small child.

"As with time, Air moves forever forward." The middle one flashed her a warning look. A teacher. Definitely.

"Speak your purpose or leave." The one on the right seemed impatient and direct, like a teenager. Tarian liked her immediately.

"We...Calliope that is...need the Air Artifact. First Mother... the former First Mother...had it, but she lost it. Do you know where it is?" She spoke to the teenager, hoping the direct approach would work best with her.

"Your perceived need is not our concern. The artifact is not lost."

"You mean it went back to First...Saorla?" Tarian said, frustration rising. "She still controls it?"

"Air cannot be controlled." The father sounded affronted.

"Air aids who it will," the teacher said.

"Air must be earned," the teenager said, her voice stern. "If that is all you require, then you should leave." The teenager gave her a significant look.

"Wait! I...we...need your help."

"What you wish needs examination," the father said.

Tarian turned to Macari, but the daemon wasn't there. Tarian whirled around, but she stood alone in the circle of Shee. "What the hell is going on? Where's my sister? Where's Macari?" She faced the three again, but they'd vanished. She stood alone on the transparent pathway surrounded by wings.

"She'll destroy the world. Is that what you want?" She shouted all the frustration and anger and anxiety that had been building for the last week.

The wings surrounding the path joined and merged and evolved into one very tall, very naked Shee Ancient. He looked regal, stern but not unkind, with pure white skin, silver eyes, and a body that blinded. He was the most perfect male specimen she'd ever seen. "As a creature of Air, you bring Water and Fire. Fire fuels the temper, but Air gives it desire." He smiled, and it almost hurt to look at, it was so perfect. "You have within you that which you need. Balance has seen it, so it will be."

The sing-song lilt, and the scent of jasmine confused her. She associated both with one particular Shee, but this was definitely not Jasmine.

He inclined his head, and dimples appeared in his cheeks as he smiled. "The Shee can be many, the Shee can be one. The Shee can move mountains, or see you undone. The Shee are Ancient, a part of the breeze…" He looked at her through long, white lashes. "The Shee are as simple and complex as the air you breathe, Keeper. We are knowledge, wisdom, and information. We are all things, or no things. Air bends the will and time and space. It shapes and binds and grows and heals. Air moves through all other elements. It is as boundless as thought, and as fluid."

She'd heard tales of an archangel called Michael. She thought they must be based on this Ancient.

He laughed, a deep belly laugh. "We are no angel, as those don't exist. We are what we are. But we like the name Michael. You may use it, if you wish. We will answer."

"You hear my thoughts."

"Keeper of Water, we *are* thought."

Tarian's gaze followed the curve of his smile to his eyes. They twinkled, but she detected hints of steel behind the amusement. It was the face of a leader. Her hopes sank. But she had to try.

"I made a promise to the Dulra, to gather the pieces my daughter will need to restore balance. And Daric...his...he can't... it can't have been for nothing." Tarian swallowed the lump in her throat that using Daric's name caused. "If Calliope has the Air Artifact, I can stop Saorla from destroying the world."

Michael gave her a kind, sympathetic look. "Your sibling already embarks on the trials of a Seeker. Air chooses as it wills and must be earned. Once begun, the quest must be completed. A prize too easily won is no prize at all. Trust and alliance come with cost and sacrifice."

"Sacrifice." She wondered what he meant by that, but could see from the look in his eyes and the set of his shoulders that he wouldn't explain any further. She had to wait and hope Calliope made it through the trials.

Tarian stared at the pathway in front of her. She could see clouds billowing below. It was serene and peaceful, and a complete lie. She knew what lay beyond those clouds. Thousands of abereil. Chaos. Death.

"Even in darkness, a spark of hope can light the way, Keeper of Water."

Tarian looked at Michael. Maybe she'd been going about this all wrong. She's asked for help, but that wasn't exactly what she wanted or needed. He'd told her that much. She needed much more than momentary aid. She needed a commitment. A bond that would last a lifetime. She thought about how to word the request and settled on a direct approach as the best one. "Will the Shee agree to an alliance with the House of Xannon?"

Michael smiled his approval, though she wasn't sure if it was her thought process or her actual request that he liked, if it even mattered. "Speak the specifics, Keeper."

Tarian considered what she needed. Ember would face her own battles with Saorla when the time came to bring balance to the world. Tarian might slow the daemon down by containing the Source abereil, but it wouldn't stop Saorla from trying again and again. The Dulra must have seen that. It was why they'd made the Agreement with her in the first place. Her job was to get Ember ready for that final battle, when she was old enough.

To do that, Ember would need knowledge of all four elements and the support of the Ancients who personified them. The dolphins would show Ember everything she'd need to know about the Water element. The Water Ancients allied with the House of Xannon thousands of years ago, and the bond had been passed from mother to daughter ever since.

Tarian already held an Agreement with the Caraigg for Ember's sake. They would show her everything she'd need to know about Earth.

She had a feeling Lasair, the Fire Ancient, merely waited for her to ask. He was a hard creature to pin down. Fire was chaos, and Lasair didn't like to remain in one place for too long. He'd had enough of that as the Guardian of the Between for thousands of years.

That left Air.

Michael smiled. "You ask for knowledge, information, and wisdom for the Scion. And what would you provide in return?"

Tarian started. "I guess reading my mind makes this faster, but I have to say it's really creepy." She thought about it. What could she ever offer beings as old, as powerful, as ancient as the Shee?

She'd broken a Stulos to free the Caraigg. But the Shee were no longer captive. They didn't need anything.

"You are mistaken, Keeper of Water. Ancients are not all powerful. We are not gods, as I see in your thoughts. We have strengths and weaknesses like all living creatures. Air alone cannot provide that which we all crave. If the Dulra are correct, only one can provide that."

She looked at him questioningly.

"Balance, Keeper. Air is the thread that strives to bind and to grow. But we are not able to achieve balance alone. We cannot unite the others without a catalyst to draw the elements together and disperse the energy with an even hand. That, Keeper, is what we hope Xannon will provide. Continue your Agreement with the Balance Court. Prepare the Scion. We will aid her, when the time is right. If we fail…" He spread his hands.

"The world fails. Game over." Tarian swallowed. "High stakes."

"For all of us." Michael nodded. His dimple had disappeared. "Do you agree?"

She hesitated. "Will you ally only with Xannon?"

"I cannot make such a promise. Other agreements already govern. They may not be negated." He looked regretful but firm.

She thought it through. There were probably loopholes. The Agreement as she'd stated it was simple and more than a little vague. And she wasn't good at contracts. She looked into Michael's eyes. He met her gaze with kindness. But she had no idea what lay in his thoughts. Ancients didn't communicate like humans. Still. Her instinct pushed her to speak the word, "Agreed."

Michael smiled. "Agreed." He bowed his head. The Agreement settled around them, the weight of it pushing on her shoulders and chest as it sank into her soul. She'd just promised the fate of her daughter to the Ancients. And they'd just promised their fate to her. It was monumental. Epic. With no real detail whatsoever.

Michael's perfect body sprouted feathers, until it was covered in white. The white revolved and separated into the three original Shee.

The father had Michael's silver eyes. The teacher had his smile and dimple. The teenager had his confidence.

"How many of you are there, really? One? A hundred?"

The teenager laughed Michael's laugh.

The three exploded into a million feathers that swirled and coalesced into giant birds that took wing and vanished into the blue like mist.

She stood alone on the pathway, surrounded by wings that began to slowly pull away. The path started to dissolve. She stared at it, disbelief flooding her. They were going to drop her. Just let her fall to her death. Anger replaced the disbelief, followed by determination and a will to live.

The path vanished, and Tarian plummeted. This time, she ignored the approach of death and looked for the bond with her sister. Calliope had come here with Macari. She had to be somewhere close by.

Calliope's location flickered, indicating rapid movement. But the direction remained constant. Tarian twisted until she'd aligned her position with Calliope.

"Leap of faith, huh?" she muttered. "I'll show you a leap of faith." She fixated on Calliope's moving signature and traveled.

—31—

Tarian popped out of travel and was immediately swept along a cold, fearsome, relentless wind. It smelled so clean and fresh it hurt her nose.

It took some effort to position her body in what she thought was an upright position. The wind carried her so fast, and the only way to move was to treat it like water and wave her arms against the flow. Below, greens, browns, reds. Above, blue, white, gray. All of it flashing by so fast she couldn't make out any details.

"Tari!" Calliope's voice whipped by, gone almost before Tarian heard it.

Calliope wobbled in the Air stream a few feet ahead of Tarian. She looked pale, almost transparent. Shades of white and gray, like a cloud gathering moisture for a storm. Her face had turned as white as clown makeup. Her hair, silver.

"Calli!" Tarian struggled to turn toward her sister and move closer, but all she managed to do was half-turn and tumble twice.

Calliope smiled, a pale watery thing. "I got it!" Her eyes glowed pure white light, with no trace of the brown they used to be.

The Air stream dipped suddenly, plummeting them

downward at a rate Tarian was sure broke the sound barrier. If there were any sound but the roaring wind. Calliope's hair stretched out behind her like a silver flag in a hurricane. The hue of the stream shifted from white to green. They sped past blobs that Tarian assumed were buildings or people or perhaps large animals. They reached the bottom of a trough, and as they started to climb once more, their momentum slowed enough that if she turned her head just right she could catch glimpses of things as they past. Enough to make out details. Horrible, deadly details.

Crumbled buildings. Bodies lying disjointed on the broken ground. The snatched wail of a child. An explosion so bright it burned into her retinas. Flashes of power. Surges of energy.

"Calli!" Tarian reached for her sister, straining to get her hand close enough to grab her.

"Tarian..." Calliope's voice barely registered. It was swallowed by the roar of the wind. Her sister's outline vanished. All that remained was the Air Artifact, glistening with its own internal light. The world rushed by, oblivious.

Tarian fixated on Calliope's signature again. The bond remained strong and vibrant and piercingly close. But Tarian couldn't see her. Not even a shadow.

They rushed through another town, where one side of the street had been flattened while the other remained untouched. More bodies. Confusion. Panic. For the barest fraction of a section, Tarian's gaze locked with a woman who stood in the middle of the street. She was tall and frumpy, with long graying hair and solid white eyes. The woman's lips pressed together, her eyes narrowed, and the feeling of absolute hatred poured from her.

Then she and the town were gone. The stream had moved them beyond it, away from the devastation and the haunting white eyes.

"Calli!" Tarian tried to shout, but the sound disappeared the second it left her lips.

"I'm here." Calliope's voice flowed past Tarian's ears. "Take my hand."

"I can't see you!"

"You don't need to." Calliope sounded amused. "I can see you."

Tarian put out her hand but felt nothing.

"Don't try so hard," Calliope said.

Tarian closed her eyes and held out her hand, fully expecting her sister to take it. Calliope grasped it tight and squeezed. The wind stopped.

Tarian opened her eyes and gaped at her sister. She'd morphed into an angelic cherub without wings. Her blond hair had turned white with streaks of silver. Her skin looked made of cotton, and her eyes had changed into pure white orbs. She grinned. "I got it." Her voice was full of pride and excitement. "The Air Artifact. It chose me!"

"Calli…" Tarian couldn't finish the sentence. Couldn't think what to say.

Calliope blinked and glanced around. "I never knew how complex the wind really is. It's so full of life, Tari. I never knew. Tari…I can see your light. It's so beautiful."

Tarian glanced down, but she saw the same dirty jeans and stupid T-shirt. No light. Nothing special. "Calli, I'm…are you okay? Do you feel okay?"

"I'm more than okay. I've never felt like this before. I'm sure I can heal more than ever now. I can see your headache. It vibrates." Calliope reached up and touched Tarian's temple. "Right here."

Tarian was so used to having a headache by now that she

hadn't really noticed until Calliope touched her and it vanished.

"Calli...what happened?"

Calliope hesitated before speaking. "It doesn't matter. What's important is I have it. We can stop her now, Tari."

"Stop who?" A raspy voice behind them made them both whirl around. The woman Tarian had seen in the small town street stood there. Her eyes no longer glowed white, but it was her. Same hate. The eyes, so pale blue they blended with the edge of the horizon, glared at Tarian with enough venom to kill a city full of people.

"You," Calliope said.

Tarian looked from Calliope to the old woman, suddenly realizing who the woman had to be. "You haven't aged well, Anadria Sha'Saorla."

Saorla's lips tightened. "You have something that belongs to me."

Tarian looked at Calliope and frowned. "I don't have anything that belongs to her. Do you?" She looked back at Saorla. "We don't have anything of yours."

Saorla turned her hateful gaze on Calliope. "You are unworthy. You defile an object so ancient you cannot fathom the depths of it. It will destroy you. You will return it to me."

Calliope held up her hands. They were both empty. "I have nothing that needs returning."

Tarian forced herself not to look behind her sister to see if she'd dropped the artifact back there.

First Mother waved a negligent hand, and a travel portal appeared beside her. She smiled, a thing that crawled along her face and never reached her eyes. "I propose an Agreement. The artifact for the child."

Tarian stared into the travel portal so long without blinking, her eyes watered. Wavering in the depths of the portal she could see a familiar living room filled with white furniture. Ruarc lay motionless on the floor, blood pooling around his head. His eyes stared at nothing. Near the windows, she saw Kia, slumped against the windows, blood trails where she'd struck it hard enough to crush her skull.

In between, two daemon guards held a young girl tightly between them.

"Ember!" Tarian rushed forward and bounced back when she struck a transparent shield.

First Mother raised an eyebrow. "Agree now, or she dies."

Tarian held up a hand to stop Calliope from moving. "You won't kill her. You need her."

"I never *needed* a daemon spawn, *Keeper*." First Mother's voice gave sarcasm a sarcastic edge. She made the title sound like the biggest insult she could conjure. "I am daemon. I am older and more powerful than you can possibly fathom. I have protected my people for thousands of years. I never *needed* anyone. You have one minute, *Keeper.*"

Tarian glanced at Calliope, giving her a shake of the head. "No deal." She was so sure First Mother would not harm Ember. Whatever the daemon might say, Tarian saw the hesitation lines in her forehead. She couldn't hide the flash of concern when she saw Tarian say no. First Mother didn't want to follow through on her threat.

But she *was* desperate. No doubt about that. She wanted the Air Artifact as badly as Tarian had wanted it.

"Tarian doesn't have it. I do." Calliope took a step forward.

"No, Calli." Tarian put a hand out, but Calliope moved it gently aside.

First Mother turned the venomous stare on Calliope. "If you

misrepresent, if you make an Agreement and do not possess the artifact, you will forfeit your life."

Within the portal, Ember screamed. Tarian couldn't make out what the guards did, but she saw the result in the obvious distress on Ember's face. "Stop!" Power welled up inside Tarian. She readied herself to strike.

Calliope rushed forward and shouted, "I'll give it to you!"

"No!" Tarian tried to stop her sister, but it was too late.

Calliope held out her hand and the Air Artifact appeared into it. It throbbed with white, silver, and blue light.

First Mother's eyes lit up with triumph.

Calliope tossed it to First Mother.

First Mother snatched it and vanished.

Tarian's gut tightened. "Crap, Calli. We could have…"

"Ember!" Calliope pointed to the portal. The guards still assaulted her daughter, and the pain on Ember's face was quite evident.

Tarian ran to the portal and dove through.

It flashed through her mind how incredibly stupid it was to jump into someone else's portal. How badly it could go wrong. But Ember was in danger. It just didn't matter—she had to get to her daughter.

She dumped out the other side, followed by Calliope. They landed on a heap, tangled together like kittens with string. Tarian pushed away from her sister and ran into something hard and sharp.

"Ow!"

They both scrambled to get to their feet. Tarian scanned the room for attack. "Ember!"

"What the fuck?" An astonished male voice said. It came from behind her somewhere.

Tarian spun, ready to strike. Power gathered in her hands, so much of it they crackled. Heat pooled in her chest. She'd reached for her most deadly combination, nearly all Fire. She planned on taking the daemon out of the equation as fast as possible, before they could react.

Except the person she faced wasn't daemon.

"Who the fuck are you? What the fuck is goin' on here?" A man in boxer shorts stood next to a kitchen island, knife in one hand, toast in the other. He'd obviously been in the middle of making breakfast.

Tarian wheeled around, but didn't see Ruarc or Kia or any sign of Ember. Calliope looked as confused as she felt. "Where is she?"

"I don't…" Calliope said.

"Where's who? Who the fuck are you, lady? How'd you get in here?" The man had a thick Brooklyn accent. "Am I being punked? Did Bernie put you up to this?"

"Bernie?" Tarian's thoughts flew by too fast to catch them all. She'd seen Ember in the portal. She'd seen Ruarc's dead body. Kia. All of them. They were here. In the portal. There was no way to fake that.

The man waved the knife around. "Yeah, bet he did. Gettin' back at me for that firehouse thing last year. Well, you can tell him he failed. I caught ya red-handed. Now you can get outta here and just you tell him he's a fucking loser. Tell him that." He used the knife to point at the door.

She had the urge to check the rest of the apartment. She even turned toward the hallway, which looked identical to Ruarc's. The layout was exactly the same.

"Tari, she's not here. They aren't here. It's a lie." Calliope grabbed her arm to stop her from running out the door. "It's a lie.

She bent reality. Air can do that."

Tarian checked for signatures. Nothing. The man with the knife didn't have a drop of magic in him. "How can she fake a portal? We're in New York. This is definitely New York!" Tarian pointed at the window. "Those are his windows, Calli."

"You bet your ass it's New York." The man took a bite of toast and spoke while chewing. "You people on meds? You escape from one of those, whatsit, facilities?" He held his hands up to make an awkward knife-filled quote symbol around the word "facilities."

"You're right. It's New York," Calliope said, putting extra emphasis on the name. "Not Mayfanata. New York."

Tarian closed her eyes, feeling like an idiot. "Shit. Shit shit shit." She opened them again. "Was any of it real?"

Calliope bit her lip. "I just don't know."

"What the fuck is wrong with your eyes? You blind or somethin'? Bernie sent me a blind chick? For what?" The man dropped the knife on the counter and took another bite of toast. "He send ya for a little somethin' somethin', eh? I ain't ever done it with a blind chick before."

"Bite me." Tarian rolled her eyes at him before grabbing Calliope's hand. "We gotta check it out. I have to be sure. Hang tight."

She pictured Ruarc's living room, with the white sofas and the guards and the pristine kitchen area, and traveled.

They landed in exactly the same spot, but in an entirely different living room in an entirely different plane. The protection of the place settled around Tarian, as if it tested her before it decided she was worthy of remaining.

Ruarc was sitting on the sofa when they appeared. He stood quickly, concern infiltrating his expression. "Keeper? What has happened?"

"You're alive." Tarian looked him up and down to be sure. "That's really you, right? Where's Ember? Is she okay?" She sniffed, reassured when Ruarc's signature hit, followed immediately by several other daemon, Ember, and Kia.

Ruarc looked confused. He gestured to one of the guards, who left the room at a run. "She's in her lessons with Kia. If anything were wrong, there'd be an alarm. What has happened?"

"First Mother hasn't been here? She's not attacking the city? Are there ercklings?"

"No." Ruarc's voice was flat and matter-of-fact. "If she tried to breach the city, she would die. That's the penalty of the Agreement."

"Shiii…" Tarian stopped the word mid curse when she saw

Ember and Kia running through the door. It took her breath away, seeing Ember looking more like a girl than a child. She looked healthy and happy and older than she had a right to be.

"Mama!" Ember ran toward her, her face bright and happy, her eyes lit with excitement. "You came! Kia said you would."

Tarian bent to give her daughter a hug and then lifted her to give her an even tighter one. "Hey, spark! I missed you."

"Missed you more." Ember sounded muffled because she'd buried her face in Tarian's hair. "Is it time to go? I miss the ocean. Ruarc says we can go swim when we go home."

"He's right. But we can't go just yet." Tarian glanced at Calliope. Her sister was smiling fondly at her niece, but it looked odd and more than a little scary in combination with the pure white of her eyes.

"Ms. Tari, if you don't mind me sayin', you look a bit put out." Kia flashed a smile of concerned understanding. She looked at Calliope. Confusion traveled across her face. "Ms. Calli? You okay?"

"I'm more than okay, Kia." Calliope smiled.

"You have been in contact with the Air Artifact," Ruarc said in a matter-of-fact tone. "You have bonded. Interesting."

Calliope turned her pure white gaze on Ruarc. Her smile was enigmatic, and she said nothing.

"You bonded?" Tarian asked. "Then how did you give the artifact to Saorla?"

Calliope turned to her. "Air can be bent. She saw what she wanted to see. Just as she tricked us, with the travel portal."

Tarian considered the words. "But, you agreed…she put the penalty as death." She looked her sister up and down. "How are you still standing here?"

"She stated her terms, but I didn't. I never agreed to anything.

It's all in the intent. I told her I'd give "it" to her. I didn't define the word "it" and she didn't ask. She assumed." Calliope smiled.

Tarian grinned at her sister, pride making it a lot wider than it probably should be given the circumstances. "You little devil. Nice one, Calli."

"Things gonna be okay now, Ms. Tari?" Kia asked.

Tarian looked at the young woman in front of her. When she'd left, Kia was sixteen years old. Now she looked early twenties, with liquid chocolate eyes that held the depths of the universe within them. "I hope so."

"What has happened?" Ruarc said. "What brought you here?"

"I…nothing. Apparently. Someone played a practical joke." She tried to keep her voice light. Her mood playful. It was a struggle. A huge one. Anxiety made her want to move on, and fast. First Mother had the Air Artifact and a clear shot at the Source abereil. But the last thing she needed was Ember reacting to her mood.

Don't worry, Mama. I'm not a baby anymore. I know how to stop.

Tarian put Ember down, startled. Ember's smile was impish and contagious. "No, you're definitely not a baby anymore." Tarian glanced at Calliope. "She takes after you, Calli."

Calliope held out her arms. "Give me a hug, you."

Ember skipped into Calliope's arms. "Aunt Calli, your eyes are so pretty! Can I go home with you?"

Calliope hesitated, looking at Tarian for an answer.

"I'm sorry, sparky, not just yet. I can't stay. There's something we need to do first."

Ember's lips pushed out in a cute pout. "But I miss the dolphins! And I promise I won't make those bubbles anymore. I didn't mean to."

Tarian frowned. She knelt next to Ember and Calliope. "Sweetie, you aren't being punished. You know that, right? You didn't do anything wrong. Nothing." Tarian tapped her on the nose. "You did a lot of things very right. You're here because it wasn't safe at home. That's all. And I promise, it'll be over soon, and then you'll be able to come home. I'm going to fix things."

She thought of Daric and nearly lost her composure.

Ember touched Tarian's hand. "Something bad happened." She said it as fact, not question. Like she already knew.

Tarian nodded. Swallowed. "But it's nothing for you to worry about. Ruarc is here to protect you. And Kia." She glanced at Kia, who nodded.

"We be just fine, Ms. Tari. One thing Mama always said, this too shall pass. It won't be long now. Things'll be right as rain. You just wait and see if they aren't. Though Mama also said sometimes it do get dark before it gets light."

"Yes, it does," Tarian said.

Take me with you. I can help.

Ember grinned, a dimple appearing to make the offer sweet and tempting. Tarian shook her head, returning the grin. *You've learned how to flirt.*

"I can. I can help." Ember said the words out loud.

Tarian let her apprehension at the very idea show on her face. "No, sparky. This is important. No matter what happens. No matter what you hear. I need you to stay here with Ruarc and Kia. Okay?"

Ember looked doubtful, and Tarian caught a flash of calculated mischief in her eyes. Tarian took her daughter by the shoulders and turned her, putting them nose to nose. She pushed her forehead into Ember's. *I need to know you're safe. You're the hope for the future, spark. I can't do what I need to do if I think you're in danger. Do you understand?*

Ember nodded, but Tarian could tell she wasn't happy about it. Tarian pulled away so she could look into Ember's eyes. "Make you a deal. You stay with Ruarc and Kia until I send for you. And when I do, we'll go on vacation. A week in the ocean, with the Ancients. Agree?"

Ember tilted her head, looking thoughtful. "What's the cost? Ruarc says every Agreement has a cost. For if you're bad and don't do the thing you promised."

Tarian flashed a I-can't-believe-you're-teaching-her-that look at Ruarc. He looked completely unaffected and proud of his protégée.

"What do you think the cost should be?" Tarian focused on her daughter. Ember thought about it, tapping a finger on the side of her face.

She brightened. "If we don't, *two* weeks' vacation."

"That doesn't sound like much of a cost, sweetheart," Ruarc said. "If you would like the person to follow through on their promise, then it must cost *them* something if they do not. I suspect your mother wouldn't mind two weeks in the ocean, right?"

Tarian couldn't help the chuckle that bubbled out. "I'd like to have a whole month. But people frown on that sort of thing."

"What if your mother had to instead let you remain with me here for those two weeks?" Ruarc suggested. Tarian could almost see two devil horns growing off the top of his head, he looked so pleased with the idea.

Ember nodded vigorously. "That sounds good!"

"I have to admit, that's quite a penalty. I wouldn't want to have that happen. Okay, sparky. The deal is, if you stay here until I send for you, then you get two weeks' vacation in the ocean with me, with the penalty of two weeks here with Ruarc instead if I don't come through."

Ember tilted her head, considering. Her brow furrowed in concentration.

"What's the missing piece?" Ruarc whispered.

"You're creating a lawyer." Calliope giggled.

"Critical thinking skills are always useful." Ruarc didn't sound the least bit concerned.

"I think we forgot the penalty for Ember," Tarian said. "Your penalty, sparky, is you forfeit the two weeks. If you don't remain here, then no vacation for you. Deal?"

Ember shook her head, still thinking. "There's something missing."

Tarian thought about the small bargain they were forming but couldn't see any missing piece. She went over each part, until finally she realized the missing element.

Ember brightened. "Time!"

Tarian gasped, feigning offense. "You totally just stole that out of my mind."

Ember giggled. Kia joined her. Calliope hid a smile behind her hand. Ruarc looked proud.

"Two weeks in the ocean the second we get home!" Ember shouted, jumping up and down.

Tarian shook her head, amused. "That's a little fast. Give me a week? One week to make sure the house isn't burning down, and then we're outta there. Deal?"

Ember thought it over, then looked to Ruarc. He smiled his encouragement. She turned back to Tarian and nodded like a bobblehead doll. "Deal. I mean, agreed."

"Agreed." Tarian grabbed her bouncing daughter and hugged her tight as the small Agreement settled around them. "I love you, little spark."

"I love you too, Mama." Ember squeezed Tarian's neck tight, then jumped back. "I made a deal. I made a deal. I made a deal."

Kia laughed and grabbed her hand. "We should get back to lessons now." Kia gave Tarian a quick hug and whispered, "He might not be dead, Ms. Tari. He might just be lost. You can help him find his way. You and Ms. Calli. Her light sure do be bright now. Seems to me it'd show the way just fine."

Kia gave her a significant look as she stepped away. "Power be a funny thing. Left to its own, it seeks balance and peace. It takes intent to make it a weapon. Ain't that so, Ember?"

"Bye, Mama!" Ember waved. "Bye, Auntie Calli."

The three of them watched the girls leave, followed by a group of guards.

"Think that'll stick?" Tarian asked.

"She's been pressing a visit to the ocean for quite some time," Ruarc said. "It should. Although I suspect you will provide quite the temptation." He glanced at Calliope, raised an eyebrow. "I am most interested in how it came into your possession. It is an object First Mother would have been most...reluctant...to relinquish."

"That's a story for another time." Calliope turned slightly away from Ruarc. Tarian watched her, curious. She wanted to hear that story. Her sister obviously didn't want to tell it. But now was not the time.

"Ruarc, what exactly was the Agreement? The one that keeps the leaders from attacking one another. I know the basics...it's in the archives. But not the specifics."

Ruarc raised an eyebrow. "Ah. I see."

"You see what?" Tarian asked.

"The Agreement has been broken. Yes, that would allow for a

new Seeker."

Tarian didn't like the light she saw in his eyes. It was calculating, greedy, and disturbing. As if he were counting up how many ways this might work to his advantage.

Ruarc considered Tarian for a moment. He came to a decision, though she couldn't tell exactly what. "When the planes were split by the Balance Court, they declared an edict that no leader of any group, be they human, daemon, Ancient, or other, could attack any other with the intent to kill without consequences. It was stipulated, I suspect, in the event that the planes ever re-joined. There are other details, which declared essentially that the daemon factions must exist independently and one could not seek to destroy the other."

"What was the cost?" Tarian asked.

"For a leader to attack another leader? It would depend on where the attack took place. If one were to visit another leader with no ill intent, and then be attacked while in their care, the penalty was loss of position, forfeiture of space such as city or, in your case, Keeper, the House of Xannon, and relinquishment of any object of power, bonded or otherwise. If Calliope has bonded with the Air Artifact, then First Mother has broken the Agreement. She has attacked with intent to kill while you visited Benata City." Ruarc's gaze traveled down Tarian's body and back up. "You appear to have survived the attempt."

Tarian flashed him a small smile for confirmation.

"What happens if First Mother attacks you, Ruarc?" Calliope asked. "Are the penalties the same?"

"If the attack is confined to only me, yes. If she were to attack the city itself, or the House of Xannon, however, the penalty is death."

Tarian mulled over the Agreement. It was complex, with

nuances that weren't readily apparent, and explained some of First Mother's actions over the past couple of years. "Wait, she attacked the House earlier…on the beach. Doesn't that count?"

Ruarc shook his head. "She did not. She attacked a specific person, on the beach, and without intent to kill."

Tarian rolled her eyes at that explanation.

"You should be aware, now that First Mother, or should I say Saorla, has broken the Agreement, she is no longer bound by it. At least, not by that particular clause. And if she is not bound by it, neither are you." Ruarc gave Tarian a significant look.

Tarian nodded her understanding. Saorla could now try to kill her without penalty. But then, she was also fair game. To anyone.

Tarian held out her hand to Calliope. "Ready?"

—33—

Tarian and Calliope landed on the now familiar mesa in the bubble field in the middle of a battlefield. To their left a daemon guard shot vapor bullets at a daemon and a Sentinel to their right. She and Calliope were perfectly positioned to serve as the net in a deadly game of ping-pong.

Bullets *bzzzzz*'d by Tarian's ear. She threw herself at Calliope, knocking them both to the ground as the volley of power sailed over their heads.

The daemon on their left wore white robes edged in green. He had to be one of First Mother's loyal guards, part of the group who deserted the city with her when it collapsed.

The daemon on the right wore the same uniform as the Sentinel, black pants and a now filthy white shirt. The Sentinel held a small version of the giant prisms in his hand, which he used to absorb the shots. The prism split the absorbed energy into a rainbow that vanished a few feet past the fighters.

The daemon, one of the Benata she assumed and new ally to the House of Xannon, launched a counterattack of Air toward the loyal guard.

Tarian rolled to the side with Calliope. She kept one arm

protectively over Calliope like a parent in a car wreck. "Stay down!"

She assessed the scene in front of them like she would any crime scene. Two Benata guards—she labeled them loyalists—fought against three Sentinels who appeared to be teamed up with three Benata. They worked in tandem, using prisms to absorb attacks.

She counted four dead or dying on the platform and wondered how many more simply fell off the edge and were lost to the Source below.

"What's that?" Calliope pointed at the furthest platform.

Something large and bright glinted in the distance above one of the other platforms, but she couldn't make out exactly what it was. The distance in between was littered with dust, debris, remnants of battles, excess energy, and far more abereil than there should be.

"Not sure. Where's the prism?" Tarian shifted, but didn't see any sign of the pyramid they'd left in place. Her stomach clenched. If they were gone, if First Mother had somehow removed them...her plan wouldn't work. She tried to think of a Plan B or, by this time, Plan F or G, but nothing came to mind. "Do you see any at all?"

"No." Calliope sounded distracted.

Tarian could understand why. Calli had never been one to jump into a battle. She preferred to strategize behind the scenes. The chaos in front of them was enough to distract seasoned war vets.

Tarian scanned the rest of the valley. Storm clouds obscured the sun and cast an eerie green haze over the scene. Energy, thick and heavy and undirected, made her skin vibrate. It was hard to breathe and hard to think.

She saw shadows moving in the middle of the valley and focused on them. It was hard to make out through the muck, but lightning helped to light it up briefly. One flash revealed First Mother, floating in the center, both arms outstretched. She seemed to be struggling with something very bright.

Darkness took over before Tarian could make out more detail. Tarian sucked in a breath. "She's here. Dammit. I can't see. What's next to her? What's she doing?"

Calliope rose to her knees for a better vantage point and gasped. One hand flew up to cover her mouth.

"What?" Tarian half-rose, but it was too dark to see much past her face.

"Alex. And Macari. I think. And…more. I don't know the others. Lots more."

Tarian glanced at her sister. "How can you see that? It's pitch black out there."

Calliope shook her head. "Not to me."

Lightning flashed, leaving the space lit up like a rocket for a second or two. Long enough for Tarian to see Alex suspended next to First Mother. His head lolled to the side, and his arms and legs wrapped painfully behind him around a nearly transparent column.

Darkness cut off the view.

"What is that column?" Tarian asked. "What's she doing to him?"

"The lubach." Calliope stood. Her voice took on a dream-like quality. "There's a stream from the lubach, through Alex, to Saorla. She's using the false artifact as if it were real. She shouldn't have been able to…oh. That's not the stone I gave her." Calliope glanced at Tarian. "It's a prism. She's using a prism to channel energy from the Source, using the lubach as a conduit."

Calliope looked back to the space in front of them. "I think... Oh Tari." Calliope choked on a sob. "She's killing him. His light is so faded, I can hardly see it. And Macari...she's brighter. But only just. She won't last long either."

Tarian shot up, heedless of the fighting that continued around them.

"Keeper, look out!" someone shouted.

Tarian ducked a shot, then lashed out with one of her own. She didn't wait to see if it hit her target. "We need the prisms to break that damn thing. Where the fuck are they?"

"They won't make it." Calliope's voice barely carried above the sounds of fighting. "I see their life force draining. It's nearly gone."

Something in her sister's voice caught Tarian's attention. "Calli. How do you know? Wait, what are you doing?"

Calliope turned toward her. Her sister's eyes glowed. They were beacons in the darkness, like two moons that lit the way. "Air told me."

Calliope turned and ran toward the edge of the platform.

"Calli! No!" Tarian sprinted after her.

Calliope reached the edge and jumped, arms stretched out wide like she dove into the water from a high dive.

Tarian stumbled over something in the dark, landed hard on her knees and slid toward the edge too fast to stop. She scrambled for a hold on something. Her head shot out over the edge. One hand found empty air. The other found a small outcropping of rock. She clutched at it with all the strength she could manage from one hand and arm. Her body continued for another foot, nearly yanking her shoulder out of the socket. Half of her dangled over the side before she stopped. She threw her free hand over and gripped the small rock with both hands.

The rock gripped back. Then pulled.

Keeper Keeper Keeper Keeper

The chorus of Caraigg voices was sweet, sweet music in her thoughts. More hands emerged through the rock to grab various body parts. They worked together to pull her back from the edge.

When her butt was on firm surface, or semi-firm given the way the whole platform shook with the explosions of abereil and lightning, she turned back for Calliope. She was just in time to see a brilliant flash of light that used to be her sister flare and rise. Light obscured Calliope's face. Light shot out of both outstretched hands. Light bloomed from her stomach. It spread over Calliope's body, until her sister was nothing but a small, newly born sun. Tarian closed her eyes and turned her face away from the brilliance, but she could still see her sister's image burned on her retinas.

When she looked back, Calliope was gone.

"Calliope!" Tarian shouted.

Keeper must hide. Keeper in danger. Keeper must hide.

Where are the prisms? Tarian moved further back from the edge. The ground lurched, tilted, then righted itself. Someone screamed, a sound of terror that faded slowly into the darkness.

Prisms remain. The Caraigg flashed images through her thoughts of all four prisms, one after the other. Three were obscured by dirt. They'd hidden them where First Mother couldn't touch them. She saw them moving and shifting in her mind and realized why the ground continued to shake. The prisms were about to surface like a submarine, pushing dirt and rocks up out of the way as they moved.

They showed the fourth prism like a movie on fast forward. At first, Tarian couldn't comprehend exactly what she was seeing. It was too dark, until lightning flashed and revealed one of the large pyramid-shaped prisms floating high above one of the platforms, out of reach to the Caraigg. Another lightning flash revealed Letta, trapped inside. Her hands were up in a surrender pose, her mouth wide open, eyes wide with shock.

Keeper must help Earth human. Earth human cannot escape prism. Prism prevents Earth Artifact from activating.

Tarian sat back, trying to get her bearings. Letta, trapped in a prism. *I need her, dammit. I need all three of them. I can't do this without Letta and Macari and Calliope.*

A scream infiltrated her thoughts. It was a primal, animalistic sound filled with frustration and absolute rage. "Where is it! I can feel it. I know it's here."

Tarian turned toward the sound just in time to see a bolt of white racing toward the platform. She ducked and rolled. The bolt landed two feet past her shoulder and exploded, showering everyone with rock like confetti at Mardi Gras.

Tarian grabbed the closest Caraigg hand. *Push this one up first. I'm going to activate it. Then get the others ready.*

The hand released hers and disappeared.

The platform shook like a master chef would shake a pan on a hot stove. It knocked loose dirt and gravel around, bouncing them like popcorn. A small fraction of prism, the tiniest tip, emerged.

Saorla shot again, a bolt of Earth that hit to the left and exploded the rocks. Tarian rolled aside, dodging the worst of it. The blow left a large crater.

"Air is mine! Give it back!" Saorla screamed, her face manic and tyrannical.

"Not anymore!" Tarian shouted back. She reached for power, digging deep past Water, always on the surface and easy to touch, through Air, to the darkest core of her elemental energy—Fire.

Saorla's face, usually so white and pale, turned a deep shade of crimson. "You wretched…this is all you. You did this. You've taken everything. You've destroyed everything. I have to stop you. I have to stop you. I have to stop you. Your death will bring balance. Your death will put it right. You death will free us all." Saorla shot another bolt at Tarian. It lit the sky with a white vapor trail and struck her shoulder. Tarian screamed in pain and lost her hold on Fire. She clutched her shoulder and dodged to the side, tripped, and fell into the small crater. Her injured shoulder struck something hard and sent searing shots of agony through her arm, shoulder, into her chest.

She lost several precious seconds to the pain of the assault. It'd only been a glancing blow, but it was enough to render her left arm useless. Her thoughts reeled at the venom in First Mother's words and the reality that the daemon was disturbed or deranged, or just old-fashioned crazy, and that she'd focused all of her anger and frustration and years of perceived injustices on Tarian. She'd leapt off the Benata Way bandwagon and landed in the pit of Me First.

Saorla rained another series of bolts. They fell randomly, with only one striking the crater. It hit the far side and pinged off. The ricochet sailed by Tarian's head and embedded in the crater wall behind her.

The ping sounded clear, like a chime tinkling in the breeze. Tarian squinted at the wall in front of her. It was too dark to make out anything. She got to her feet and nearly fell. Her hand shot out to steady herself and touched a smooth, glass-like surface.

It was the top of the prism. The tip of it extended just past her head from what she could tell. So only about a third of it showed.

She glanced up but realized Saorla, without her Air Artifact bond, couldn't see any better in the dark than she could. It gave her a few seconds to do what she needed.

She reached for Fire again. It took longer to push through her outer pool of resources this time. Pain made it hard to concentrate. Anger usually helped her get past this part, but at the moment pain overrode that emotion too. Finally, a small spark flickered to life deep in her core. She focused on it, grappled with it, coaxed it into a bigger flame. Then finally took hold and tugged.

It took a lot more effort to touch and still more to pull it out from the center of her soul. It seared as it answered her call, leaving a hot trail through her chest. It licked the Water Artifact and emerged, hungry and volatile and deadly.

Tarian snatched Water energy through the artifact and wrapped it around the Fire, then used Air to shape it into a laser beam that rocketed to the tip of the prism.

It struck and penetrated the prism, sending shivers through the diamond like a lover in orgasm. Something in the center of the prism activated and began to glow. The small light pulsed brighter and brighter until she couldn't see anything but the millions of colors of a rainbow.

She stared, her mouth falling open. She'd never seen anything so beautiful. So awe-inspiring. So amazingly perfect.

Then the prism made a sound like a deep gong, the kind used to call gods. It shook the ground, crumbled rocks, and woke the sky. It grumbled like a hungry teenager. And then it began to eat as it siphoned power from everything.

Tarian remained frozen in place, but now it was because the prism held her tightly in its grasp. It worked like a giant magnet, and she was a piece of steel. She clung to the side of it while the ground crumbled, revealing more of the vast pyramid as a crater formed around it.

The edge of the crater continued to spread outward, devouring the platform as it went. It sounded almost like popcorn popping as the rocks struck other rocks and continued.

Saorla struggled against the call of the prism as well. Instead of attacking Tarian, she worked on putting distance between herself and the object. Panic flared in her eyes as she put more and more energy into the effort.

Nearby abereil flocked to the prism like teens to a bonfire. Tarian watched, horrified, as the first one approached. She expected it to explode. She expected it to destroy the entire mountain, with her on it. She had the brief thought that at least it would destroy Saorla along with it, but then Saorla stopped struggling. Serenity replaced the panic in her eyes, and she vanished.

Tarian blinked at the empty spot where the daemon used to

be. The abereil inched closer. It picked up momentum the closer it got. In seconds it would slam into the prism. She had no idea what would happen after that and didn't want to find out while she stood so close.

Tarian reached for any energy she could control. Found the stream still steady beneath the grip of the prism. She could use it for something internal. Saorla had realized the same thing, faster.

Feeling like an idiot, Tarian pictured the opposite platform and traveled.

When she landed, she immediately crouched low and twisted to survey the area. This mesa was twice the size of the last. The ground shook but she was in no danger of falling off the side. Thankful for small miracles, she counted the number of loyalists still fighting Sentinels and Benata. At least five, though there might be more she couldn't see. The loyalists were holding their own against far superior numbers. At first she couldn't understand how it was possible. They were elite guard, but she had daemon on her side too. A lot of them. Plus Sentinels, with prisms and other special weapons.

Then she saw that most of the shots Sentinels hurled at the loyalists were deflected. With so much elemental energy running loose, she couldn't tell how they did it but she could guess. They used some sort of shield, one made with pure Air and probably amplified a thousand times by Saorla.

Once again she couldn't see any sign of the prism she knew lay just below the surface. She also didn't see any sign of the Caraigg. But it was dark, and the space was large. She moved to the center to get a better look. It put her closer to the fighting, and she had to dodge random jets of power as Sentinels deflected or shots went wild.

"Guards! To me!" Saorla's voice rang out above the lightning crackles and clash of power.

Loyalists flashed away to circle around Saorla. Tarian crouched low and ran toward the back of the platform. She hoped the daemon hadn't seen her land. If she just had a minute or two to focus, she could activate the second prism.

It left the Benata and Sentinels with nobody to fight. They clustered in small groups, and watched Saorla and her guards. Some helped the wounded move back away from the front lines. A few up front noticed Tarian, but she waved them away. If they all moved toward her location, Saorla would know where she landed. She needed an element of surprise.

Saorla spoke, her voice carrying above the noise. "By ancient Agreement, I command of thee, be present this day and hear my plea. By ancient bond I demand the right to petition the Shee for relief from my plight. Appear before me, Council of Three, that my will be done, as you agreed."

The atmosphere churned around Saorla and her guards. Wind kicked up and tossed Tarian's hair, making it difficult to see. White clouds bloomed into giant birds, which circled the daemon, their wingspans more than eight feet across, their feathers white and silver. One by one they appeared until hundreds of them filled the space. Their presence changed something in the atmosphere. For a moment, the abereil settled, and it seemed the entire world held its breath.

One bird flew deliberately toward First Mother. It buffeted her with wind. Saorla somehow stood her ground, though Tarian saw her teeter just a bit. The wings came together with a loud clap and collapsed down into a human form. Tarian detected the scent of jasmine, but it wasn't Jasmine who appeared. It was the father figure.

Soon another bird joined him. It held there, wings flapping

slowly, while another joined. The two shifted to human form that Tarian recognized as the teacher and the teenager.

"By Agreement and bond, we respond to thy plea," the father said. His tone sounded like a grandpa interrupted from his nap.

"Saorla, what is it you wish of we three?" the teacher added.

"This space is not stable, Saorla. Explain," the teenager said. "We respond to your call, but we will not remain."

Saorla clasped her hands in front of her, looking regal and dignified. Only the odd light in her eyes betrayed the insanity inside. "I require the Air Artifact. It was stolen from me, and I wish it returned. Now."

The teacher answered, "By Agreement we are bound to comply."

"What you seek, Saorla, may not be wise," the teenager said.

"It is not possible to hold the wind in the palm of one's hand," the father said. "The wind goes where it wills. You may not command."

"Think carefully, Saorla, this cannot be undone," the teacher said. "This request, once served, will sever the bond."

"I didn't ask for your opinion. Do as you promised. I need that artifact. I will have it. I fulfilled my side of the Agreement decades hence. It is time for you to fulfill yours."

"As you wish." The Shee spoke in unison. "By ancient Agreement, we answer the plea. We call upon Air to appear here before the daemon Saorla."

They bowed their heads. Energy churned around the Ancients. "The Agreement is fulfilled" reverberated around them. Lightning flashed, the crackle of it making Tarian's skin tingle. The crash of thunder, which followed interrupted her heartbeat for a second, jarring her insides and setting her teeth on edge.

In the next flash of lightning, Calliope appeared directly

between the trinity and Saorla, her skin glittering in the flashes of light, her expression shocked and confused.

Saorla stared at Calliope, her face twisted and red. "What is this? Where is the artifact?"

The three Shee dissolved into brilliant white feathers that separated into the most magnificent white birds Tarian had ever seen. They winged up to join the rest of the flock, and the entire group vanished into the clouds.

"The Agreement is *not* fulfilled! It is not! I demand the artifact. It is not here. You have not delivered." First Mother's face looked distorted, the veins on her forehead throbbing. Her lip and eye twitched.

Tarian looked from her sister's shocked expression at having been summoned to Saorla's angry one at having been duped. Saorla didn't see the Air Artifact because Calliope *was* the artifact. Like Letta, the physical object had merged with the host. It was now a part of Calliope, and she it. Just as the Earth Artifact was a part of Letta. The Shee had done as they agreed, but Saorla was too blind to understand.

«It's not possible to hold Air in the palm of your hand, daemon," Calliope replied.

Saorla lashed out, shooting a bolt of ice toward Calliope. It froze her in place before she could do more than gape at the daemon.

"Calli!" Tarian shouted. She ran forward, pushing through the Sentinels and daemon in her way. Her heart pounded so loud she thought everyone would hear the beat. "Let her go!"

Saorla turned her gaze to Tarian. It was cold, calculating, and callous. Any trace of what the daemon might have been had long since vanished, replaced by the frenetic thing that glared back at Tarian with the hatred of a thousand suppressed years.

The daemon's eyes narrowed. Vapor swirled around her hands. She raised an eyebrow, and her gaze flicked to one of the guards.

The guards vanished.

Saorla flicked her hand toward Calliope.

The guards, five in total, appeared around Tarian and attacked with bullets of Air that struck her shield and ricocheted out. She saw one Sentinel fall, then another.

It was like getting caught in an old-fashioned mob hit like the ones she'd seen on TV, the hail of bullets came so fast and furious.

Calliope dropped.

"No!" Tarian lunged forward. Two guards grabbed her arms. She dropped to the ground, breaking their hold, and rolled toward one, knocking him off his feet.

Sentinels rushed forward. They fought the two loyalists using small prisms to block any power they tried to focus. In close physical combat, the daemon were no match for Sentinels. The two who'd tried to hold her were on the ground unconscious or dead within seconds.

Tarian crawled to the edge as fast as she could. Rocks ripped her jeans and tore holes in her knees and hands. She reached the edge in time to see Calliope plunge into the Source abereil.

"Calli!"

The surface bent with the weight of her sister, then swallowed her. Just as it had swallowed Daric.

For a few precious seconds, she crouched on hands and knees, too stunned to move. Memories of Daric as he fell mixed with Calliope's frozen form. She couldn't grasp it. Numbness crept into her heart. It played there for a few minutes while the fighting went on around her.

Saorla appeared in front of Tarian. "I will command all

four artifacts." The three remaining daemon guards formed a protective triangle around Saorla.

"You can't." Tarian could barely push the words out. She continued to stare at the place where Calliope had entered the Source abereil. It looked unblemished, as though nothing had broken the surface.

Saorla narrowed her eyes. "I can. A lubach gives me access and control of all the elements. It returns what was stolen when the Stulos were formed. It puts the elements back in their rightful place."

Tarian shook her head. The idea that Saorla clung to was just so wrong. She couldn't fathom how anyone could think they owned something so natural, so much a part of life itself. Saorla's misguided beliefs had taken Daric and Calliope. Tarian looked up. "The elements of magic belong to the world, and everyone in it."

"No human should ever have touched the sacred elements. No human was ever worthy." Saorla said the words as if her mouth was full of something extremely bitter.

Tarian gave one last glance to the Source, then stood. "The artifacts don't belong to you. They never did. Each one chooses who it will serve. Who it will bond with. By an ancient Agreement, Water belongs to Xannon. Always."

"Any Agreement can be broken, human. No Agreement lasts forever. But I don't need to break that particular bond, do I? Humans are so foolish when making agreements. They leave so much to chance." Saorla's tone took on a sing-song quality. Her eyes lit up with insane excitement. "I can call her back, you know. Bring your daughter to me, *human*, and your sister lives. "

Tarian wondered at the request. The all-powerful daemon knew exactly where Ember was hiding. "Why don't you just go get her yourself, *daemon?*" She put extra emphasis on the word "daemon," hoping it carried the same amount of derision that Saorla's inflection held.

Saorla swirled, turning her back on Tarian.

"You can't, can you? Ruarc told me if you breach his city, or attack him, you forfeit your life. And *you* would have to attack him, wouldn't you? You're the only one who could even come close to defeating Ruarc, and he would protect Ember with his life. You'd have to kill him, to get to her. And if you did that... now that's irony."

Saorla glanced over her shoulder at Tarian. "You care so little for your sister?" She spun around to face Tarian. A white glow engulfed Saorla's hands and lit her eyes with demonic silver. Tarian smelled the daemon's signature, strong and nauseating.

Tarian turned and sprinted for the center of the platform. She pushed a Sentinel and shouted, "Get off this! Get off this!"

She tapped a Benata daemon. "Get them off this platform!"

Tarian continued to shout, hoping they understood. She couldn't wait to find out, she had seconds to act. Energy gathered. Saorla readied a killing blow. The power pinched Tarian's back as it rose, ready to strike.

Tarian tapped into her own resources, dragging Fire up and through Air and Water, binding them together and forging a weapon. It was a lot easier this time. This time, she used Calliope's face as fuel.

Something crackled behind her. Tarian jumped and twisted and used both hands to aim down at her target. Rods shot from her hands, thick and stronger than steel. Forged by rage and need. The rods slammed into the ground in rapid succession, like missiles from a rocket. Dirt and rocks billowed up, obscuring everything for a few seconds.

Air held her body aloft longer than normal. Saorla's shot lanced part of Tarian's thigh and continued on past her to strike the abereil directly behind.

Tarian dropped to the ground, hard, and rolled with it. Another lance buzzed past her ear and struck the ground. She whirled away and scrambled for the hole she'd just made. She hoped she hit the prism. But shooting blind, she couldn't be sure.

Lightning crashed, startling her enough to take a leap forward. Electricity sizzled the air and her hair. Saorla shot another lance, and another, so fast they lit the sky. Tarian kept moving and crouched low, using the debris to hide her movements.

She stumbled on a rock, then another. Her hands were raw and bloody. Her knees ached. The blast she'd used to get to the prism took a lot out of her and left her weak.

The air vibrated and shimmered and charged every hair on Tarian's body. She looked behind her, dreading what she'd see.

An abereil emerged from nothing and expanded twice, then three times.

Tarian froze and looked behind her. Between her and Saorla stood a very determined looking group of Sentinels and daemon. They lobbed a counterattack that kept Saorla and her three guards busy. Too busy to notice what was happening with the abereil.

Tarian looked from them, to the abereil, to the crater. She could just make out the edge of the prism still mostly buried in solid granite. It clearly hadn't activated. Her shot had been slowed and absorbed by so much rock.

She didn't know if she could manage another shot so soon. She'd used everything she had, tied it all into the one try. It hadn't been enough. Even with the artifact, it wasn't enough.

Tarian looked back at the abereil and the Sentinels. First

Mother had taken out three. They lay sprawled on the ground, eyes wide, staring at nothing. Dead.

The Benata fared a little better. So far only one had dropped.

The abereil stretched a bit further but didn't explode. It needed another hit. A push. Something other than Air.

It needed a little chaos.

Tarian pulled herself to her feet and sprinted for the abereil. This time, she grabbed a daemon and dragged him with her long enough to shout, "It's going to blow! Get them out!"

She made sure he saw the abereil and understood, before dropping his arm and running as fast as she could. She wanted to get close enough for the Water Artifact to take over. Just a few more feet. And a little shove.

When the artifact heated, she stopped running and yanked power through it. She pelted the abereil like a firefighter with a hose, dousing it in pure Water. The abereil shimmered, drank in the elemental pureness, and began to split. The cell divided into two smaller, brighter abereil. As their connection severed, an explosion of power pushed them away and traveled like a wave on the ocean. A loud sonic boom shook the ground.

Tarian opened herself to it. As it reached her, she reversed her own flow to pull the power inside instead of push it out. She'd done it once before, with Calliope to help. Now she stood alone. Just her, and the power of a thousand-year-old trinket.

Energy poured into her, infiltrated her body and mind and thoughts. The force of it tossed her body up, then slammed her to the ground. Air rushed out of her lungs and left her gasping, and still the power kept coming.

Now she knew how Ember's talent worked. Well, part of it. She didn't think she could magnify what she held like Ember could. She just hoped she could use it.

As energy pushed her along the ground like patio furniture in a tornado, she caught a glimpse of the other two abereil. Both had already begun to divide. They'd go at the same time. It was now or never. She couldn't survive another.

Tarian pictured the prism below her in her mind, as well as she could. Her thoughts were wired, a cocaine addict on caffeine. The buzz overwhelmed her. The prism. She had to get to the prism.

She pushed and teleported the remaining few feet, landing next to it in the small crater. She threw her arms across it, turned her thoughts to the ocean, and released.

Pain rocketed through Tarian as the energy she'd taken launched out of her and into the prism. The diamond vibrated and groaned and lit up with an internal glow that radiated blues and greens and reds and whites.

It flared to life and pulled. Tarian pressed against it, the Water Artifact melded to the surface like a sucker fish. She couldn't push back, even if her arms weren't made of jello.

The prism convulsed, and the ground around it began to crumble. A large crack split the platform in two. Rocks struck her back, one after the other. The final blow knocked her loose from the prism. She tumbled backward, riding the wave of dirt and rocks as it cascaded toward the Source below.

Two platforms left. Choose one. Choose.

Tarian picked one and teleported.

—35—

Tarian landed hard on unforgiving rock. She collapsed to the ground and rolled onto her back, then lay there, arms and legs wherever they landed. She couldn't get a breath. They came hard and fast, shallow and painful. Her body ached, her head pounded and her heart broke. Calliope. Daric. Both lost. Alex, almost gone. Macari. Letta.

"Keeper?" Voices broke through the haze of guilt and exhaustion. She didn't recognize any of them. Hands lifted her up, dragged her away from the edge to the darker corners of the platform. She let them. She didn't have the strength to argue.

Someone sat her upright. Handed her a small flask of water. Someone else put hands on her head and pushed healing into her brain. It felt foreign and sticky, instead of soothing and warm like Calliope's healing. She waved a hand at whoever it was but didn't bother looking at them. She stared straight ahead, transfixed and overwhelmed by what she saw.

The first prism hung suspended over the spot where the first platform used to be. It no longer touched anything at all. It pulsed alternating red, green, blue, and white light. Even at this distance she could feel a pull, the tug of a rope. It hungered for more. No abereil existed anywhere near it. It glowed like a jellyfish in a sea of black.

To the right, the second prism alternated colors as well. But the glow wasn't as bright, and some colors appeared muted. It was new, and some abereil remained in the area. They flocked to the diamond. It sucked them up, slow but steady. Each one consumed made it a brighter beacon.

Below, the Source abereil had grown darker, deep shades of gray and silver with a black rift that scarred the bubble where the lubach broke the surface.

But the thing that grabbed her attention more than anything was the lubach itself. It extended from the Source upward to a pinnacle that pierced the sky. It pulsed an eerie alternating rainbow of colors. Whatever had shielded it before had been removed. She could see Alex. He hung suspended from the outside of the column, arms bent around it behind him at an awkward angle, his chin dropped down to his chest. She couldn't tell if he was breathing.

Other bodies hung suspended from the column. At least ten, maybe more. None of them looked alive. Some looked like shriveled skeletons. She thought they must have been the first to be used as batteries for the construct.

A network of filaments extended outward from the lubach like delicate ropes. They formed an intricate pattern of pearlescent nodes and glistening strands that stretched toward the three visible prisms. It looked like a giant spider's web, and the lubach was the spider. Or, she thought, Saorla was the spider.

"What the hell is that?" Tarian said the words out loud, though she hadn't meant to.

Someone crouching next to her spoke softly, as if he didn't want to disturb the mood. "It is a net, intended to contain and control. Such is often used to harness a child's talent. It is not usually expanded to this extent. The filaments are usually too small to see with unaided vision."

Movement near the lubach caught Tarian's attention, and she honed in on it. Saorla moved around the side of the column. She looked old and haggard and maniacal, like a deranged bag lady toting a bright yellow sack. Tarian squinted, trying to make out what it was.

"Macari." Tarian clenched her fists.

Macari had been trapped inside some sort of shield or... no. "She trapped Macari in an abereil." Tarian almost hissed the words.

"Yes. We have been formulating plans, but so far have been unable to conceive of anything that would free our leader without killing her in the process."

Tarian glanced at the person speaking. It didn't surprise her to see the First Advisor kneeling next to her. "And Alex?"

"Your friend may be too far gone, Keeper. I am sorry." First Advisor kept his gaze transfixed on the column.

She had a feeling he would pounce the second he saw an opening. She couldn't blame him. She'd do the same.

Tarian returned her attention to First Mother. The daemon touched Alex's face, with an almost tender expression. When she let go, Alex began to drift slowly down the column toward the Source, as if it drank him in through a giant straw.

"Alex." Tarian whispered her friend's name. It hurt too much to say anything else. She added his name to the growing list of people she'd lost. She couldn't process it. Couldn't focus on it. She couldn't afford to. If she lost herself to the grief, she wouldn't be able to function. She stared at Alex as he drifted slowly down. She didn't bother to wipe away the tears that fell.

Saorla watched Alex for a moment, then turned to Macari. She pulled the abereil holding Macari around until it was between herself and the lubach.

Macari was so pale, she looked almost transparent. Her dress was ripped, her face and arms scratched, and the Fire Artifact that rested in her naval glowed an angry, malevolent red.

With the Fire Artifact, Macari made a far better battery to power the lubach than Alex. Once Macari with her daemon power and the artifact were bound to that column, Saorla could add Fire to her arsenal.

The filaments continued to stretch toward the prisms. She wondered what would happen once they reached the prisms. Flashes of explosions, chaos, destruction, and terror filled her thoughts. A world, destroyed. An evil bitch, holding all the power.

"We have to stop this. Now." She looked at First Advisor. "Do we have enough to attack?"

He continued to watch Macari, but she could tell he considered her question. "As things stand, no."

She caught the hesitation and pushed him further. "And if they changed?"

First Advisor finally turned to look at her. His face looked impassive, but she saw the slightest twitch near the corner of his mouth. It betrayed just how upset the daemon actually was. "What change do you suggest?"

Tarian kept her gaze locked on his. "We get Macari and Letta back. Three artifacts, on our side. If I have access to them, I can stop her."

"With the aid of the lubach, she is nearly immune to attack."

"So we break the lubach. Isn't that what you suggested?"

He tilted his head slightly, considering. "And you know how

to accomplish such a feat?"

Tarian looked back at the column and the spider web extending out from it. In some other time and some other place, with less at stake, it would have been a beautiful site. Awe-inspiring, even.

"It's not all that different from a Stulos. If I can get the other two artifacts, I can break it." She thought of the fourth and Calliope, and her chest tightened. "All I need is a merge."

He watched, silent for a full minute, before replying. "We have enough to distract her. Briefly. She has lost more than half of her guards. Those who remain are stationed around the object on the far side. The...prism, I think it was called. If we focus our efforts there, it will draw her attention and give you a small amount of time to free First Mother."

Tarian put a hand on his arm and squeezed. "Do it. Oh, and First Advisor? The Caraigg are allies. Be ready for helping hands from the ground."

First Advisor gave her an appraising look. "Good fortune in your endeavors, Keeper."

"Break a leg, daemon." Tarian patted his shoulder and stood. Her knees buckled and her head spun, but she managed to stay upright.

First Advisor looked momentarily confused by her broken leg wish. It flashed through his eyes for a fraction of a second before he clearly decided it wasn't worth worrying about. He stood and held out both hands in an I-mean-no-harm sort of way. "Keeper, if you would permit. A joining will replenish your reserves."

Tarian hesitated. Took an internal pulse and knew he was right. But she'd never joined with anyone besides Daric, and Ruarc of course. Not like that. She remembered the experience as one highly sexually charged and couldn't fathom doing it with the

First Advisor.

"It is a natural and normal thing, among daemon, to share energy stores. I mean no harm or disrespect."

"It's not that. I'm just not sure you're my type... Never mind." Tarian held out her hands. "Let's do it."

First Advisor held his hands over hers, palms facing palms. The warmth of the joining embraced her, but instead of beginning in her nether regions as part of an orgasm, it spread from her hands to her chest and then worked through the rest of her body. It was like being dunked in a luscious hot bath. When it reached the peak, she almost moaned. It was sensual, luxurious, life-affirming. When First Advisor withdrew his hands, and the connection severed, the warmth faded and she shivered against the sudden cold.

"Well, okay then." Tarian nodded, assuring herself. "Good. That was...yeah, thanks. That's better." She tested the Water Artifact, and it warmed to her touch, ready. She felt tired, but not exhausted. It might be enough.

She glanced at the assembled group of Sentinels and Benata. She wanted to say something inspiring. Something about how they should all be careful. That they should come home alive. But she knew they probably wouldn't and couldn't promise something like that. It would be a miracle if she ever saw any of them ever again. With all that, she couldn't think of any words at all to say. So she gave them a quick nod and a half salute to show her gratitude. The Benata saluted her in their own way, both fists to chest. The Sentinels half-mimicked their approach, one fist pump on their chest.

First Advisor organized them into pairs or groups of three. Then as one, they teleported, and she stood alone on the platform.

"Now for my part of the distraction." Tarian touched the

Water Artifact for luck, then tugged at the power lying ready just below the surface. She wove Water with Air, then used it to dig a trench that burrowed into the granite. The trench filled with water touched with the salt of the sea. The minerals in it helped funnel down through the earth, aided by the Air element she wove into the mix.

It took a few precious minutes to work into the ground far enough. When she felt the resistance of something more than stone, the ping of something *other*, she added Fire to the Water in the trench and coaxed it hotter and hotter and hotter until water became hot and thick as lava.

The ground shook. The edges of the platform began to crumble. She pulsed, then hit it again, then again.

One more push. She screamed with the effort, and something below gave way. The quake that shook the platform knocked her off her feet and split the granite. A rift quickly traveled across the plane, and the prism convulsed as it activated.

Tarian got to hands and knees and looked at the lubach. She focused on Macari. Saorla had heard the noise and seen the destruction of the platform. She watched the rise of the fourth prism with interest, but then something caught her attention and she turned away. Whatever she saw, whatever the daemon and Sentinels were doing, it worked. Saorla teleported away from the lubach, leaving Macari to dangle alone.

"Now or never." Tarian focused on the lubach and traveled.

—36—

Tarian clung to Macari, one arm wrapped around the daemon's neck and her legs wrapped around the daemon's waist. It was tenuous at best. She wished she could see the pathways Macari and Calliope both seemed able to use.

She touched one of the web strands and tried to sever it with a bolt of Water, but it held like steel forged in the pits of hell. The more she worked on it, the harder it seemed to become.

"Macari! Macari, wake up. I need you. Macari!" Tarian shook the daemon's shoulders, but she didn't answer. Her right eye ticked, the only sign that life remained at all besides her unsteady heartbeat.

The Fire Artifact burned so hot, it should have consumed the daemon already, but instead the energy funneled straight into the lubach and down to the Source. Tarian tested with her own artifact, but couldn't penetrate the web surrounding the column. Macari was the only way in.

Tarian leaned her forehead against Macari's. *How can I destroy this thing if you're still attached? It'll take you with it.*

Save...Letta. Save Earth. First.

Tarian pulled way, startled. She hadn't expected an answer.

Not really. "Save Letta…how the hell do I do that without you?"

Don't need me. Need…artifacts…Earth…absorbs. Earth…can eat…shields.

Tarian stared down at the Fire Artifact. The spark of an idea flashed through her mind and took hold. She turned her gaze back to Letta. Her friend remained frozen inside the enlarged prism where it hung suspended above the last remaining platform.

Saorla and four loyal guards stood underneath the base of the diamond pyramid. Tarian couldn't tell exactly what they did at this distance, but she saw the result. The prism lifted further away from the ground. Caraigg definitely wouldn't be able to help.

But something disrupted those standing below it. Saorla seemed to be the only one unaffected. She stared at the diamond, her arms held high. Small pulses of white shot from her hands into the prism. Tarian held her breath. If Saorla activated the prism, it might just solve a lot of problems. Or it might end up killing Letta.

The prism shuddered, then appeared to grow. Slow at first, almost like an optical illusion. Tarian blinked. Blinked again. It was definitely getting larger. How that would affect the woman trapped inside it, she didn't know. But if Saorla was orchestrating things, it couldn't be good.

Tarian searched for a good place to land. One that would give her some cover, long enough to try merging with Letta. She had to get close. Very close.

The prism expanded a bit further. Something inside it beamed a feeble green light. It ping-ponged off the sides of the pyramid as if trying to find a way out.

She thought she knew what the green represented. The Earth Artifact responded to the threat. It was trying to unleash protections for Letta, the shadowy forms that always appeared whenever Letta was in danger. They were trapped inside the prism and looking for a way out.

Tarian tapped Macari on the shoulder. "I'm going for Letta. Be ready. If this works, this column is going down. Don't go with it. I don't wanna have to chase you. I suck at flying."

Macari didn't respond.

Tarian teleported from Macari to Letta in one smooth jump. She placed herself at the apex of the prism and threw her arms around it, clinging like plastic wrap. Her hands were sweaty and slick, and she slipped a few inches.

"Finish her!" Saorla's scream was barely understandable, but the volley of white bullets spoke loud and clear.

One hit Tarian's shoulder, and she couldn't stop the shout of pain. Another hit her thigh. Two more struck in her right calf and left arm.

Blood poured from the wounds, leaving hot sticky trails. She had one chance. A few more hits, and she'd be dead from blood loss if nothing else.

Tarian opened herself to the Water Artifact and dragged Fire through it. She used all of her anger, her fear, her determination, and her hate. The artifact flared with heat and the sound of dolphin cries. She slammed all of it into the apex of the prism, at the most vulnerable point. One direct blow.

Saorla had expanded the prism so much it was no longer as solid. No longer as strong. And the pinnacle had already been struck with Air too many times. Tarian's blast hit like a hammer, and the prism was a gong. A loud clang, off-key and violent, ripped through the air.

The force of the prism activating tossed everything near it. Tarian lost her grip and fell. She hit the ground and bounced once, twice, then stopped. She couldn't get her breath. She couldn't see. Everything shook. The ground cracked and split as the sonic boom continued to roar.

Then something howled. It was a low, haunted sound. Like a thousand hellhounds with the scent of blood. Shadows moved. Three black ghosts raced along the ground and out into the web. They sped toward the lubach, so fast Tarian couldn't track them.

The apex of the prism had disintegrated, leaving a gaping hole. Saorla hovered next to the apex and stared at it in disbelief. More black shadows, all shaped like Letta, streamed through the hole. Hundreds of them. They surrounded Saorla and the remaining guards, and their howls were a haunting, terrifying chorus.

One guard dropped like a swatted fly. Then another. The shadows moved from one to the other, but Saorla was too strong for them. She erected a shield around herself and turned her focus to Tarian. Her eyes blazed with enough hatred to fuel a thousand suns.

Tarian didn't bother getting to her feet. She didn't have the strength or the time. Instead, she reached for her tracking ability and found the bond that tied her to Letta. It snapped into place, strong and vibrant. Letta was very much alive.

Tarian used it to send Air and Water to Letta, along with a single thought. *Merge.*

Letta resisted for a fraction of a second before she opened up and let Tarian through.

It was like moving through sludge at first. Earth didn't mix well with Air or Water. It wanted to suppress. To insulate. To absorb. Tarian fought back, sending a little Fire along with it.

Fire hardened the connection and suddenly Letta's thoughts merged with Tarian's.

For fuck's sake get me the fuck outta this thing what the fuck!

Tarian almost laughed. She would have if it didn't hurt so much.

We need Macari. Gotta break the column.

It'd only taken a second. Maybe two. But Saorla had used that time to move back to the lubach. She now floated in front of Macari, her hands on Macari's face.

Tarian looked for the bond she held with her friend and found it. Again, vibrant. Macari still lived. Relief surged through her. Then she took a stream of all the elements she controlled and shot them in one hit through the bond and into Macari.

Macari had been waiting. But her mother had reached her first. Tarian felt the assault and conflict the second she and Letta entered Macari's consciousness.

You will give me Fire. I am your mother.

You are no mother to me. You never were.

I am your leader! You will do as I command.

You are no one's leader. Not anymore. Get out of my head!

Macari flexed, giving her mother a mental shove. It didn't do much, but it was enough of a distraction. Tarian grabbed the opportunity and pushed her way in.

Saorla remained connected. Tarian wove a link with Macari and caught Saorla in the middle of it. The daemon's surprise, fear, and panic trickled through the merge.

Tarian took the combined energy into herself and let it fill her with power and potency. It made her feel alive and vibrant and frazzled. She couldn't hold it long. It was too much. She'd merged all four of them. Saorla was now a helpless member of their merge. She was along for the ride and terrified.

Tarian struggled to her feet. She held so much power, all four elements, and it enhanced everything. She could now see the web, the pathways, and the filaments of Air. She could see

Saorla standing on a pathway. She saw Macari's Fire as it throbbed and stretched, barely contained by the artifact in her naval. She smelled the sunshine scent of Macari's signature, and the wet earthy grass of Letta, and the cold mountain breeze of Saorla. A dozen other scents swirled around her nose, but she didn't recognize them.

She was vaguely aware that the fighting had stopped. The shadow forms that always appeared when Letta was in danger swarmed the column now, looking for a target. Tarian tugged and pulled them in. They didn't want to come. They fought and struggled. Letta uttered a command through the merge, but they didn't listen.

Tarian focused on the lubach and their need to destroy it. She thought of how it would save Macari and Letta.

The shadows zoomed around the column in a tight circle, then one after another struck the lubach with the force of laser guided missiles.

Saorla screamed. She thrashed and tried to use her power to fend them off. She tried to get control of the merge. But it was three against one. She couldn't take it. Even her thousand-year-old daemon magic wasn't strong enough to control a merge of three powered by artifacts.

The column shuddered. Cracked. Split.

Tarian pulsed again.

Saorla resisted. The shot skewed to the left and missed. Tarian tried again. Again Saorla thwarted her attempts.

Their merge faltered. The three of them had been abused, and their reserves weren't high. The shadows drained Letta to the point of breaking. It wasn't going to be enough.

She could feel the prisms siphoning off a portion of power. Even this far away from them, they took more than she had to give. The column remained. Weakened, but not broken.

Tarian thought of the Stulos and what she'd done to break them. She thought of the abereil and how they released the most power when they split. The idea struck a nerve.

Through the bond, she felt Saorla recoil.

That's it, isn't it? Release is a powerful thing, isn't it, Saorla? People always tell me I need to let it go.

Do it, Letta thought.

We'll pick up the excess, Macari thought.

You'll destroy us all! Saorla raged.

Tarian put her hands on the lubach. The power of it made her arms go instantly numb. It tried to suck her in, pull her down. She clenched her teeth and released the merge.

The backwash of release lashed out like a tidal wave. She pushed at it with pure Water. Macari added Fire. Letta added Earth. The column sucked all of the elements inside, and reality bent. Then the column exploded in a flash of colors and power and vapor. The energy roared out and enveloped them all.

The Fire Artifact flashed and bathed Macari in flames that fed the wave of power and crashed into Saorla. The daemon screamed and tumbled backward, carried by it into the spider web. She thrashed, caught up in the web until it began to dissolve.

Saorla lashed out with a pulse of power, pure Air that raced toward Tarian. It was a killing blow.

Time slowed to a stop. She saw the strike coming. She heard Ruarc's words as they echoed through her thoughts. *She is no longer bound by the Agreement. And neither are you.*

And she saw with absolute clarity what she needed to do. She acted without any hesitation, instinct and need driving every beat of her heart and every action.

Tarian used her tracking sense to form a bond with the

daemon she'd just merged with and pulsed a shot of Fire, powered by Air. It struck Saorla in the chest. A flash of fire burned a hole the size of a grapefruit where the heart should be.

Saorla's face froze in an expression of shock. Her eyes, wide and unseeing, stared out at nothing as the web evaporated around her. The daemon dropped like an anchor into the Source below. Tarian watched. The expression on Saorla's face burned into her memory. The silhouette of white robes, silver hair, and decayed skin against the boiling white of the Source abereil as it accepted another tribute.

And then the Source swallowed Saorla.

—37—

Tarian dropped, no longer supported by any pathway. She'd let the merge go and, with it, the ability to support herself. She flailed and tried to focus on a platform. Tried to push Air to travel. Nothing happened.

"Oh no, you don't." Macari zoomed by, threw her arms around Tarian, and popped them both out of the center of the valley and onto the last remaining platform. Exhaustion and reality knocked Tarian onto her knees. Saorla. She'd killed the leader…former leader…of the Benata. She couldn't wrap her head around it. She'd never killed anyone other than the laghairtine that had attacked her what seemed like a decade ago. It was the event that had started off this whole mess. He'd been trying to kill her and her family at the time. He'd taken over her mind and her magic, and she'd justified his death as self-defense. She hadn't felt guilty when he died. She'd been too wrapped up in her mother's death to care about an obvious murderer.

This was…she wasn't sure what this was. She hadn't expected to do it. She'd wanted to stop the daemon from destroying the world, but other than destroying the lubach she hadn't worked through what "stop" might entail. Not really.

She didn't know what to think. Or feel. Or what to do. Reality slammed into her with a vengeance. Daric. Alex. Calliope. They were all trapped in the Source abereil. She didn't know if they were dead or alive, but either way, she wasn't leaving them there to rot.

Tarian dragged herself to her feet. Patted Macari on the arm. Forced one foot in front of the other. She had to get to them. A quick glance at the prism told her most of the small abereil had been absorbed, but the prism burned with brilliant light. It couldn't hold much more. She was sure the rest were near capacity as well. And the Source remained.

She needed to use them, now, to create a shield that would contain the Source abereil. She had to do it before anything else went wrong. She had to do it before she wasn't capable of channeling any more magic.

She refused to do it while there was a chance. A hope.

"A little help?" A desperate voice from above broke through her thoughts and captured her attention. Tarian glanced up.

Letta dangled from the top of the prism, half in and half out. "It's weak but not dead. It's got a little juice left. Enough to hold me here like a damn fool."

Macari put a hand out to stop Tarian. She smelled of sunshine and burnt hair. The Fire Artifact remained active, and a good portion of her dress had burned away. "Can we make the shield without Calliope?" Macari looked as if she instantly regretted her words.

Tarian glared at the Source below. "I'm not leaving them in there." She glanced at Macari. "Help Letta. Get everybody else out of here."

She ran to the edge of the platform, ready to leap off.

"Tari, wait! Take this!" Macari threw a white stream of vapor toward Tarian. Tarian caught it, and Fire flared up her arm and hardened the stream of vapor into a translucent rope that connected her to the daemon. She tied it around her waist and dove off.

When she struck the Source, it didn't feel at all like she'd expected. She'd expected something squishy like jello. She'd expected to be sucked inside like quicksand. Instead, it was like drifting into space. The world around her shattered into a million colors and a thousand scents and a lifetime of thoughts and memories and worlds.

A hundred universes opened up in front of her. Galaxies and stars and planets floated in them, each one vibrant and alive. She felt like an astronaut viewing Earth from space for the first time. She'd seen the pictures. Heard the stories. But no story would ever compare to this. She never knew so many worlds existed. And she knew, somehow knew, that each one teamed with life and magic.

She didn't know how long she stared at it like a kid at a toy store window. She almost forgot why she came.

He just be lost, Ms. Tari. But Calliope, she be a bright light. Maybe she can guide the way.

Kia's words haunted and teased. Tarian couldn't see the light Kia saw in her sister. Even if she could, it wouldn't compete with the stars and suns inside this abereil.

The rope around her waist tugged a reminder. She looked at it, surprised it remained. It seemed solid, even if it extended out into the void and disappeared. Macari had given her a lifeline.

She realized something else. She could feel her tracking bonds, all of them. Some were far away and faint, like Ember's and Kia's. But some were very close. Solid and strong and steady.

She pulled on the one that led to Calliope and turned until she had a direction. Her thoughts took her along the filament that stretched between her and her sister.

It took seconds, or a thousand years, she wasn't sure which, but she bumped into Calliope with a reassuringly real thump. Calliope's eyes glowed white in the darkness.

Tari!

Calli! Are you okay?

Alex is next to me. He was close. But I can't find Daric. It's hard to see.

Tarian checked her tracking ability. *He's that way.*

They moved together toward Daric. It was like doing a space walk from one planet to another. A vast expanse of darkness punctuated by brilliant points of light stretched on and on and on.

Tarian bumped into something old and clingy and recoiled, feeling repulsed.

The former First Mother drifted beside them. Wrinkles and pockmarks and scars marked her face. Large black orbs stared at nothing. White hair wafted out around her like a sail. Her arms and legs splayed out at awkward unnatural angles, and Tarian saw stars through the hole in her chest. She looked broken and decayed and defeated. A husk of the former great power. Tarian looked at her for a long moment. Swallowed. She'd never understood the daemon. Didn't get what drove her to extremes. Didn't understand the fear or the anger or the hate.

But then, she'd never really understand the Benata Way either. The good of the many must outweigh the good of the few seemed archaic and simplistic. Life was more complex than that. Every situation needed a unique answer. There was no one-size-fits-all approach to life. And leadership was knowing and embracing that fact.

She closed her eyes.

Calliope squeezed her shoulder. *I see Daric.*

Tarian turned in the direction the bond indicated, and the two of them took off, leaving the empty shell that used to be First Mother behind and alone in the void.

—38—

Tarian pulled Daric close, and Calliope did the same with Alex. Tarian used the rope Macari had provided to tie the four of them together. They'd get out as one or stay here forever. Either way, she wasn't losing them again.

Now, Macari. She tugged on the rope, hard.

The rope tightened and hauled them up up up. They sailed past lights and through darkness until they reached the surface of the giant abereil.

It didn't want to let go. It clung to their bodies and fought against the release of its prisoners. Tarian thought about shooting at it, but she was afraid using energy in that way would only spawn more abereil. It was, after all, how Saorla had first constructed the lubach, and it was how she'd first launched abereil into Fort Worth. There were plenty of abereil to deal with already. She didn't want to risk any more.

Calliope reached out, touched the edge of it, and did something. Whatever it was, it made her hands and arms glow and her eyes shine and filled the air with a signature Tarian had never detected from her sister before. The breezy forest scent now mingled with hints of jasmine.

The abereil relaxed. They popped free and shot away like rockets. They landed on the remaining platform in a heap, surrounded by Caraigg and Sentinels and daemon.

"Hot damn!" Letta cheered. "Now that's how you kick some ass."

Macari worked to unravel the rope she'd created. It took more effort than it should have. Tarian had tied special knots they used for traps and nets, and they were hard to untangle. In the end it took all three of them, with Macari and Calliope using Air to expand the filaments of the rope and Tarian to untie them. Sentinels caught Daric and Alex before they lost the support of the rope and lowered them carefully to the ground.

They lay so still, Tarian thought they might be dead. She leaned over, watching for them to take a breath. Alex's chest rose. The movement was slight, but it was enough. For now. She moved to Daric and put her ear near his mouth. The faintest hint of breath caressed her cheek. She closed her eyes, grateful.

The three prisms burned bright and hot, surrounded by darkness. Very few abereil remained, and those that did were close to being taken in by the prisms.

The Source had grown since she saw it last. It now filled the valley and oozed outward. It extended up the side of the platform they stood on to within about ten feet of the top. It would overtake them soon if it didn't stabilize.

"We have to seal it. Now." She glanced at the First Advisor. "Get them out of here. Please. Take them to Xannon. They need healers." Tarian stood, then swayed as the world spun around her for a second. Her time in the Source left her drained and off-balance. Or it might have been the overload she'd held to destroy the lubach. Whatever it was, she wasn't sure she had enough left to finish what she'd started. "Everybody out! I don't know what will happen when we try to seal the Source. We have enough dead or injured. You've done all you can. Time to go home."

Tarian moved closer to Macari, Calliope, and Letta. They looked ragged and beyond tired. The three of them sported ripped clothes, drooped shoulders, and worn expressions. But Macari's Fire Artifact burned bright red, and Letta's three main shadows circled like prowling cats. They might have enough left for one more thing. Maybe.

The Caraigg who were clustered nearby looked agitated. One grabbed her leg. *Hurry.*

The one word repeated over and over and over, along with an image of the platform collapsing under the weight of the Source abereil.

"Ready to merge again?" Tarian looked from Macari, to Calliope, to Letta.

"Yes," Macari said.

"Do we have enough?" Calliope asked.

"Let's sink this bitch." Letta stared back at Tarian, determination in her eyes. "Whatcha waitin' for? This platform's gonna blow."

She didn't want to admit her energy reserves had sunk dangerously low. A merge took an enormous amount of power. More power than she had left. Maybe. If she couldn't manage it, then it was all for nothing.

Macari took her hand and squeezed. "You don't have to do this alone. We'll help."

Tarian smiled, grateful for the reassurance. "Okay, Calli first."

One by one, Tarian reached through her bonds to pull them into a merge. When each woman entered, she brought her thoughts, emotions, and memories along with her magic and talent. The power from all four artifacts bombarded Tarian, fighting for dominance. It was like trying to wrestle a room full of cats. The elements collided and resisted. Tarian struggled against the force of it. She staggered back a few steps and bumped into a Caraigg.

The touch sent a flood of Caraigg thoughts and images into the mix. It was too much. Pain rocketed through her skull. She gasped and fell.

Macari's arms wrapped around her, and an intense warmth flooded into her. She recognized the feel of it. It was a joining, split four ways. It called all four elements and shared the load among the four of them.

She felt Letta's shock, Calliope's surprise, and Macari's joy. She loved these women, more than she ever thought possible. They returned it, and the four of them lifted past the pain and the exhaustion. It was an emotion so deep, so timeless, so all-encompassing that it almost hurt.

Now, Tari. Macari urged her with a thought.

Tarian reached for the prisms. They were like toys now. She used pure Air to pull them all closer together. They moved slowly into the center of the valley, like four stars on a collision course.

They collided and jostled for position. Tarian reached for Letta's Earth abilities. She needed one large prism, but she had no idea how Letta made them in the first place.

Just ask. Letta's voice was the loudest whisper Tarian had ever heard.

You do it. Tarian opened further, and Letta stepped to the forefront of the merge. She saw in her thoughts what Letta intended. Witnessed the girl ask for approval. Experienced the rock's response of love and affection and approval.

The four prisms merged, bit by bit, into one large piece. It moved like liquid glass at first, fluid and sensual.

Calli, stretch it out, Macari whispered.

Letta's awareness stepped away to allow Calliope to take control of the merge. Tarian felt her sister's gentle touch with Air. She wove it like fabric, her skill with needle and thread shining through as she molded and shifted the prism into a curved mirror-like object. It expanded to fill the valley, covering the abereil completely.

Calliope lowered the newly formed diamond shield until it touched the surface of the abereil.

Make it hard, Tarian whispered.

Macari took the focus from Calliope and shot Fire into the prism. Letta added a jet of Earth. Tarian finished with Water, using it to make a crust and shield that bent toward the ground and plunged through the surface for several feet. It formed a complete dome over the abereil.

Tarian looked down at their work. The diamond surface gleamed with every flash of lightning. It was beautiful and brilliant and would attract attention from neighboring galaxies if they left it like this. She was sure it could be seen from satellites. The reflection of the sun in the morning would be enough to bring thousands to the site.

Can we hide it?

Oh yes. Macari touched Air, wove it with Water, and created a reflective surface that mirrored the surrounding valley so completely it hid the diamond-encrusted abereil like an invisibility cloak. She touched it with Fire to tie it off.

When she was done, it looked like a normal valley filled with trees and rocks. Impassable, but innocently beautiful.

It's done, Tarian thought.

Feels stable, Letta answered.

Tarian let Macari go first, then followed with Letta, and last her sister. Calliope soothed Tarian's headache on her way out.

When the merge released, they all dropped to the ground. Her nerves were raw and sore, her body was broken, and her thoughts were a jumbled mess.

But she looked out at the valley and smiled. It was almost dawn, and the storms were moving out. The abereil rested. She'd call it a win.

Several hours or a lifetime later, she'd never be sure which, Tarian paced in front of the monitors in the receiving hall like a panther with a caffeine high. She couldn't sit still. Anxiety ate at her. When the side door opened, she yelped.

Calliope ran through the door. She looked excited. "Tari, he's awake!"

Tarian's heart leapt into her throat and pounded. "Daric?" She started toward her sister, then stopped when her sister hesitated. It lasted a fraction of a second, but it was long enough to fill her stomach with dread. Again.

"Alex, I mean. Alex is awake. He's groggy and a little disoriented, but he's asking about you and Ember and he wants a sandwich." Calliope smiled. "It's a good sign. A really good sign."

Tarian bit her lip. "And Daric?"

Her sister watched her with understanding and sympathy. At least, Tarian assumed that's what the expression meant. Calliope's eyes remained solid white orbs. She looked like one of those possessed dolls in horror movies.

"I'm sure Daric isn't far behind. I'm sure of it. Just give him time. Daric was in the Source a lot longer than the rest of us. I've looked…there's nothing physically wrong."

Tarian nodded, but the adrenaline and excitement now wandered around with anxiety and looked for a new home in her stomach. She must have three ulcers by now. Or four. The roller coaster of emotions in the last few hours left her beyond wired and beyond exhausted.

She turned back to the monitors so her sister wouldn't see the tears forming in her eyes. She'd left the news blaring on all of them, because the noise helped drown out her own thoughts.

The fallout from her battle with Saorla would probably fill a library of history books when it was all done. Abereil by the thousands popped up all over the world during their fight. Some places got heavier concentrations than others, but it was all random and there was no way to track them. The only good thing was the stockpile of small prisms Letta created. The Sentinels and Benata worked in teams of two armed with four prisms each. Daemon proved better at locating the abereil, while Sentinels were better at using the prisms to absorb the bubbles.

She caught a glimpse of Letta on one news report and tried to catch the detail. "I assured the president that cleanup will continue around the clock until all the elemental abnormalities have been contained. We urge anyone who has located one of these abereil to call the special hotline at the bottom of the screen and report the location as soon as possible, and in the meantime, don't be stupid. Maintain your distance."

Tarian grinned at the way her friend couldn't help showing her personality. She'd appeared on TV several times over the last couple of days, but looked uncomfortable and had difficulty not using swear words. But she was a master at organizing the teams, and her ability with Earth surpassed everyone. She could capture dozens of abereil in just a few hours, if she knew where to look.

Tarian glanced at the logo for the news channel. It was a progressive take on the whole thing. One that recognized the word abereil and saw the task force as helpful. But several other newscasts had headlines flashing on the screen like "apocalypse" and "terrorists," and one still showed her own picture as a fugitive.

It was a mess. A cluster of the highest level. And at the moment, she didn't care. She was exhausted and worried, and her daughter would be home in a second, and that was simply all she could take.

Calliope touched her shoulder and wafted a soothing wave of comfort into her body. She leaned against her sister and let it travel. It helped a little. Not a lot, but a little.

"Come see him when you can. It'll make you feel better."

Tarian shook her head at the monitors. "I've made a mess."

"You'll clean it up. You always do." Calliope patted her arm. "Bring Ember."

Calliope left, closing the door softly behind her. A few seconds later, a portal formed in the center of the room.

Ruarc and Ember stepped through, followed by Kia. Tarian offered a greeting to Ruarc and Kia, but she had eyes only for Ember. Her daughter looked like a child of seven or eight. She wore jeans and a blue T-shirt and sandals. She'd put her hair up in a ponytail. She was looking at a miniature version of herself. Ember had the black hair, the tan, and the fashion sense of her mother. But her eyes...those were the most amazing part. Twin sapphires, so deep and mysterious Tarian thought she could see another universe there.

Tarian held out her arms to Ember. "Welcome home!"

"Mama!" Ember raced forward.

Tarian hugged her daughter, enjoying the sweet smell of her. The signature that combined all four elements. The soft skin, and the mental connection that grew every day.

I missed you, sparky.

Ember backed up a bit and giggled. *I missed you too, Mama. Look what I can do!*

Ember held out her hand, a mischievous look in her eye. A small round bubble formed in her palm. It looked suspiciously like a miniature abereil. It flashed blue, green, white, and red in a hypnotic pattern and contained enough power to raise the hair on Tarian's arms.

"Sweetie…" Tarian glanced at Ruarc, startled. "Where did you…"

Ruarc gave her a significant look. "Your daughter has a very strong connection with you, Keeper. You might learn how to block your thoughts."

"Look!" Ember held it in front of Tarian's face. Her hand glowed with a silvery white light, and the ball sank into it and vanished. The glow intensified, then evaporated. "I can blow bubbles!"

"I…uh…right." Tarian stared at her daughter with fascination. She'd learned to create an abereil, and pop it, in the palm of her hand. From a distance. Just from watching Tarian's thoughts and memories. It was an interesting development. Interesting and disturbing, and more than a little amazing. "Well, let's not do that in the house, okay?"

Ember nodded.

Tarian gave Ember another quick hug before standing to face Ruarc and Kia. Kia had matured into a young woman during her time with the Mayfanata. She'd given up her teen years to supervise and protect Ember. They didn't make enough greeting cards in the world to give the girl thanks for that service. Tarian pulled Kia into a big hug. "I owe you," she whispered.

"Ain't no thing, Ms. Tari." Kia hugged back. "If you don't mind, I thought I'd check in with the healers. Why don't you come with me, Ember? I bet there's people there want to see you. And it'll give your mama some time with your daddy." She ruffled Ember's hair and winked at Tarian.

Kia and Ember left by the side door, with Ember chatting excitedly about the beach and the things she wanted to do on her vacation. "Don't forget our Agreement, Mama!"

"Oh, I'm not likely to forget that." Tarian laughed. When the door closed, she turned back to Ruarc. She didn't quite know what to say, now that she had him alone. The daemon was the most infuriating, dishonest, loyal man she'd ever known. She wanted to throttle him, and thank him. At the same time.

Ruarc's lip twitched, as if he sensed her thoughts and found them amusing. He glanced at the monitors. "All is not yet resolved I see."

Tarian waved her hand to turn them off. "Yeah, well, it probably won't ever be. That's just humans for ya." She faced the daemon who'd stolen Ember's childhood via a shitty Agreement she hadn't understood and marveled at how much had happened in the short time between Ember's first birthday and now. So many places, destroyed. So many lives lost. One huge source of power, contained. One baby, now not a baby anymore. One evil bitch, destroyed. "First Mother is dead."

Ruarc looked at her with a tell-me-something-I-don't-know expression. But what he said was "Anadria Sha'Saorla is dead. First Mother is alive and well and currently working to rebuild Benata City. With Mayfanata support and assistance."

"Seriously? She's letting you help?" It shocked the hell out of her, to hear Macari the I-can't-stand-Mayfanata daemon accepted help from the very same.

"Apparently she feels I have earned her trust." The faintest glint of a smile flashed across Ruarc's face.

Tarian glanced at the door, where Ember and Kia had just recently passed through. "She loves you."

"Does she?"

Tarian caught another expression traveling across Ruarc's face, and her surprise deepened. She'd meant Ember. She thought maybe Ruarc meant someone else. It was an interesting development. Perhaps the irritation and angst on Macari's part had been something else. Like foreplay.

Tarian glanced at the door again. "I should go. Alex just woke up. And Daric…well, I should go."

"As you wish, Keeper." Ruarc bowed his head slightly. "Until next year?"

"Until whenever you like. You're welcome here, Ruarc. Anytime. Always."

Ruarc looked startled, then intrigued, then his eyes held an expression she thought was probably gratitude. Or appreciation. Or…well, she'd stick with gratitude.

"As you wish. May your partner and friends heal fully and completely." He gave her a long look before stepping through the portal.

She took one more look at the monitors and then turned her back on them.

A few minutes later, Tarian stood in the healer's ward with Kia and Ember. This one contained six beds, all of which were occupied, four with Sentinels injured during the attack at the bubble field and two with Alex and Daric. There were two other rooms equally full, and a large portion of the practice yard had been turned into an infirmary. Several Benata daemon worked there, healing and nurturing the wounded.

Ember and Kia chatted with two of the Sentinels a couple of beds away. They looked mostly healed and amused with Ember's enthusiasm.

Tarian was able to give her undivided attention to the two men who meant the most. Daric had yet to wake up. Alex had drifted back to sleep before she got there, but Ember assured her Alex had already said hello and he was fine and could they go play?

Tarian stared down at Alex, trying her best not to let the tears escape her lashes. It hurt to see them like this. It hurt to see the strongest, most capable men she'd ever known so vulnerable. It hurt to know they were in that position because they'd supported her. Protected her. They'd offered their lives for her. More than that, they'd offered their love.

She owed them so much. More than she could ever repay.

A tear threatened to make a run for it. She sniffed and brushed it away.

Alex's eyes fluttered open. He saw her staring and smiled in a sleepy-sexy-adorable way. "Hey, *chica*."

"Alex!" She hicuped a sob. "Oh. I thought…I thought you were…shit. I'm sorry. I'm so sorry."

"*Nada*. No." He shook his head and grimaced. "Nothing to be sorry for. Bitch better look out. I get outta this bed…" He rolled onto his side and groaned.

"The bitch is dead." Tarian grinned when she saw a satisfied look cross his face. "You probably shouldn't look so happy about it."

"Why the hell not? The wicked witch is dead, *chica*."

"She was a normal person, once. She had dreams and hopes and…I killed her." It felt wrong. Sounded wrong. But it had been the right thing to do. The *only* thing.

"She lost that a long time ago. What she became had to be put down. We need to celebrate. Let's get a beer."

"No getting out of that bed, Alex Hernandez. That's an order." Healer Chloe swept into the room carrying a small tray with assorted fruits and a bottle of something Tarian suspected was not beer. "You don't get out until I say so. Now eat. And be sure you drink all that."

Alex eyed the tray with suspicion. "What the hell is that?"

"Drink," Chloe demanded. She set the tray on a small table next to him.

Alex took a swig and looked as if he wanted to spit it back out.

"Drink!" Chloe said again.

"What about him?" Alex nodded toward Daric.

"He's still sleeping." Tarian sniffed again and turned away before Alex could see the tears in her eyes. She dragged a chair over to the side of Daric's bed and sat. She held his hand in both of hers, grateful that he felt warm to the touch. His dark hair stuck out in odd directions, and his face looked peaceful. A slight snore escaped half-parted lips.

"He be okay, Ms. Tari. You just wait 'n see." Kia gently pushed a stray bit of hair away from Daric's forehead before laying her hand against his face. "He still lost, but Ms. Calli, she be a bright light. She'll show him the way home."

"Healer Chloe doesn't seem to think so." Tarian glanced over at the corner where Calliope and Chloe conferred while both of them watched Tarian with sympathetic eyes. Or Chloe did. Calliope's eyes looked more alien than sympathetic. But she knew what her sister felt. She'd always known. Calliope had an excellent bedside manner.

"She be faced with something new, that's all. You'll see. I'm thinking maybe Ember will help out a bit." Kia kept her hand on Daric's face, and she stared at him so intently Tarian wondered exactly what Kia was doing. Kia's talent worked like insulation. But she couldn't see how blocking power from Daric would help him out of the coma he'd slipped into while in the Source abereil.

Kia grunted, as if she'd just shifted something really heavy. She blew out a breath, then whispered, "Ms. Calli. I think you best take a look now."

Calliope hurried over, followed by a very curious Ember. Kia backed away to make room for Calliope to lean over Daric. She put a hand on his forehead just as Kia had done.

Ember took Calliope's other hand. Calliope's hands glowed as she began to hum. The light moved from Calliope to Ember, where it traveled up her arm and into her face. For a few seconds Ember's eyes lit up bright white, so full it obscured the irises, making her a small twin to Calliope. Then the glow faded and receded back into Calliope.

Daric coughed. Snorted. Coughed again. He gasped, as if he'd been underwater. His eyes flew open, and he stared around like a man under attack. He struggled to sit up, frantic. "Tari!"

Tarian leapt up and pushed him back down onto the bed. "It's okay. I'm here. It's safe. Calm down!" Her voice got progressively louder until Daric finally heard and stopped struggling.

"Daric! Daric! Daric!" Ember jumped up and down, clapping her hands. "Daddy Daric! I missed you!"

Daric looked confused. She could tell he was trying to process the words and the seven-year-old shouting them.

"Dude, 'bout time!" Alex grunted as he shifted to a sitting position. "Slacker."

Daric grimaced as if pain shot through somewhere. "Hey, sparky. I missed you more." He pulled Ember in for a hug and a kiss on her forehead. "Missed you lots more. A billion times more."

"A billion *times* a billion!" Ember declared.

Calliope laughed. "Okay, sweetie, he needs to rest."

"I'll take her, Ms. Calli." Kia took Ember's hand and led her away. She sounded tired.

Ember smiled and pretended to whisper, "I'll sneak back in later."

They all laughed and waited until the door closed behind the two.

Tarian looked at her sister for reassurance. "Calli, is he okay?"

"He needs some rest, some food, and maybe a little bit of alone time with you." Calliope smiled an open, genuine, I'm-not-lying smile.

"Hey, I'm right here," Daric said. He sounded like a chain-smoker.

"Yeah, so am I," Alex said. "No doing that shit with me in the room."

Calliope patted Daric's arm. "I'll go get a snack for both of you."

"Tari? You okay? Ember..." Daric looked at her like she might sprout another set of eyes or two heads. Or a tail.

"I'm fine."

Daric gave her a doubtful look. She had to laugh.

"I know I didn't handle the last reunion so well, but this time...I'm really okay. Ember is happy. Ruarc kept her safe. Well, Ruarc and Kia. And an entire city of Mayfanata. That's what matters. Not to mention the older she gets, the more she's in my head. Distance doesn't seem to matter at all. If I want to hear her voice, I can. And vice versa. We're probably closer than any mother and daughter should ever be."

The men both laughed. Or Alex laughed. Daric chuckled in a painful sort of way. He sounded and acted like he'd punctured a lung and broken some ribs. Maybe he had—she had no way of knowing what really happened in the abereil.

She looked at Daric. "First Mother…Saorla…is dead. The Source is contained."

"Oh." He shifted a little. Nodded. His eyelids drooped. "All is right with the world?" Daric yawned, and his eyes slid closed.

She snorted. "Not even close. But…I think it will be. Someday."

—40—

Several days later, Tarian stood in a place she'd visited only once before in her life. A place where she'd taken an oath to protect and provide for her daughter so that her daughter could, in turn, bring balance to the world. The Balance Court, home of the Dulra. Ancient beings whose origin she didn't understand but who commanded more respect, more power, and more magic than anything or anyone anywhere on the planet. Their influence, she suspected, extended far beyond Earth. But she didn't ask. She wasn't sure she wanted to know.

She'd made the Agreement thinking that she would gather the pieces and Ember would use them to fulfill her destiny. She'd thought that her daughter's destiny involved the destruction of the most evil daemon history had ever known. She'd thought Ember, with the help of all four artifacts, was meant to bring down First Mother and that one act would, in turn, bring balance and peace to the world.

She'd thought wrong. So very wrong. It was a wrongness of monumental, epic proportions.

Tarian waited now in the place where she'd taken that oath and embarked on the mission to destroy the Stulos, in complete confusion. The former First Mother was dead. No getting around that simple truth. The bitch was dead and Ember was still a child, if a bit older, and balance, it seemed, had not been achieved after all. She'd wrapped elements up in a neat little, or rather large, package but the Source remained the single largest deposit of element power on Earth, a symbol of the fact that things were very much *not* in balance. If they were in balance, there wouldn't be one large deposit of anything. It would be spread evenly throughout the world. The elements would infiltrate everything, even the rocks and the birds and the clouds in the sky. Every person would be able to touch magic, and none would be more powerful than any other.

Thinking about it that way made balance seem like nothing more than a dream. A goal that would never be achieved. A distant prize that would never be won. It seemed impossible.

She studied the font of energy at the center of the Balance Court. It remained intact, an endless supply of power that fed the Court and who knew what else. Just looking at it made her feel insignificant and small.

"Keeper Tarian Xannon, of the House of Xannon, of the Water Artifact. Welcome. Be at ease." Dulcet tones filled the cavernous space as the Dulra entered.

Tarian faced them, suddenly feeling stupid. But her need for answers burned hotter than the stupid feeling, so she waited for the Court to assemble. They formed a semicircle around the font of power, standing in pairs. Silence extended far past the comfortable stage and into the incredibly uncomfortable stage, the stage where she wondered who was supposed to speak first and exactly what the protocol was for speaking to supernatural, immortal beings.

For their part, the Dulra waited with clasped hands, rainbow-colored hair, and two toned faces, staring back at her with patient, alien expressions.

Tarian cleared her throat. It echoed.

They waited.

"Screw it," she muttered to herself. She was never good with protocol. Why start now? "I need answers."

"To what questions, Keeper?" The Dulra asked in unison.

Tarian blew out a long breath. Closed her eyes for a second. Straightened her shoulders. They intimidated the hell out of her, but she plunged forward anyway. "The former First Mother is dead."

The Dulra bowed their heads in acknowledgment. They made no judgment that she could see. Just...accepted.

"I thought...I mean, the Agreement...I destroyed the Stulos like you asked." She took another breath. Tried her best to channel her mother's poise and cool head. "I have gathered the artifacts as agreed. I thought they were for Ember. So that she could bring balance to the world. I thought...I thought First Mother...Saorla...was the one standing in the way of that balance. I thought Ember would be the one to fight her. But she wasn't."

They watched her and still didn't speak.

"If Saorla is dead, what is left for Ember to do?" There, let them answer *that*.

"Balance has not been achieved. Your daughter's destiny lies ahead." Their tone was matter-of-fact and non-judgmental.

"I don't understand. If it wasn't to kill Saorla, then what?"

"The Scion is needed to restore to the world that which was lost."

Tarian waited for them to continue, but they didn't. They stood there, hundreds of them, just staring at her. It was the most frustrating thing she'd ever seen. All those faces and all that knowledge, and all they did was stare.

She motioned for them to continue. "Care to throw a little more information my way?"

They didn't answer. Not one of them even so much as flinched.

She tried to deflect a temper tantrum with sarcasm. "Nah, wouldn't want to actually *tell* me what it is I'm supposed to be doing. That'd make things too easy, wouldn't it?"

It wouldn't do any good to have a fit. Not here. They were judge, jury, and, she supposed, executioner, should it come to that. They might as well be gods. And she was merely mortal.

They waited with pleasant expressions and kind eyes. They looked far too kind for her mood. She almost wished they'd shout or something. She tried one more time to get information she could actually use. "The Agreement's done. So now what?"

"The Agreement is not complete, Keeper. Our obligation has not been met. We will aid your daughter when the time comes for her to right the ancient wrong."

"And when will that be?"

They didn't answer. Of course. Tarian crossed her arms and studied her feet for a moment. She tried to remember the exact Agreement. It'd been too long, and she hadn't exactly paid attention to all the details that day. She'd been more focused on First Mother and Macari. But she thought one thing stood out. She looked up. "You said the keys would be returned. What keys?"

"The keys of balance."

"And have they been returned? I assumed by keys you meant the artifacts. Was I wrong?"

"Assumptions are often incorrect. The objects of power will aid the Seeker in finding the keys."

She mulled over that statement. "Who is the Seeker?"

"Ember, Scion to the House of Xannon, daughter of the Keeper."

"And when is she supposed to do this seeking?"

"When the time is right, the Seeker will know."

Tarian thought about their statement. Ember would just know, when the time was right. She might be ten years old or a hundred. "What if she doesn't know? What if she doesn't want to do...whatever it is?"

"The choice to answer a call of duty will be hers to make, just as it was yours, Keeper. We all make our choices. We all live with the consequences. None are gods or immortal. Not even the Balance Court." They spread their hands wide in a choreographed movement that would have been impressive if she weren't so frustrated. "Do you regret your choices, Keeper?"

She considered that. Even though most of her choices ended in some sort of disaster, they'd also resulted in some pretty good things. Her relationship with Daric. Her daughter. "Everything I've done led to this moment and to the friendships I've formed. Every choice I made led me to Ember. How could I ever regret that?"

"We will fulfill our part of the Agreement when the time comes, Keeper. We do not regret our choices. We stand with you, and we stand ready to aid the Scion."

The Dulra bowed, then turned as one and walked away. They melted into the far shadows without another word, or thought, or any indication of what she should do next.

They were the most frustrating beings Tarian had ever encountered. But she still had an Agreement with them. They'd promised, and they would deliver.

Someday.

###

Did you know that the best way to tell an author you appreciate their work is to leave a review? Just a few words of review at your vendor of choice boosts sales, and sends little fuzzies that warm the author's heart at the end of a long day of fussing over letters and words, sentences and paragraphs, fueled by far too much caffeine.

If you'd like to know more about me, the Xannon series, or future book plans, you can find me here:

Website: *http://melindavan.com*
Facebook: *https://www.facebook.com/MelindaVanLone*
Twitter: *MelindaVan*
Instagram: *http://instagram.com/mvanlone*
Email: *melinda.van@gmail.com*